This volume contains INU-YASHA PART 4 #1 through INU-YASHA PART 4 #5 in their entirety.

STORY AND ART BY
RUMIKO TAKAHASHI

ENGLISH ADAPTATION BY
GERARD JONES

Translation/Mari Morimoto
Touch-Up Art & Lettering/Wayne Truman
Cover Design/Hidemi Sahara
Graphics & Layout/Sean Lee

Editor/Julie Davis
Editor-in-Chief/Hyoe Narita
Publisher/Seiji Horibuchi

Printed in Canada

Published by Viz Communications, Inc.
P.O. Box 77010 • San Francisco, CA 94107
www.viz.com and **www.j-pop.com**

10 9 8 7 6 5 4 3 2 1
First printing, September 2000

INU-YASHA GRAPHIC NOVELS TO DATE:

INU-YASHA VOL. 1
INU-YASHA VOL. 2
INU-YASHA VOL. 3
INU-YASHA VOL. 4
INU-YASHA VOL. 5
INU-YASHA VOL. 6
INU-YASHA VOL. 7

VIZ GRAPHIC NOVEL

INU-YASHA

A FEUDAL FAIRY TALE™

VOL. 7

STORY AND ART BY

RUMIKO TAKAHASHI

CONTENTS

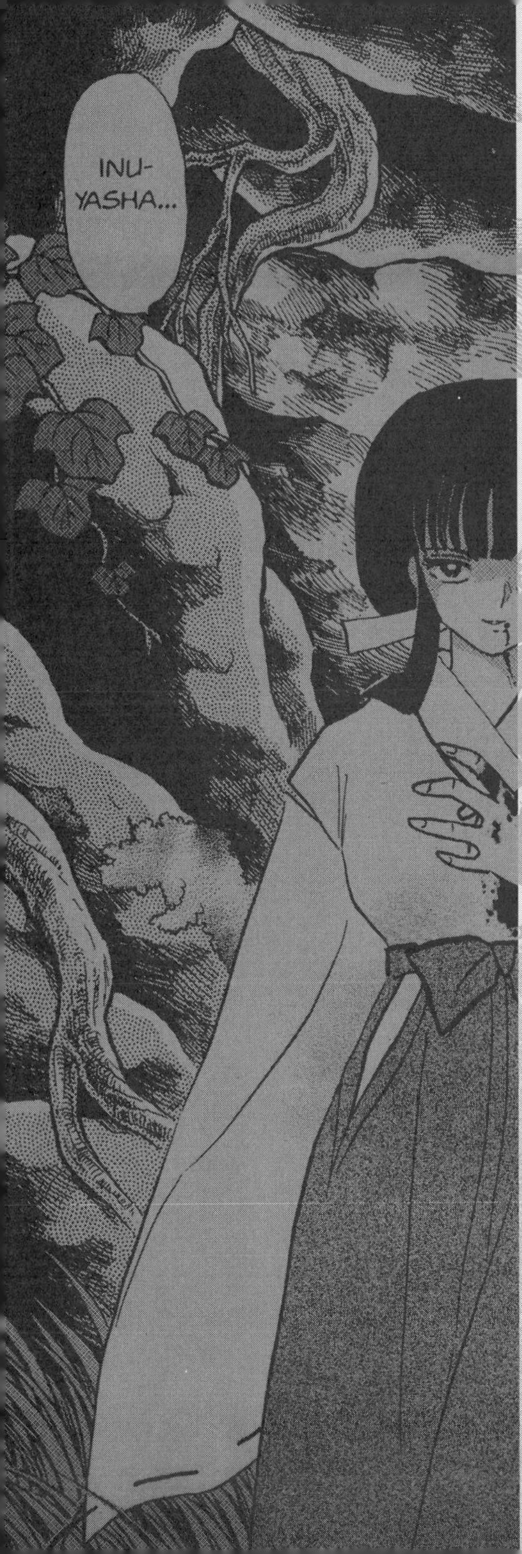
INU-YASHA...
I HAVE BEEN WAITING FOR YOU TO COME HERE...

THE STORY THUS FAR

Long ago, in Japan's era of the "Warring States"—the Muromachi period (*Sengoku-jidai*, approximately 1467-1568 CE)—a legendary doglike half-demon called "Inu-Yasha" attempted to steal the Shikon Jewel, or "Jewel of Four Souls," from a village, but was stopped by the enchanted arrow of the village priestess, Kikyo. Inu-Yasha fell into a deep sleep, pinned to a tree by Kikyo's arrow, while the mortally wounded Kikyo took the Shikon Jewel with her into the fires of her funeral pyre. Years passed.

Fast forward to the present day. Kagome, a Japanese high-school girl, is pulled into a well one day by mysterious centipede monster, and finds herself transported into the past, only to come face to face with the trapped Inu-Yasha. She frees him, and Inu-Yasha readily defeats the centipede monster.

The residents of the village, now fifty years older, readily accept Kagome as the reincarnation of their deceased priestess Kikyo, a claim supported by the fact that the Shikon Jewel emerges from a cut on Kagome's body. Unfortunately, the jewel's rediscovery means that the village is soon under attack by a variety of demons in search of this treasure. Then, the jewel is accidentally shattered into many shards, each of which may have the fearsome power of the entire jewel.

Although Inu-Yasha says he hates Kagome because of her resemblance to Kikyo, the woman who "killed" him, he is forced to team up with her when Kaede, the village leader, binds him to Kagome with a powerful spell. Now the two grudging companions must fight to reclaim and reassemble the shattered shards of the Shikon Jewel before they fall into the wrong hands.

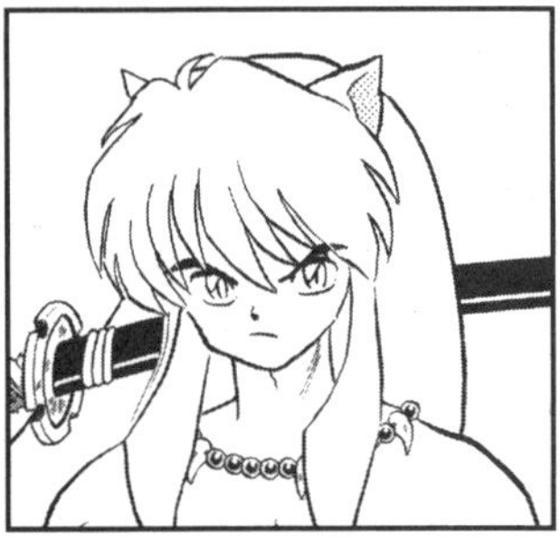

INU-YASHA
A half-human, half-demon hybrid son of a human mother and a demon father, Inu-Yasha resembles a human but has the claws of a demon, a thick mane of white hair, and ears rather like a dog's. The necklace he wears carries a powerful spell which allows Kagome to control him with a single word. Because of his human half, Inu-Yasha's powers are different from those of full-blooded monsters—a fact that the Shikon Jewel has the power to change.

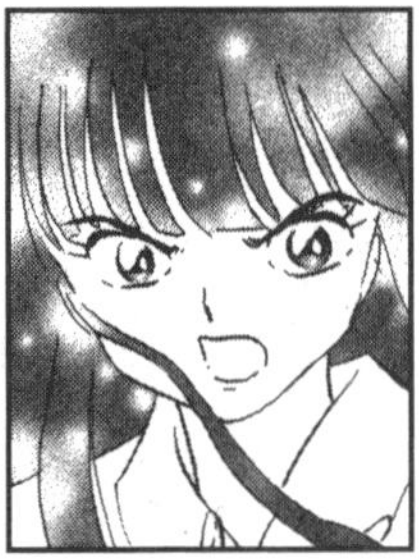

KIKYO
A powerful priestess, Kikyo was charged with the awesome responsibility of protecting the Shikon Jewel from demons and humans who coveted its power. She died after firing the enchanted arrow that kept Inu-Yasha imprisoned for fifty years.

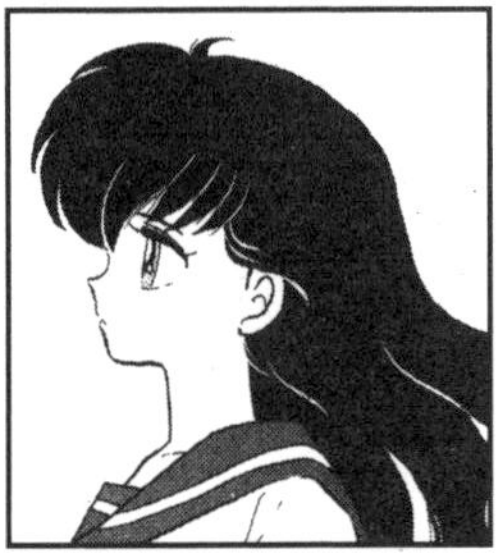

KAGOME
Working with Inu-Yasha to recover the shattered shards of the Shikon Jewel, Kagome routinely travels into Japan's past through an old, magical well on her family's property. All this time travel means she's stuck with living two separate lives in two separate centuries, and she's beginning to worry that she'll *never* be able to catch up to her schoolwork.

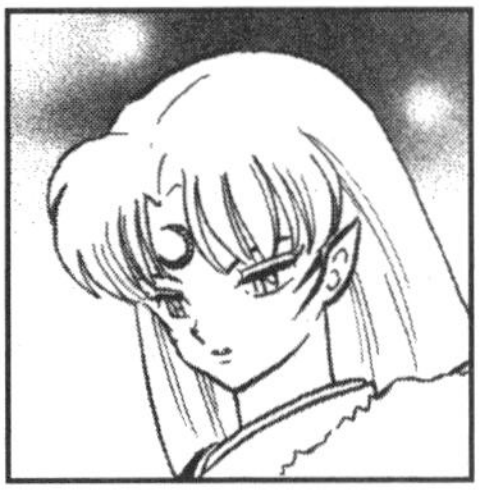

SESSHÔ-MARU
Inu-Yasha's half-brother, Sesshô-maru shares the same father, but has none of the human blood that taints his brother's powers. When the two previously clashed over their father's sword, the Tetsusaiga, or "Steel-Cleaving Fang," Sesshô-maru lost an arm. Now, he's taken care of that troublesome handicap....

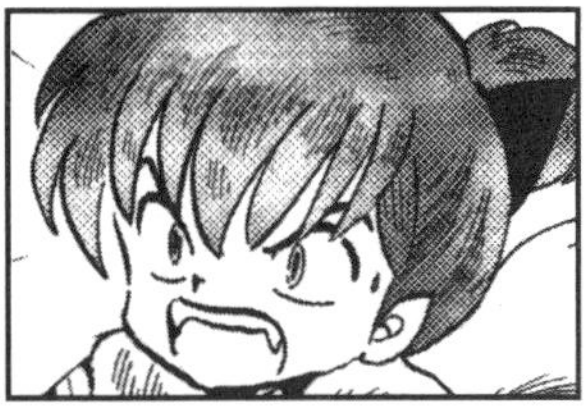

SHIPPÔ
A young fox-demon, orphaned by two other demons whose powers had been boosted by the Shikon Jewel, the mischievous Shippô enjoys goading Inu-Yasha and playing tricks with his shape-changing abilities.

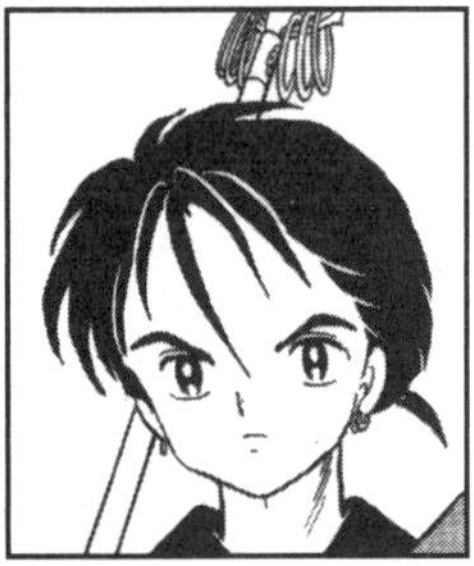

MIROKU
An easygoing Buddhist priest with questionable morals, Miroku is the carrier of a curse passed down from his grandfather. He is searching for the demon Naraku, who first inflicted the curse in hopes of finding a cure.

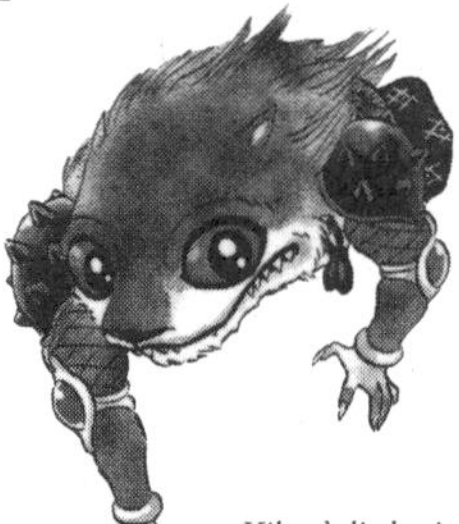

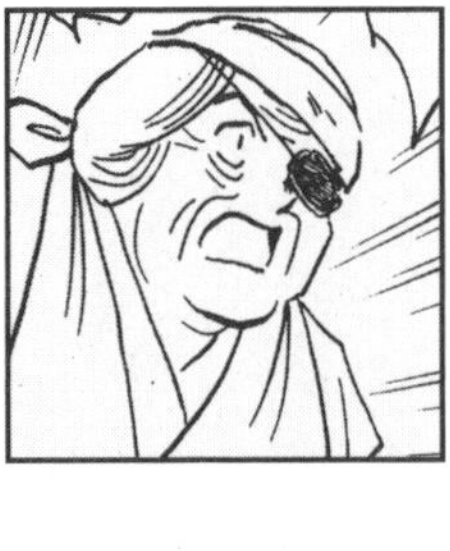

KAEDE
Kikyo's little sister who carried out the priestess' wish that the Shikon Jewel should be burned with her remains. Now fifty years older, Kaede is head of the village. It is Kaede's spell that binds Inu-Yasha to Kagome by means of a string of prayer beads and Kagome's spoken word—"Sit!"

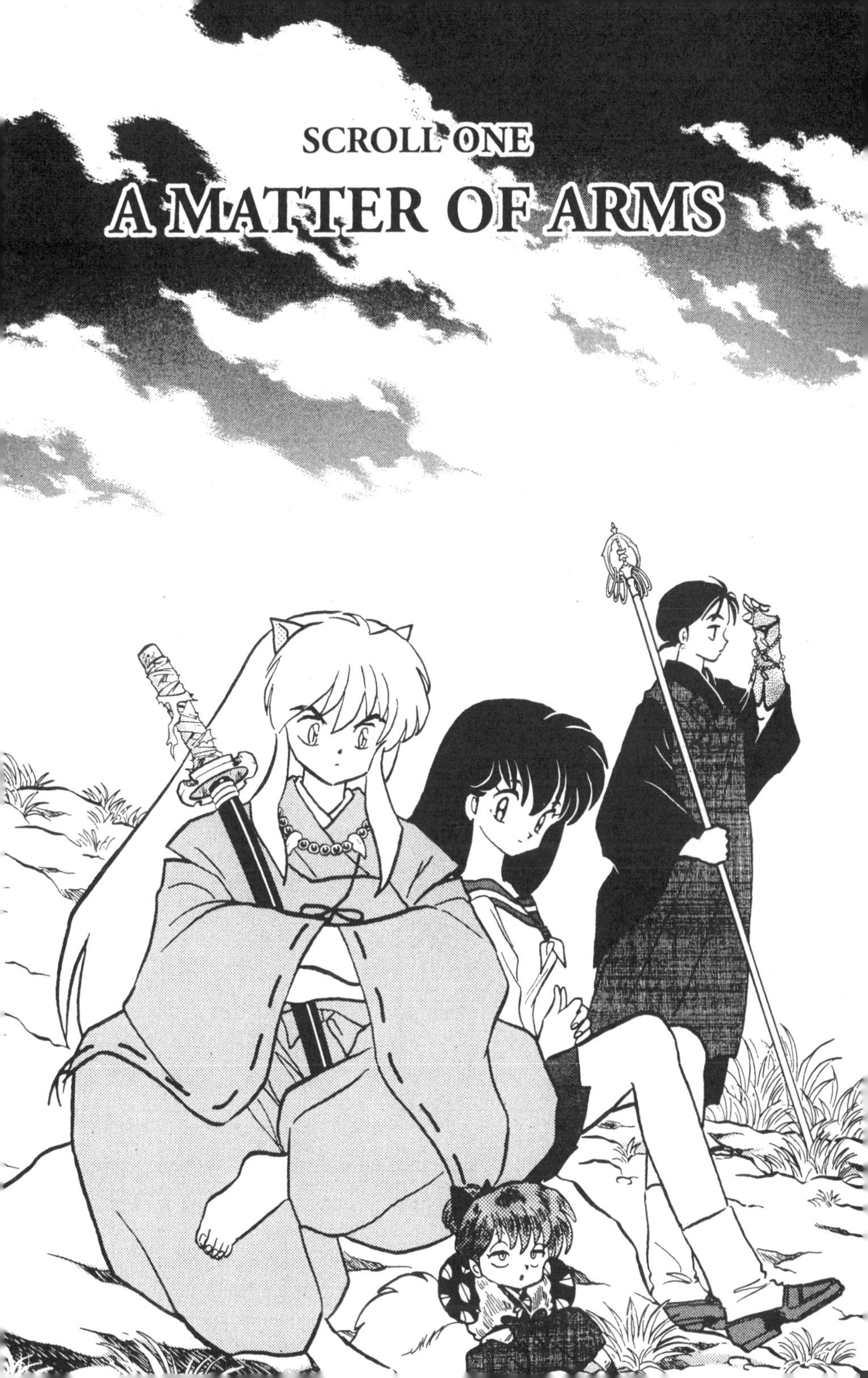
SCROLL ONE
A MATTER OF ARMS

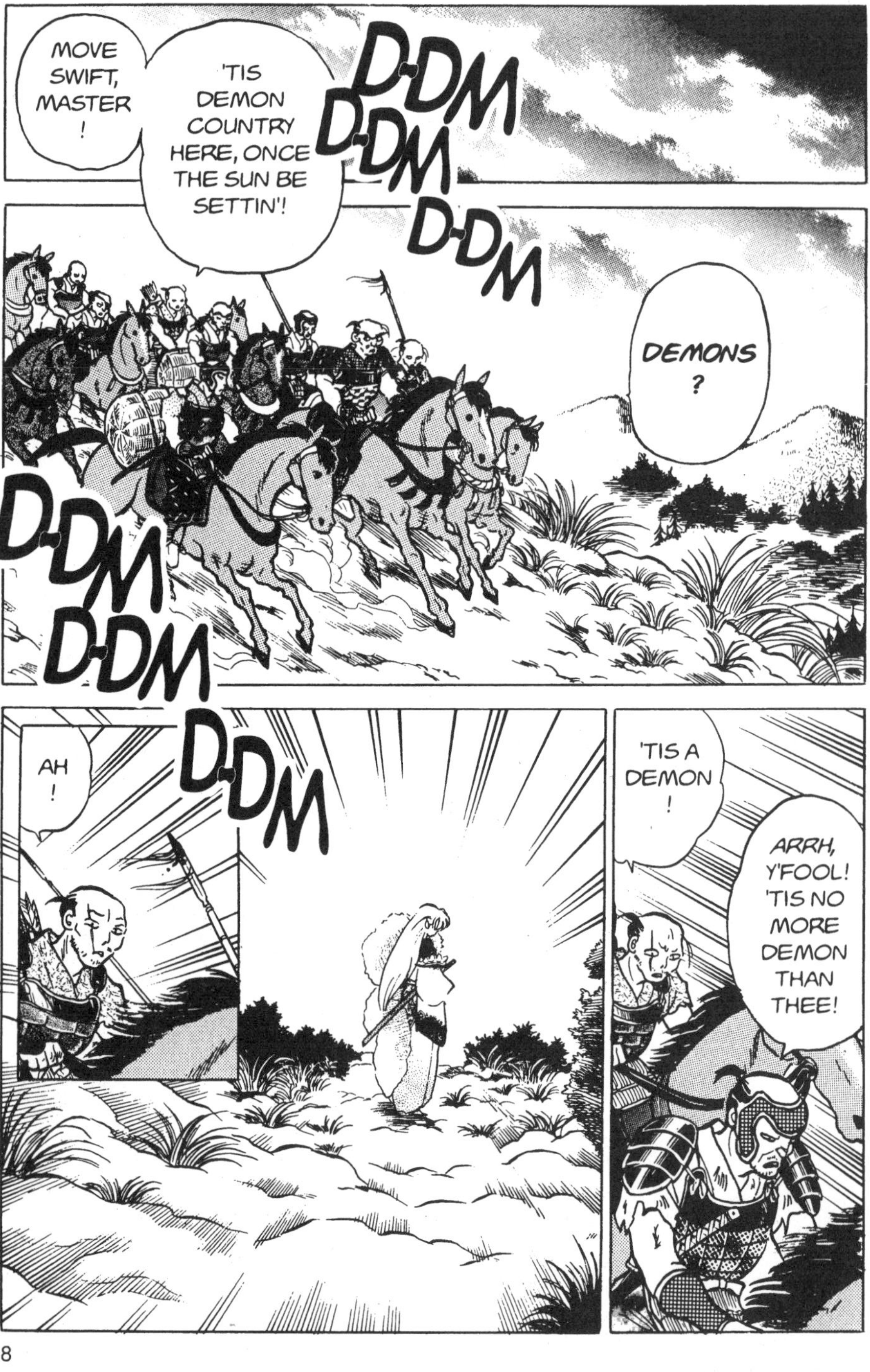
MOVE SWIFT, MASTER!
'TIS DEMON COUNTRY HERE, ONCE THE SUN BE SETTIN'!
D-DM
D-DM
D-DM
DEMONS?
D-DM
D-DM
D-DM
AH!
'TIS A DEMON!
ARRH, Y'FOOL! 'TIS NO MORE DEMON THAN THEE!

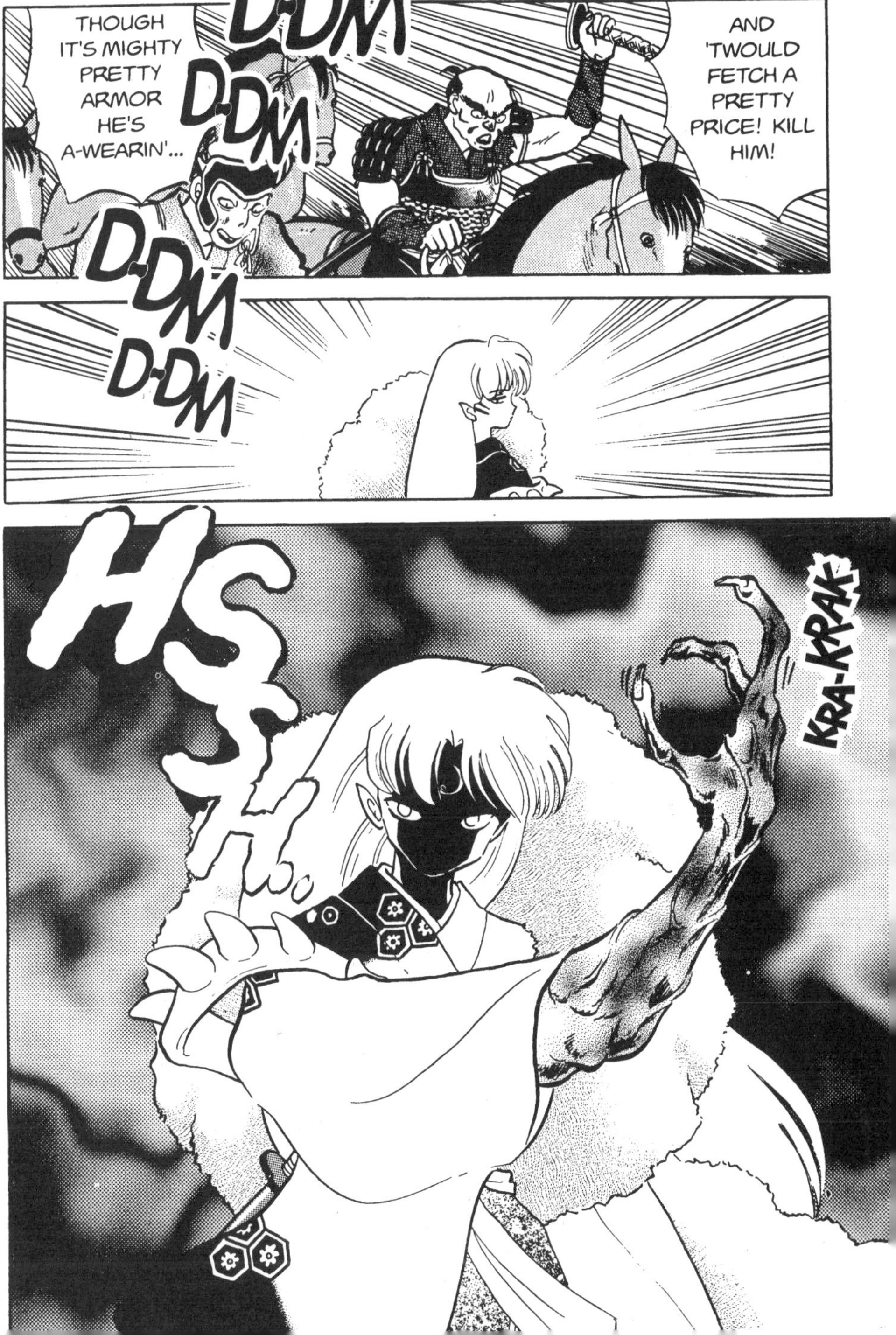
THOUGH IT'S MIGHTY PRETTY ARMOR HE'S A-WEARIN'...
D-DM
D-DM
AND 'TWOULD FETCH A PRETTY PRICE! KILL HIM!
D-DM
D-DM
HSSH...
KRA-KRAK

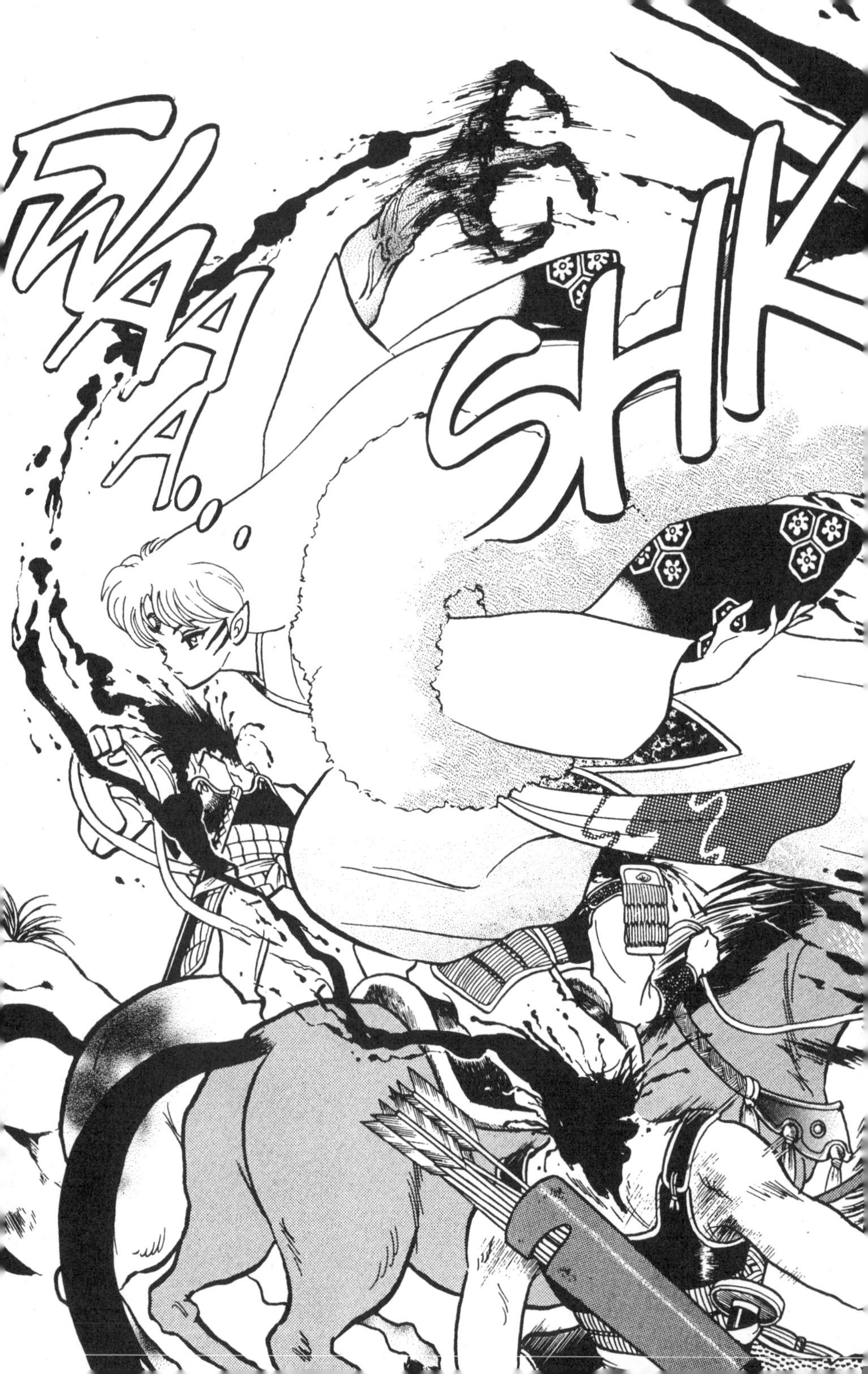
FWAAA...
SHK

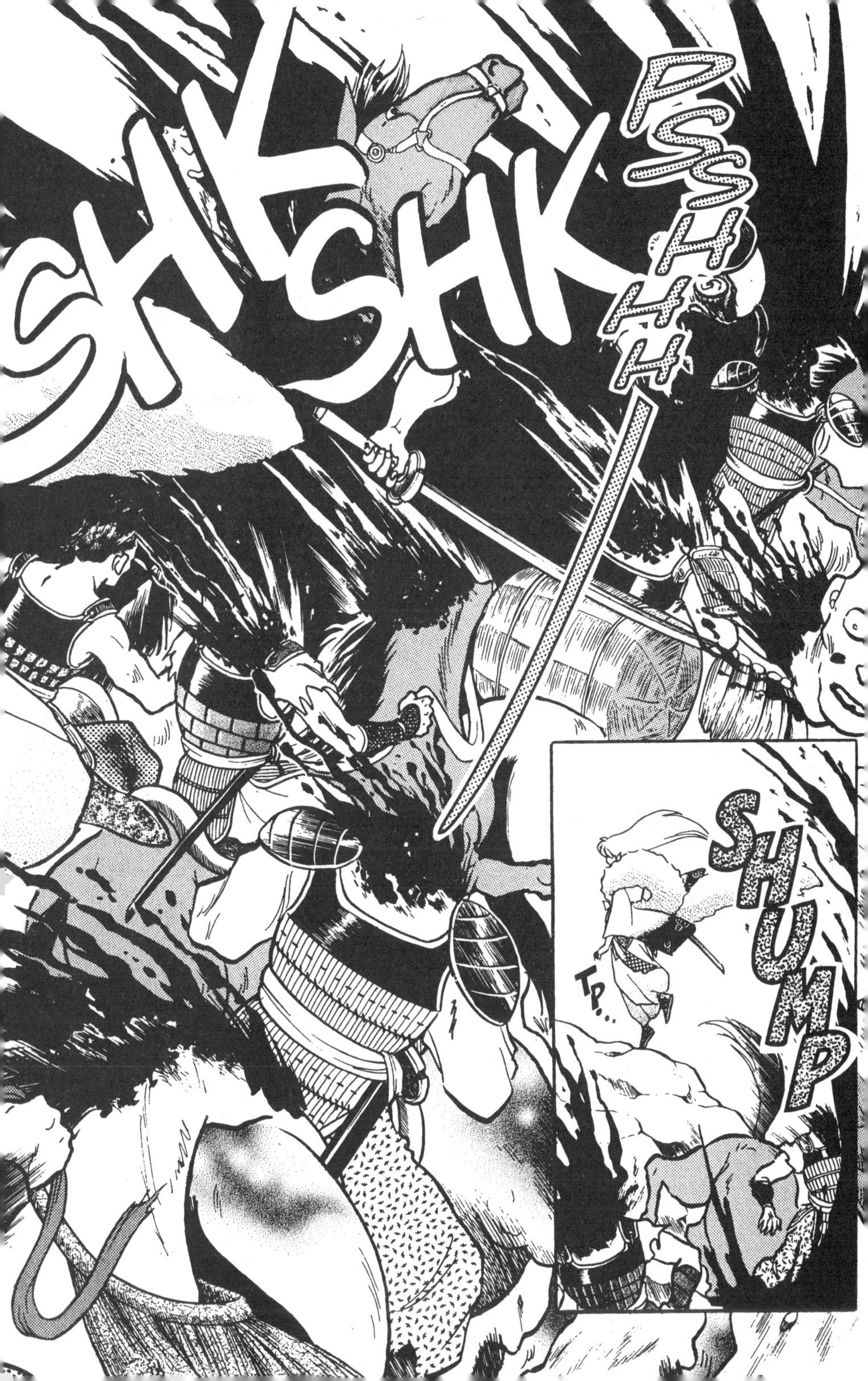
SHK SHK
PSSHHHH
SHUMP
TP...

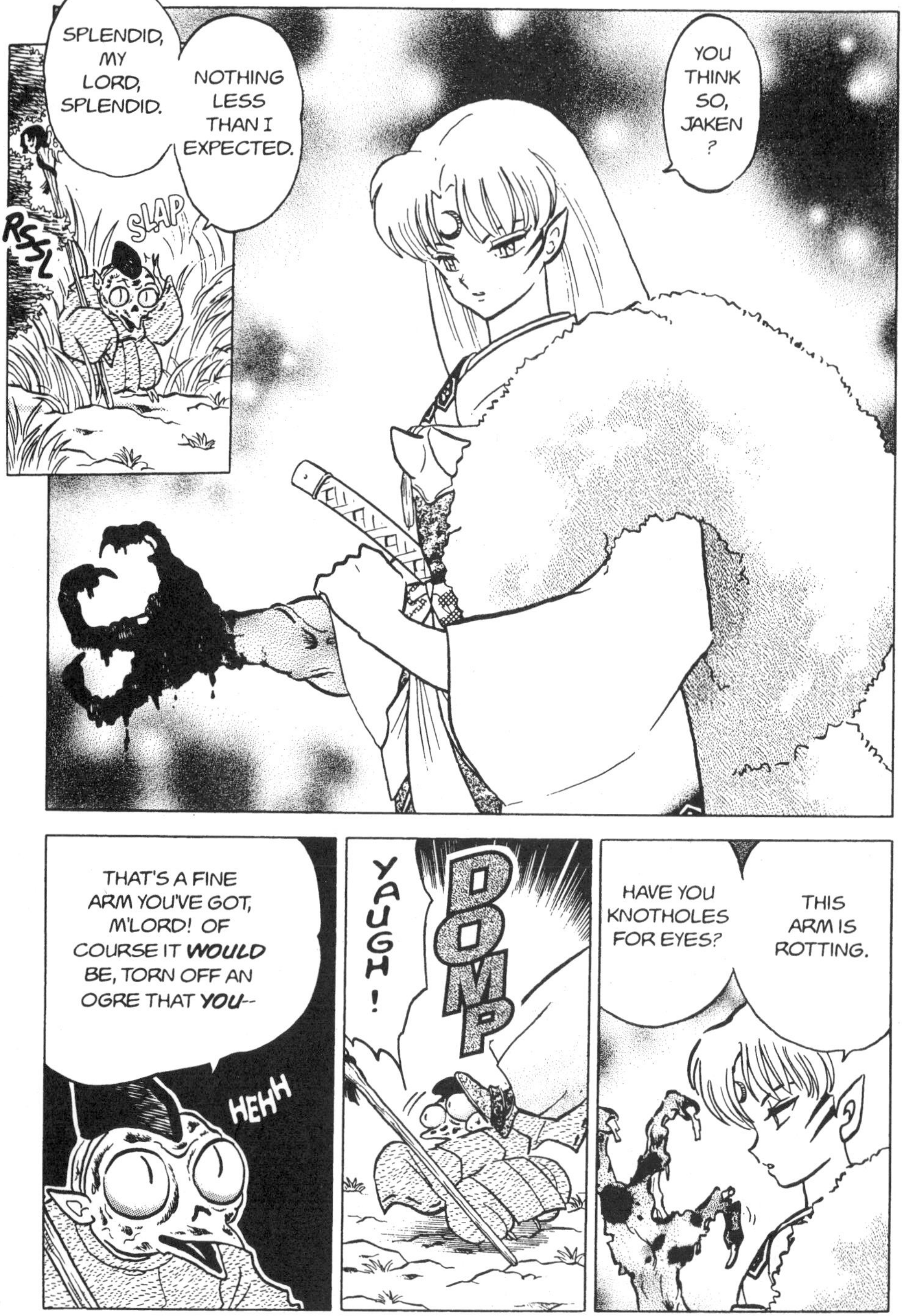
SPLENDID, MY LORD, SPLENDID.
NOTHING LESS THAN I EXPECTED.
SLAP
RSSL
YOU THINK SO, JAKEN?
THAT'S A FINE ARM YOU'VE GOT, M'LORD! OF COURSE IT **WOULD** BE, TORN OFF AN OGRE THAT **YOU**--
HEHH
YAUGH!
DOMP
HAVE YOU KNOTHOLES FOR EYES?
THIS ARM IS ROTTING.

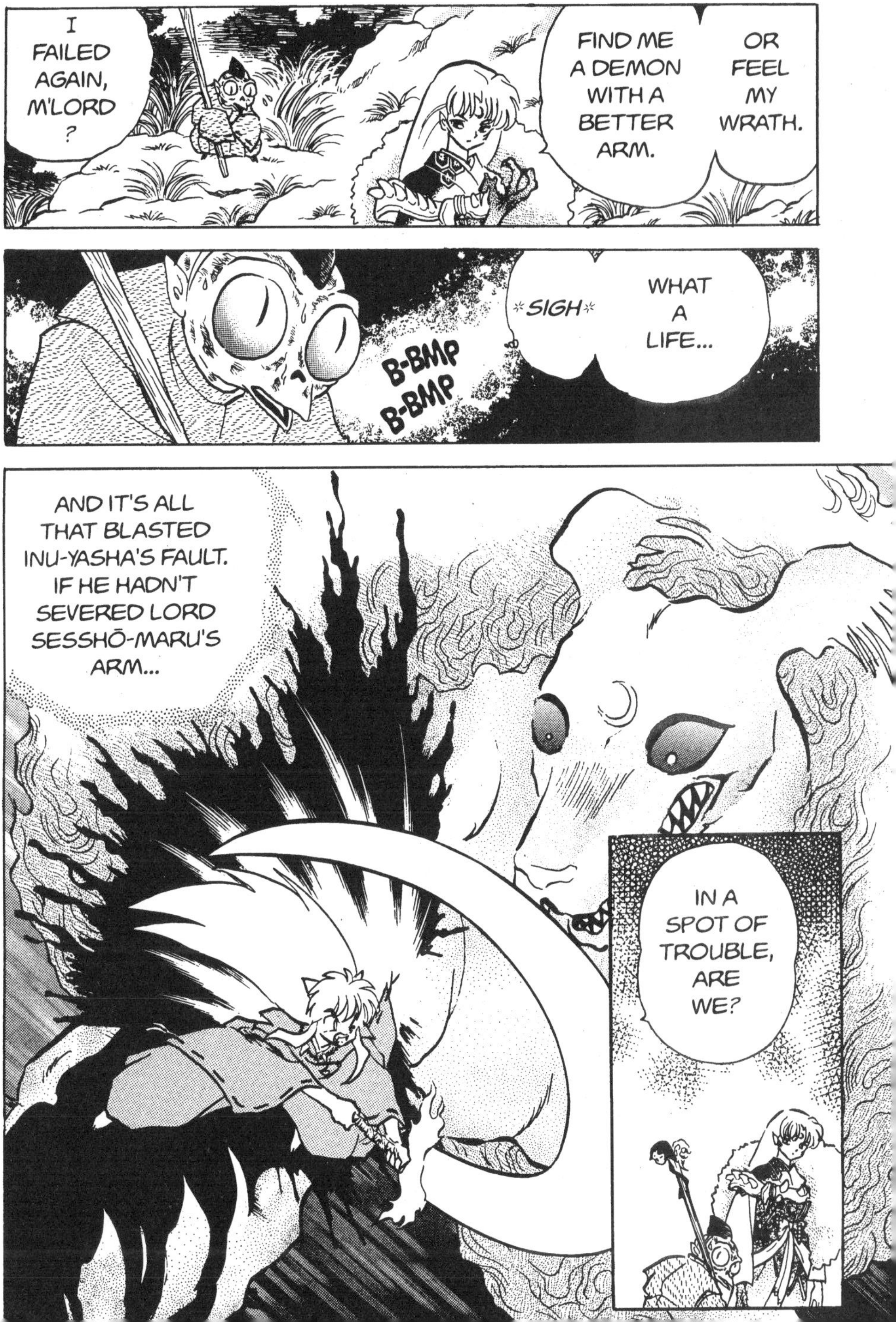
I FAILED AGAIN, M'LORD?
FIND ME A DEMON WITH A BETTER ARM.
OR FEEL MY WRATH.
B-BMP B-BMP
SIGH
WHAT A LIFE...
AND IT'S ALL THAT BLASTED INU-YASHA'S FAULT. IF HE HADN'T SEVERED LORD SESSHŌ-MARU'S ARM...
IN A SPOT OF TROUBLE, ARE WE?

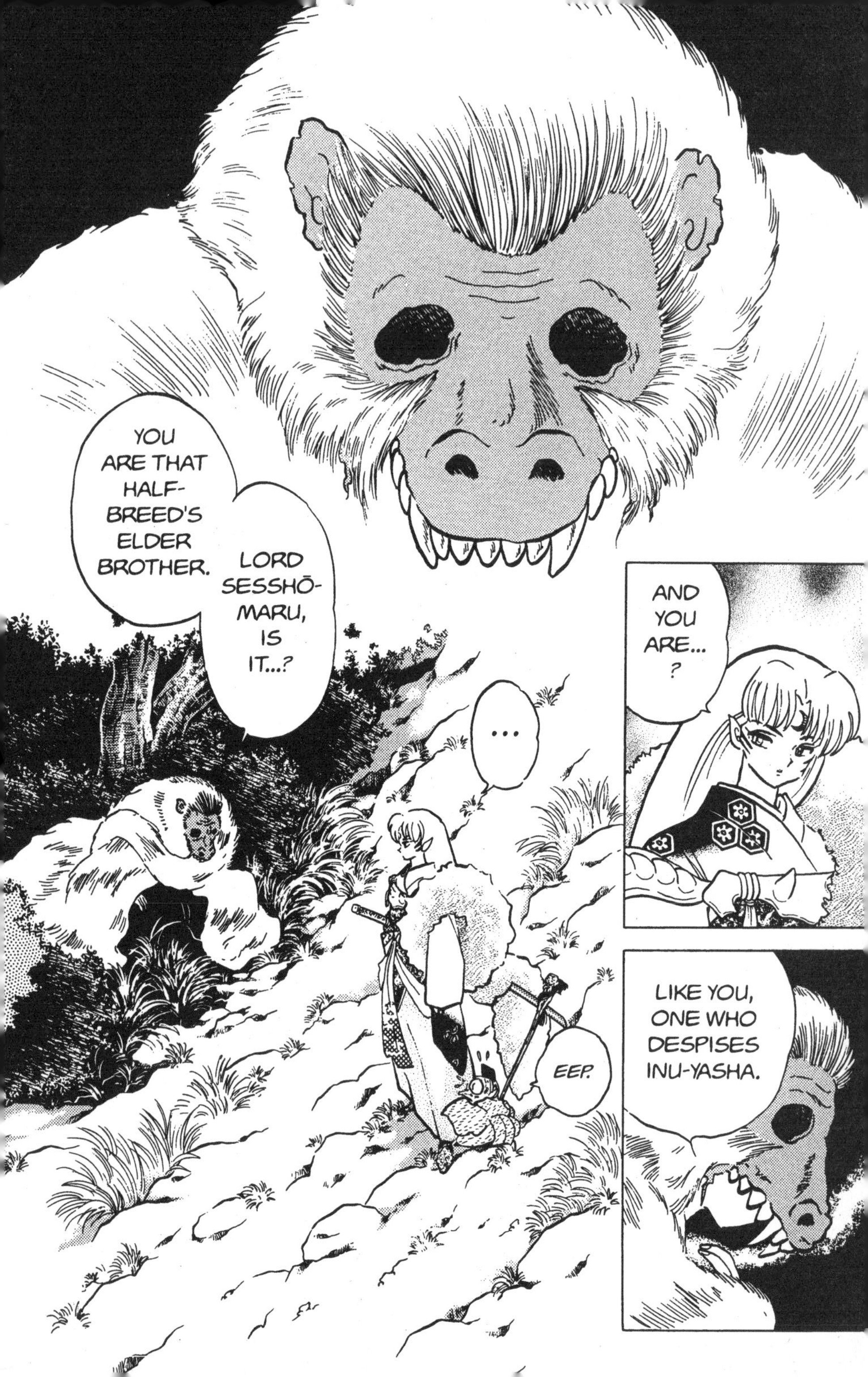
YOU ARE THAT HALF-BREED'S ELDER BROTHER.
LORD SESSHŌ-MARU, IS IT...?
...
EEP.
AND YOU ARE...?
LIKE YOU, ONE WHO DESPISES INU-YASHA.

HERE. USE THIS ARM.

···

WHAT--?!

DO NOT MOCK MY LORD!

THAT IS A **HUMAN** ARM!

MORE PRECISELY...

...A HUMAN ARM IMPREGNATED WITH A SHIKON SHARD.

A SHUH... SHIKON...?

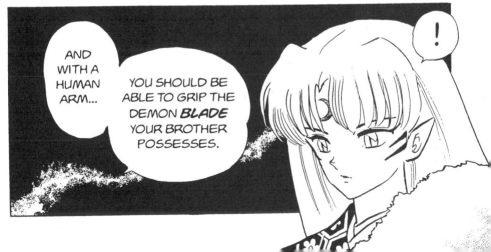

AND WITH A HUMAN ARM...

YOU SHOULD BE ABLE TO GRIP THE DEMON **BLADE** YOUR BROTHER POSSESSES.

!

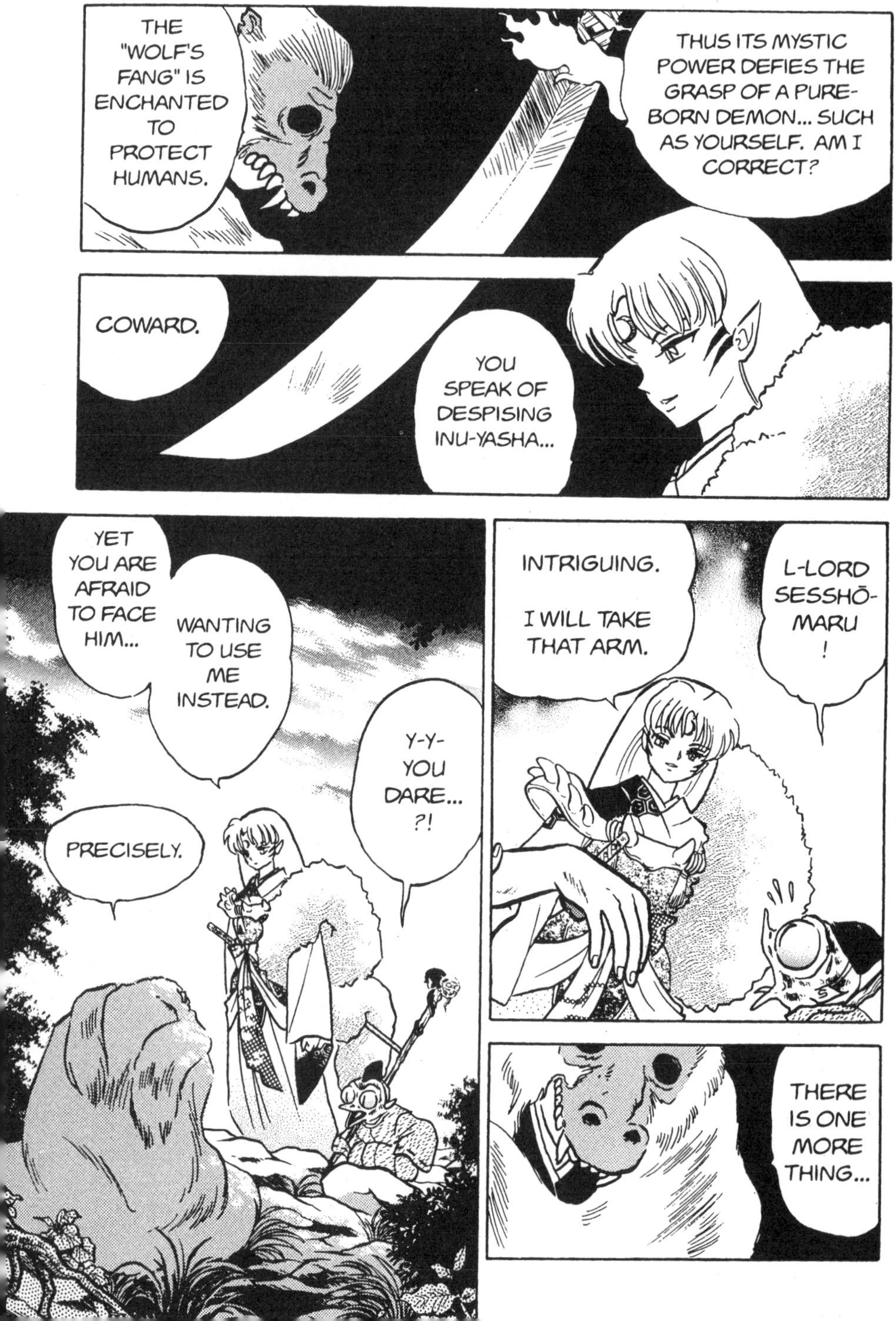
THE "WOLF'S FANG" IS ENCHANTED TO PROTECT HUMANS.
THUS ITS MYSTIC POWER DEFIES THE GRASP OF A PURE-BORN DEMON... SUCH AS YOURSELF. AM I CORRECT?
COWARD.
YOU SPEAK OF DESPISING INU-YASHA...
YET YOU ARE AFRAID TO FACE HIM...
WANTING TO USE ME INSTEAD.
Y-Y-YOU DARE...?!
PRECISELY.
INTRIGUING.
I WILL TAKE THAT ARM.
L-LORD SESSHŌ-MARU!
THERE IS ONE MORE THING...

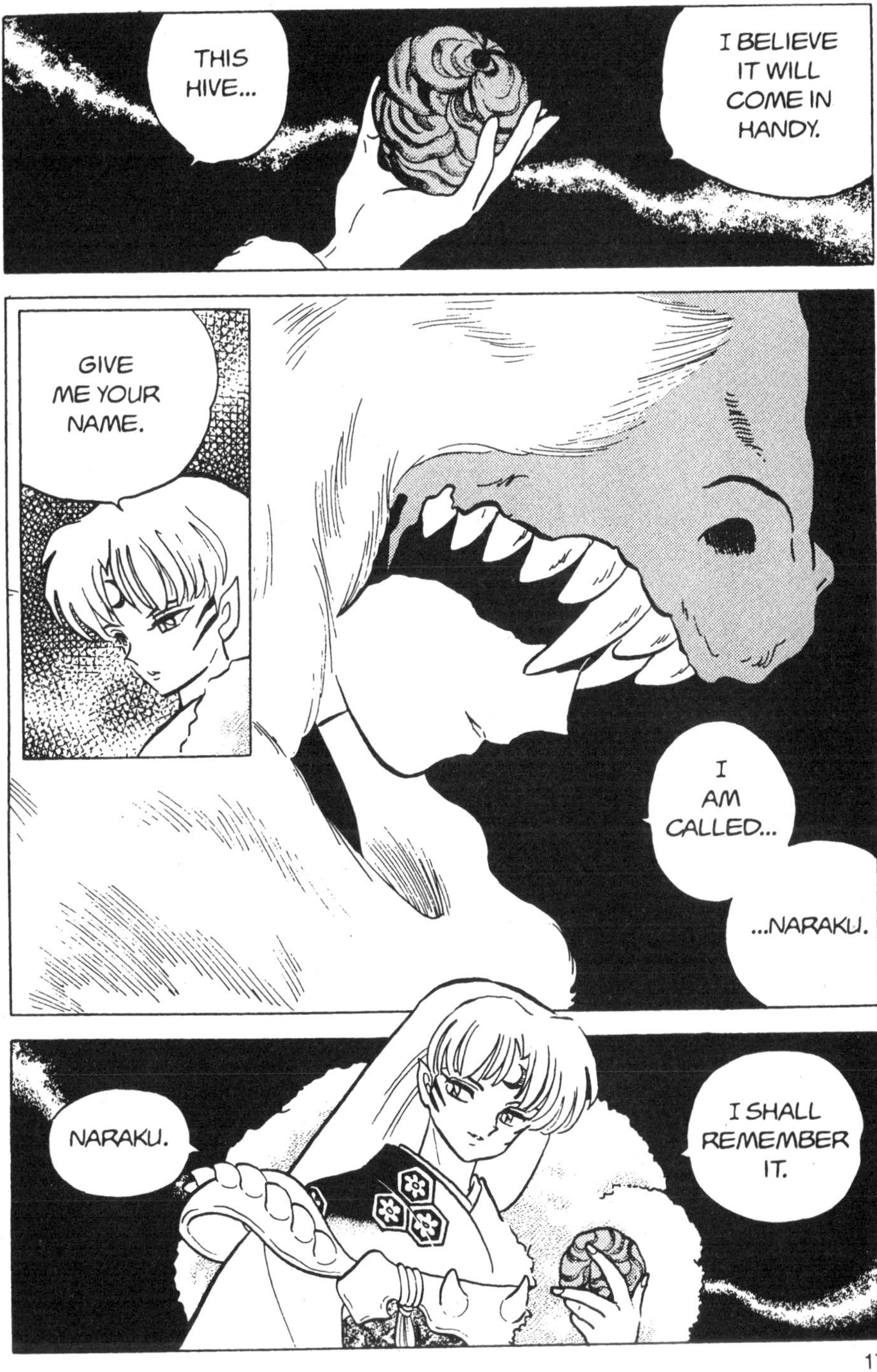
THIS HIVE...
I BELIEVE IT WILL COME IN HANDY.
GIVE ME YOUR NAME.
I AM CALLED...
...NARAKU.
NARAKU.
I SHALL REMEMBER IT.

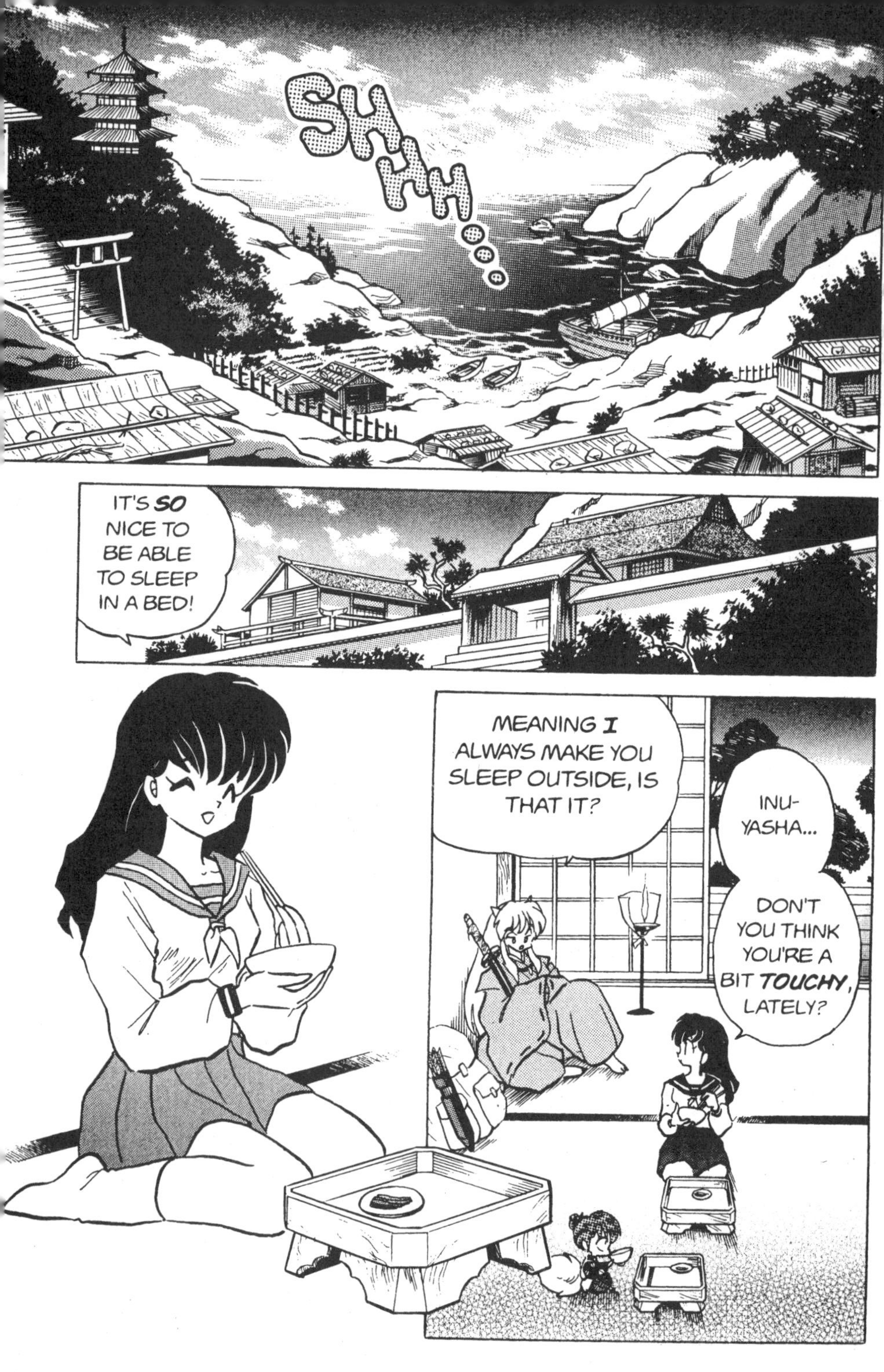
SHHH...
IT'S SO NICE TO BE ABLE TO SLEEP IN A BED!
MEANING I ALWAYS MAKE YOU SLEEP OUTSIDE, IS THAT IT?
INU-YASHA...
DON'T YOU THINK YOU'RE A BIT TOUCHY, LATELY?

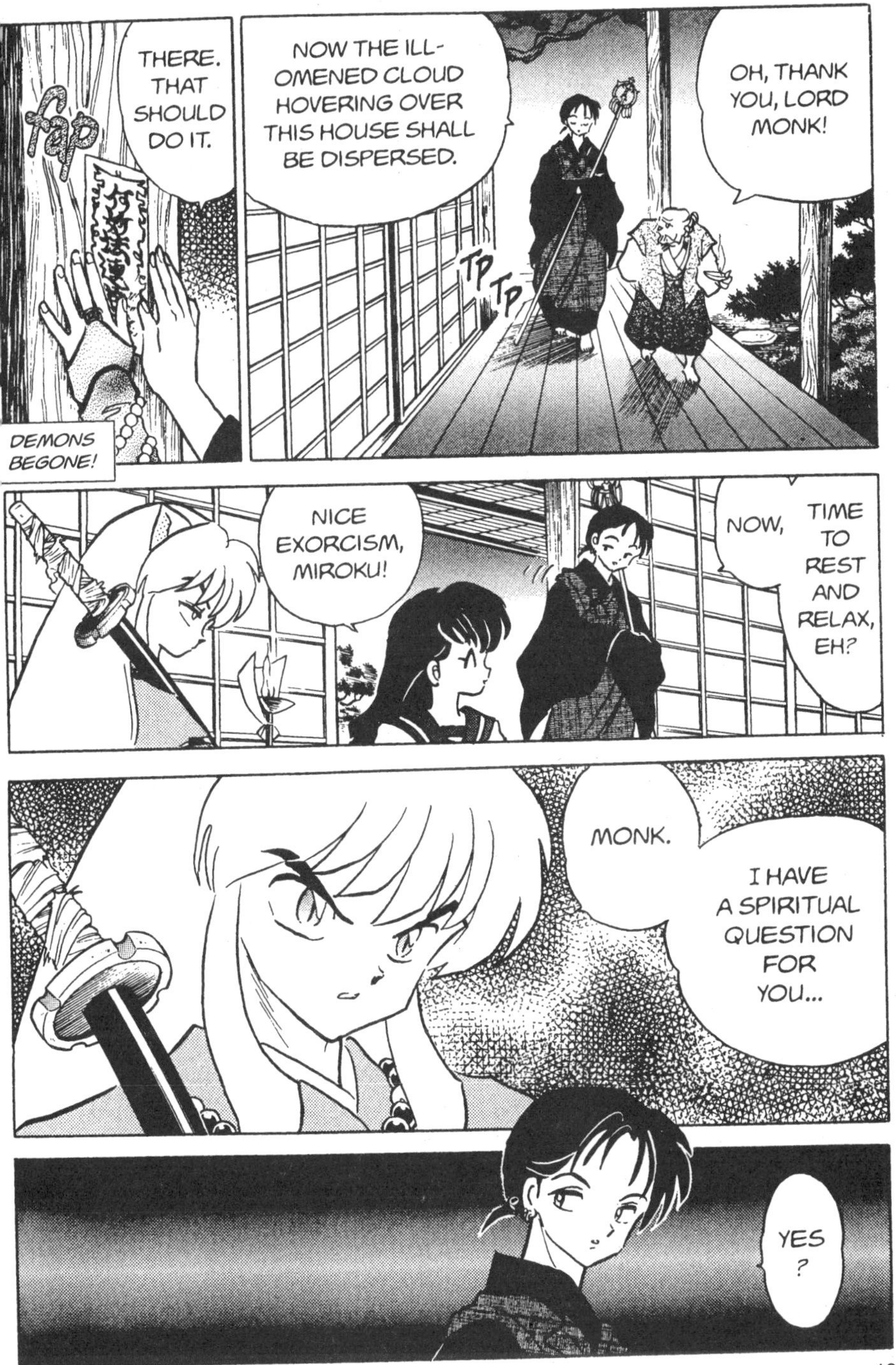
fap
THERE. THAT SHOULD DO IT.
DEMONS BEGONE!
NOW THE ILL-OMENED CLOUD HOVERING OVER THIS HOUSE SHALL BE DISPERSED.
Tp Tp
OH, THANK YOU, LORD MONK!
NICE EXORCISM, MIROKU!
NOW, TIME TO REST AND RELAX, EH?
MONK.
I HAVE A SPIRITUAL QUESTION FOR YOU...
YES ?

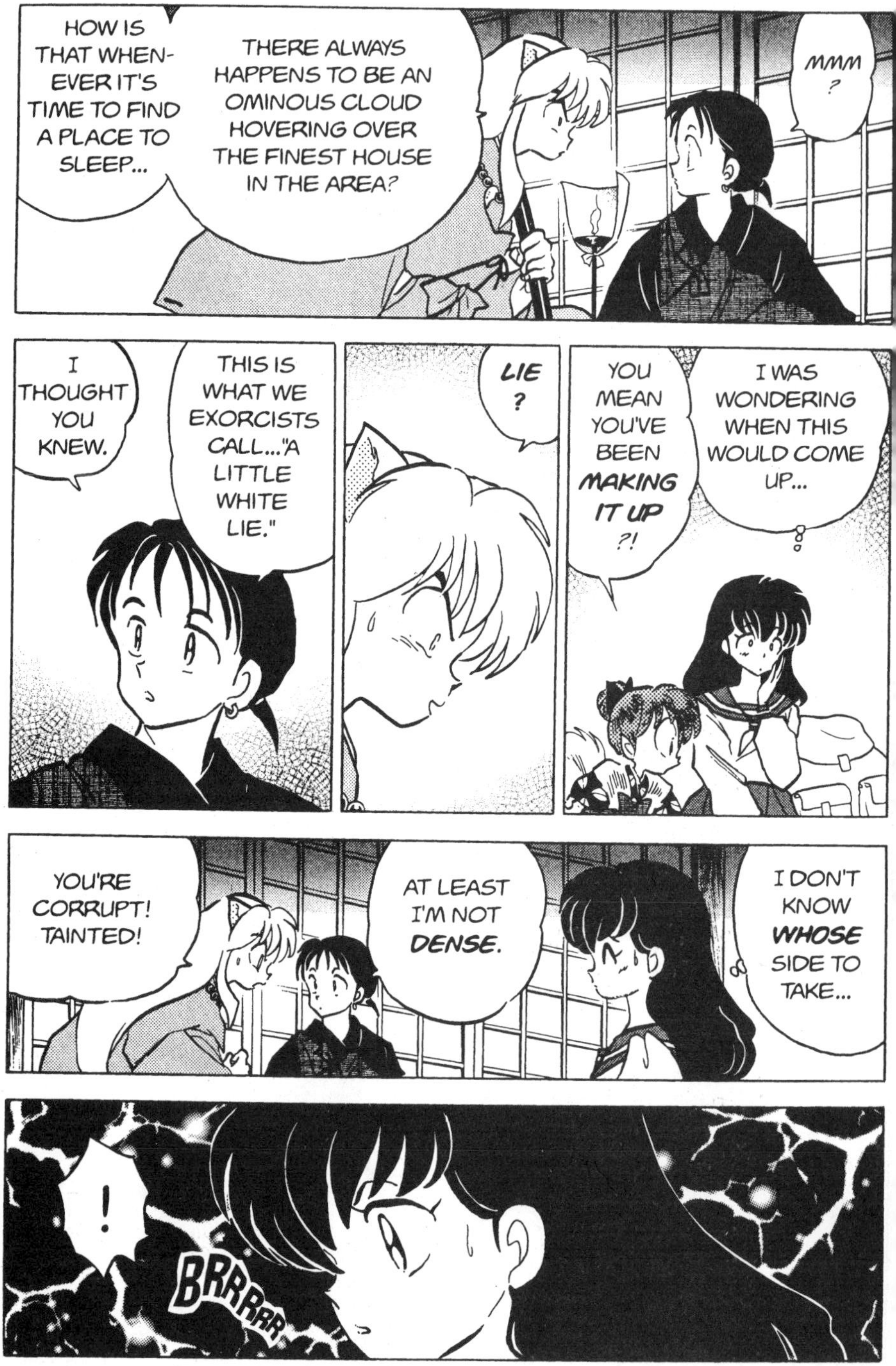
HOW IS THAT WHENEVER IT'S TIME TO FIND A PLACE TO SLEEP...
THERE ALWAYS HAPPENS TO BE AN OMINOUS CLOUD HOVERING OVER THE FINEST HOUSE IN THE AREA?
MMM ?
I THOUGHT YOU KNEW.
THIS IS WHAT WE EXORCISTS CALL..."A LITTLE WHITE LIE."
LIE ?
YOU MEAN YOU'VE BEEN MAKING IT UP ?!
I WAS WONDERING WHEN THIS WOULD COME UP...
YOU'RE CORRUPT! TAINTED!
AT LEAST I'M NOT DENSE.
I DON'T KNOW WHOSE SIDE TO TAKE...
!
BRRRRRR

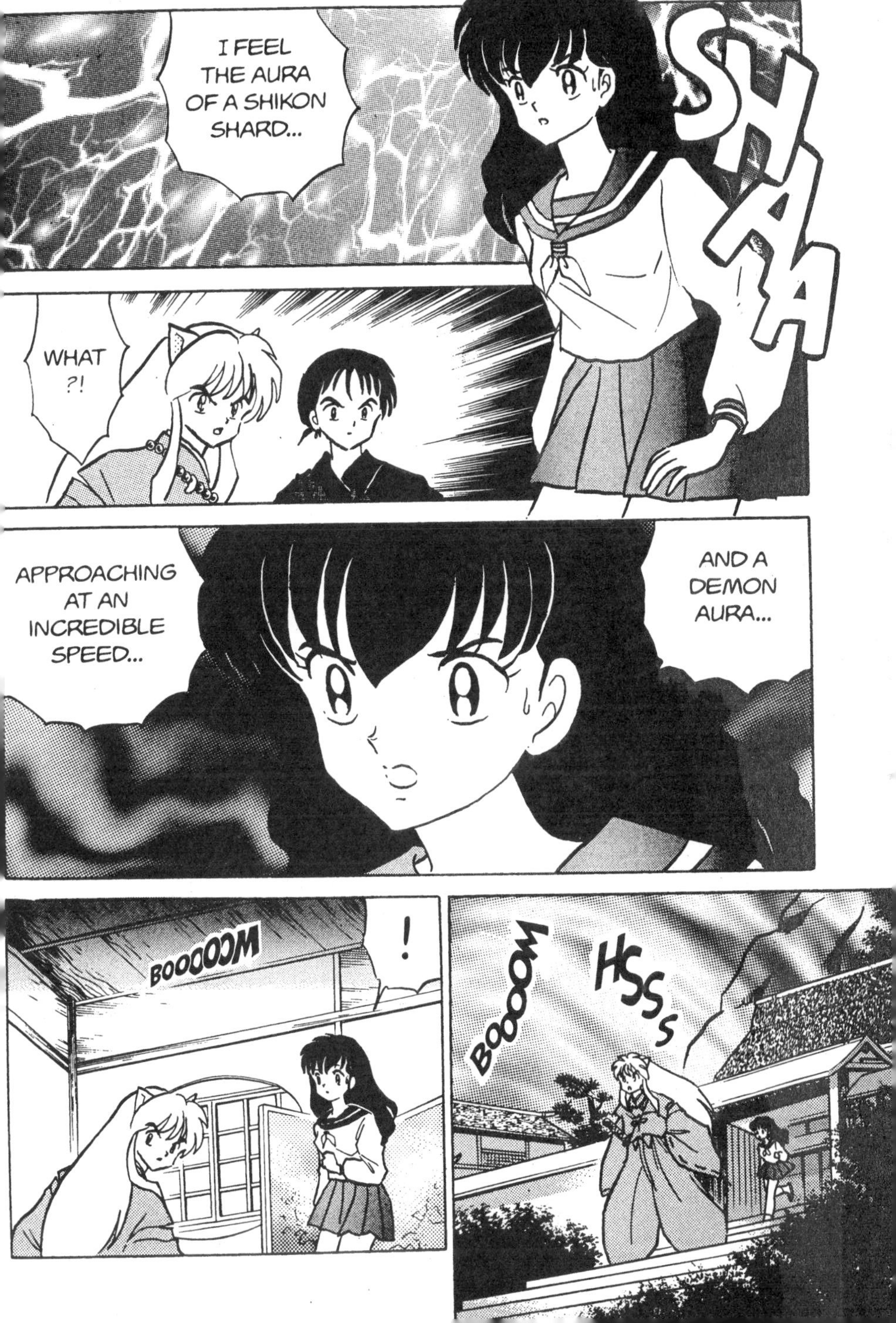
I FEEL THE AURA OF A SHIKON SHARD...
SHAA
WHAT ?!
APPROACHING AT AN INCREDIBLE SPEED...
AND A DEMON AURA...
BOOOOOM
!
BOOOOM
HSSSS

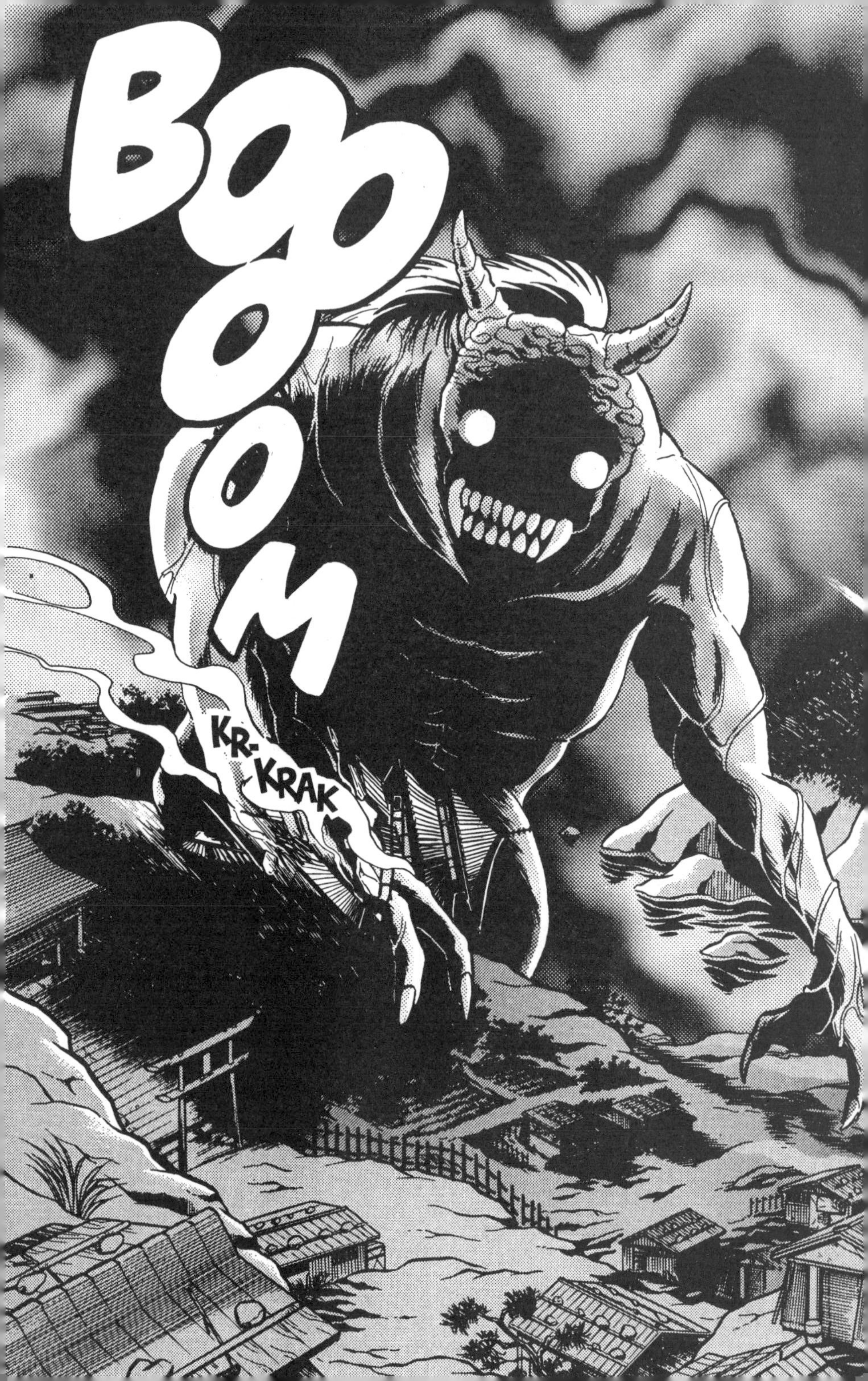
BOOOOM
KR-KRAK

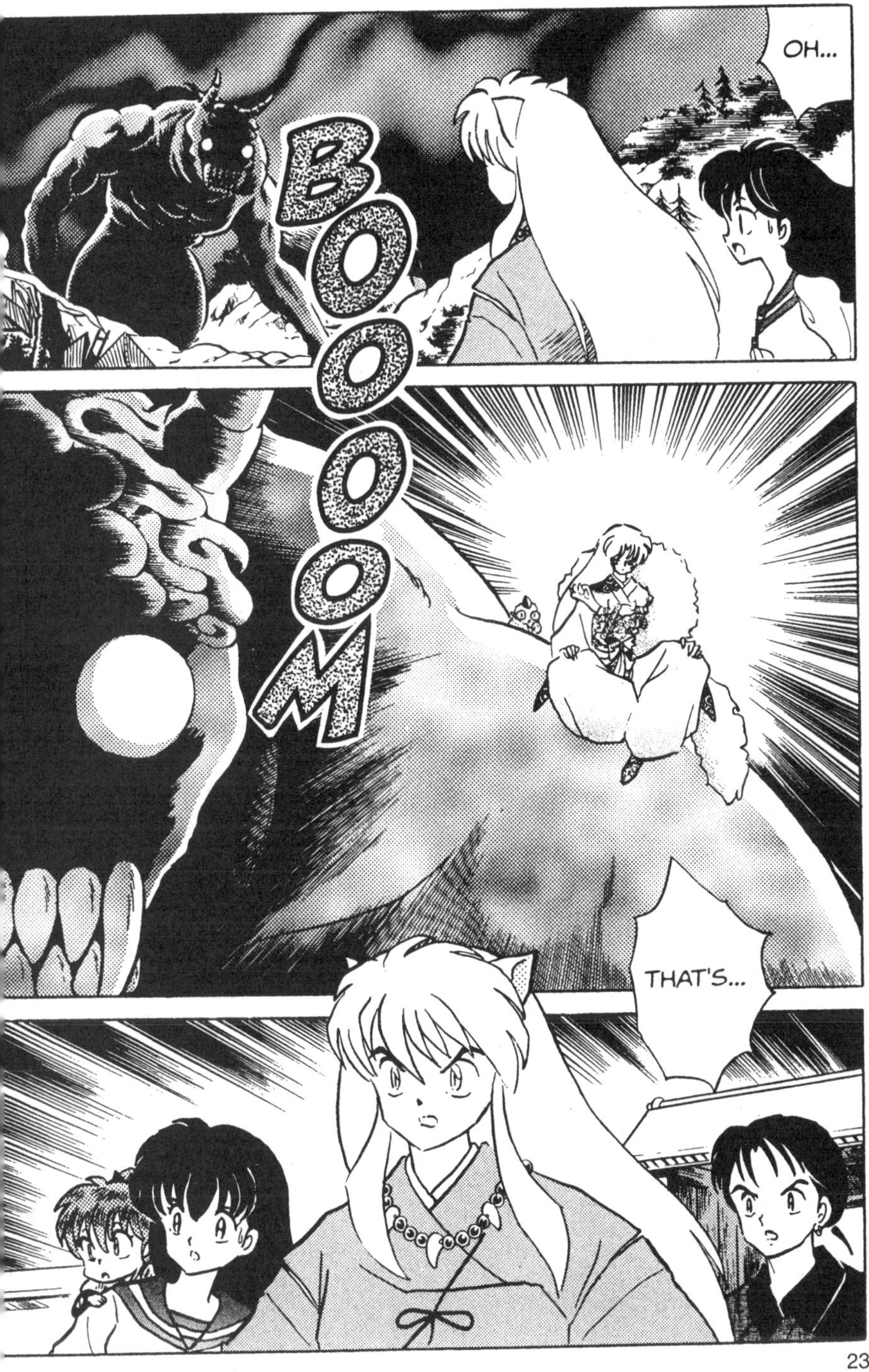
BOOOOOM
OH...
THAT'S...

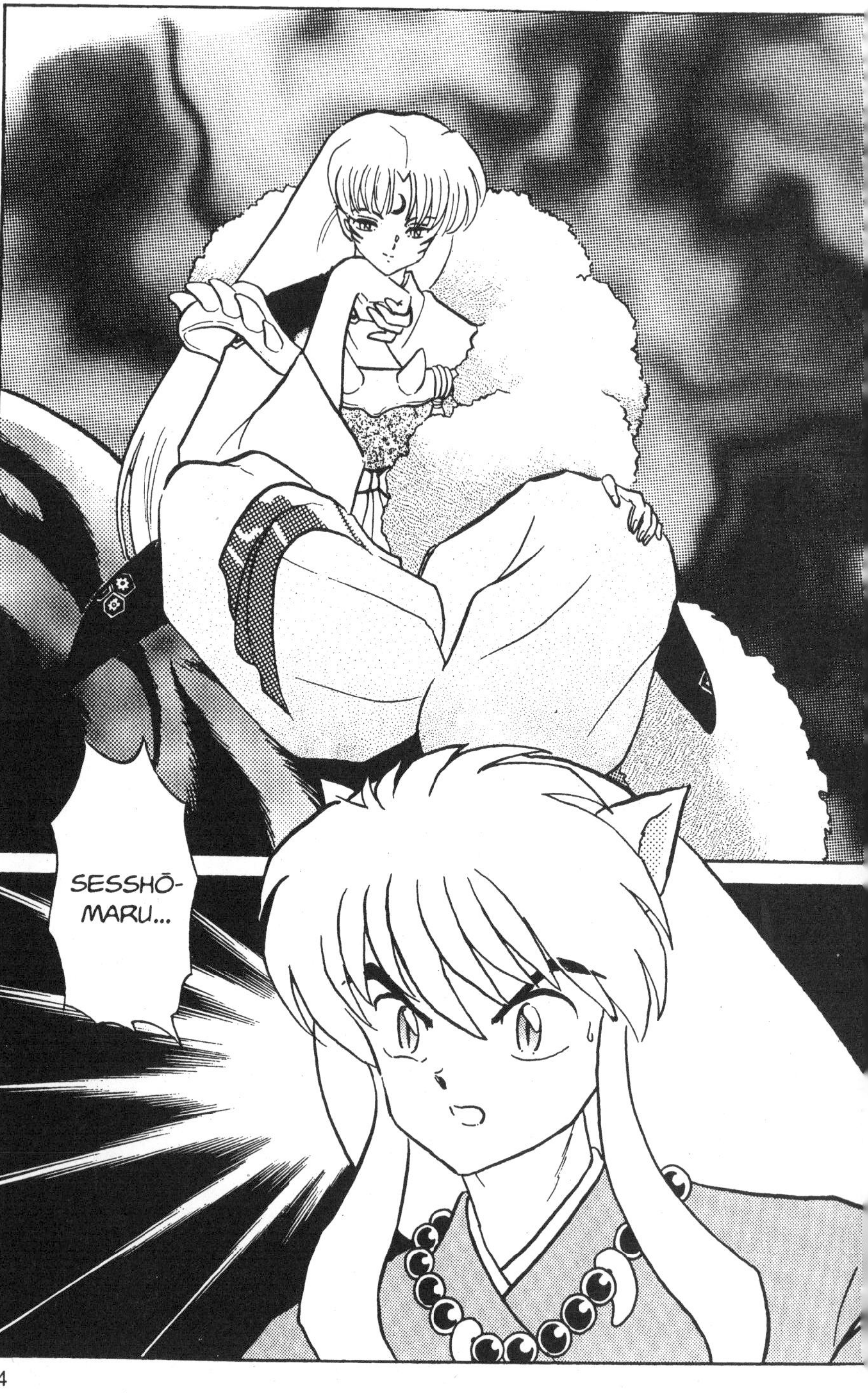
SESSHŌ-
MARU...

SCROLL TWO

THE POWER OF THE WOLF'S FANG

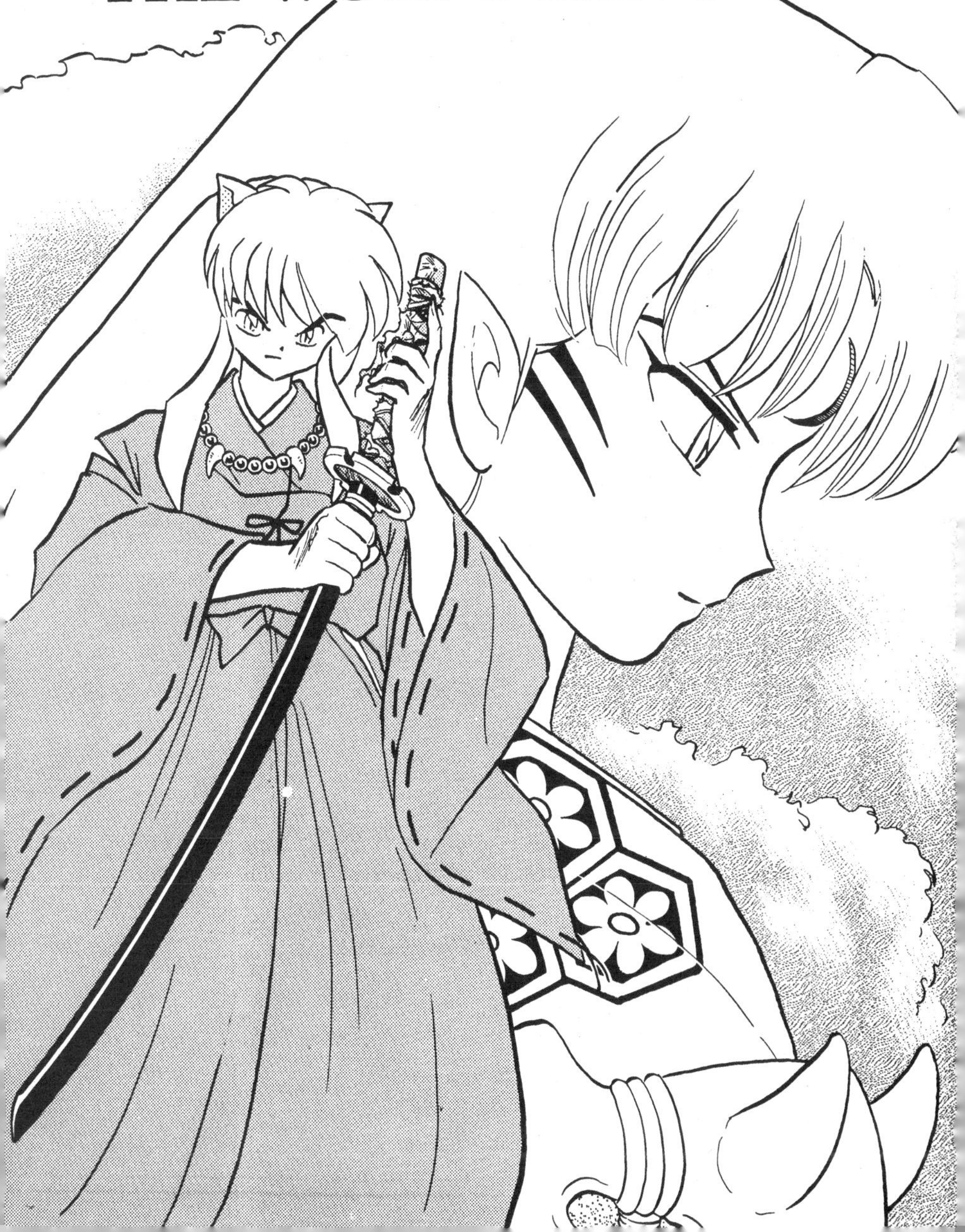

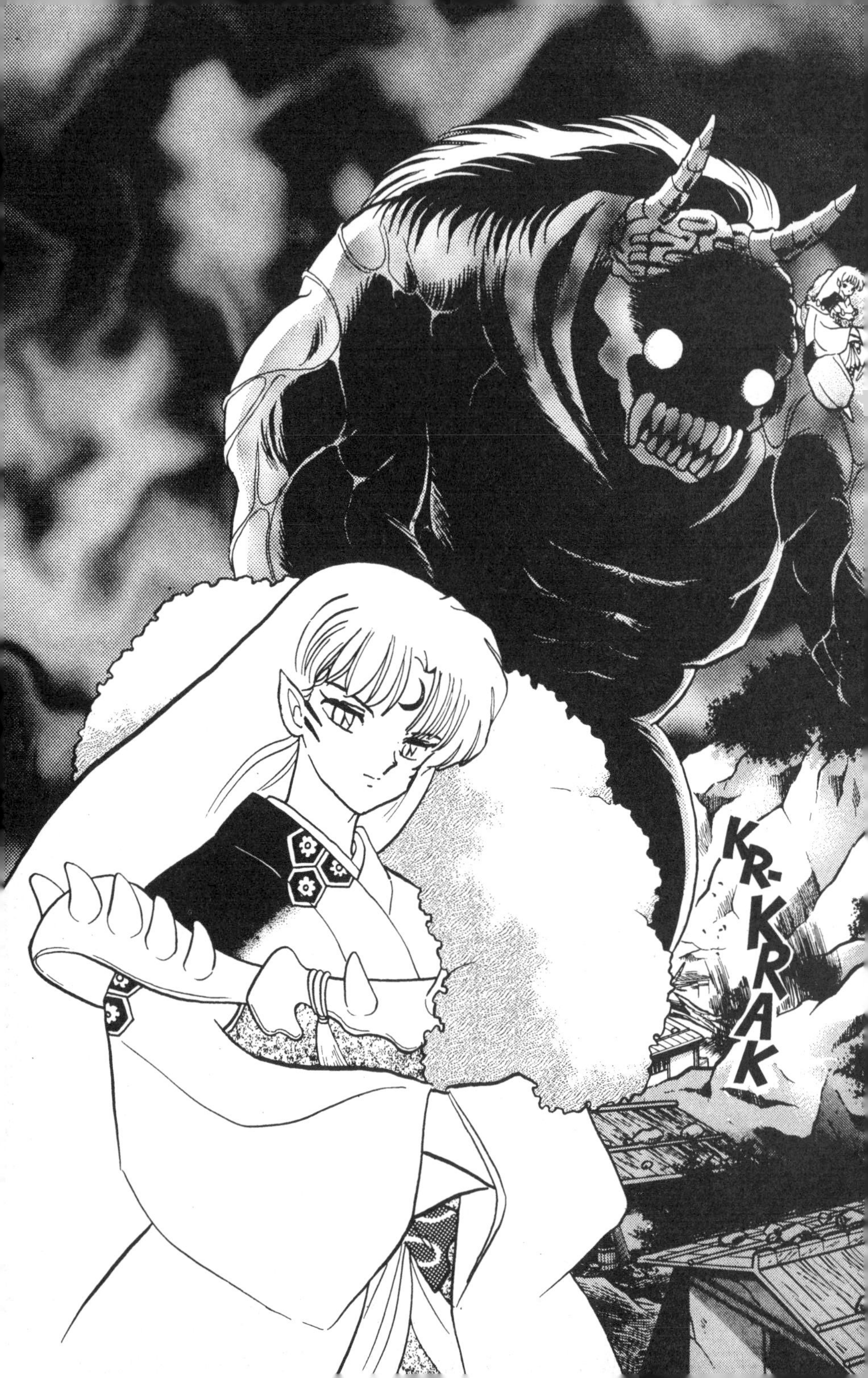
KR-KRAK

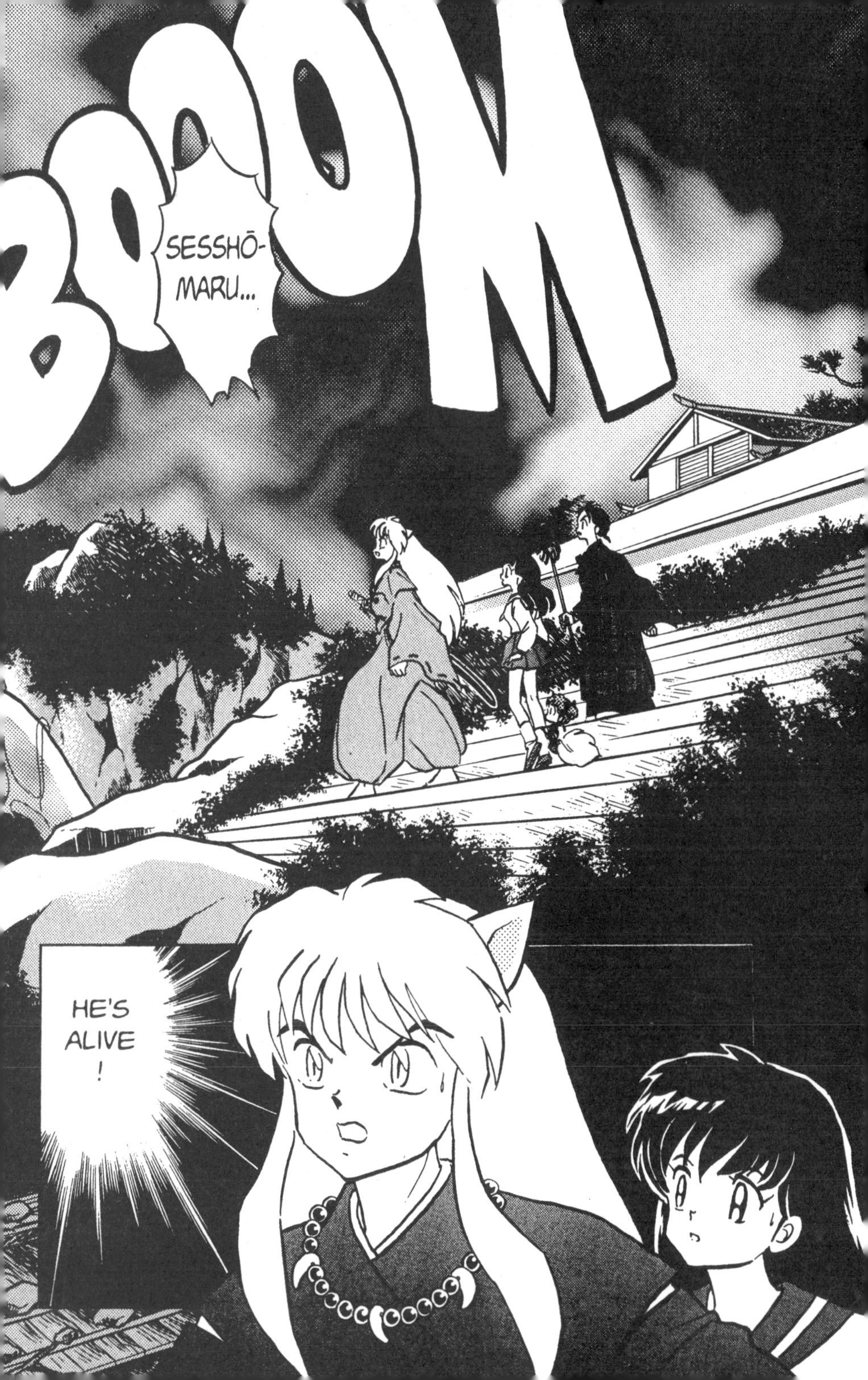
BOOOOM
SESSHŌ-MARU...
HE'S ALIVE!

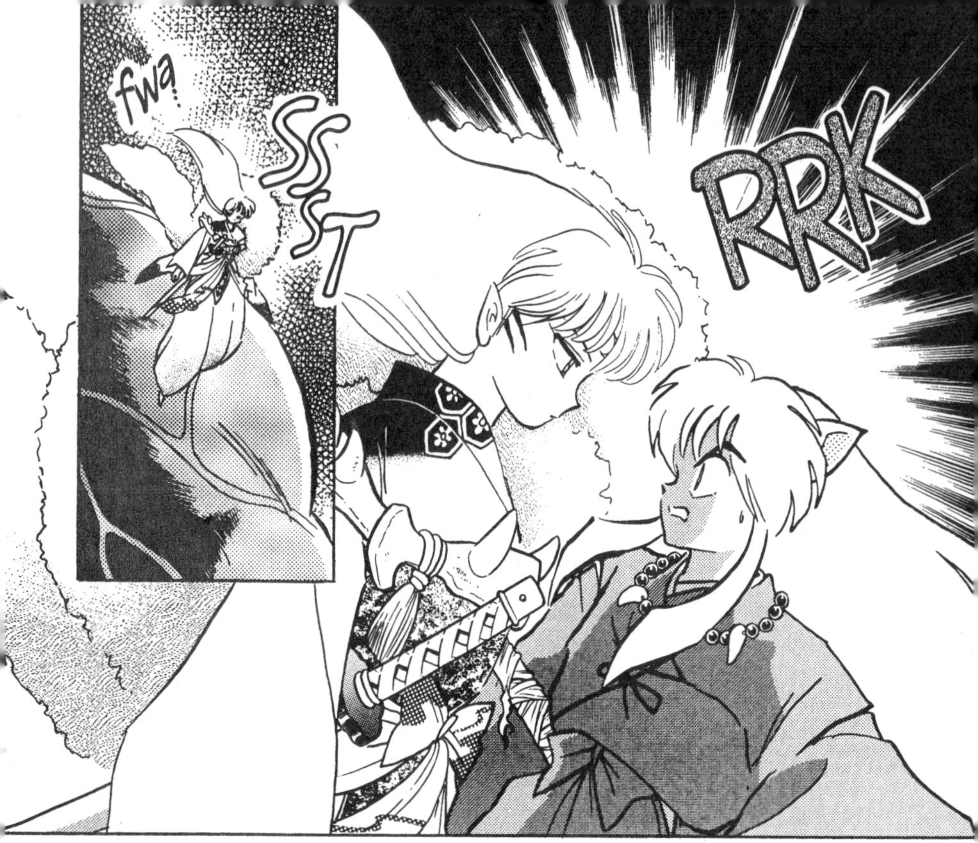
fwa
SSST
RRK

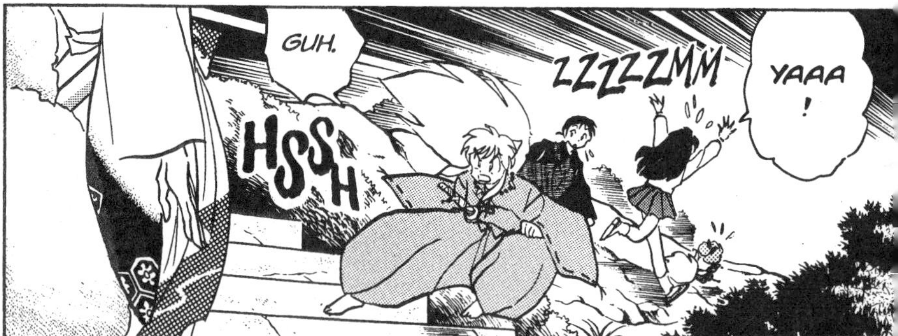
GUH.
HSSH
ZZZZZMM
YAAA!

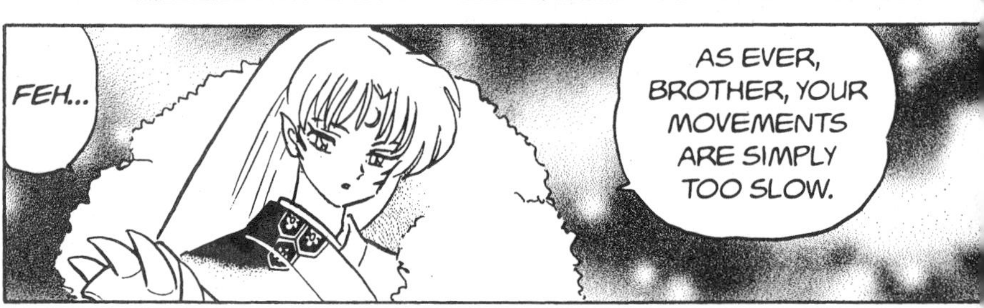
FEH...
AS EVER, BROTHER, YOUR MOVEMENTS ARE SIMPLY TOO SLOW.

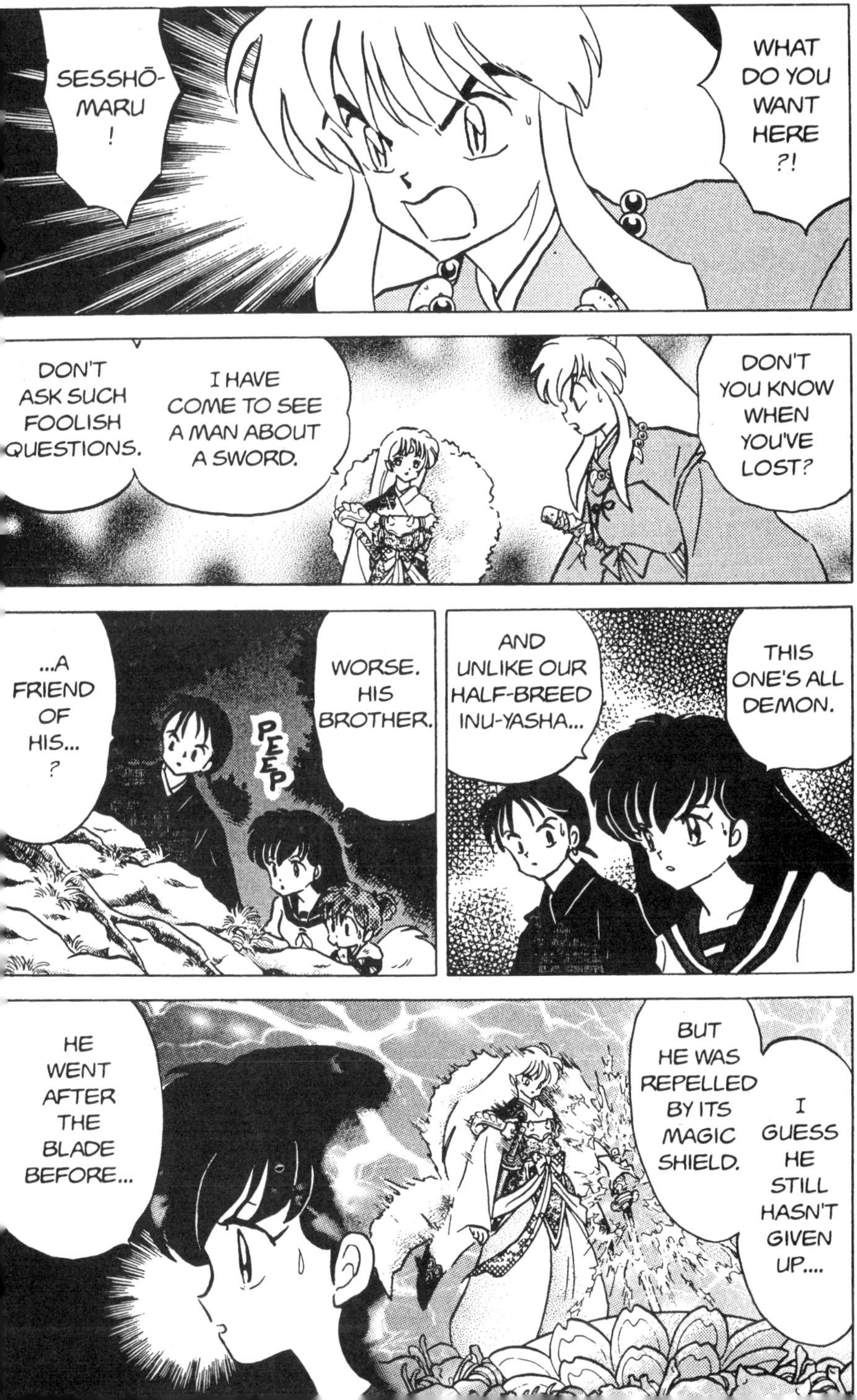
SESSHŌ-MARU!
WHAT DO YOU WANT HERE?!
DON'T ASK SUCH FOOLISH QUESTIONS.
I HAVE COME TO SEE A MAN ABOUT A SWORD.
DON'T YOU KNOW WHEN YOU'VE LOST?
...A FRIEND OF HIS...?
PEEP
WORSE. HIS BROTHER.
AND UNLIKE OUR HALF-BREED INU-YASHA...
THIS ONE'S ALL DEMON.
HE WENT AFTER THE BLADE BEFORE...
BUT HE WAS REPELLED BY ITS MAGIC SHIELD.
I GUESS HE STILL HASN'T GIVEN UP....

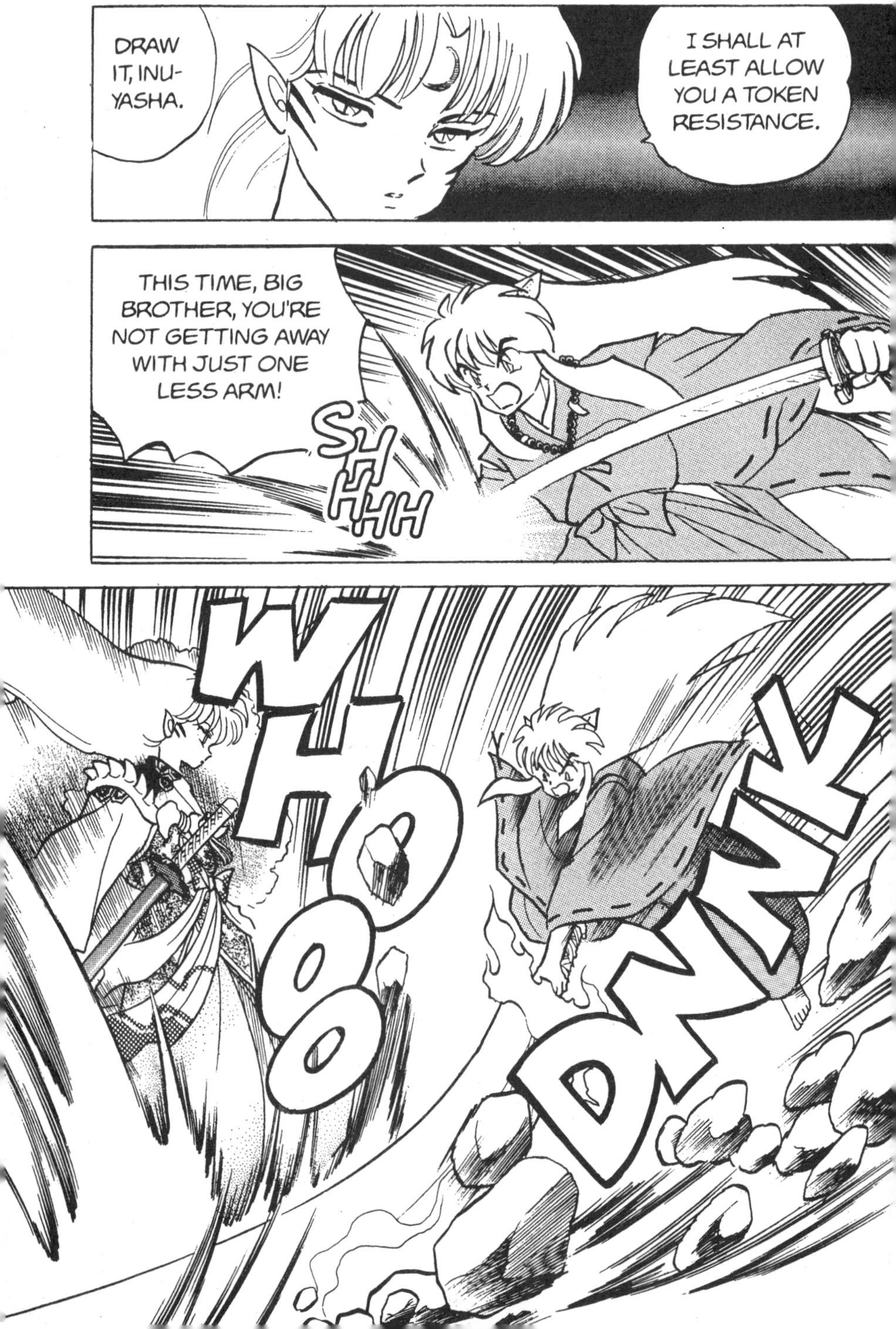
DRAW IT, INU-YASHA.
I SHALL AT LEAST ALLOW YOU A TOKEN RESISTANCE.
THIS TIME, BIG BROTHER, YOU'RE NOT GETTING AWAY WITH JUST ONE LESS ARM!
SHHHH
WHOOO
DNNK

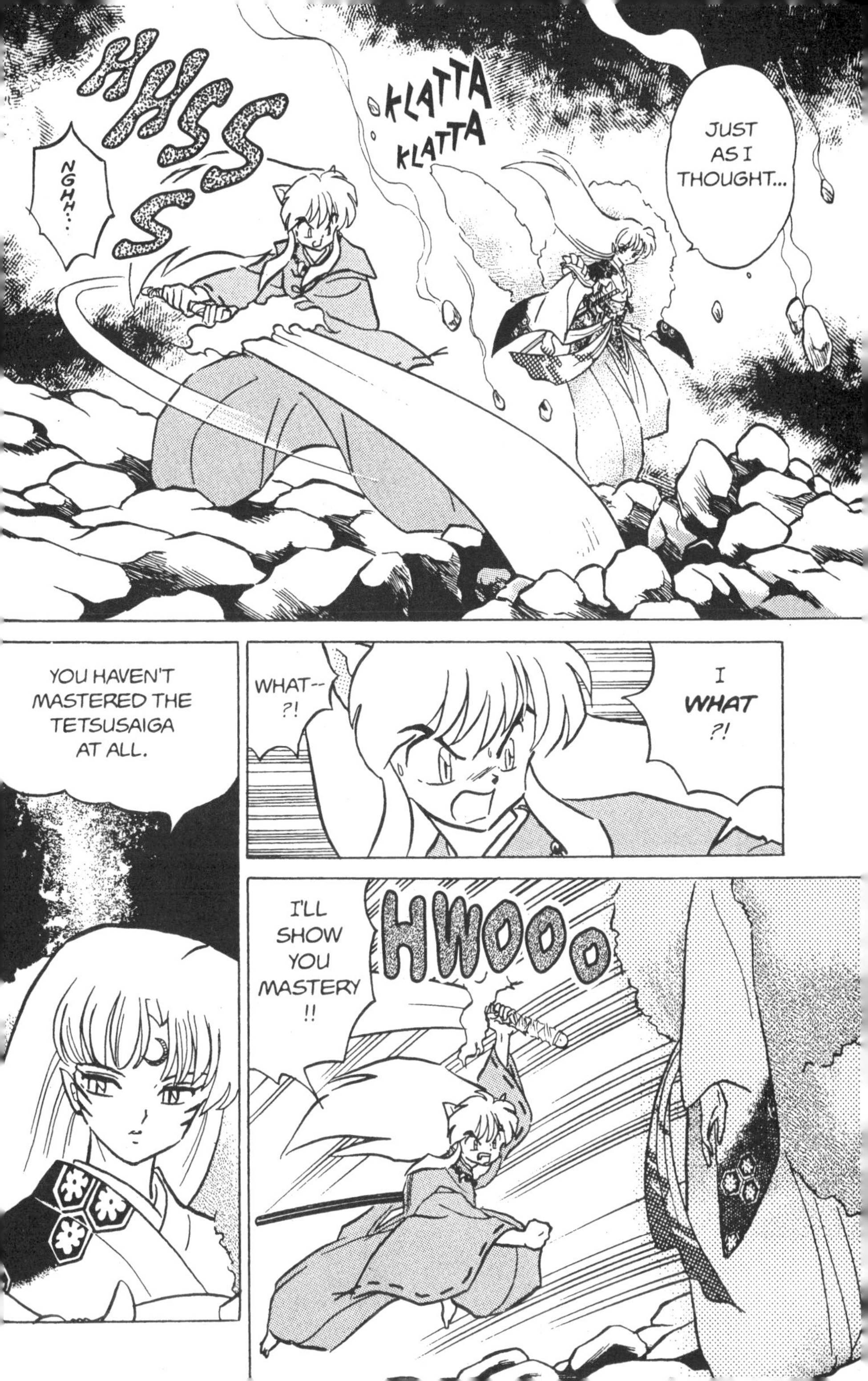
NGHH...
HHSSS
KLATTA KLATTA
JUST AS I THOUGHT...
YOU HAVEN'T MASTERED THE TETSUSAIGA AT ALL.
WHAT--?!
I WHAT?!
I'LL SHOW YOU MASTERY!!
HWOOO

GGGG

!

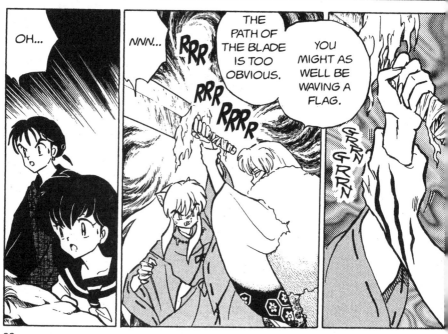

OH...

NNN...

RRR

RRR

RRRR

THE PATH OF THE BLADE IS TOO OBVIOUS.

YOU MIGHT AS WELL BE WAVING A FLAG.

GRRN GRRN

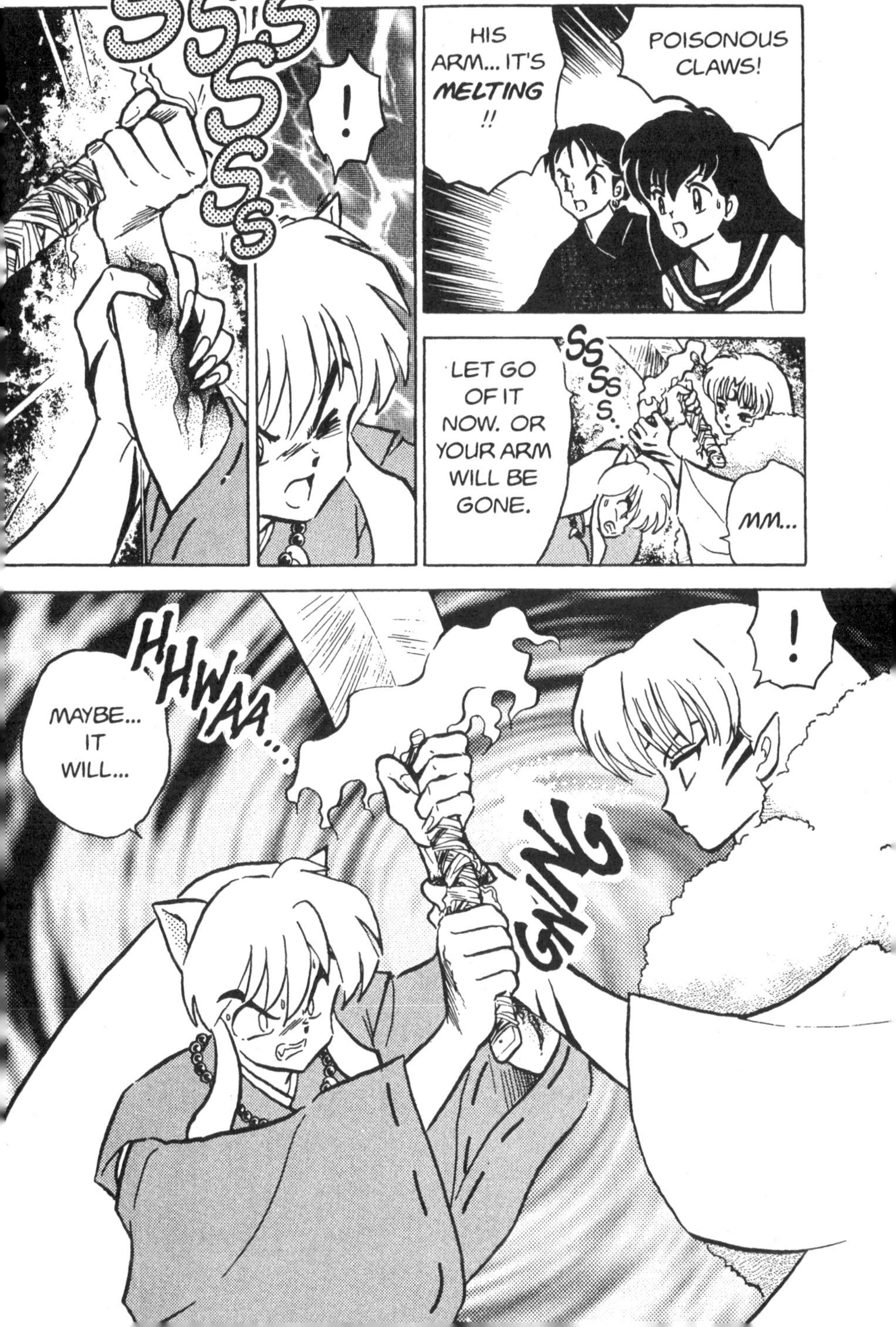
!
HIS ARM... IT'S MELTING !!
POISONOUS CLAWS!
SSSSS...
LET GO OF IT NOW. OR YOUR ARM WILL BE GONE.
MM...
HHWAAA...
MAYBE... IT WILL...
!

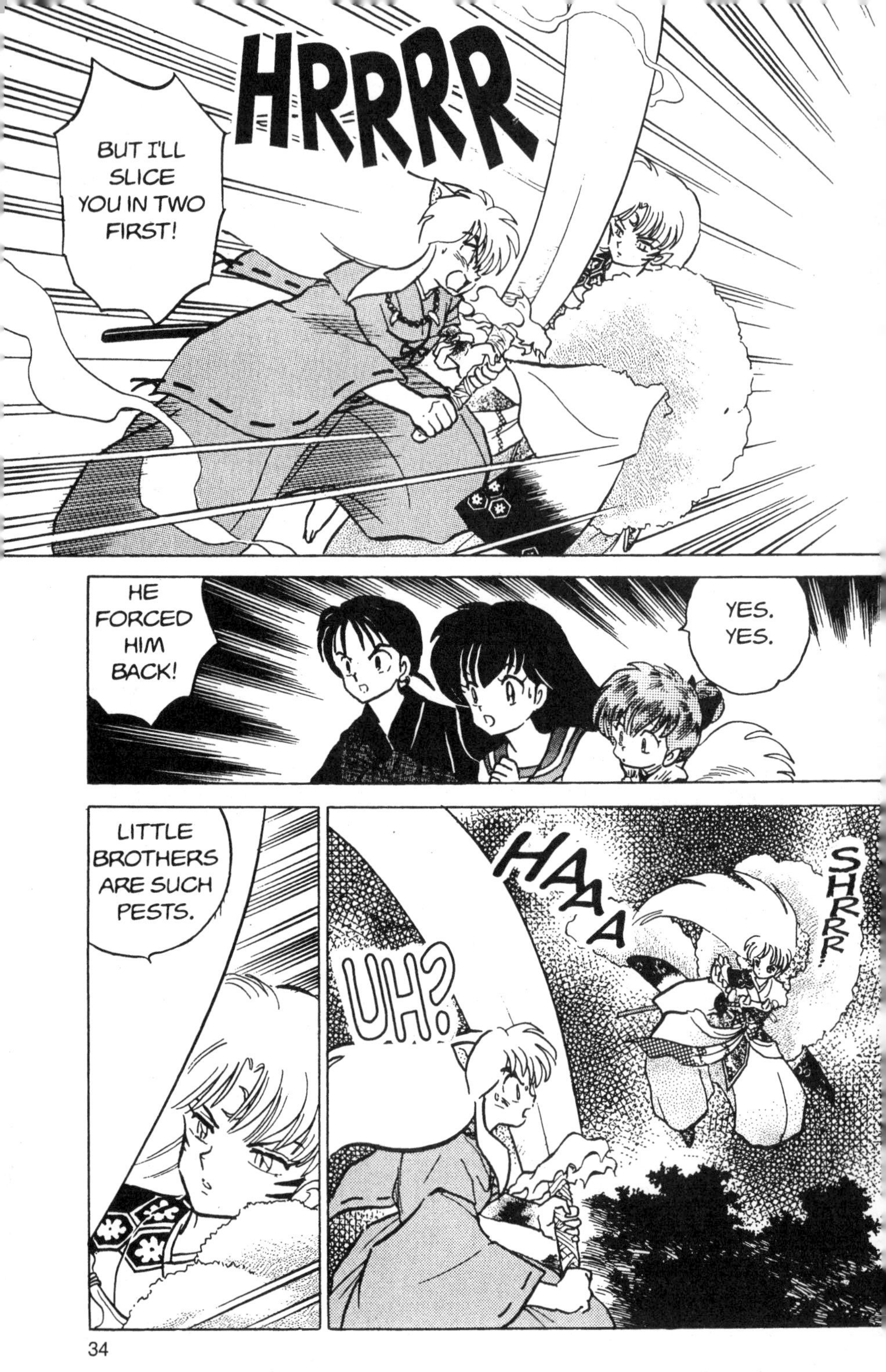
BUT I'LL SLICE YOU IN TWO FIRST!
HRRRR
HE FORCED HIM BACK!
YES. YES.
LITTLE BROTHERS ARE SUCH PESTS.
HAAAA
SHRRR
UH?

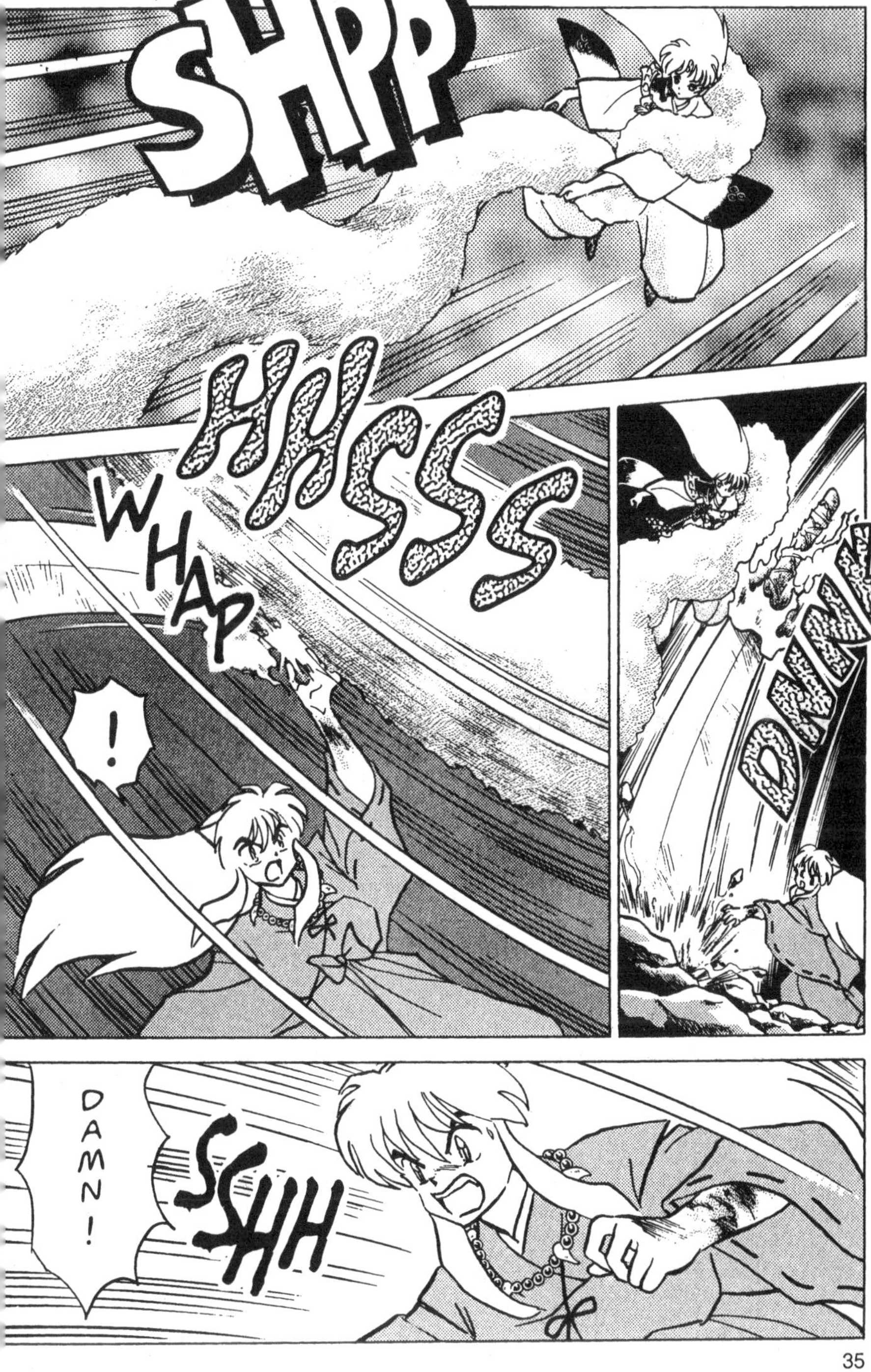
SHPP
HHSSSS
WHAP
!
DWNNK
DAMN!
SSHH

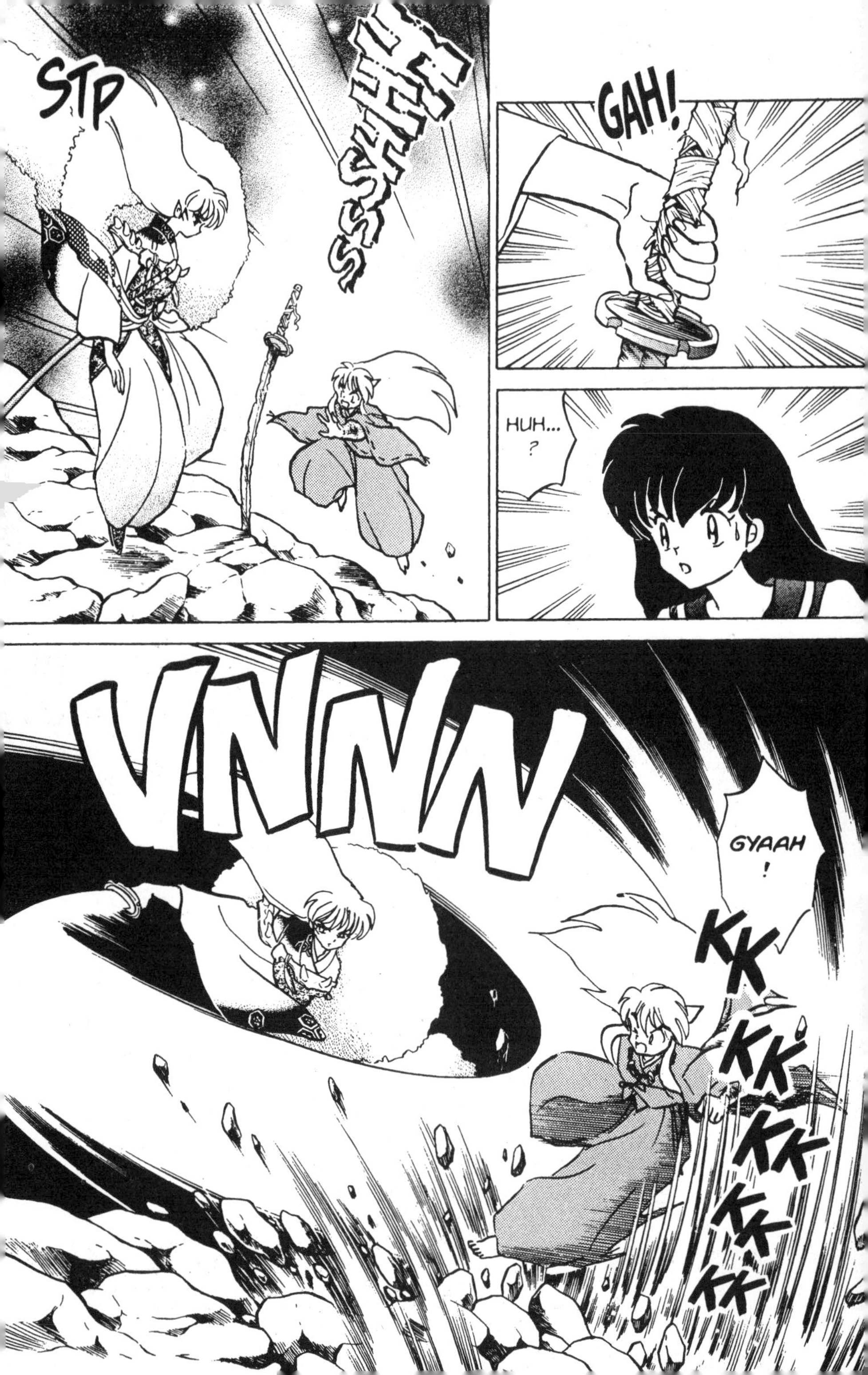
STP
GAH!
HUH...?
VNNN
GYAAH!
KKKKKKKKKKKK

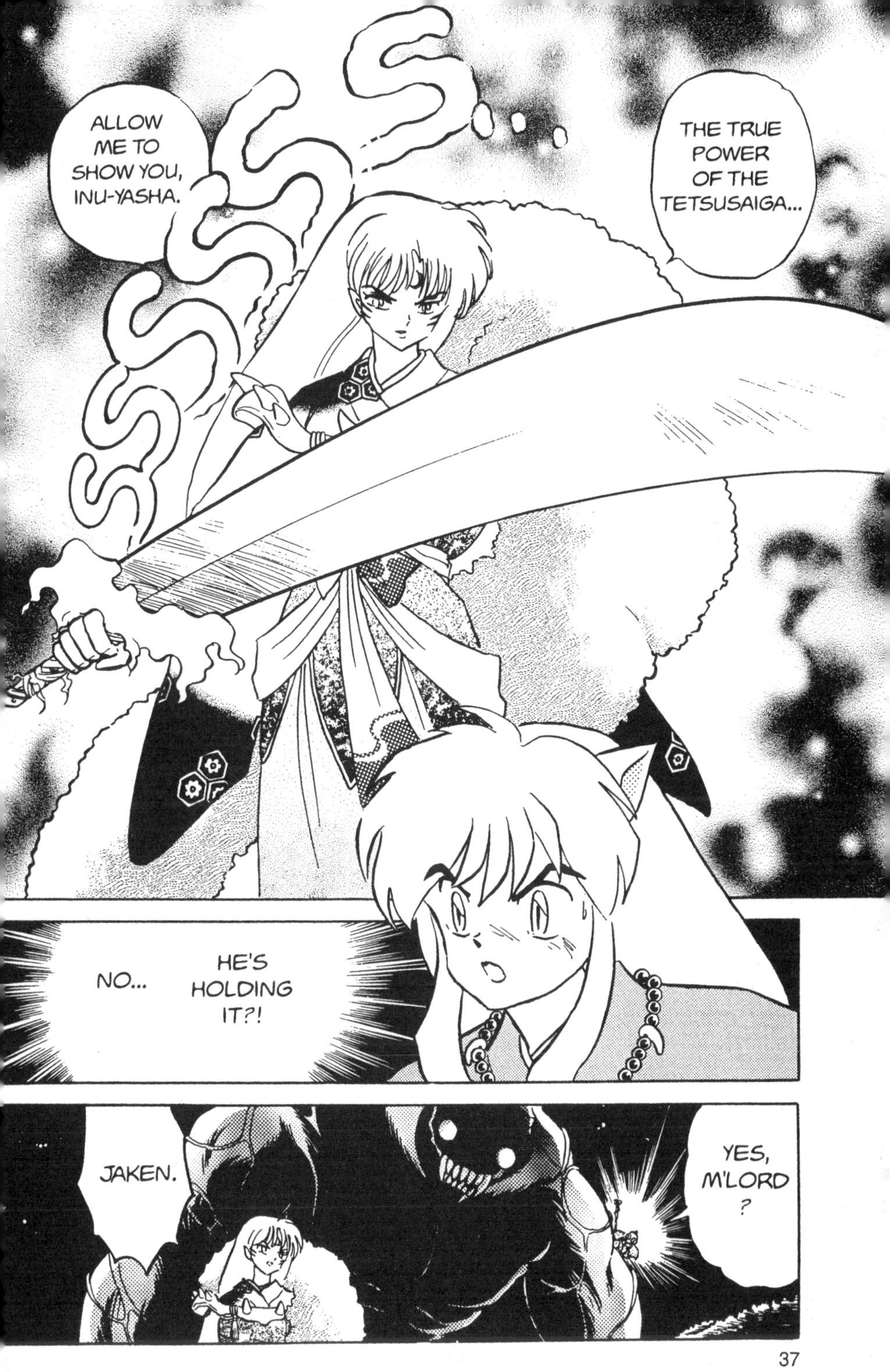
ALLOW ME TO SHOW YOU, INU-YASHA.
SSSS...
THE TRUE POWER OF THE TETSUSAIGA...
NO...
HE'S HOLDING IT?!
JAKEN.
YES, M'LORD?

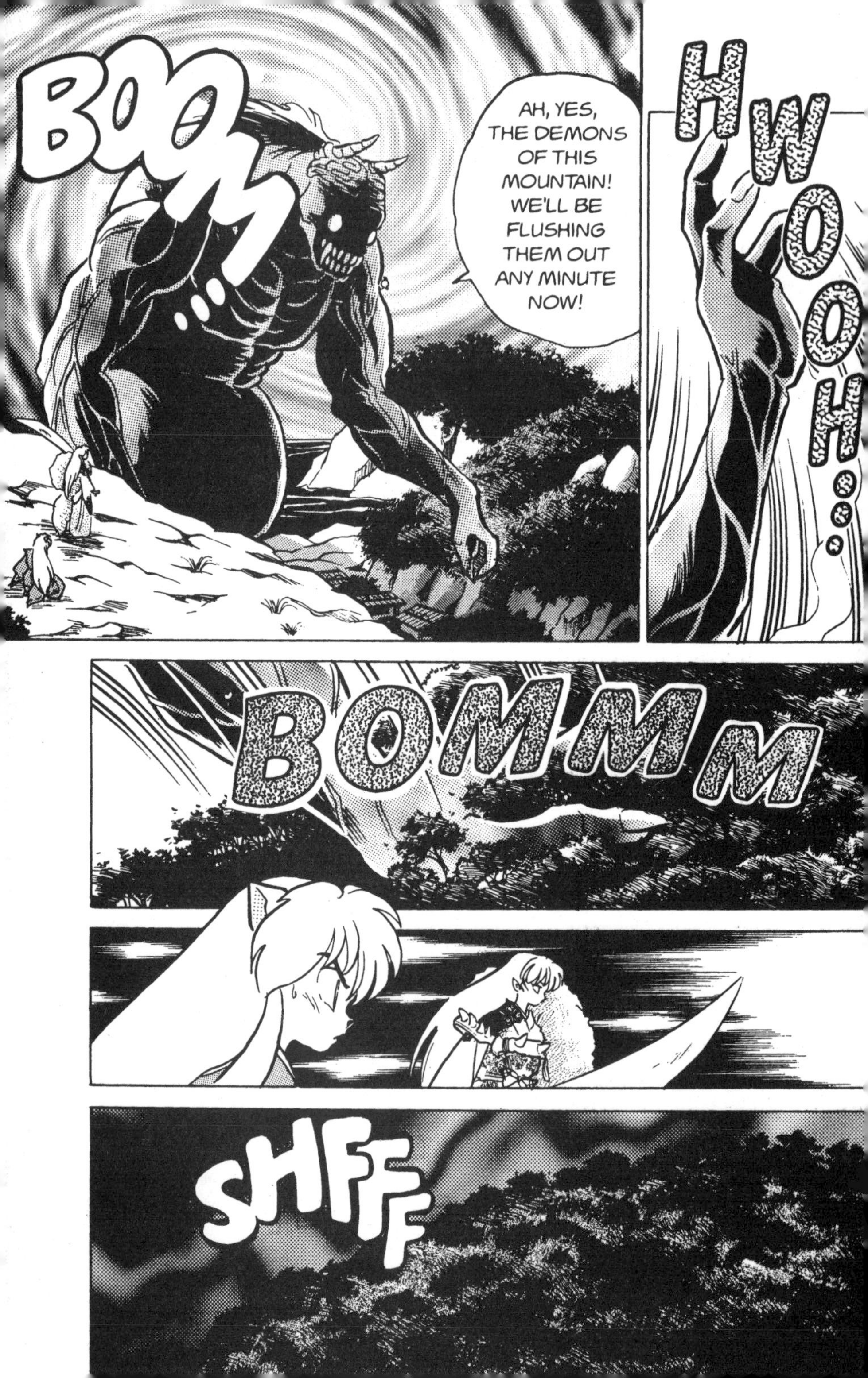
BOOM...
AH, YES, THE DEMONS OF THIS MOUNTAIN! WE'LL BE FLUSHING THEM OUT ANY MINUTE NOW!
HWOOH...
BOMMM
SHFFF

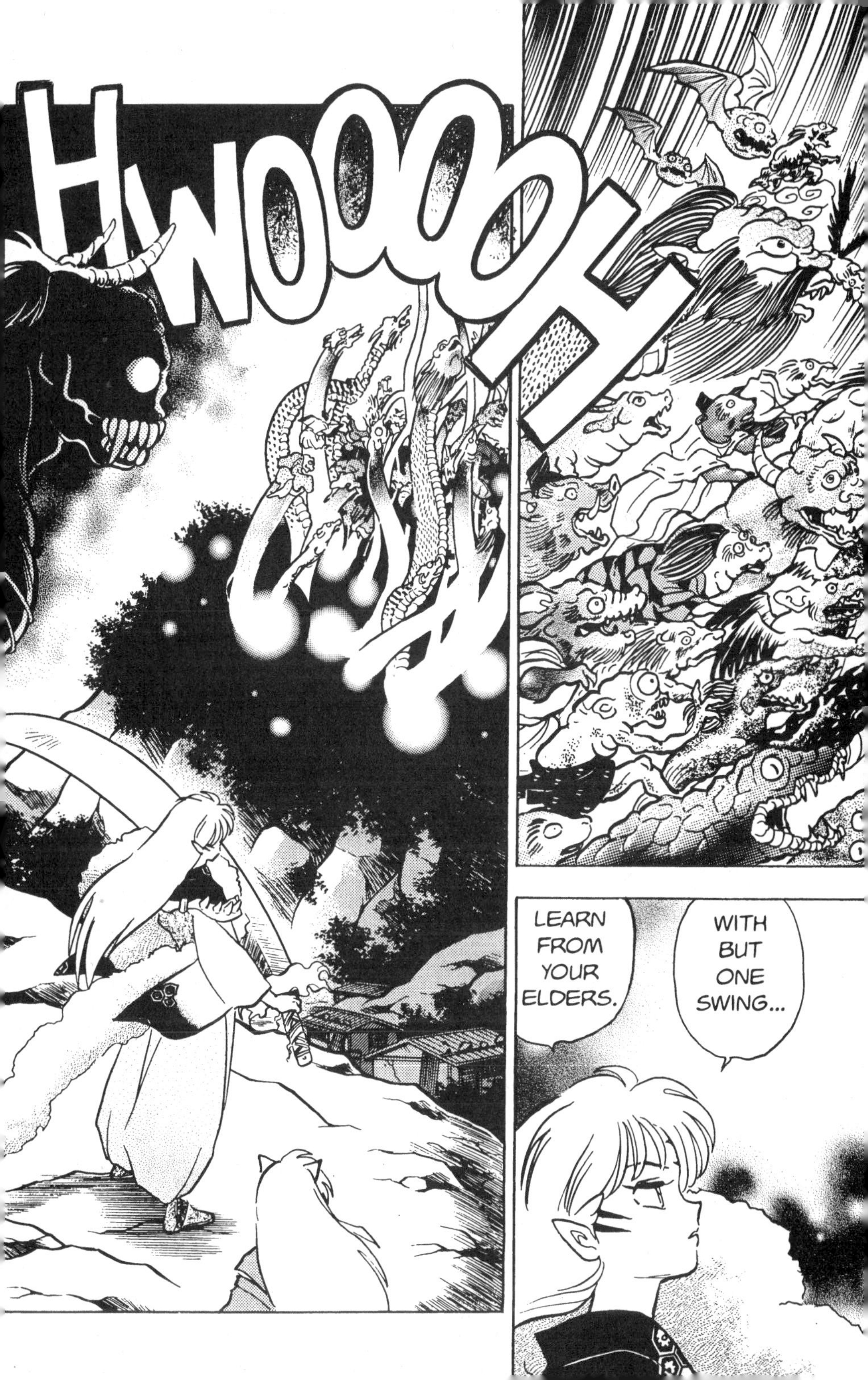
HWOOOOH
LEARN FROM YOUR ELDERS.
WITH BUT ONE SWING...

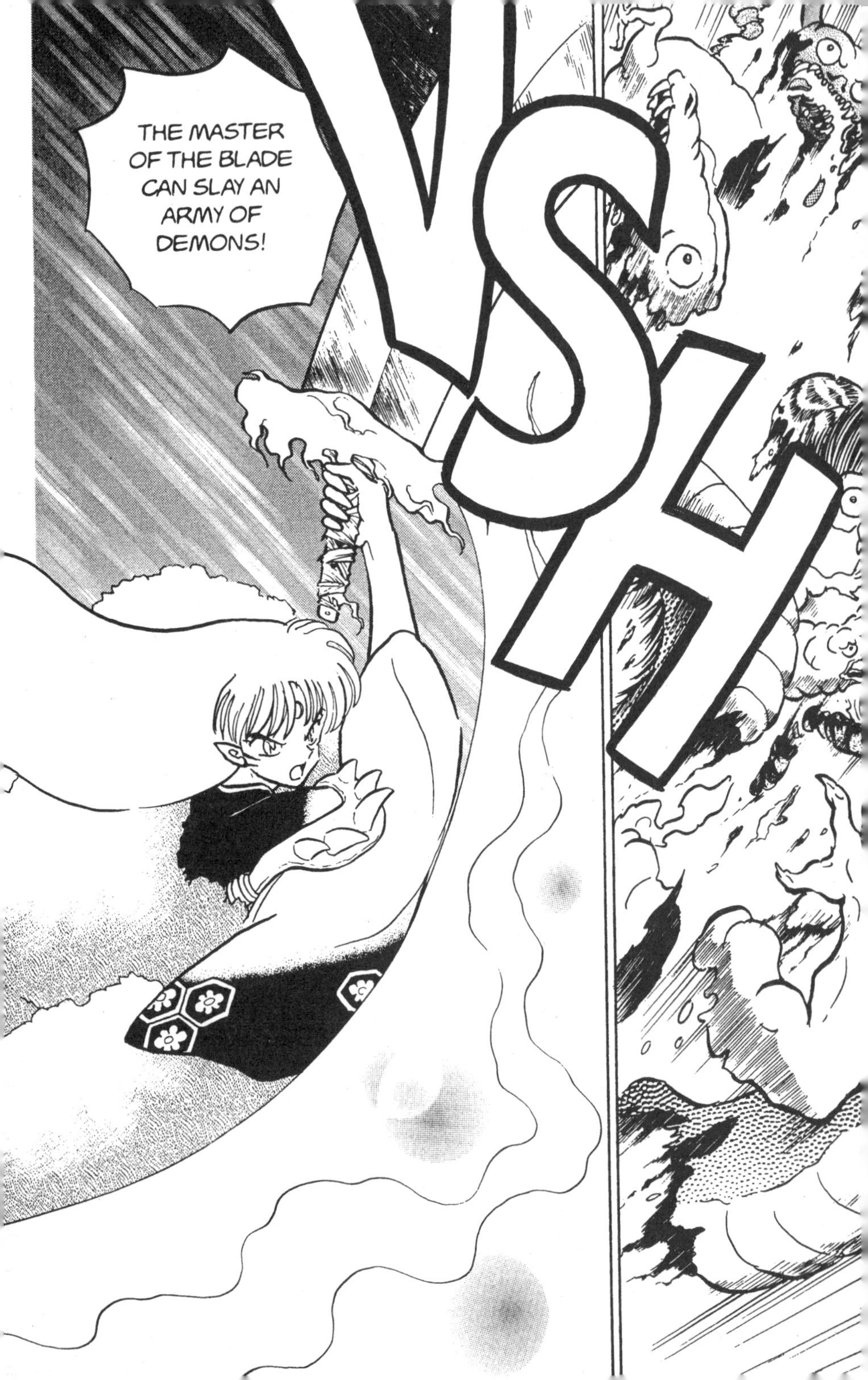
THE MASTER OF THE BLADE CAN SLAY AN ARMY OF DEMONS!
VSSH

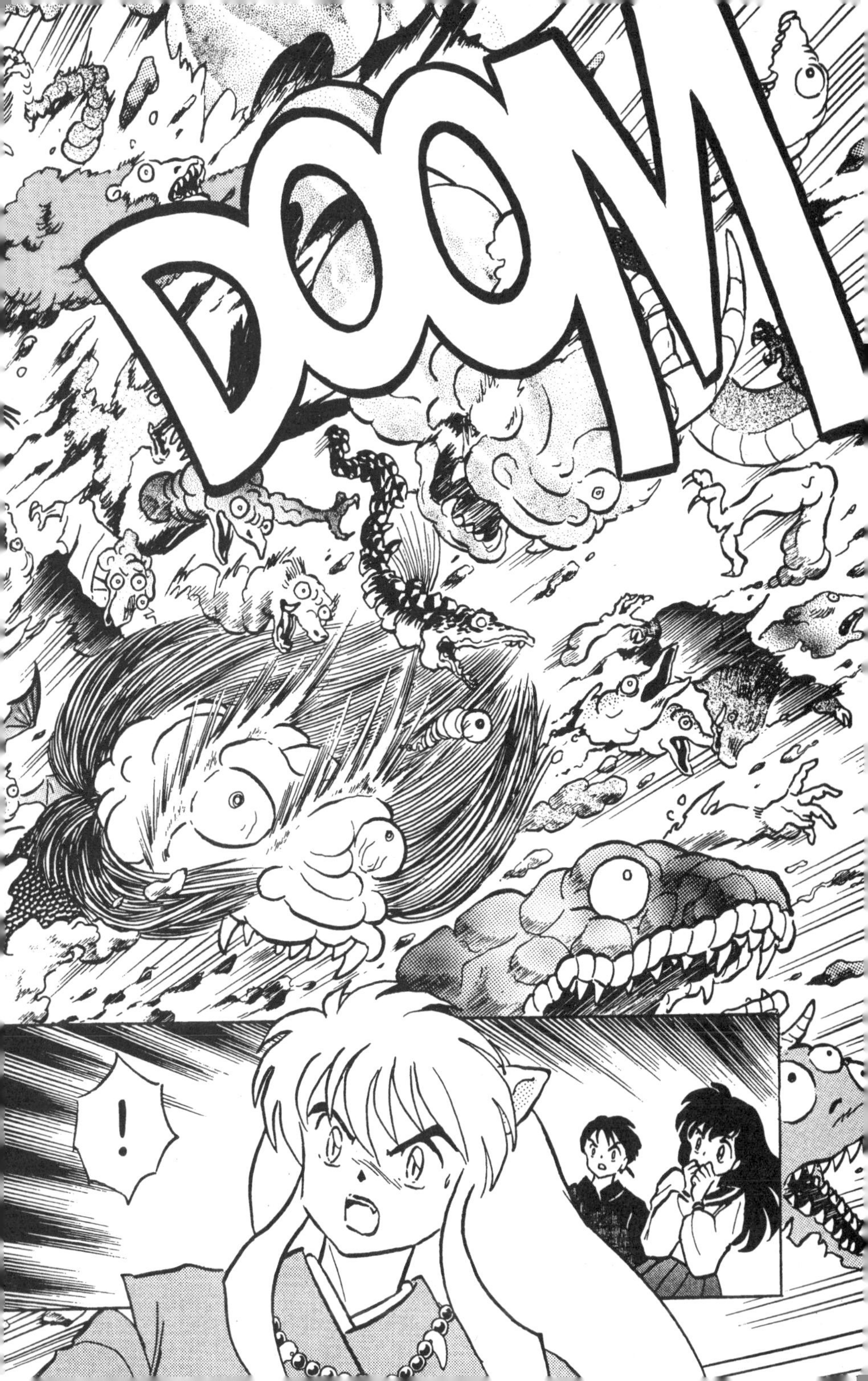
DOOM
!

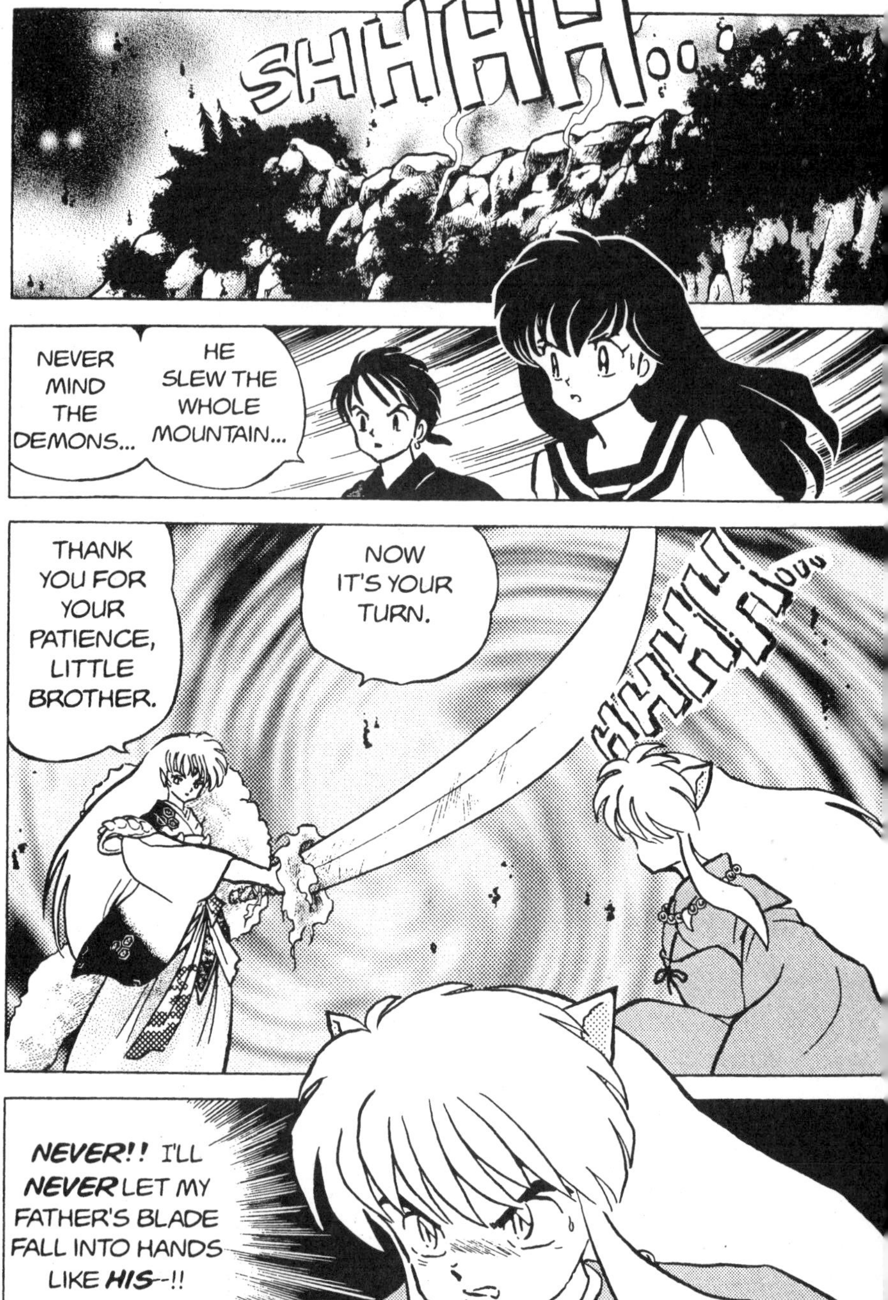
SHHHHH...
NEVER MIND THE DEMONS...
HE SLEW THE WHOLE MOUNTAIN...
THANK YOU FOR YOUR PATIENCE, LITTLE BROTHER.
NOW IT'S YOUR TURN.
SHHHHH...
NEVER!! I'LL **NEVER** LET MY FATHER'S BLADE FALL INTO HANDS LIKE **HIS**--!!

SCROLL THREE

THE STING OF VICTORY

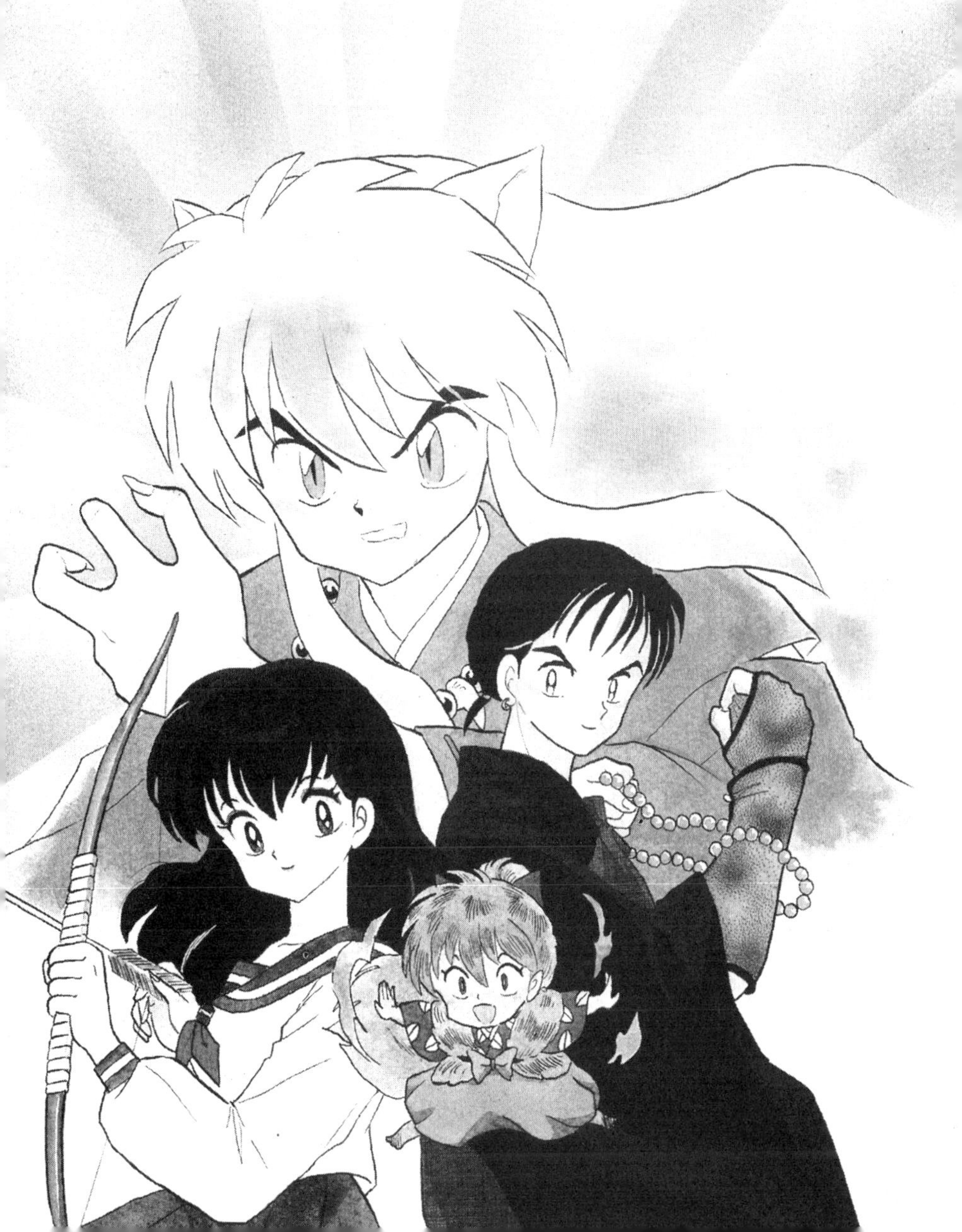

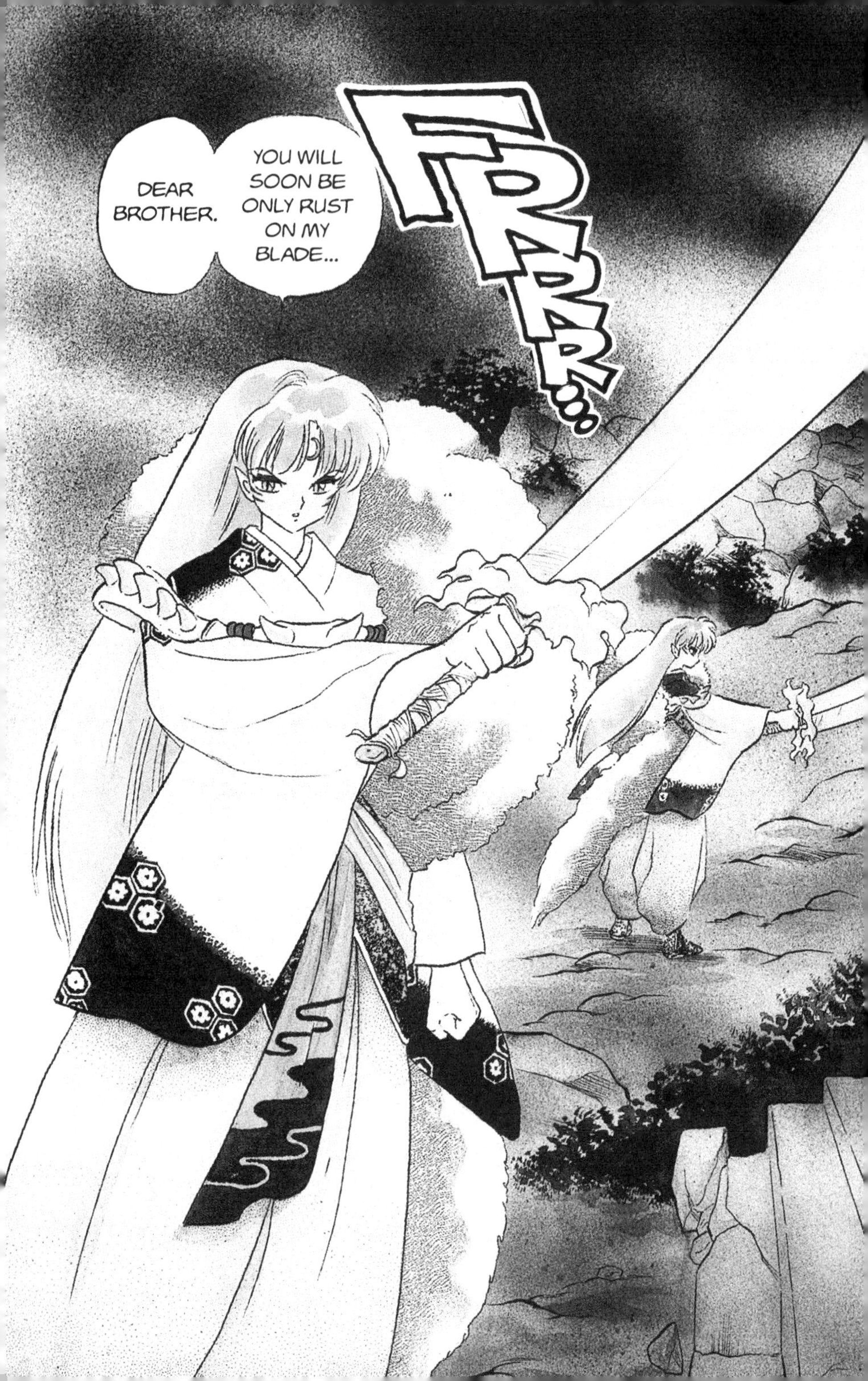
DEAR BROTHER.
YOU WILL SOON BE ONLY RUST ON MY BLADE...
FRRRR...

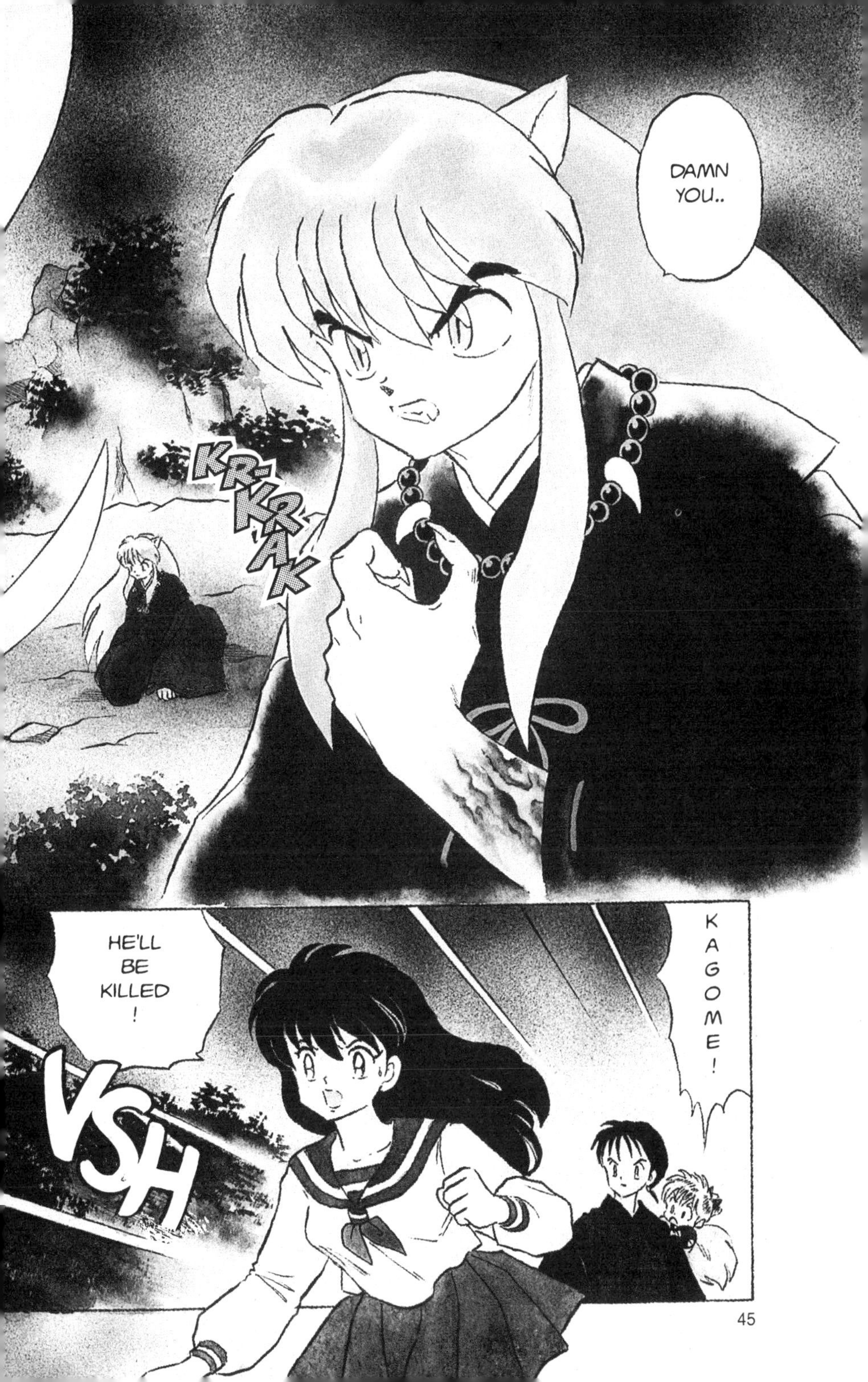
DAMN YOU..
KR-KR-KRAK
HE'LL BE KILLED!
VSH
KAGOME!

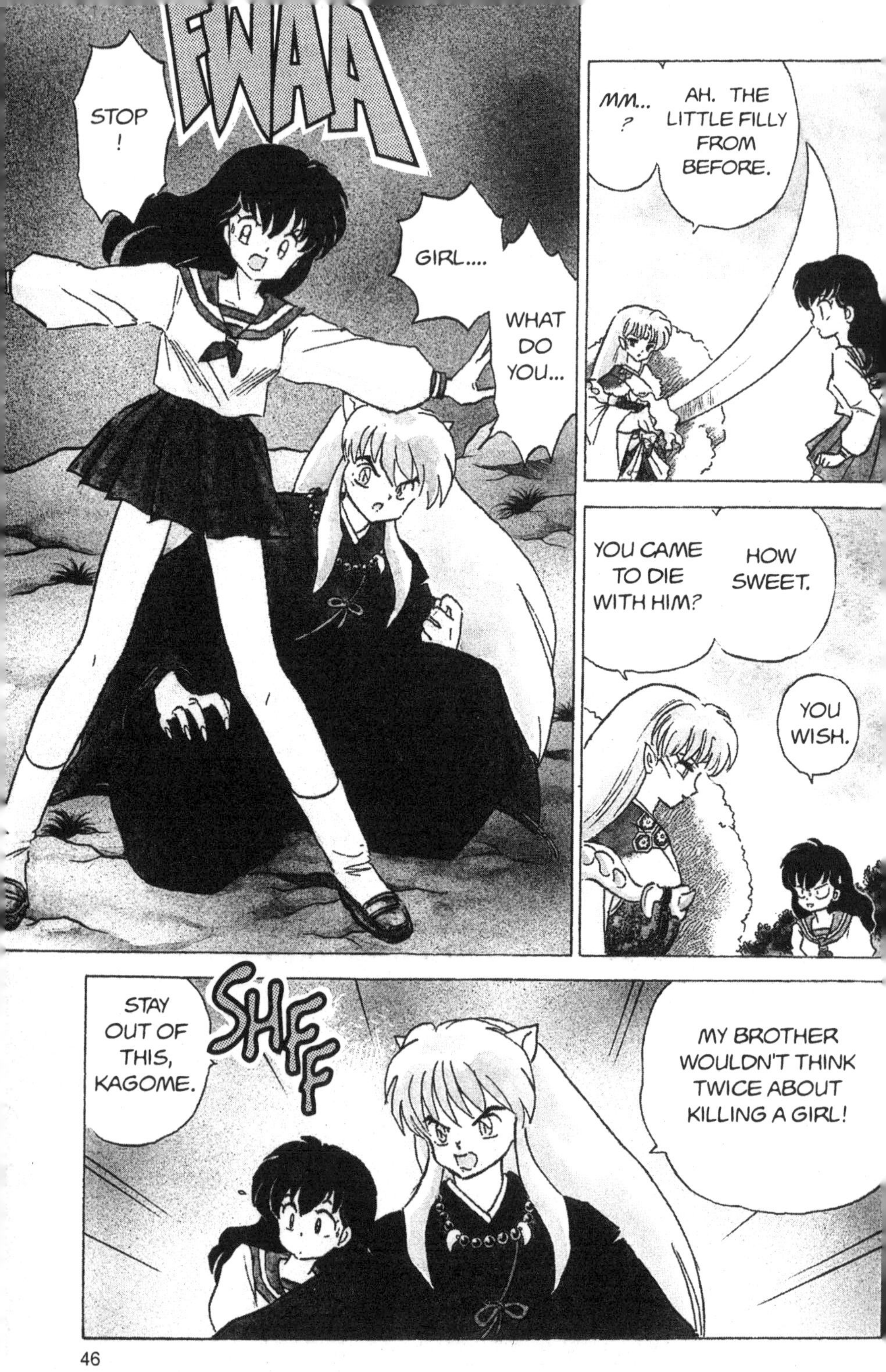
STOP !
FWAA
GIRL....
WHAT DO YOU...
MM... ?
AH. THE LITTLE FILLY FROM BEFORE.
YOU CAME TO DIE WITH HIM?
HOW SWEET.
YOU WISH.
STAY OUT OF THIS, KAGOME.
SHFF
MY BROTHER WOULDN'T THINK TWICE ABOUT KILLING A GIRL!

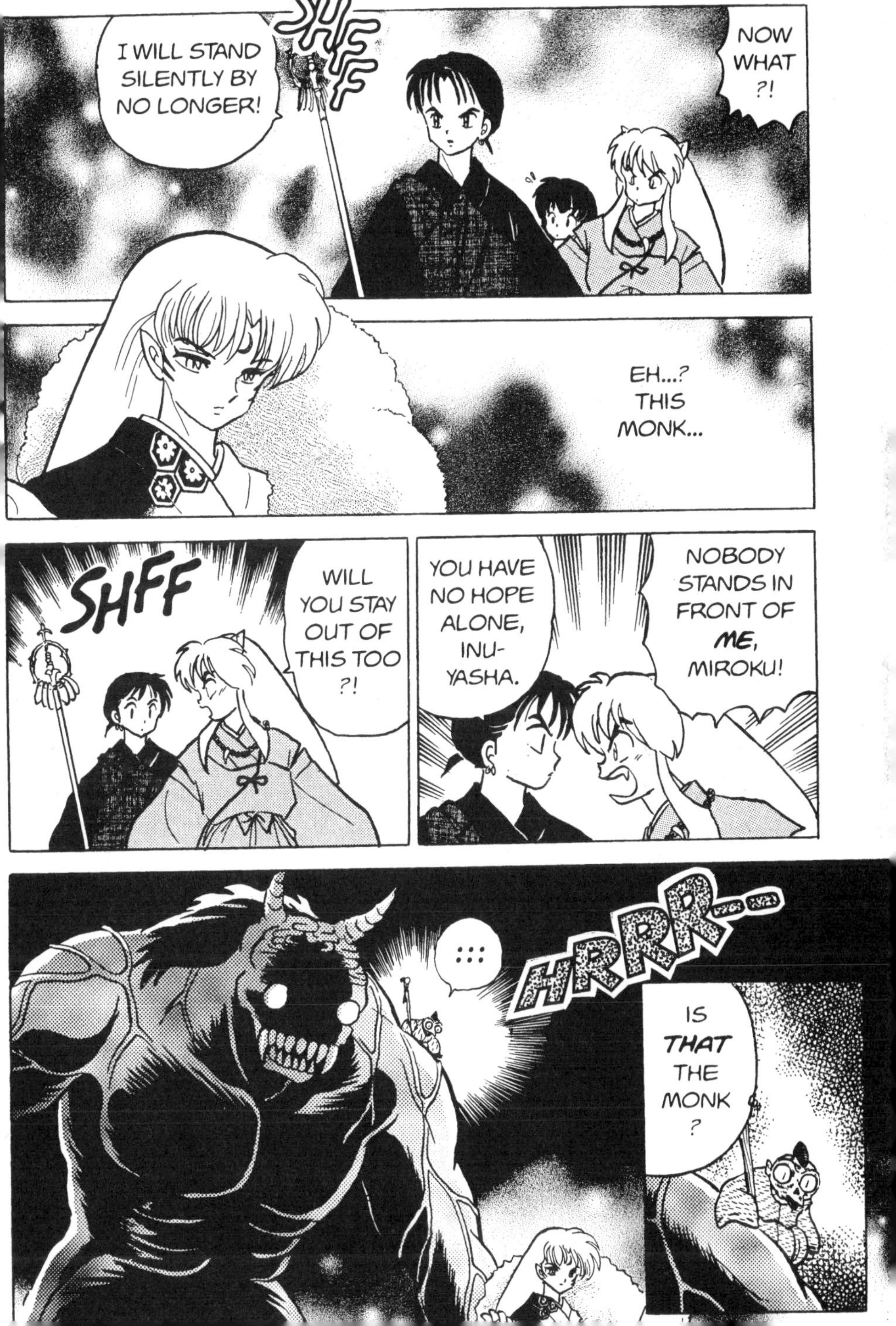
I WILL STAND SILENTLY BY NO LONGER!
SHFF
NOW WHAT ?!
EH...? THIS MONK...
SHFF
WILL YOU STAY OUT OF THIS TOO ?!
YOU HAVE NO HOPE ALONE, INU-YASHA.
NOBODY STANDS IN FRONT OF *ME*, MIROKU!
HRRR--
IS *THAT* THE MONK ?

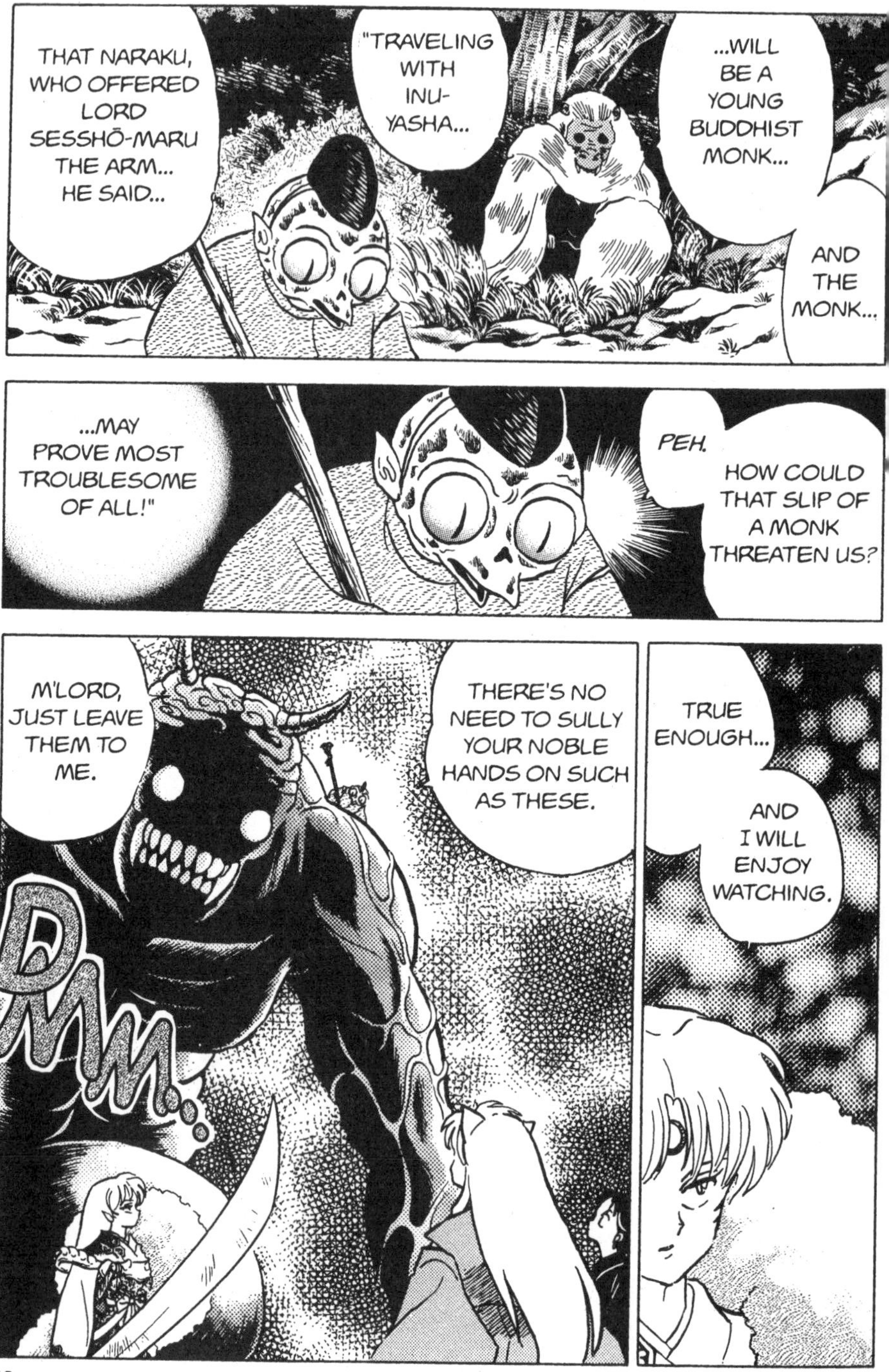
THAT NARAKU, WHO OFFERED LORD SESSHŌ-MARU THE ARM... HE SAID...
"TRAVELING WITH INU-YASHA...
...WILL BE A YOUNG BUDDHIST MONK...
AND THE MONK...
...MAY PROVE MOST TROUBLESOME OF ALL!"
PEH.
HOW COULD THAT SLIP OF A MONK THREATEN US?
M'LORD, JUST LEAVE THEM TO ME.
THERE'S NO NEED TO SULLY YOUR NOBLE HANDS ON SUCH AS THESE.
DMM...
TRUE ENOUGH...
AND I WILL ENJOY WATCHING.

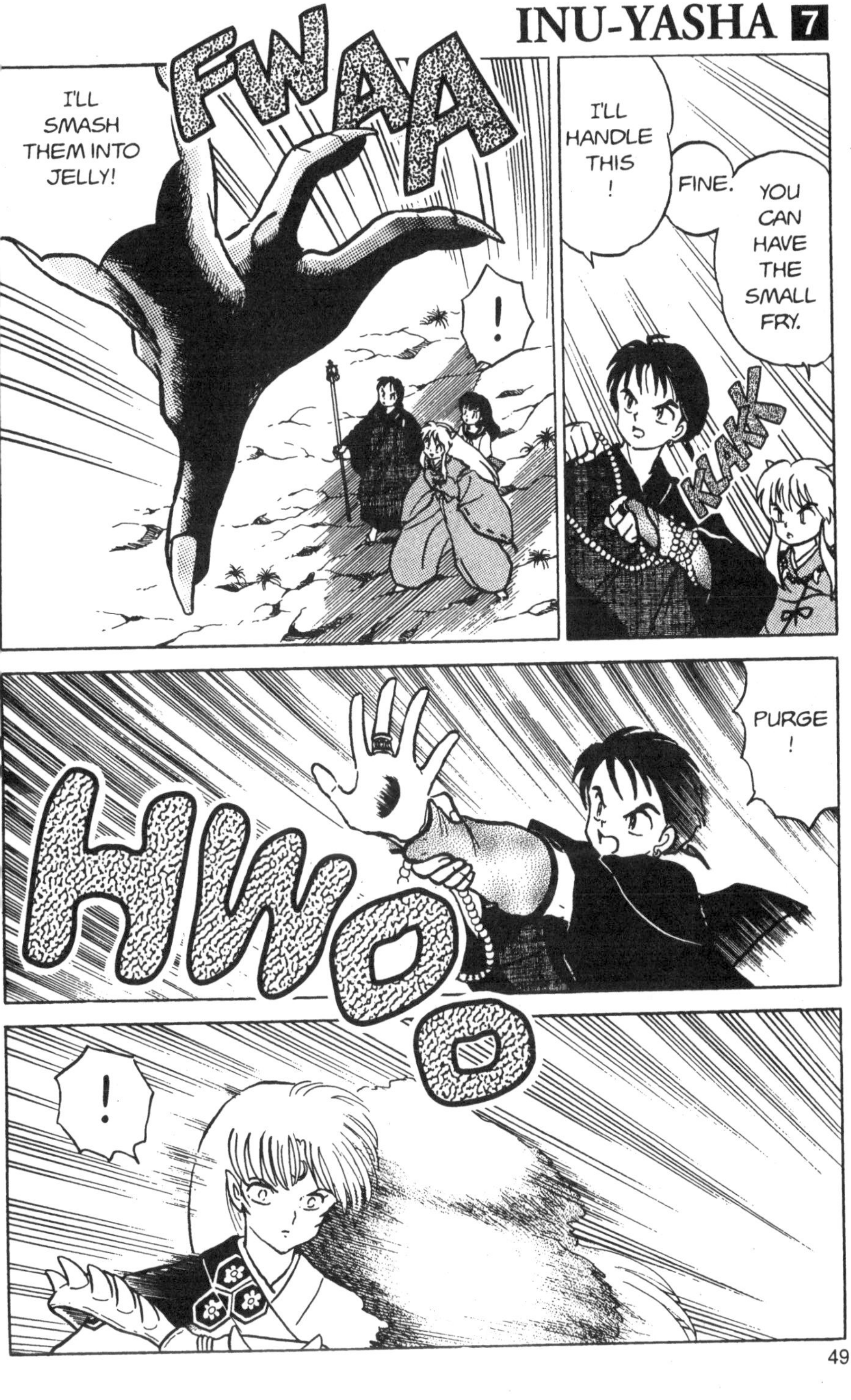
FWAA
I'LL SMASH THEM INTO JELLY!
!
I'LL HANDLE THIS!
FINE.
YOU CAN HAVE THE SMALL FRY.
KLAK
HWOO
PURGE!
O
!

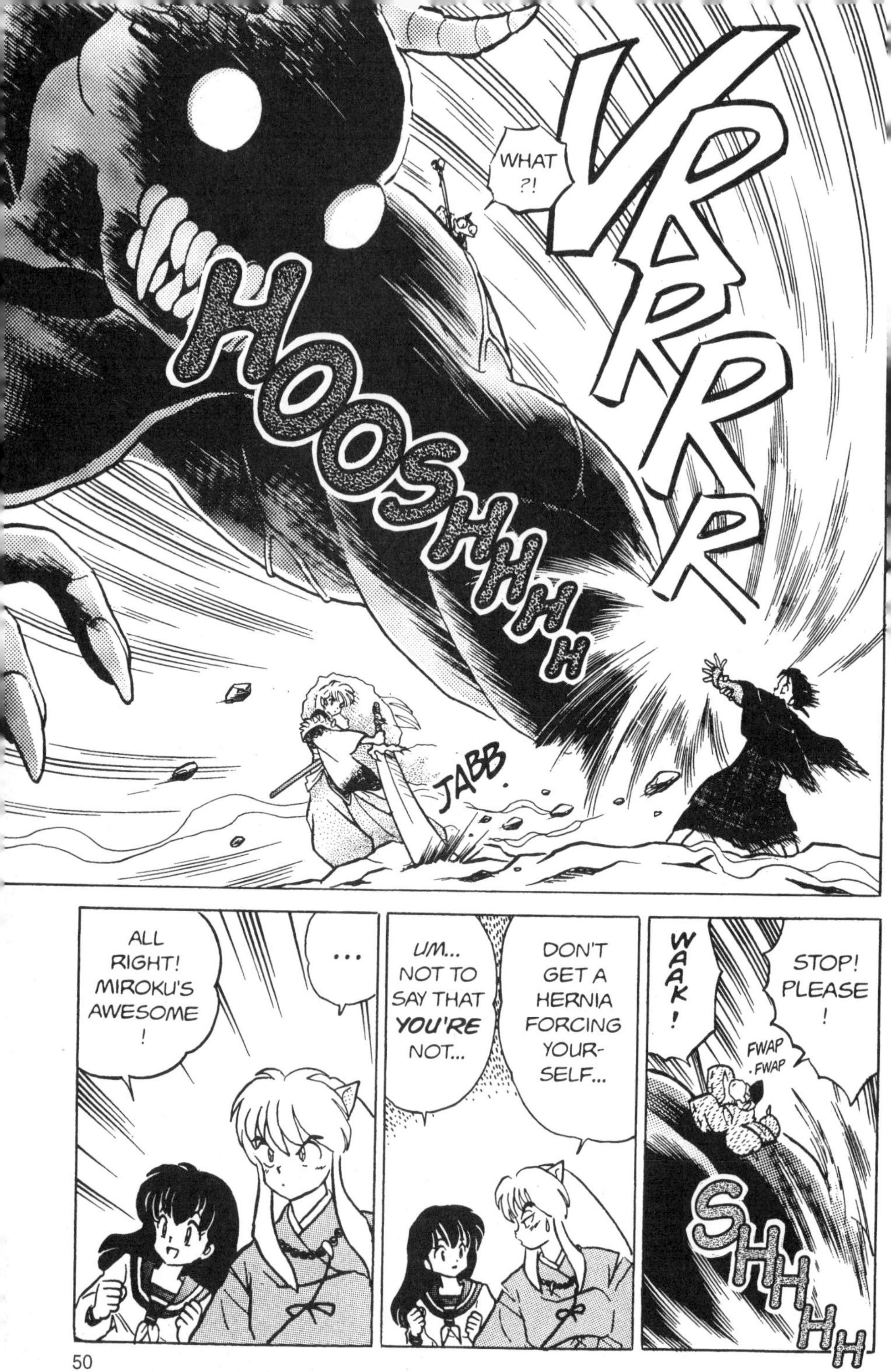
WHAT ?!
VRRRRR
HOOSHHHHH
JABB
ALL RIGHT! MIROKU'S AWESOME !
...
UM... NOT TO SAY THAT YOU'RE NOT...
DON'T GET A HERNIA FORCING YOUR-SELF...
WAAK !
STOP! PLEASE !
FWAP FWAP
SHHHHH

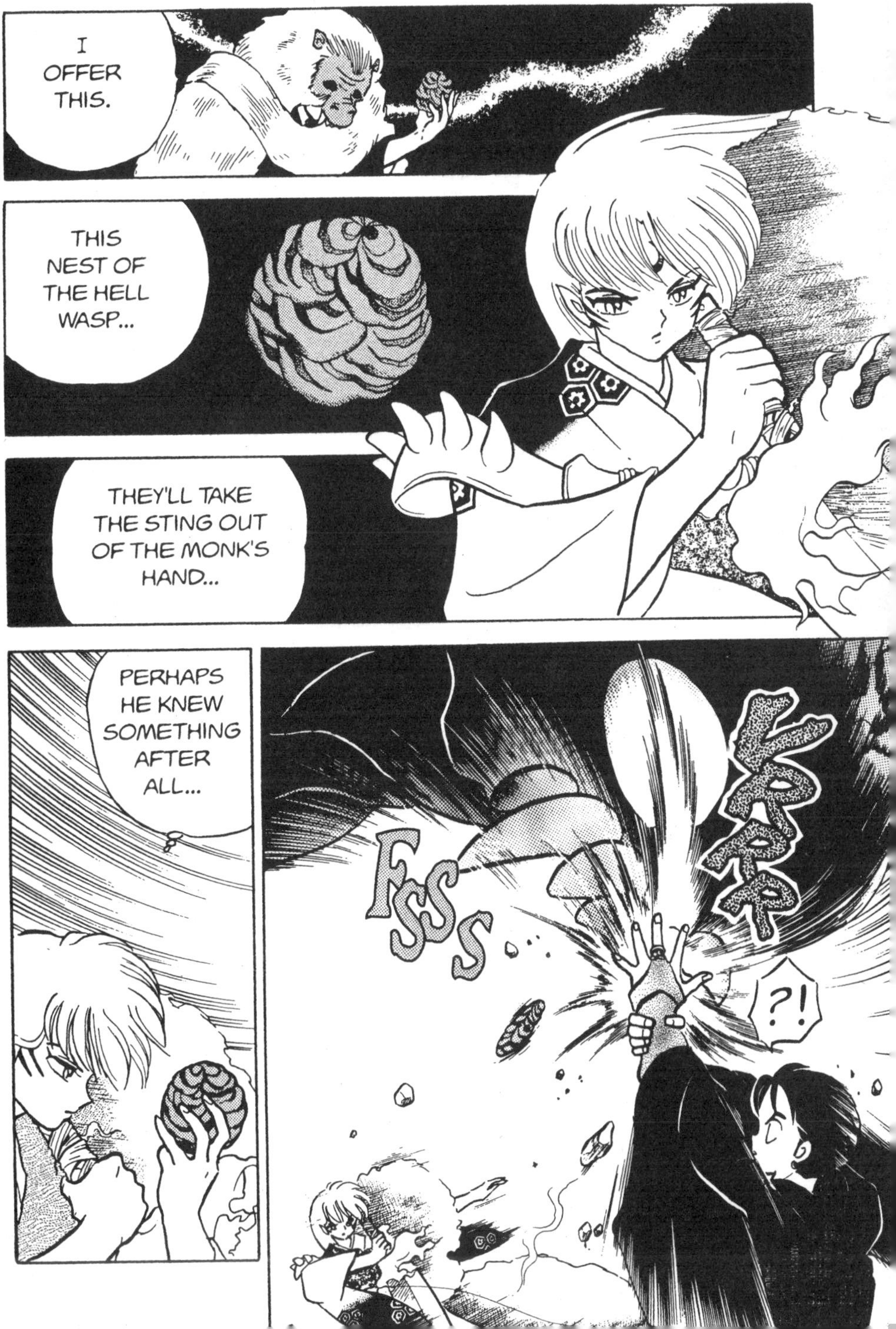
I OFFER THIS.
THIS NEST OF THE HELL WASP...
THEY'LL TAKE THE STING OUT OF THE MONK'S HAND...
PERHAPS HE KNEW SOMETHING AFTER ALL...
FSSS
VRRR
?!

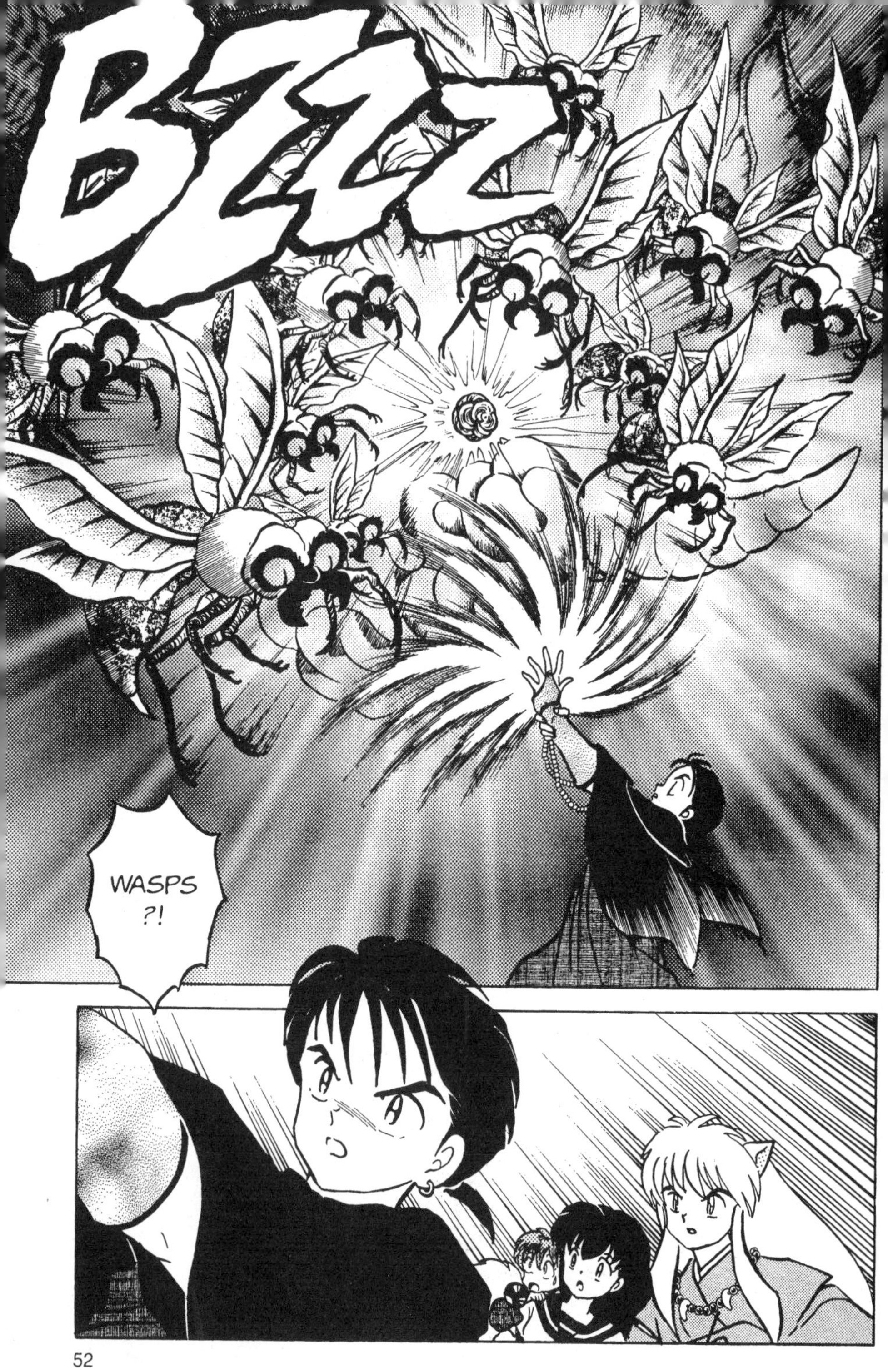
BZZZ
WASPS ?!

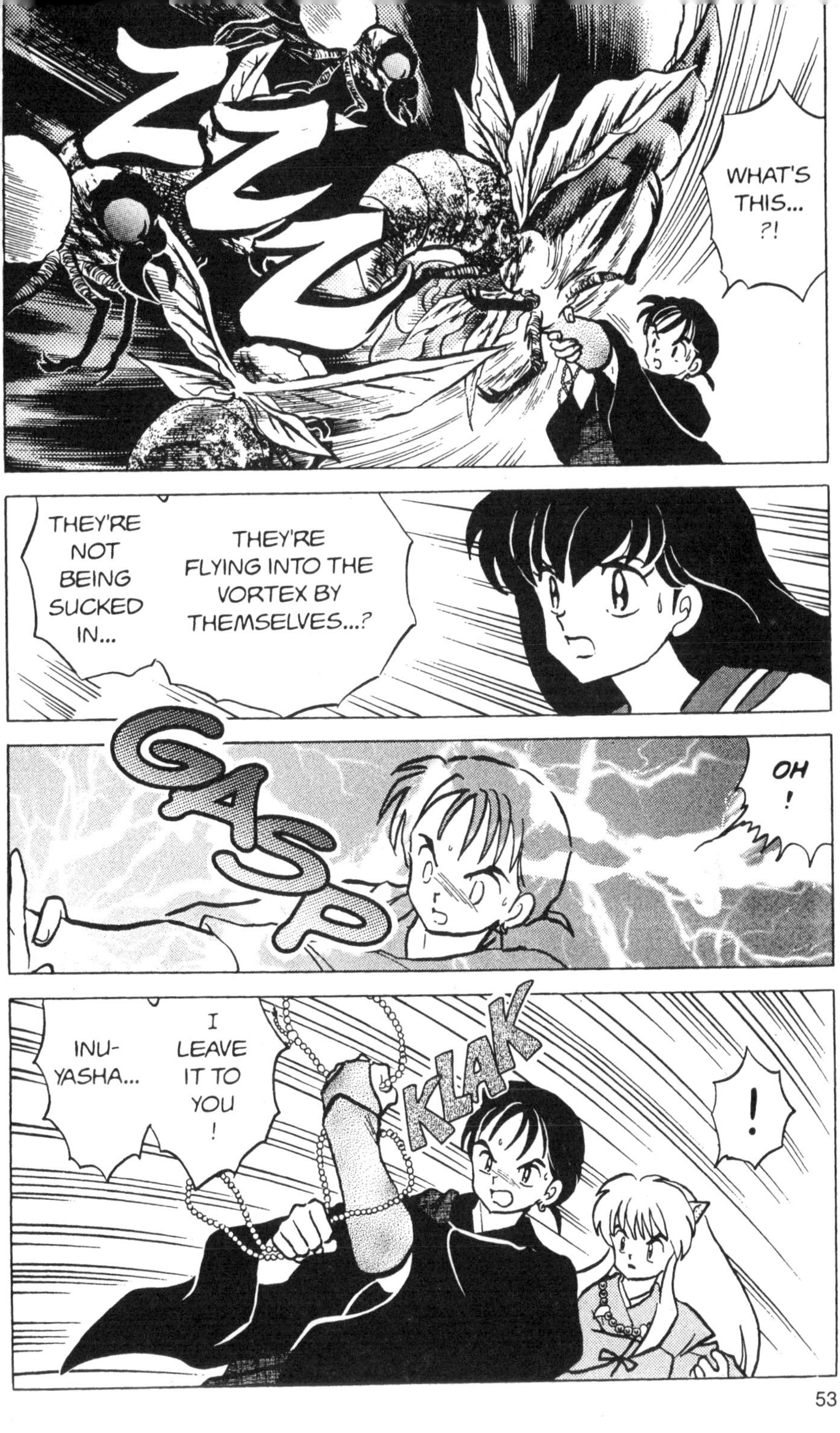
WHAT'S THIS... ?!
THEY'RE NOT BEING SUCKED IN...
THEY'RE FLYING INTO THE VORTEX BY THEMSELVES...?
GASP
OH !
INU-YASHA...
I LEAVE IT TO YOU !
KLAK
!

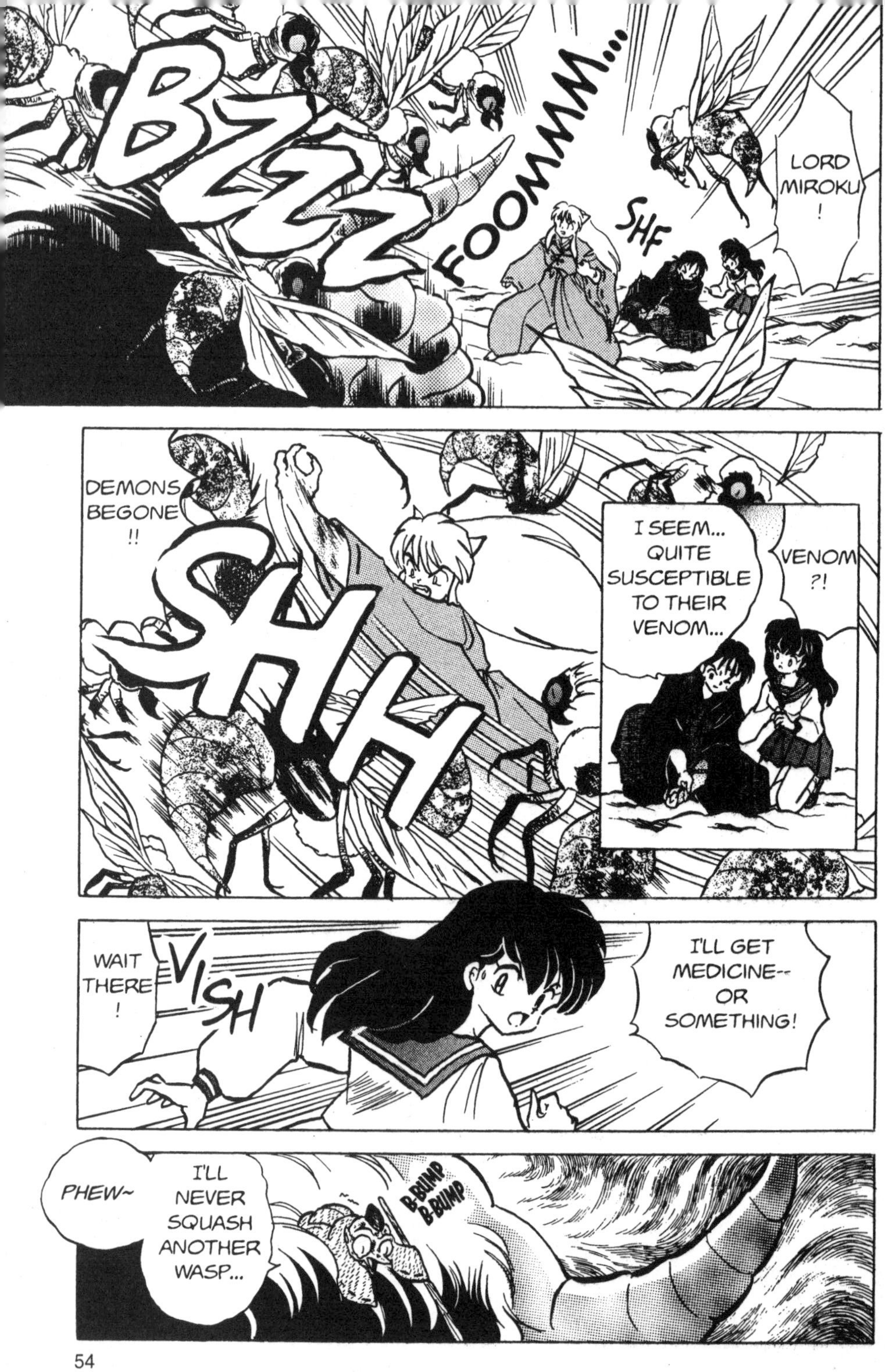
BZZZ
FOOMMM...
SHF
LORD MIROKU!
DEMONS BEGONE!!
SHHH
I SEEM... QUITE SUSCEPTIBLE TO THEIR VENOM...
VENOM?!
WAIT THERE!
VISH
I'LL GET MEDICINE--OR SOMETHING!
PHEW~
I'LL NEVER SQUASH ANOTHER WASP...
B-BUMP B-BUMP

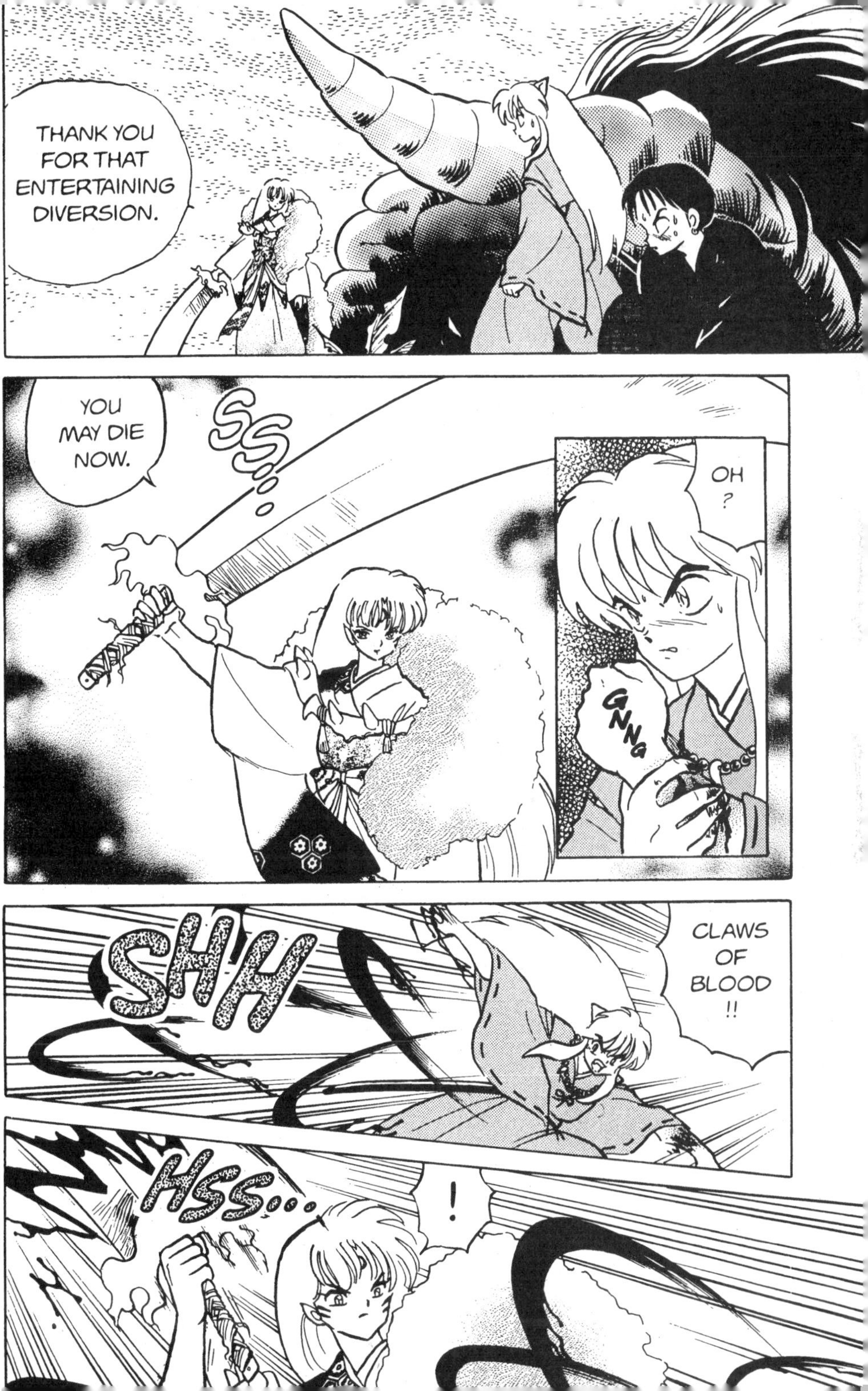
THANK YOU FOR THAT ENTERTAINING DIVERSION.
YOU MAY DIE NOW.
SS...
OH?
GNNG
SHH
CLAWS OF BLOOD!!
HSS...
!

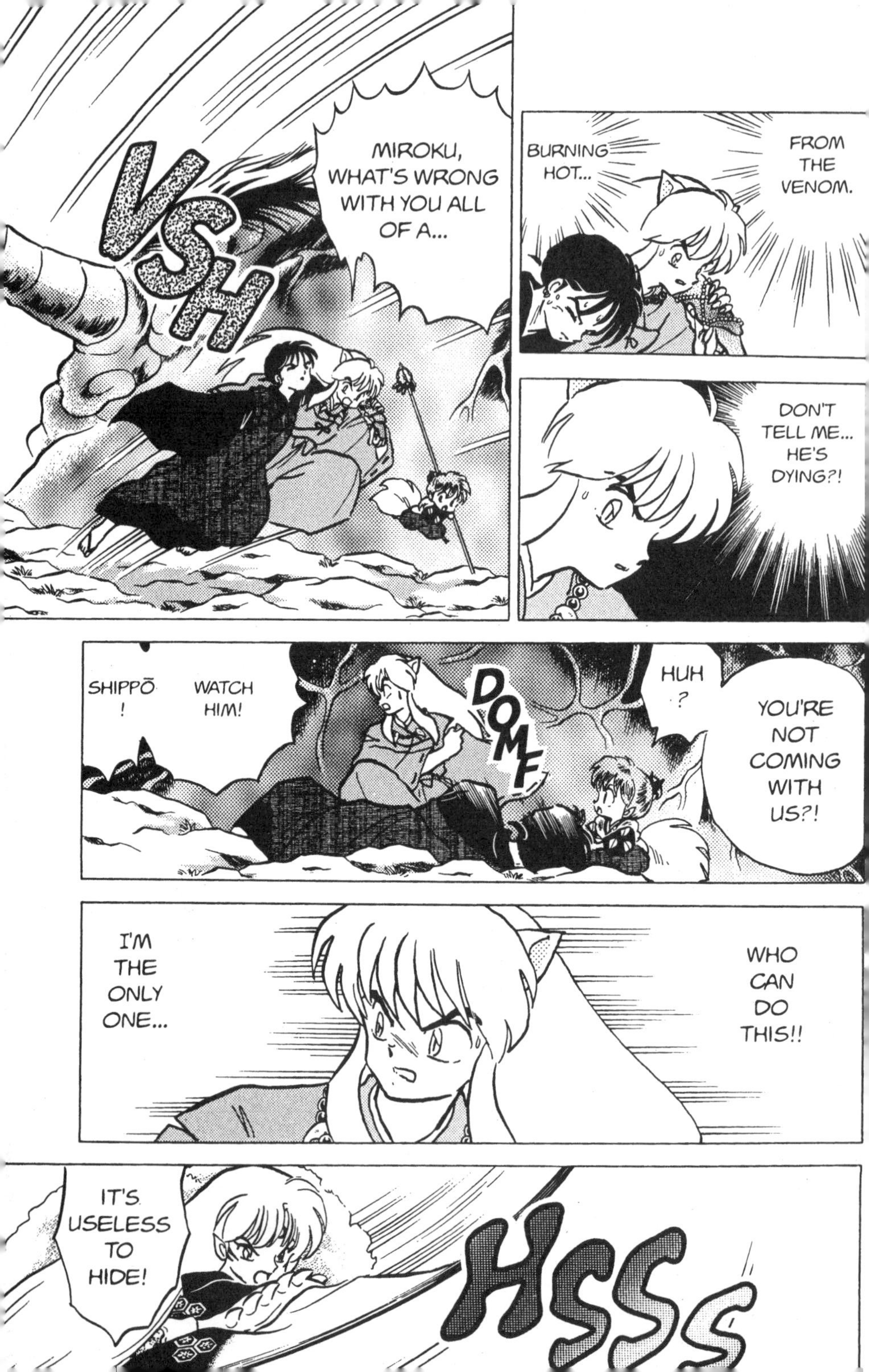
VSH
MIROKU, WHAT'S WRONG WITH YOU ALL OF A...
BURNING HOT...
FROM THE VENOM.
DON'T TELL ME... HE'S DYING?!
SHIPPŌ!
WATCH HIM!
DOMF
HUH?
YOU'RE NOT COMING WITH US?!
I'M THE ONLY ONE...
WHO CAN DO THIS!!
IT'S USELESS TO HIDE!
HSSS

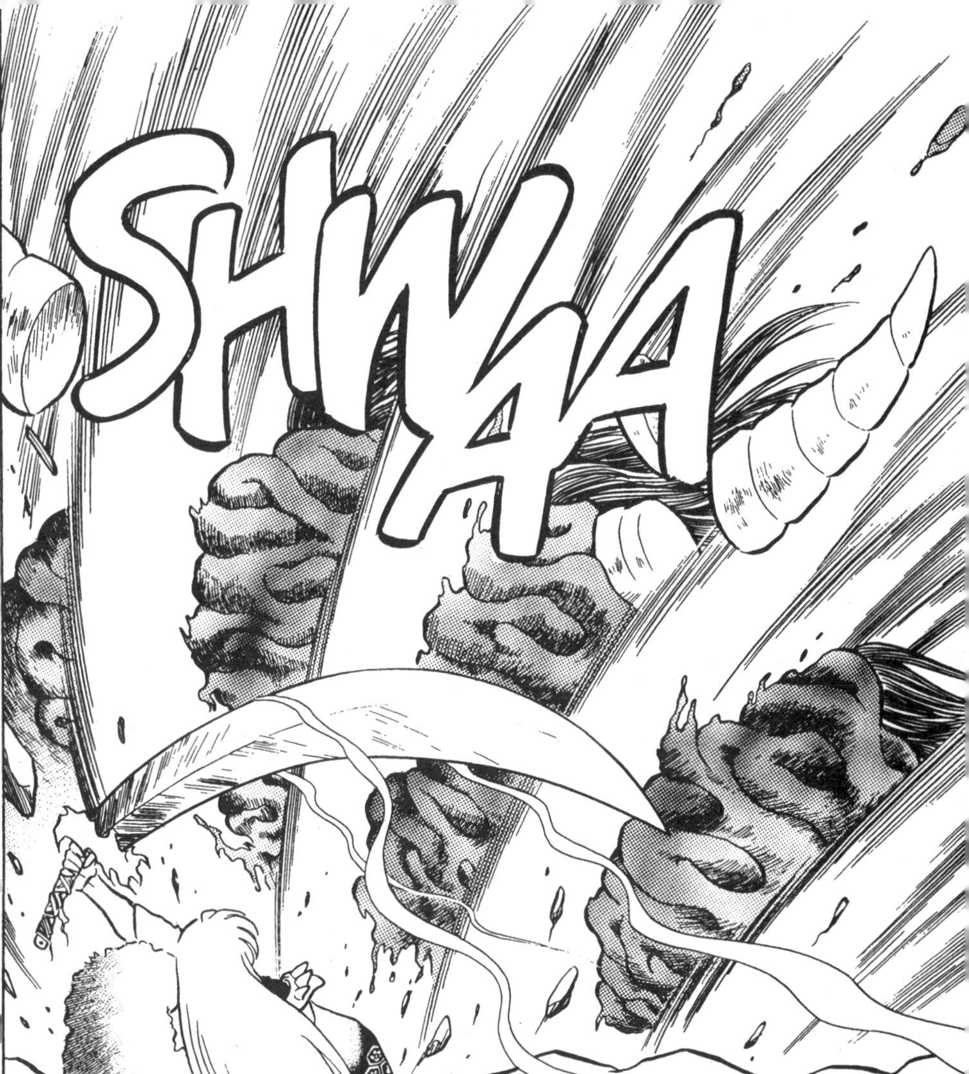
SHWAA
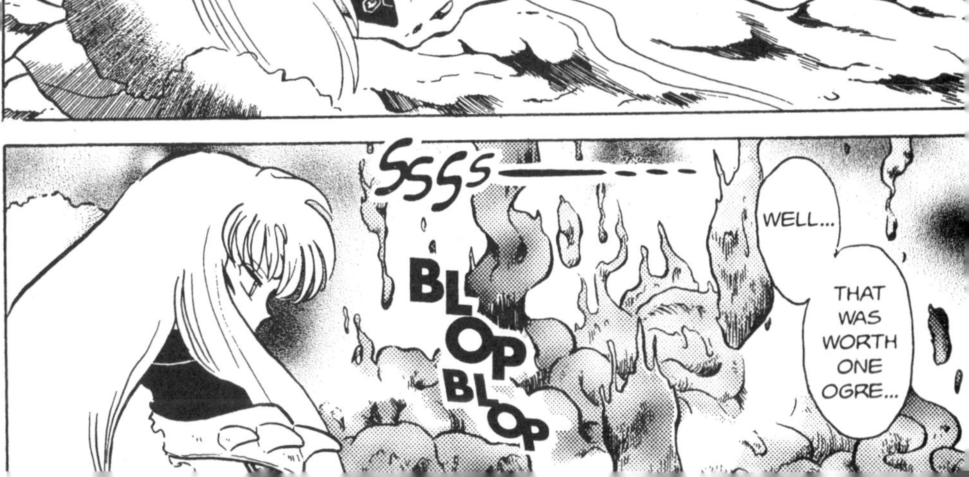
SSSS
BLLOP BLLOP
WELL...
THAT WAS WORTH ONE OGRE...

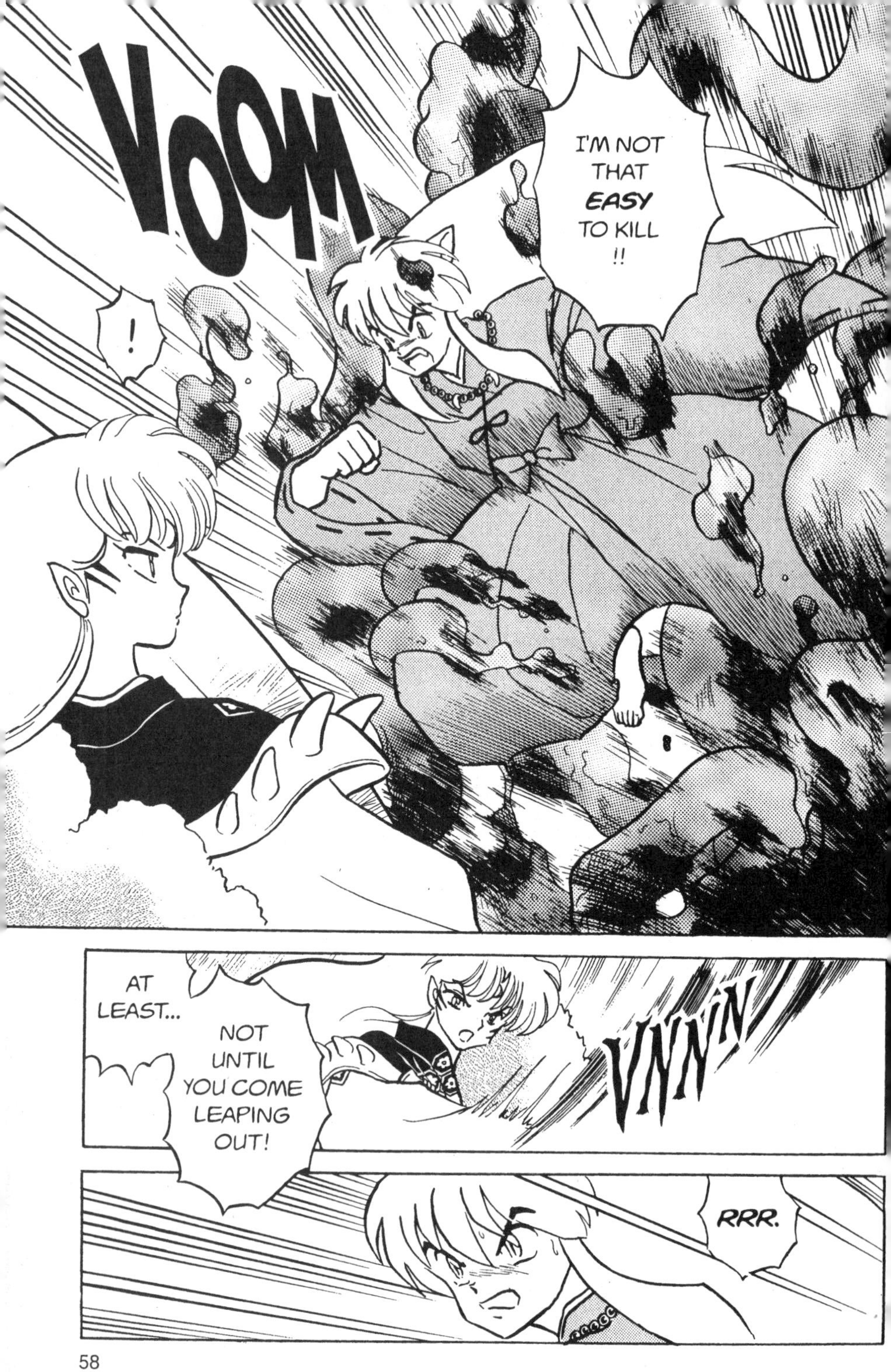
VOOM
!
I'M NOT THAT **EASY** TO KILL !!
AT LEAST...
NOT UNTIL YOU COME LEAPING OUT!
VNNN
RRR.

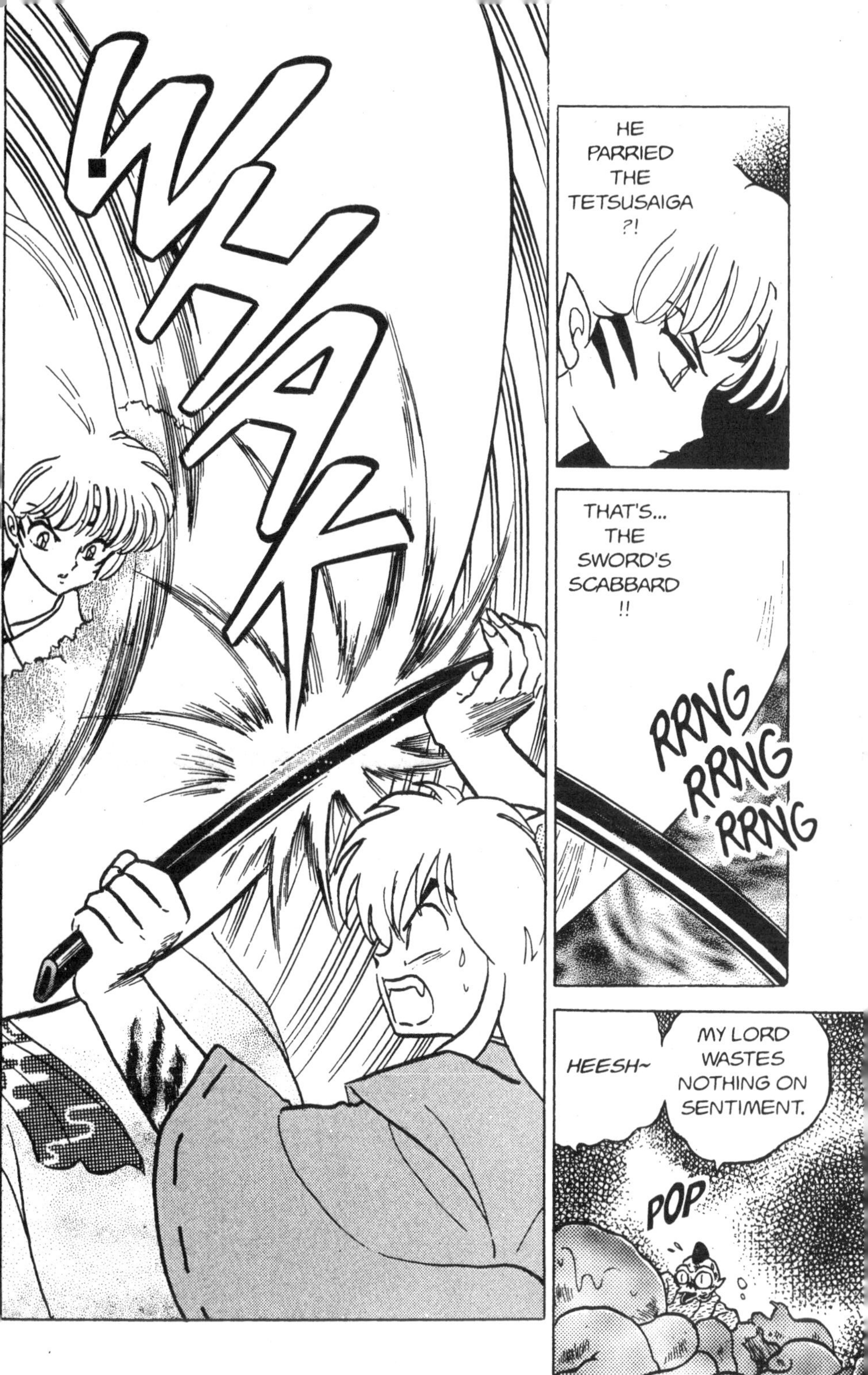
WHAAK
HE PARRIED THE TETSUSAIGA ?!
THAT'S... THE SWORD'S SCABBARD !!
RRNG RRNG RRNG
HEESH~
MY LORD WASTES NOTHING ON SENTIMENT.
POP

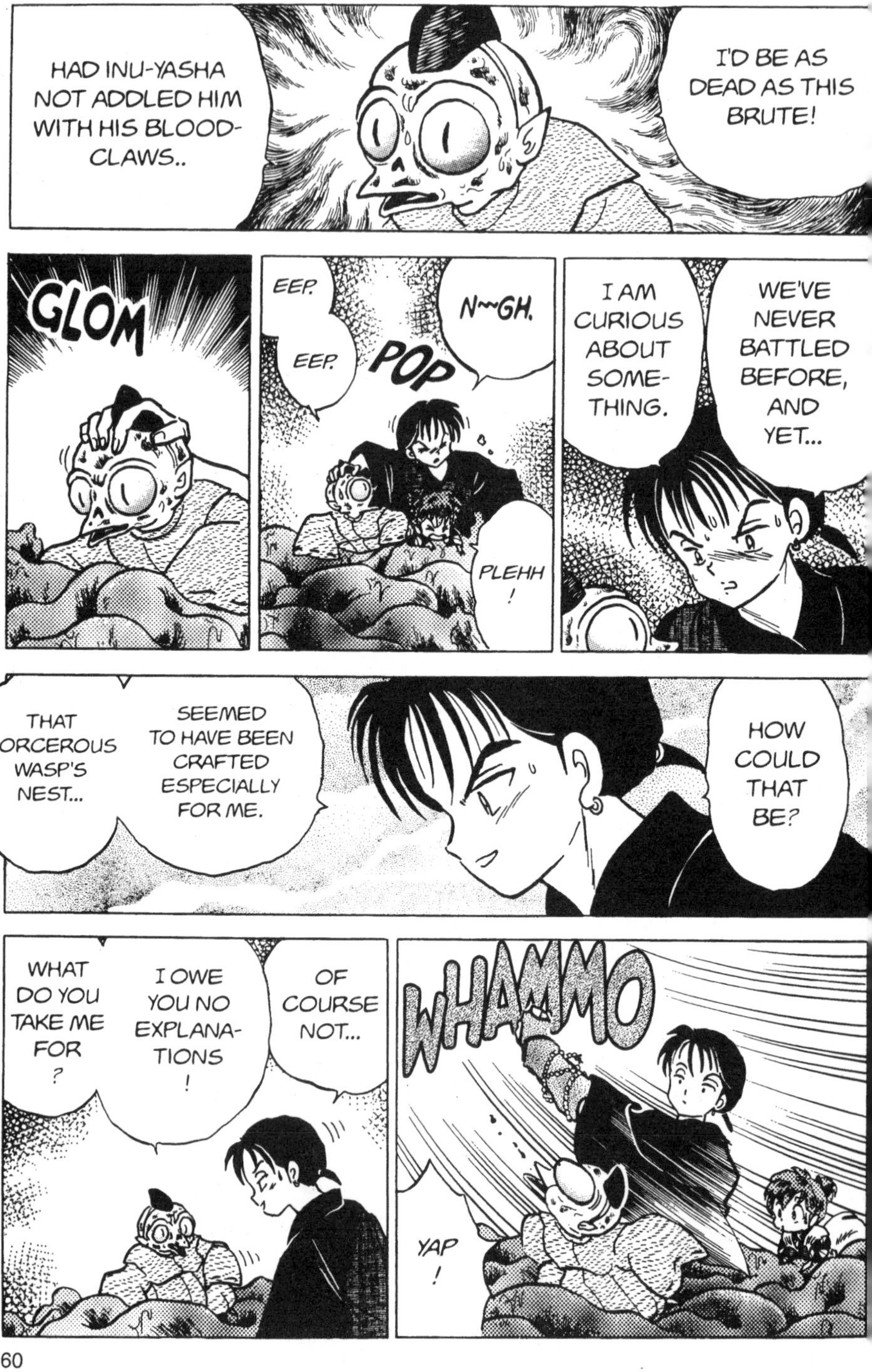

HAD INU-YASHA NOT ADDLED HIM WITH HIS BLOOD-CLAWS..
I'D BE AS DEAD AS THIS BRUTE!
GLOM
EEP.
EEP.
POP
N~~GH.
PLEHH!
I AM CURIOUS ABOUT SOME-THING.
WE'VE NEVER BATTLED BEFORE, AND YET...
THAT SORCEROUS WASP'S NEST...
SEEMED TO HAVE BEEN CRAFTED ESPECIALLY FOR ME.
HOW COULD THAT BE?
WHAT DO YOU TAKE ME FOR?
I OWE YOU NO EXPLANA-TIONS!
OF COURSE NOT...
WHAMMO
YAP!

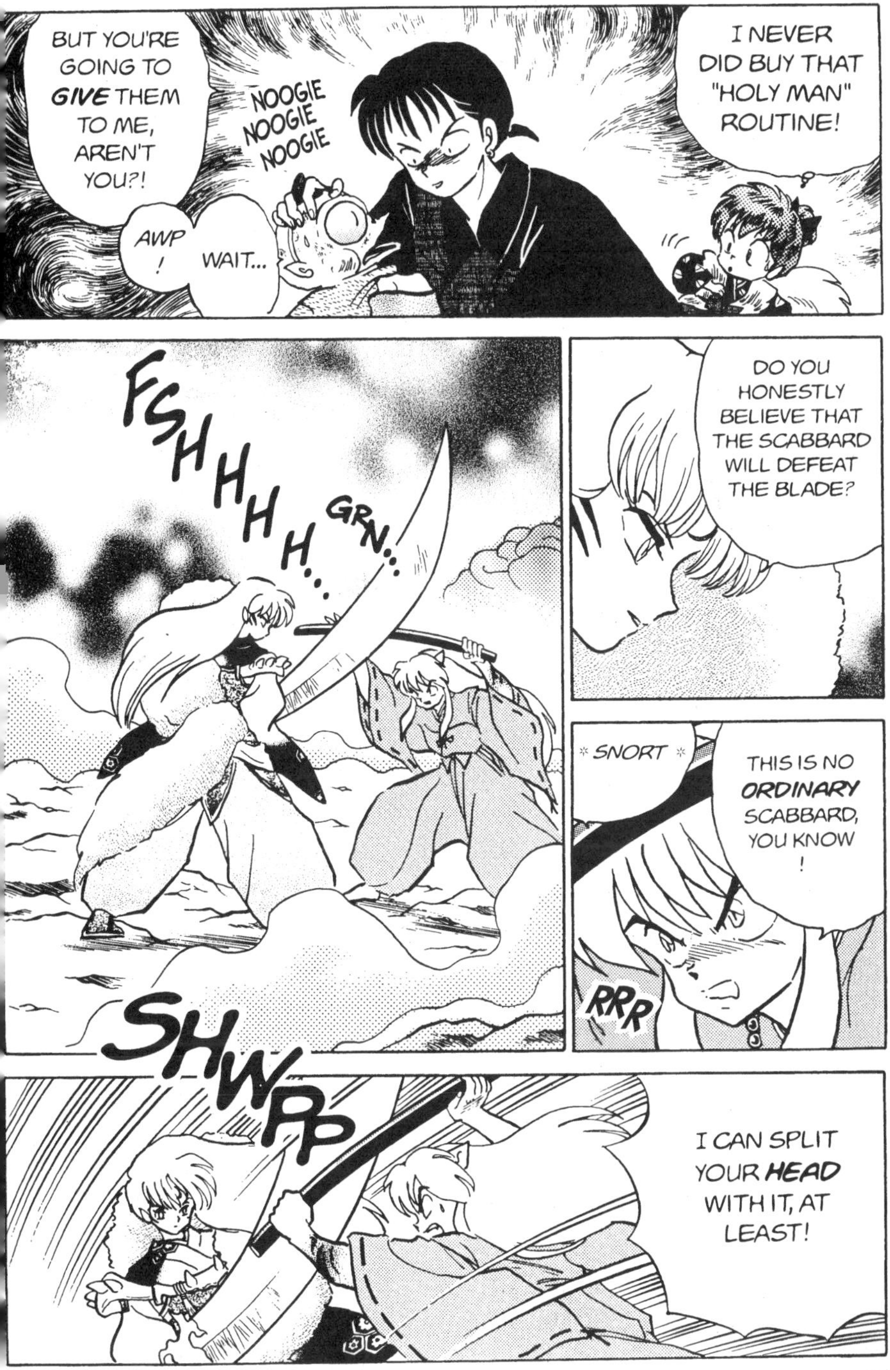
BUT YOU'RE GOING TO **GIVE** THEM TO ME, AREN'T YOU?!
NOOGIE NOOGIE NOOGIE
AWP !
WAIT...
I NEVER DID BUY THAT "HOLY MAN" ROUTINE!
FSHHHH...
GRN...
SHWPP
DO YOU HONESTLY BELIEVE THAT THE SCABBARD WILL DEFEAT THE BLADE?
* SNORT *
THIS IS NO **ORDINARY** SCABBARD, YOU KNOW !
RRR
I CAN SPLIT YOUR **HEAD** WITH IT, AT LEAST!

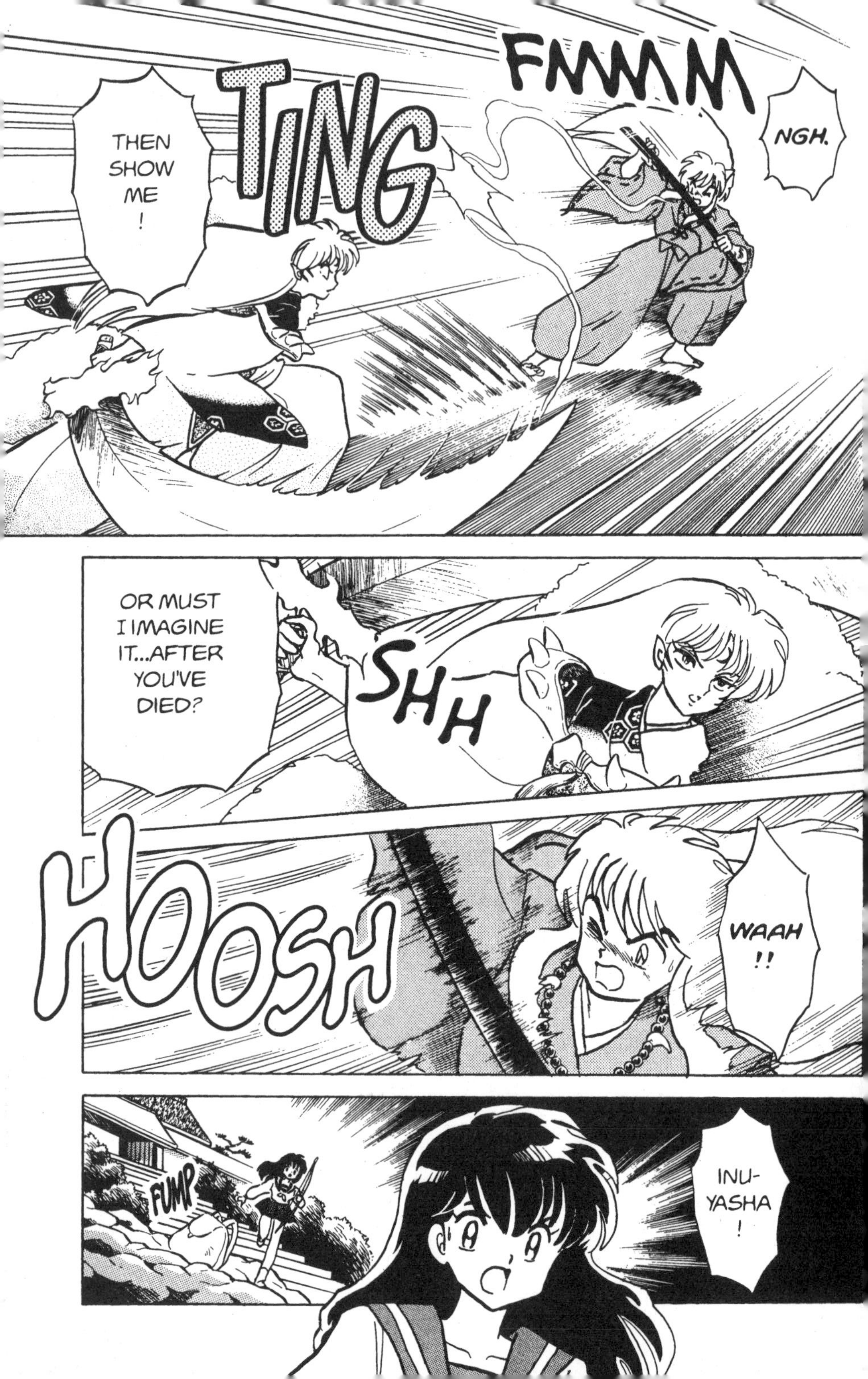
NGH.
FMMM
TING
THEN SHOW ME !
SHH
OR MUST I IMAGINE IT...AFTER YOU'VE DIED?
WAAH !!
HOOSH
INU-YASHA !
FUMP

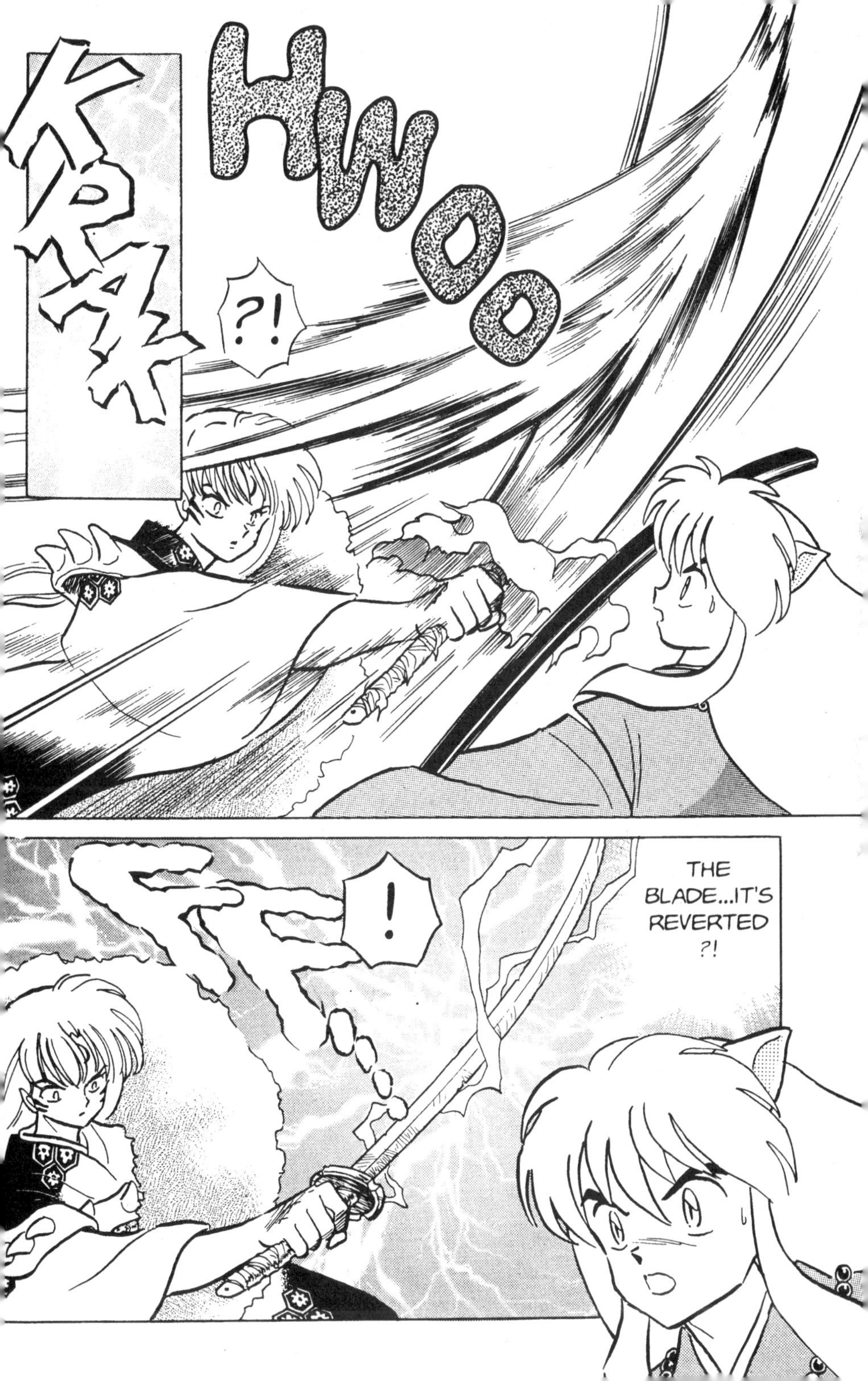
KRAK
HWOOO
?!
!
THE BLADE...IT'S REVERTED ?!

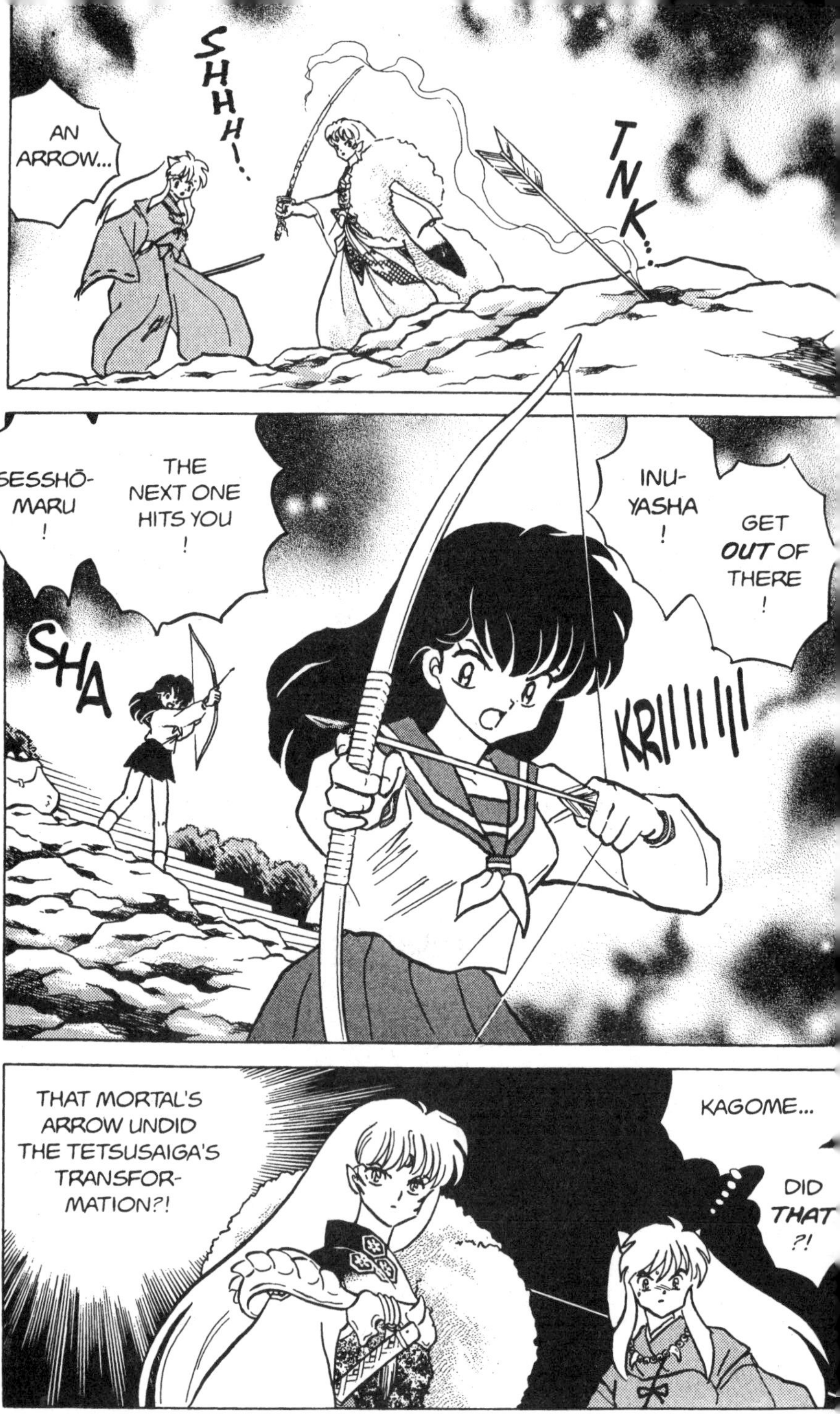
AN ARROW...
SHHH!...
TNK...
SESSHŌ-MARU!
THE NEXT ONE HITS YOU!
INU-YASHA!
GET OUT OF THERE!
SHA
KRIIIIIII
THAT MORTAL'S ARROW UNDID THE TETSUSAIGA'S TRANSFOR-MATION?!
KAGOME...
DID THAT?!

SCROLL FOUR

ARM ROBBERY

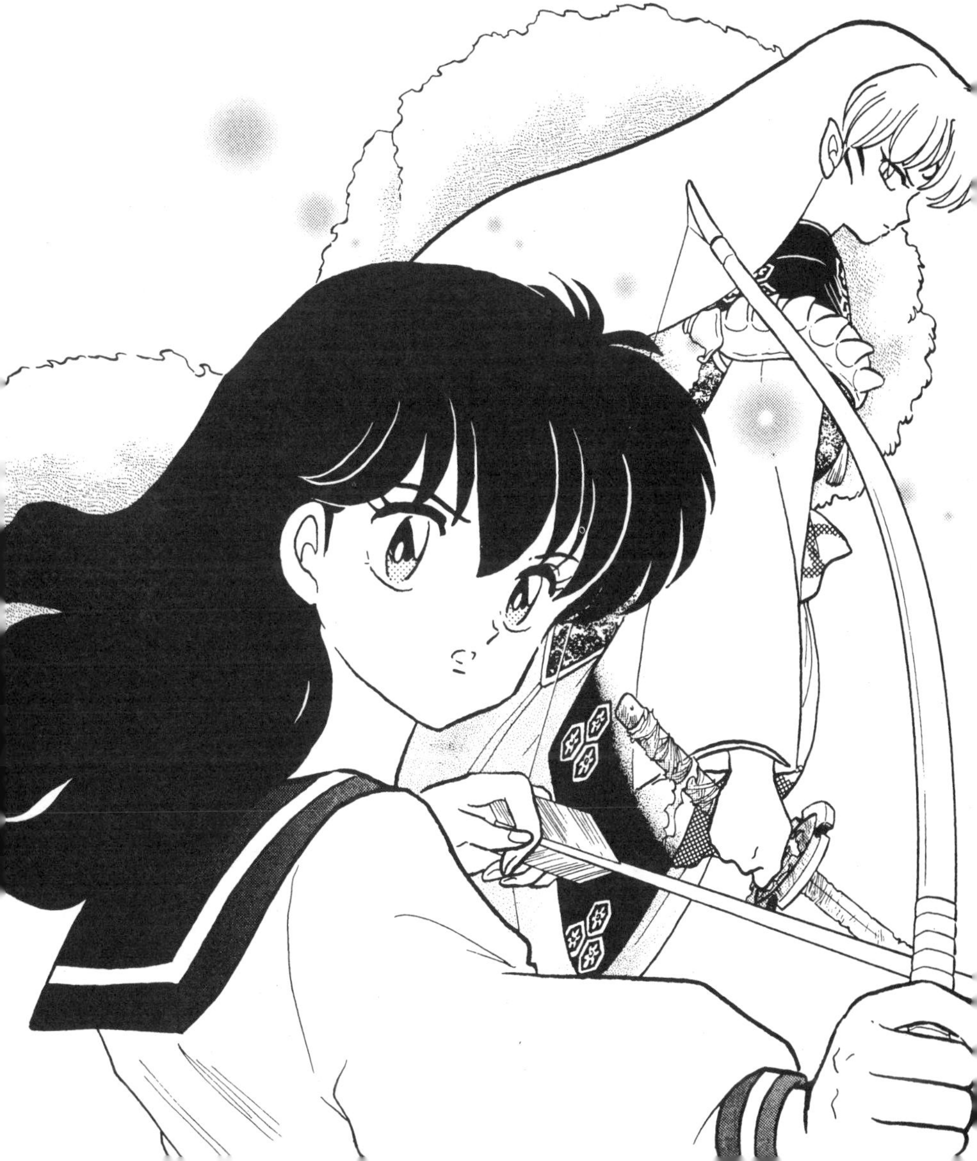

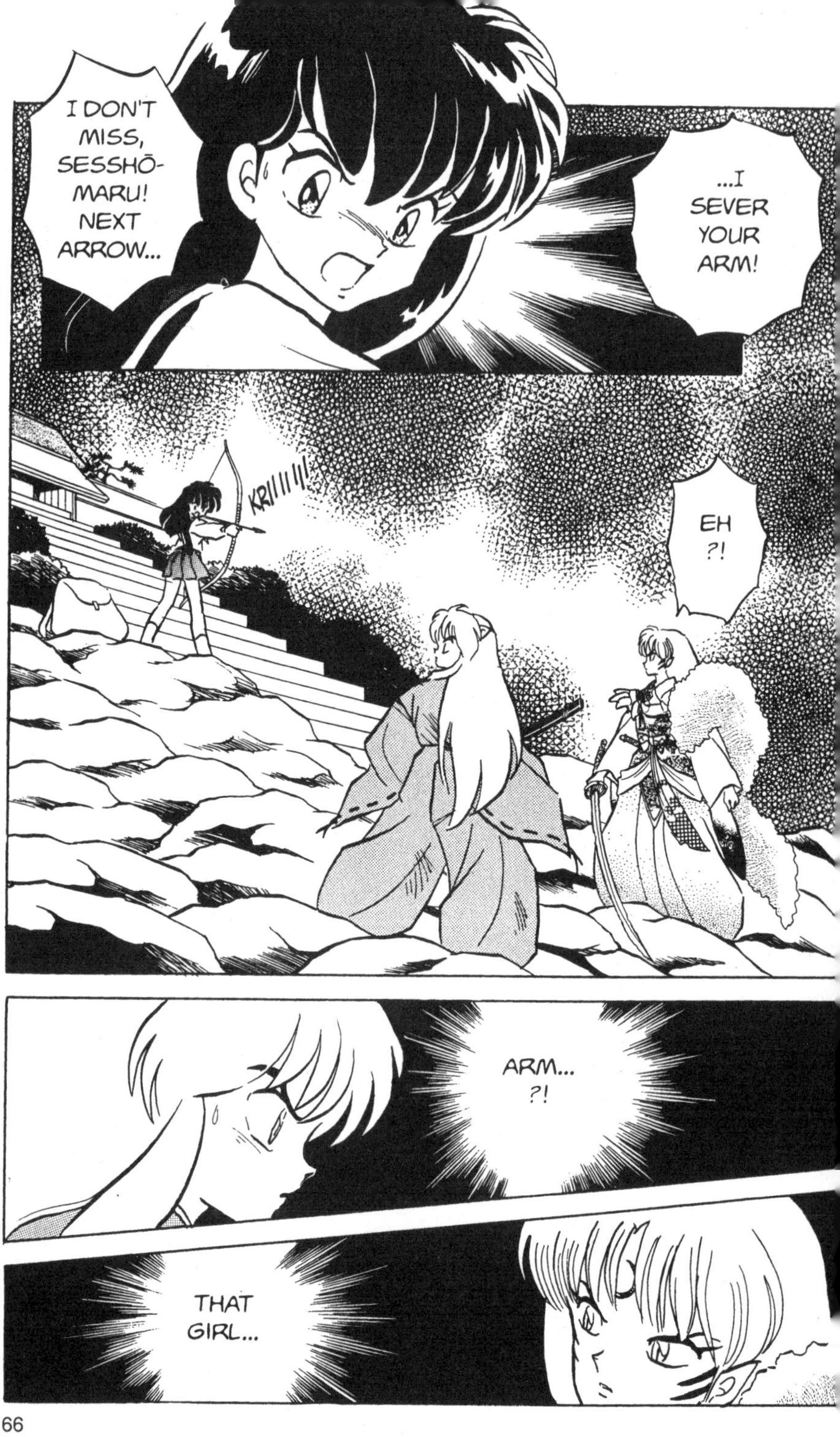
I DON'T MISS, SESSHŌ-MARU! NEXT ARROW...
...I SEVER YOUR ARM!
KRIIIIII
EH ?!
ARM... ?!
THAT GIRL...

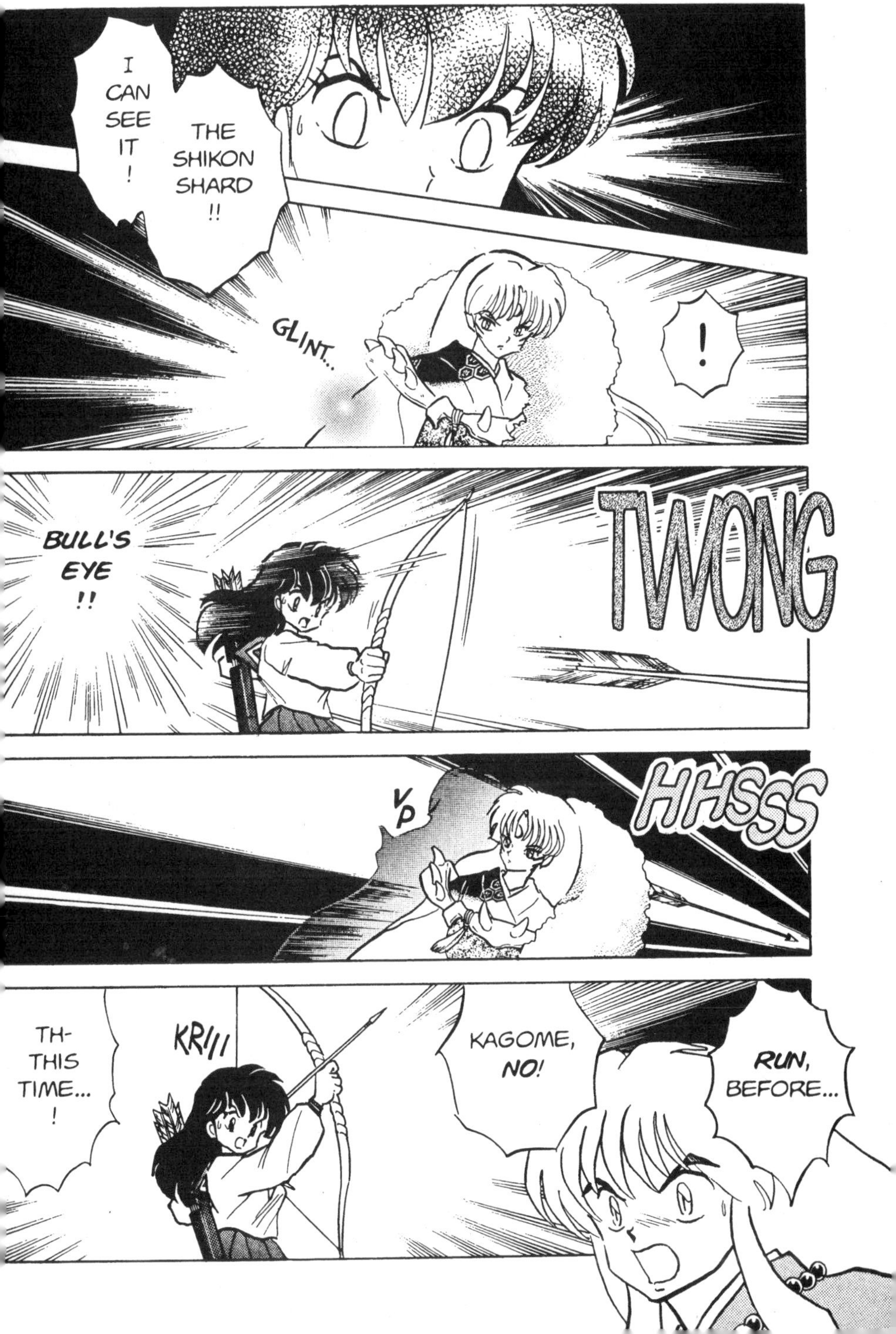
I CAN SEE IT !
THE SHIKON SHARD !!
GLINT...
!
BULL'S EYE !!
TWONG
VP
HHSSS
TH- THIS TIME... !
KRI//
KAGOME, NO!
RUN, BEFORE...

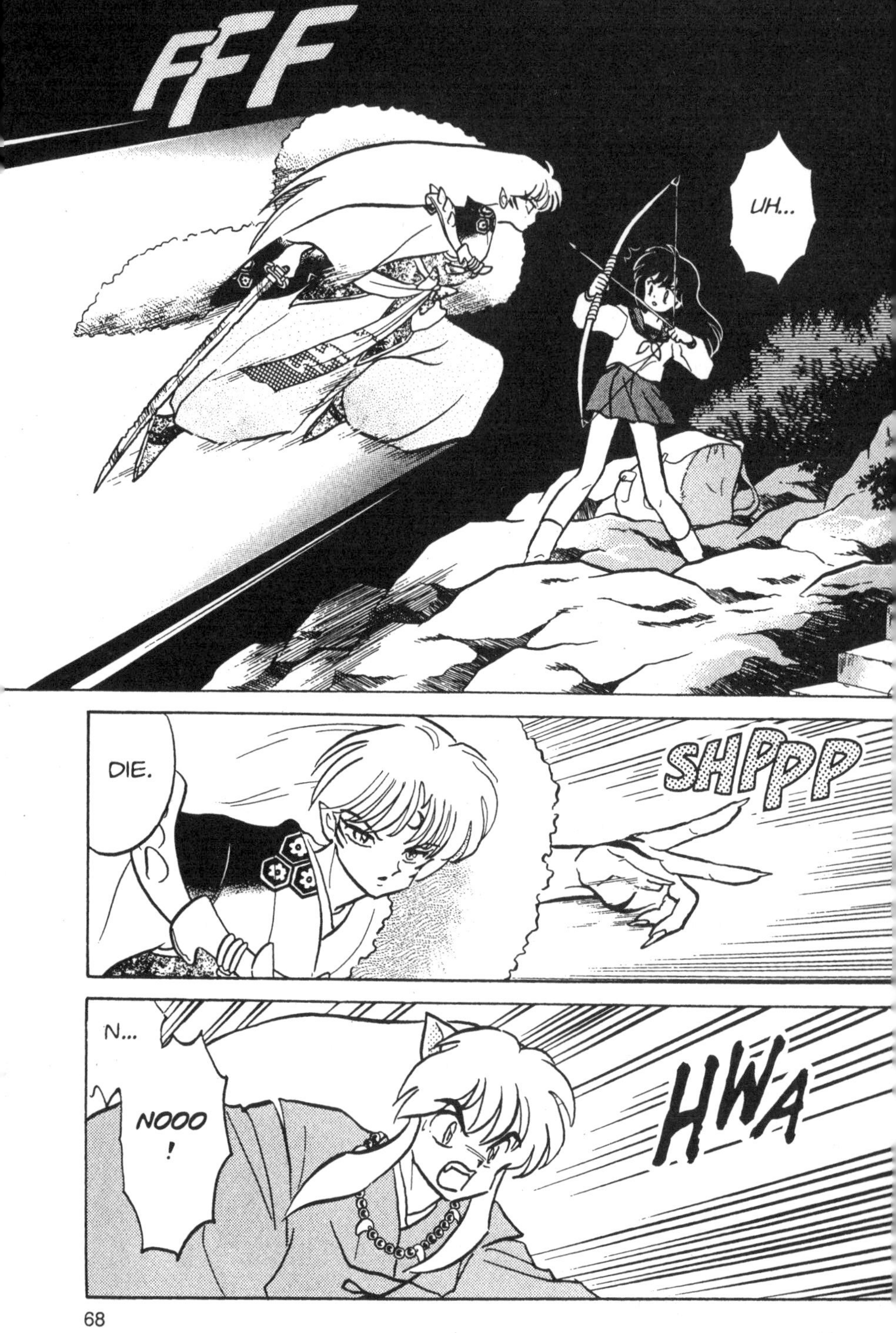
FFF
UH...
DIE.
SHPPP
N...
NOOO
!
HWA

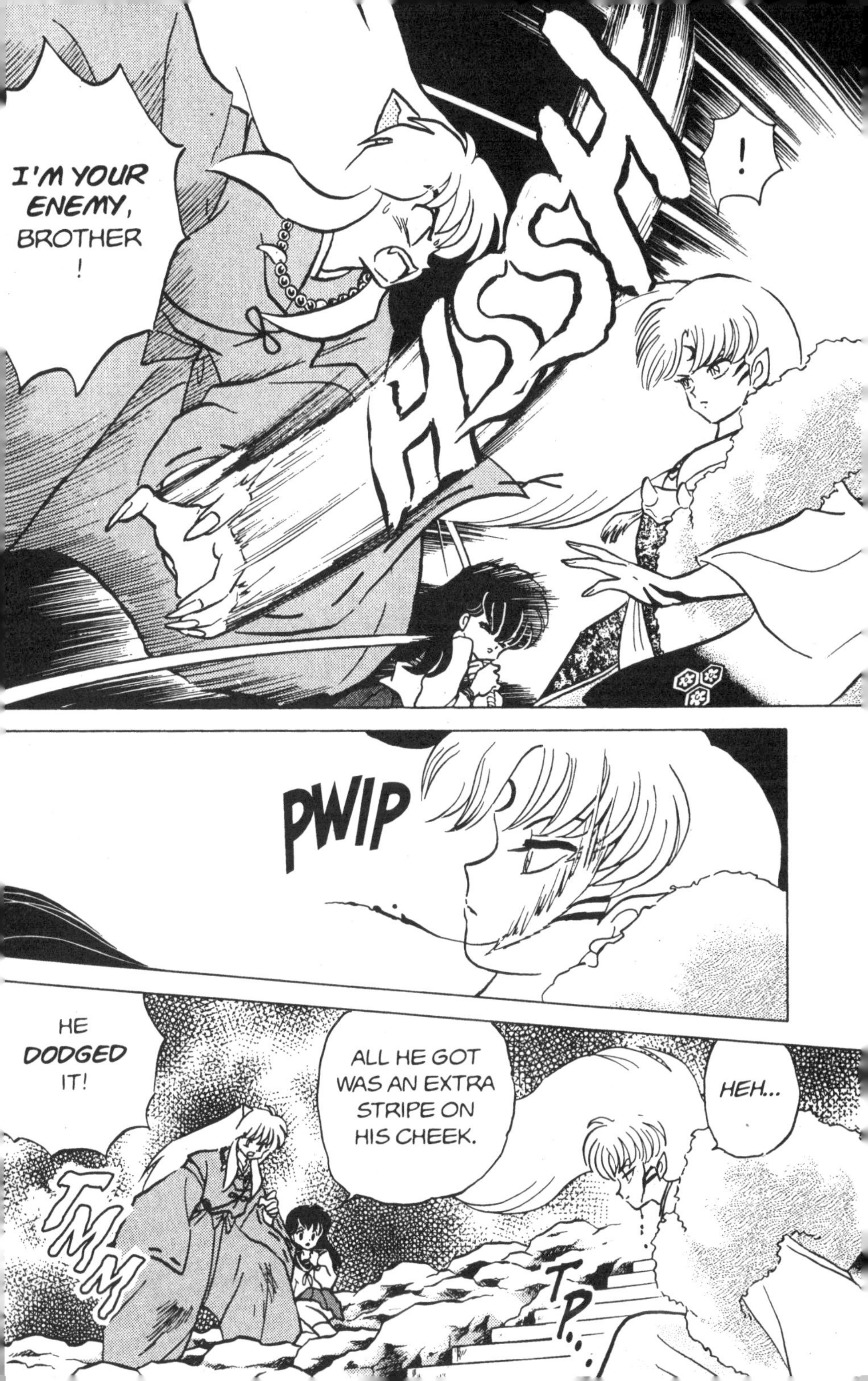
I'M YOUR ENEMY, BROTHER!
HISSH
!
PWIP
HE DODGED IT!
ALL HE GOT WAS AN EXTRA STRIPE ON HIS CHEEK.
HEH...
TMM
TP...

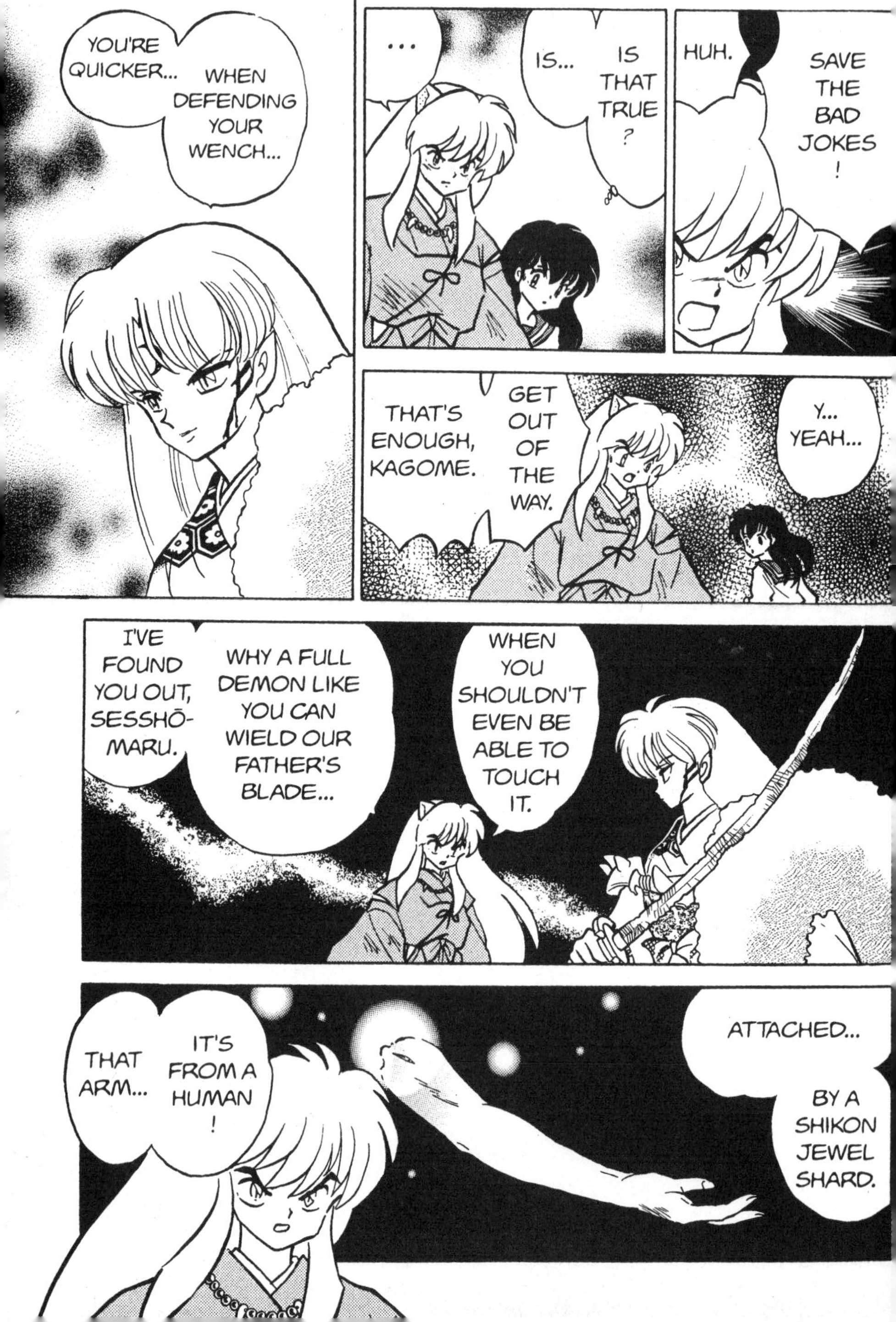
YOU'RE QUICKER... WHEN DEFENDING YOUR WENCH...
...
IS... IS THAT TRUE?
HUH.
SAVE THE BAD JOKES!
THAT'S ENOUGH, KAGOME.
GET OUT OF THE WAY.
Y... YEAH...
I'VE FOUND YOU OUT, SESSHŌ-MARU.
WHY A FULL DEMON LIKE YOU CAN WIELD OUR FATHER'S BLADE...
WHEN YOU SHOULDN'T EVEN BE ABLE TO TOUCH IT.
THAT ARM...
IT'S FROM A HUMAN!
ATTACHED...
BY A SHIKON JEWEL SHARD.

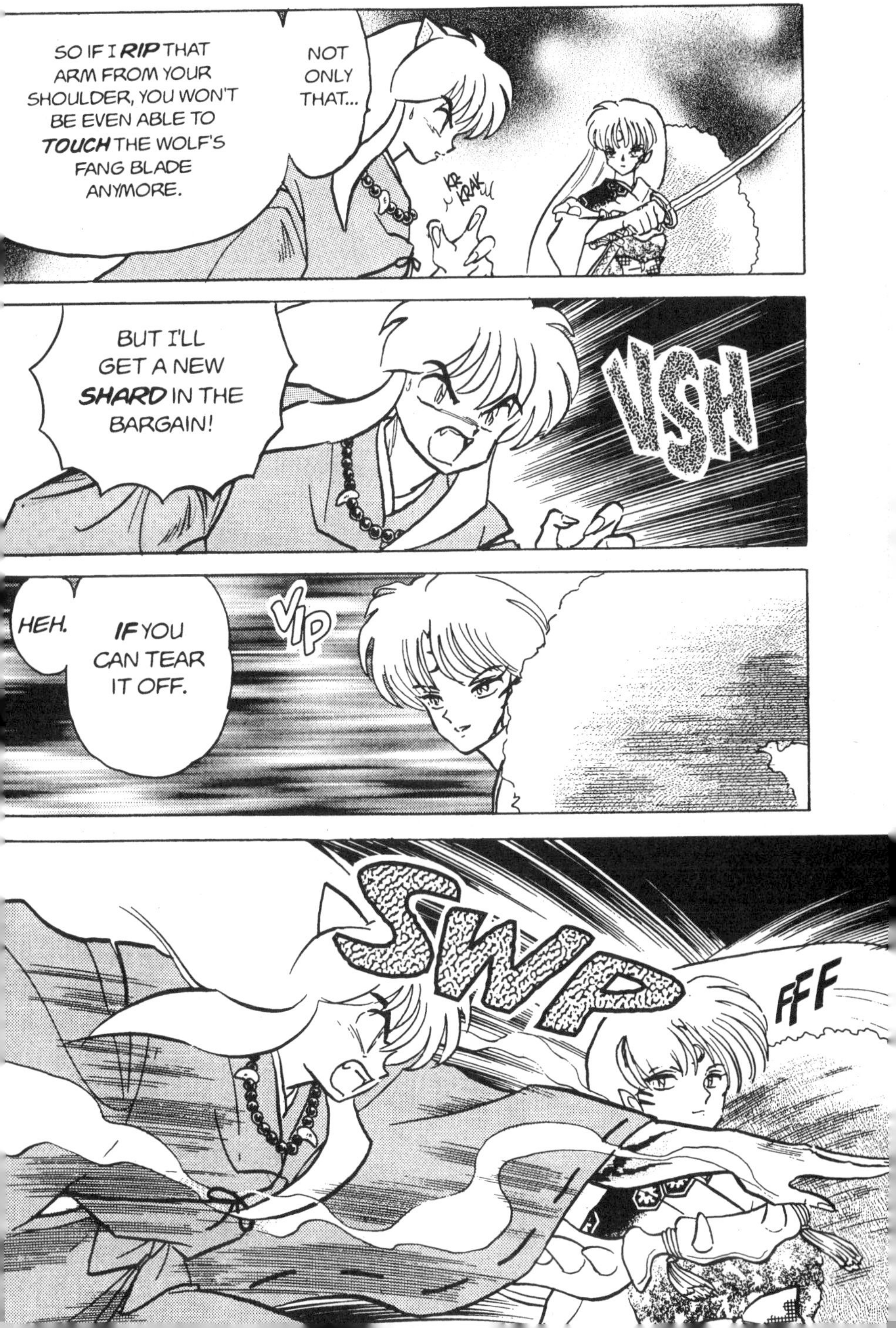
SO IF I RIP THAT ARM FROM YOUR SHOULDER, YOU WON'T BE EVEN ABLE TO TOUCH THE WOLF'S FANG BLADE ANYMORE.
NOT ONLY THAT...
KR KRAK
BUT I'LL GET A NEW SHARD IN THE BARGAIN!
VSH
HEH.
IF YOU CAN TEAR IT OFF.
VIP
SWP
FFF

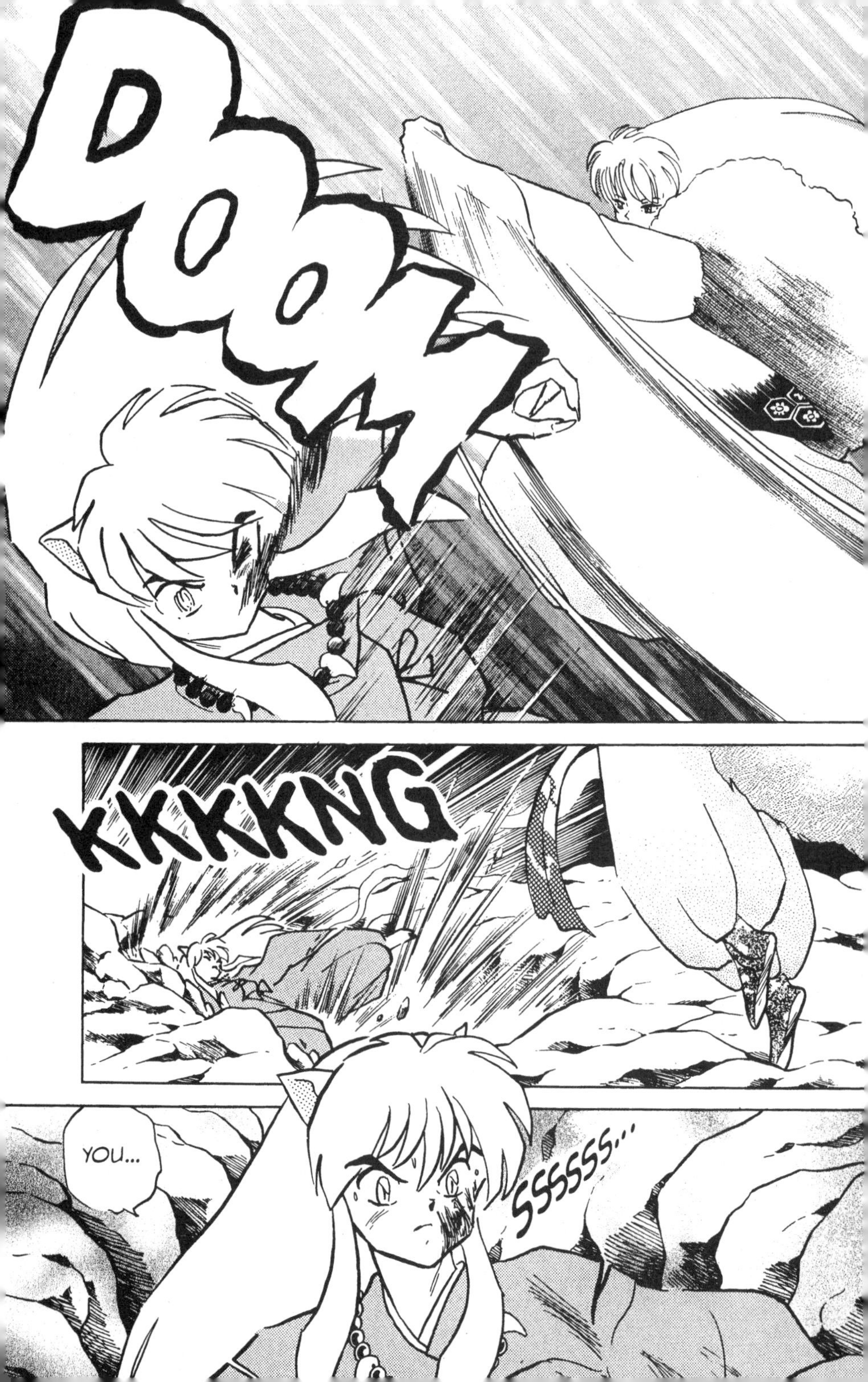
DOOOM
KKKKNG
YOU...
SSSSSS...

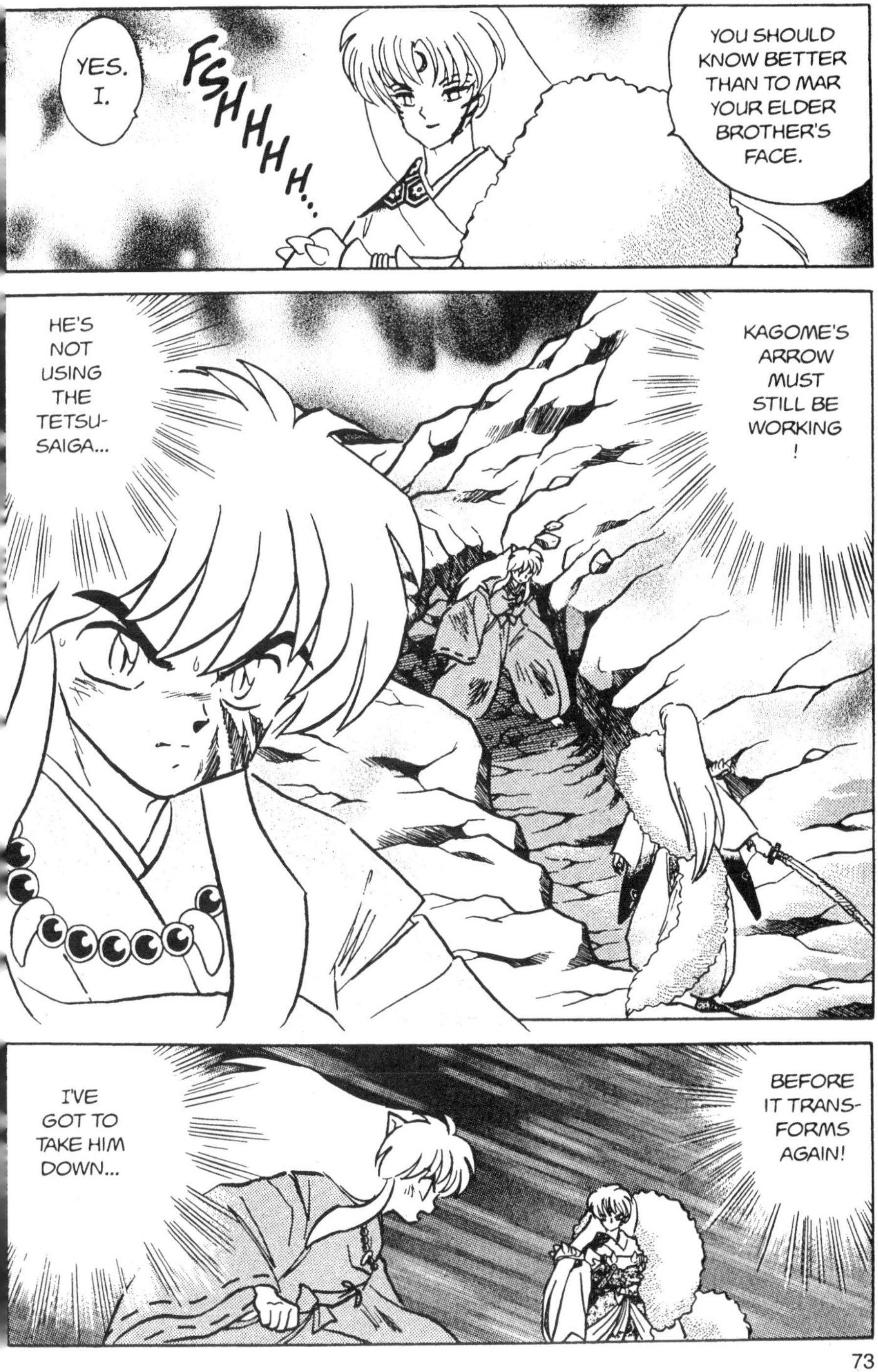
YES. I.
FSHHHHH...
YOU SHOULD KNOW BETTER THAN TO MAR YOUR ELDER BROTHER'S FACE.
HE'S NOT USING THE TETSU-SAIGA...
KAGOME'S ARROW MUST STILL BE WORKING!
I'VE GOT TO TAKE HIM DOWN...
BEFORE IT TRANS-FORMS AGAIN!

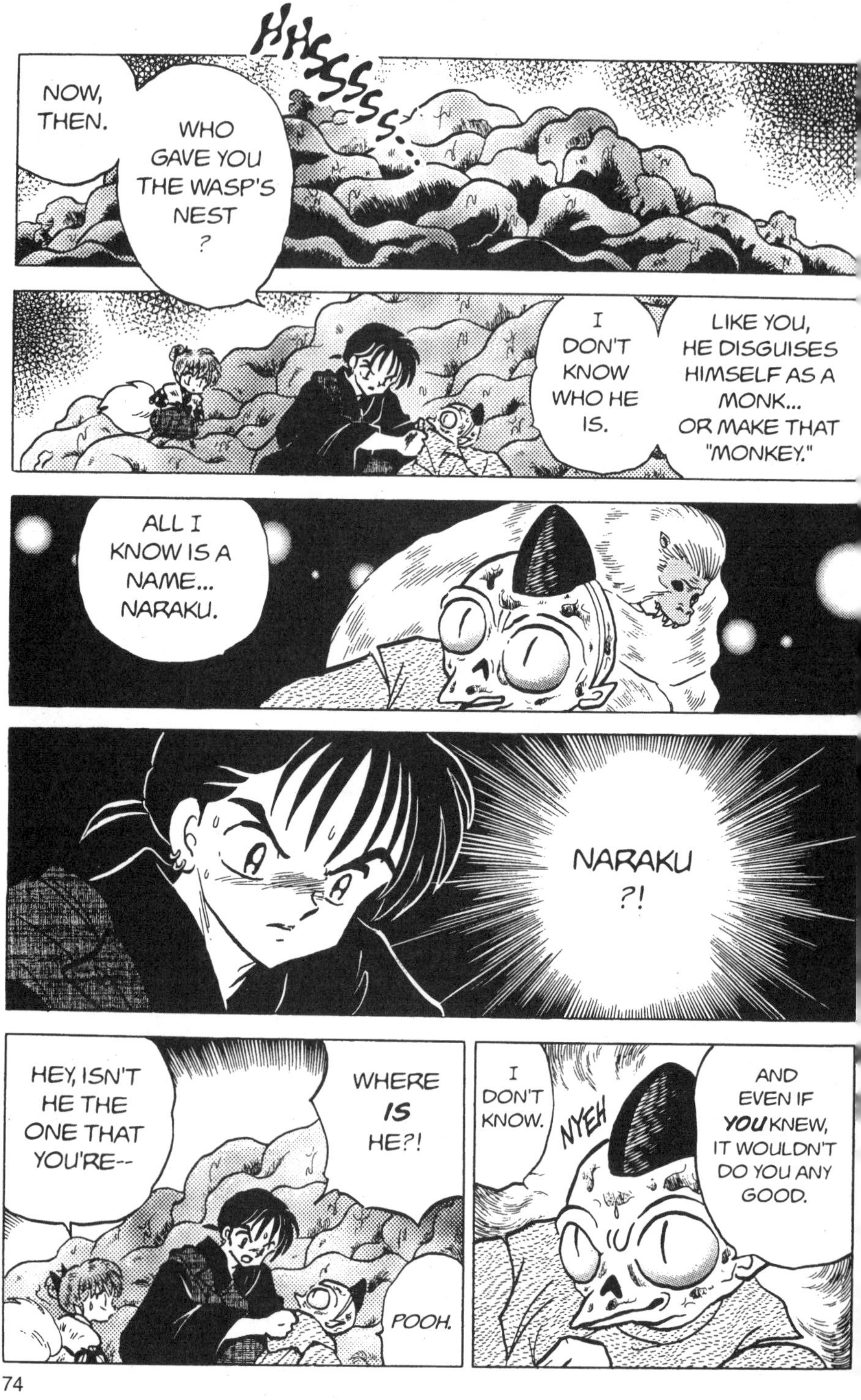
HHSSSSSS
NOW, THEN.
WHO GAVE YOU THE WASP'S NEST ?
I DON'T KNOW WHO HE IS.
LIKE YOU, HE DISGUISES HIMSELF AS A MONK... OR MAKE THAT "MONKEY."
ALL I KNOW IS A NAME... NARAKU.
NARAKU ?!
HEY, ISN'T HE THE ONE THAT YOU'RE--
WHERE *IS* HE?!
POOH.
I DON'T KNOW.
NYEH
AND EVEN IF ***YOU*** KNEW, IT WOULDN'T DO YOU ANY GOOD.

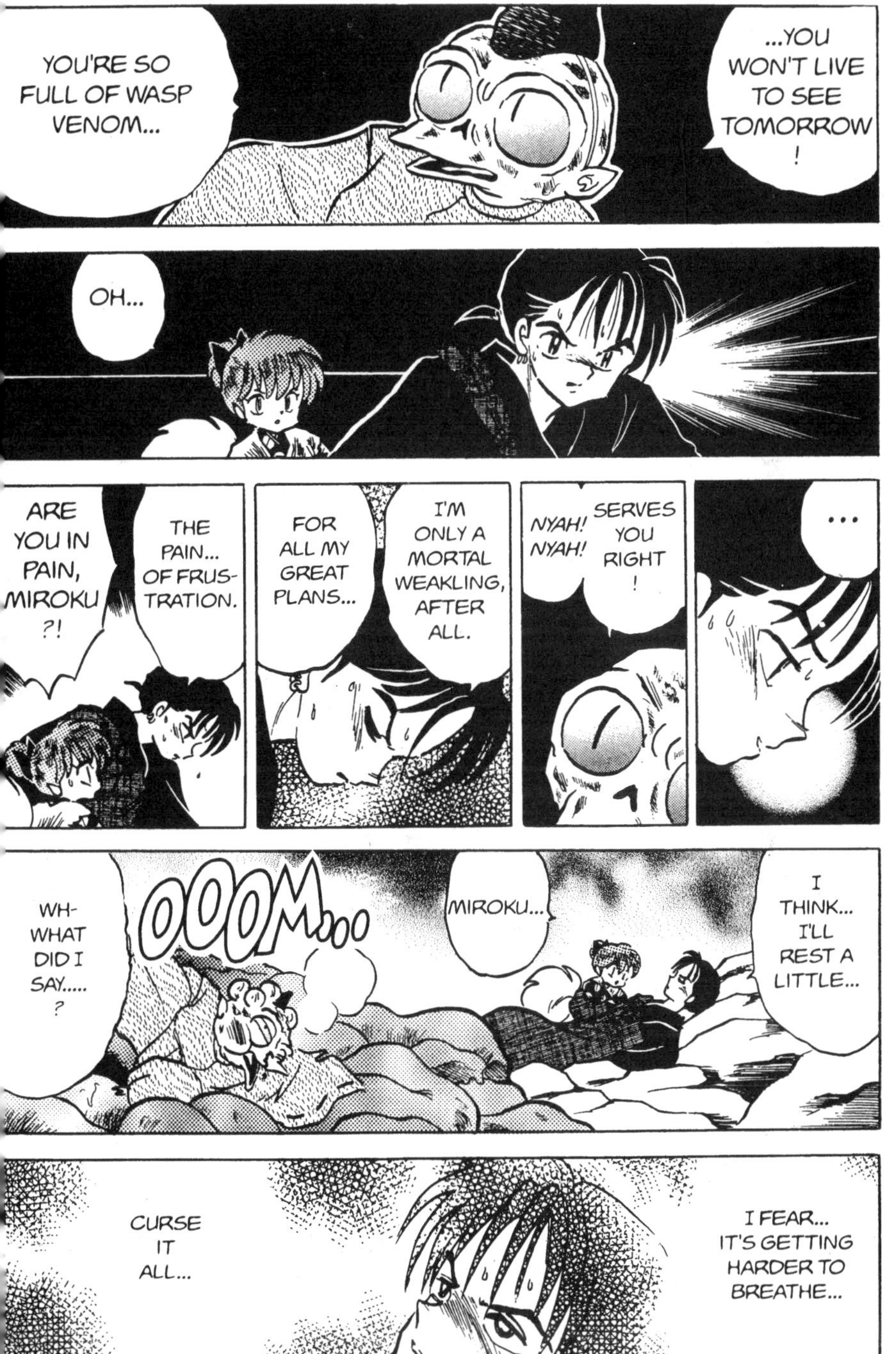
YOU'RE SO FULL OF WASP VENOM...
...YOU WON'T LIVE TO SEE TOMORROW!
OH...
ARE YOU IN PAIN, MIROKU?!
THE PAIN... OF FRUS-TRATION.
FOR ALL MY GREAT PLANS...
I'M ONLY A MORTAL WEAKLING, AFTER ALL.
NYAH! NYAH!
SERVES YOU RIGHT!
...
WH-WHAT DID I SAY.....?
OOOM...
MIROKU...
I THINK... I'LL REST A LITTLE...
CURSE IT ALL...
I FEAR... IT'S GETTING HARDER TO BREATHE...

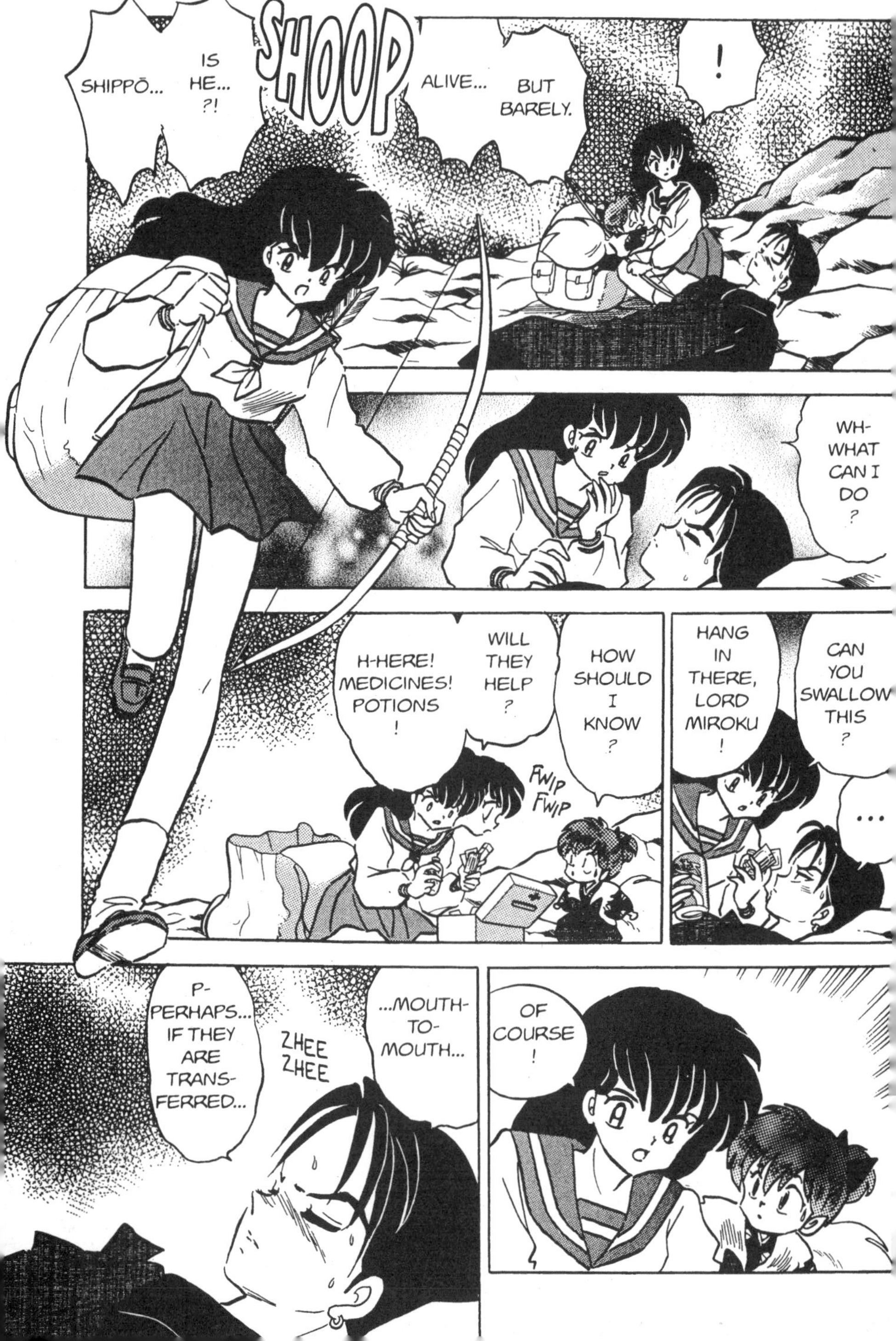
SHIPPŌ...
IS HE... ?!
SHOOP
ALIVE...
BUT BARELY.
!
WH-WHAT CAN I DO ?
H-HERE! MEDICINES! POTIONS !
WILL THEY HELP ?
HOW SHOULD I KNOW ?
FWIP FWIP
HANG IN THERE, LORD MIROKU !
CAN YOU SWALLOW THIS ?
...
P-PERHAPS... IF THEY ARE TRANS-FERRED...
ZHEE ZHEE
...MOUTH-TO-MOUTH...
OF COURSE !

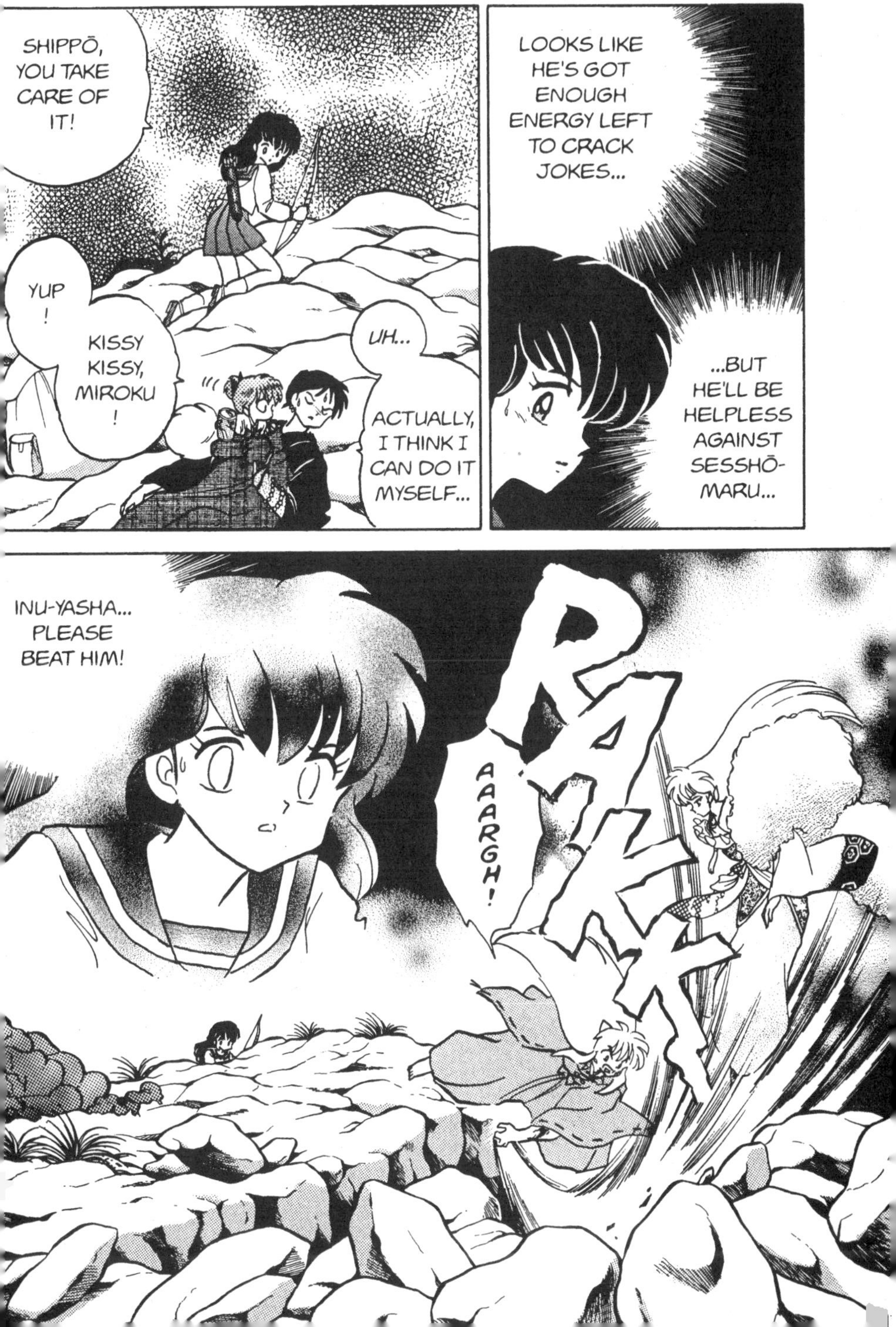
SHIPPŌ, YOU TAKE CARE OF IT!
YUP!
KISSY KISSY, MIROKU!
UH...
ACTUALLY, I THINK I CAN DO IT MYSELF...
LOOKS LIKE HE'S GOT ENOUGH ENERGY LEFT TO CRACK JOKES...
...BUT HE'LL BE HELPLESS AGAINST SESSHŌ-MARU...
INU-YASHA... PLEASE BEAT HIM!
PAKK
AAARGH!

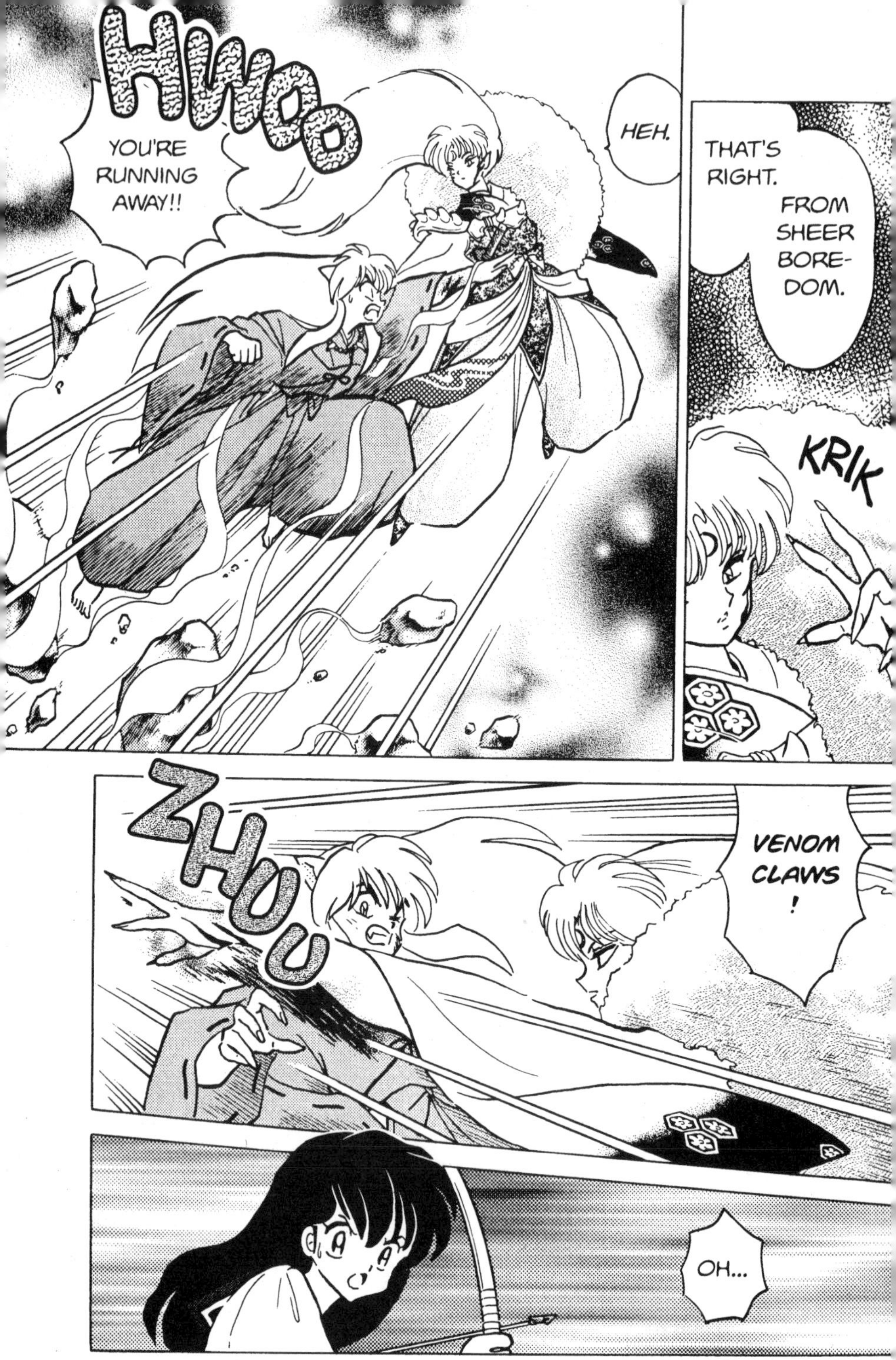
HWOO
YOU'RE RUNNING AWAY!!
HEH.
THAT'S RIGHT.
FROM SHEER BORE-DOM.
KRIK
ZHUU
VENOM CLAWS!
OH...

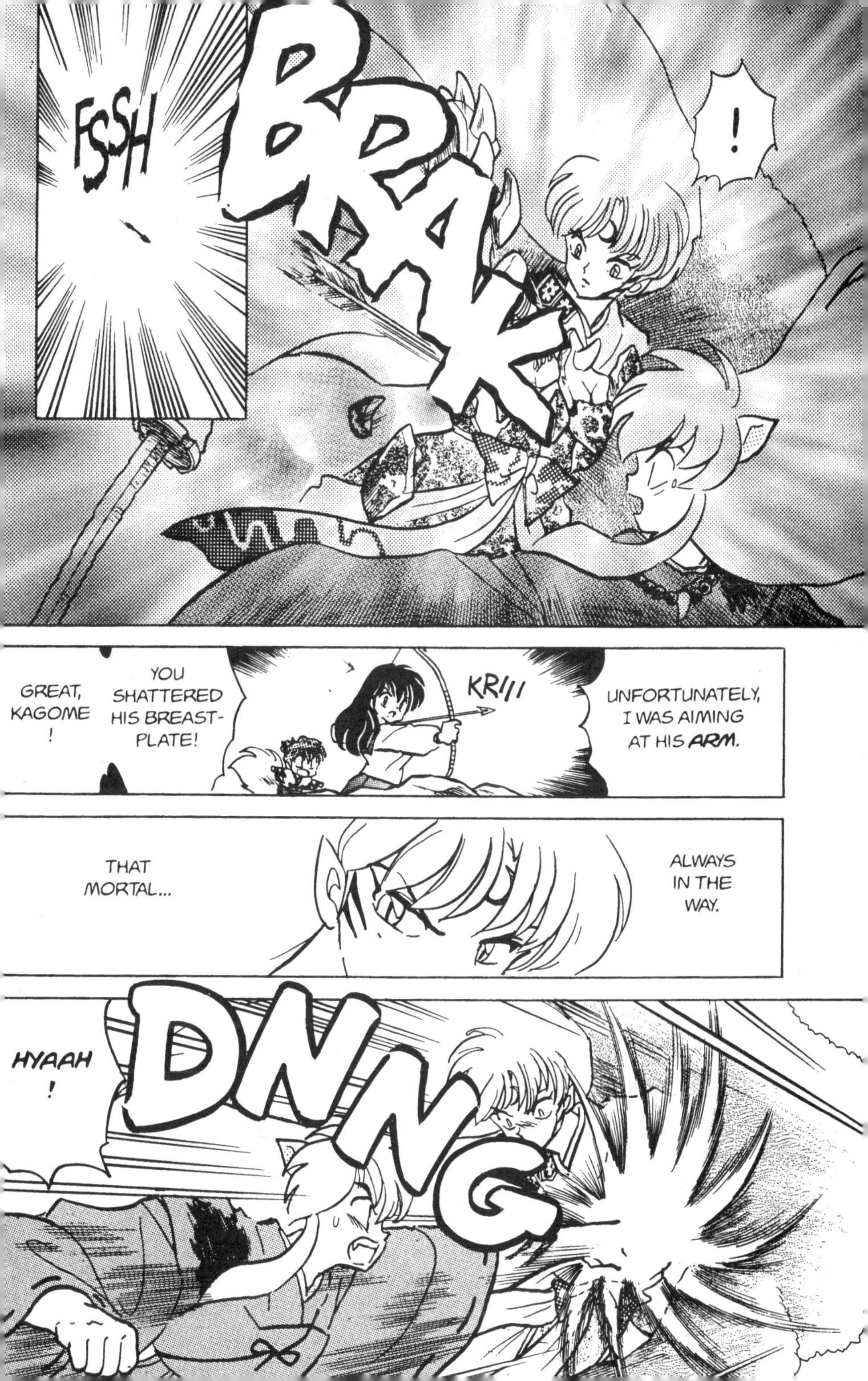
FSSH
BRAK
!
GREAT, KAGOME!
YOU SHATTERED HIS BREAST-PLATE!
KRIII
UNFORTUNATELY, I WAS AIMING AT HIS ARM.
THAT MORTAL...
ALWAYS IN THE WAY.
HYAAH!
DNNG

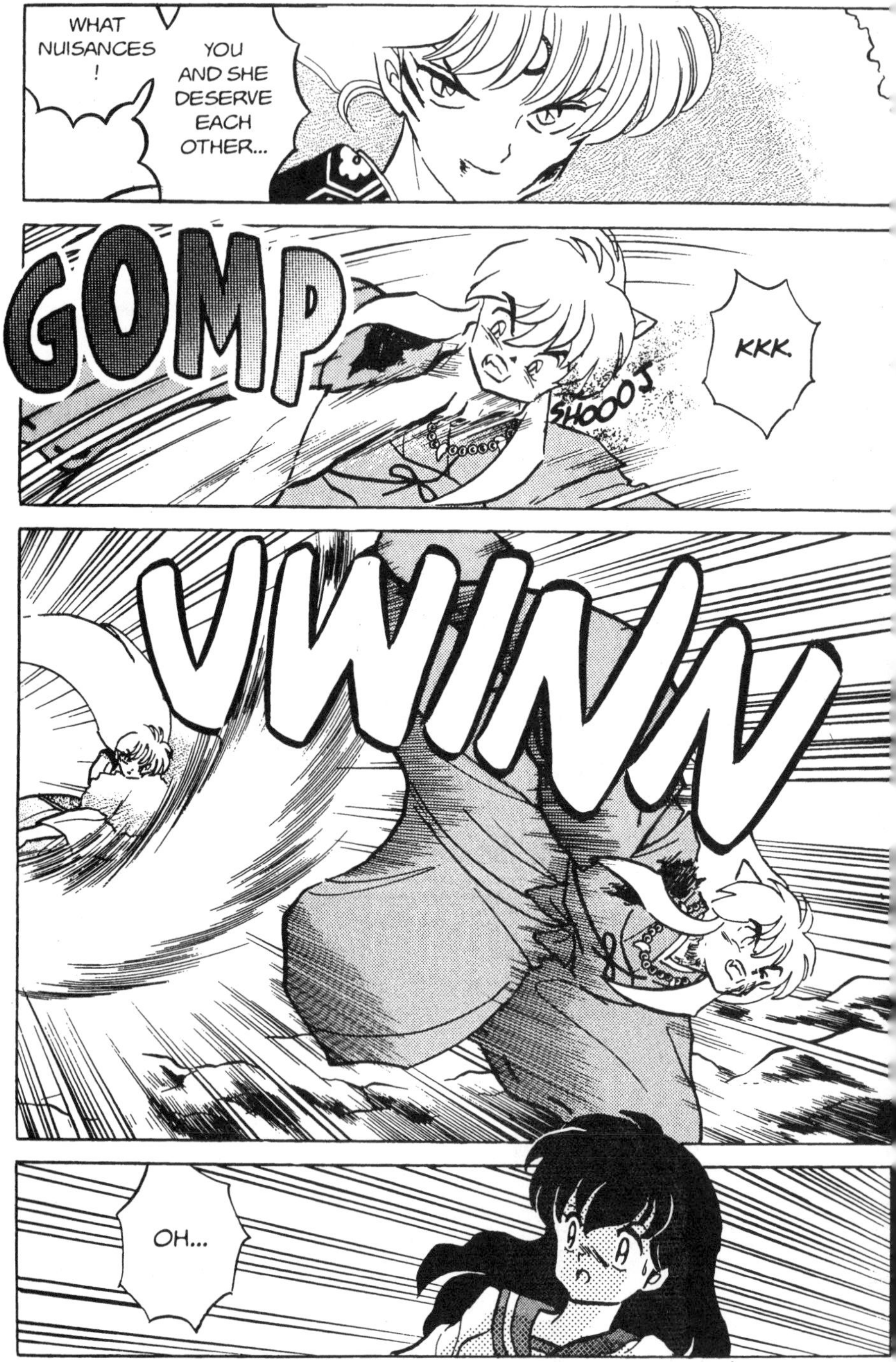
WHAT NUISANCES !
YOU AND SHE DESERVE EACH OTHER...
GOMP
SHOOOJ
KKK.
VWINN
OH...

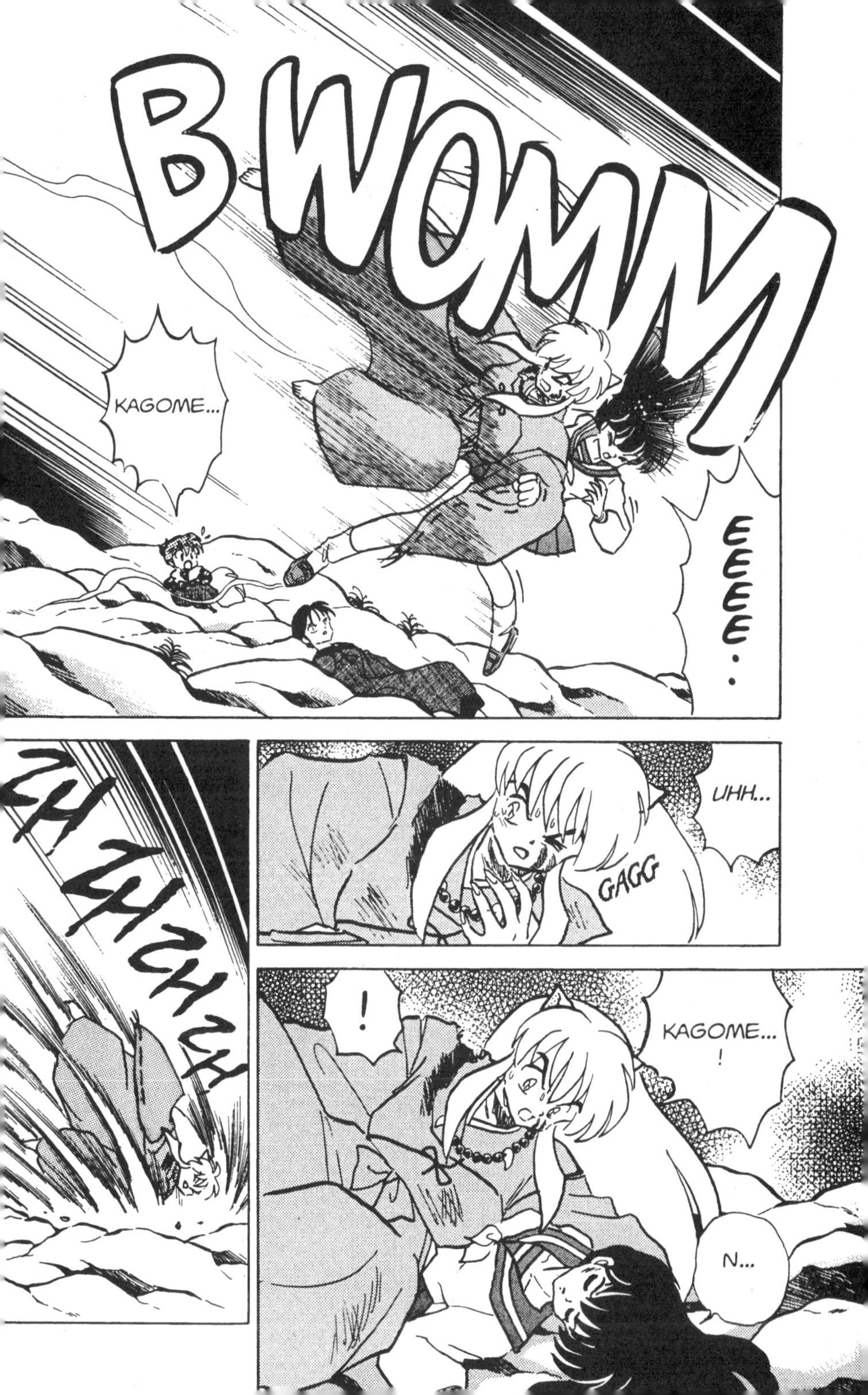
BWOMM
KAGOME...
EEEEE...
UHH...
GAGG
!
KAGOME... !
N...

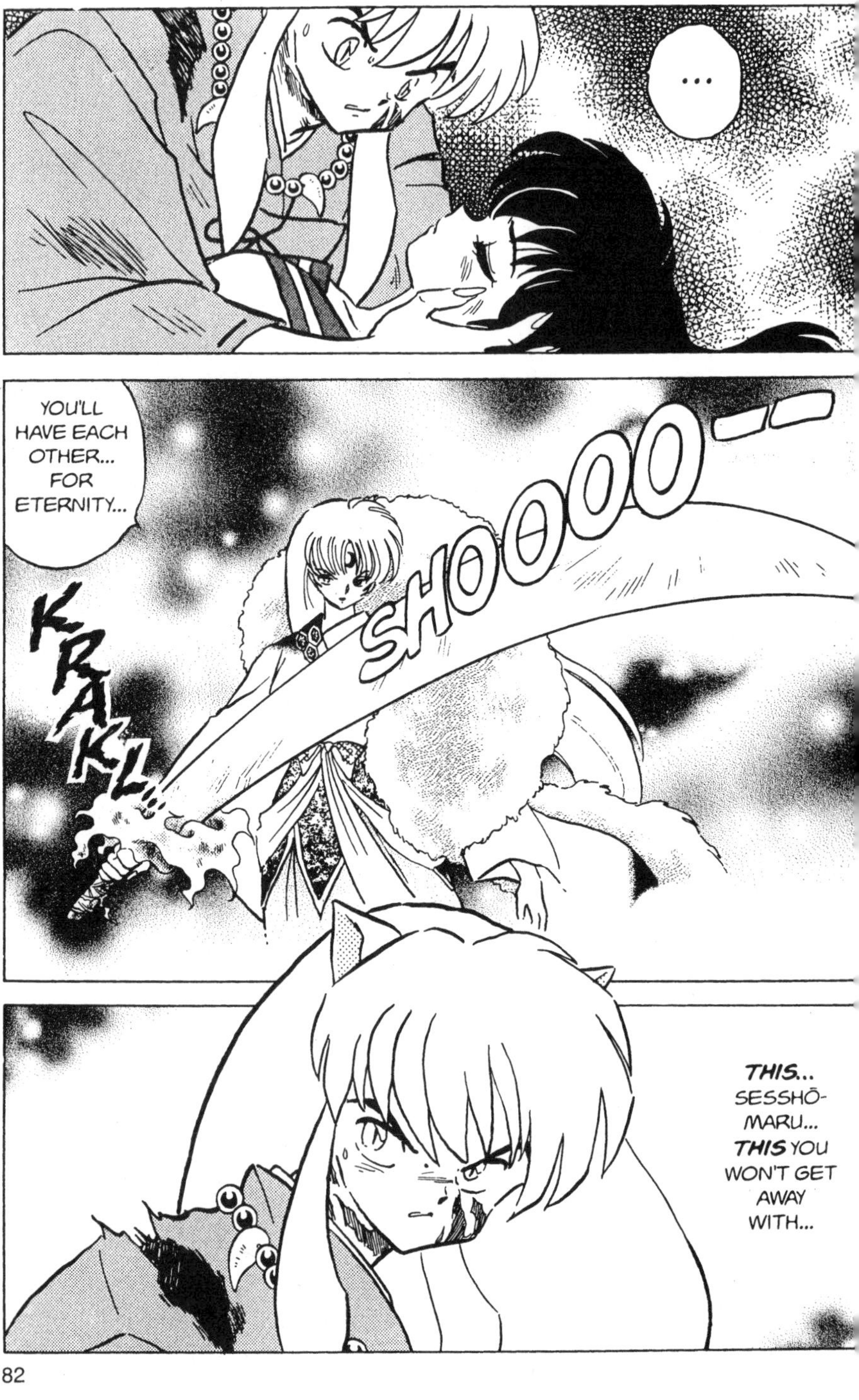
...
YOU'LL HAVE EACH OTHER... FOR ETERNITY...
SHOOOOO--
KRAKL
THIS... SESSHŌ-MARU... THIS YOU WON'T GET AWAY WITH...

SCROLL FIVE

RECLAMATION

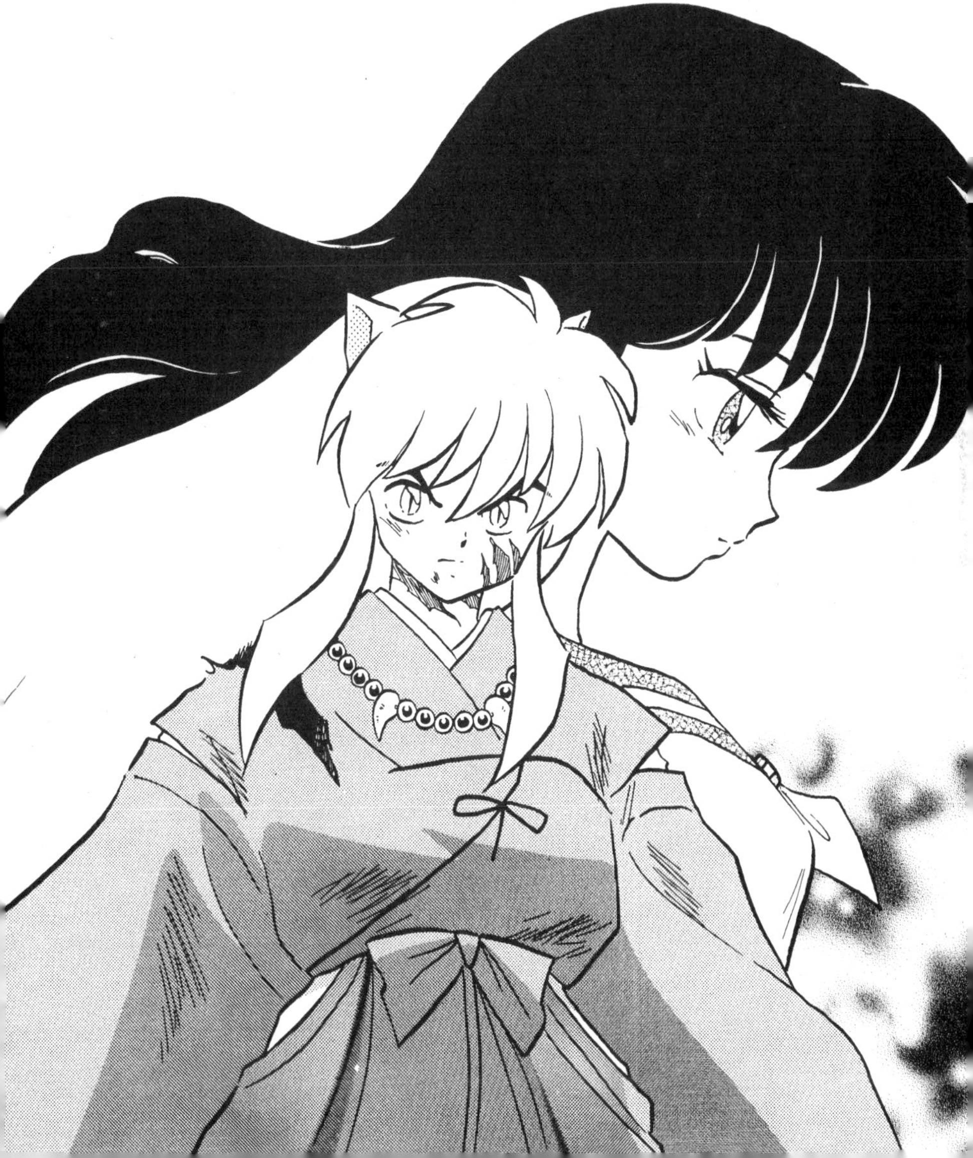

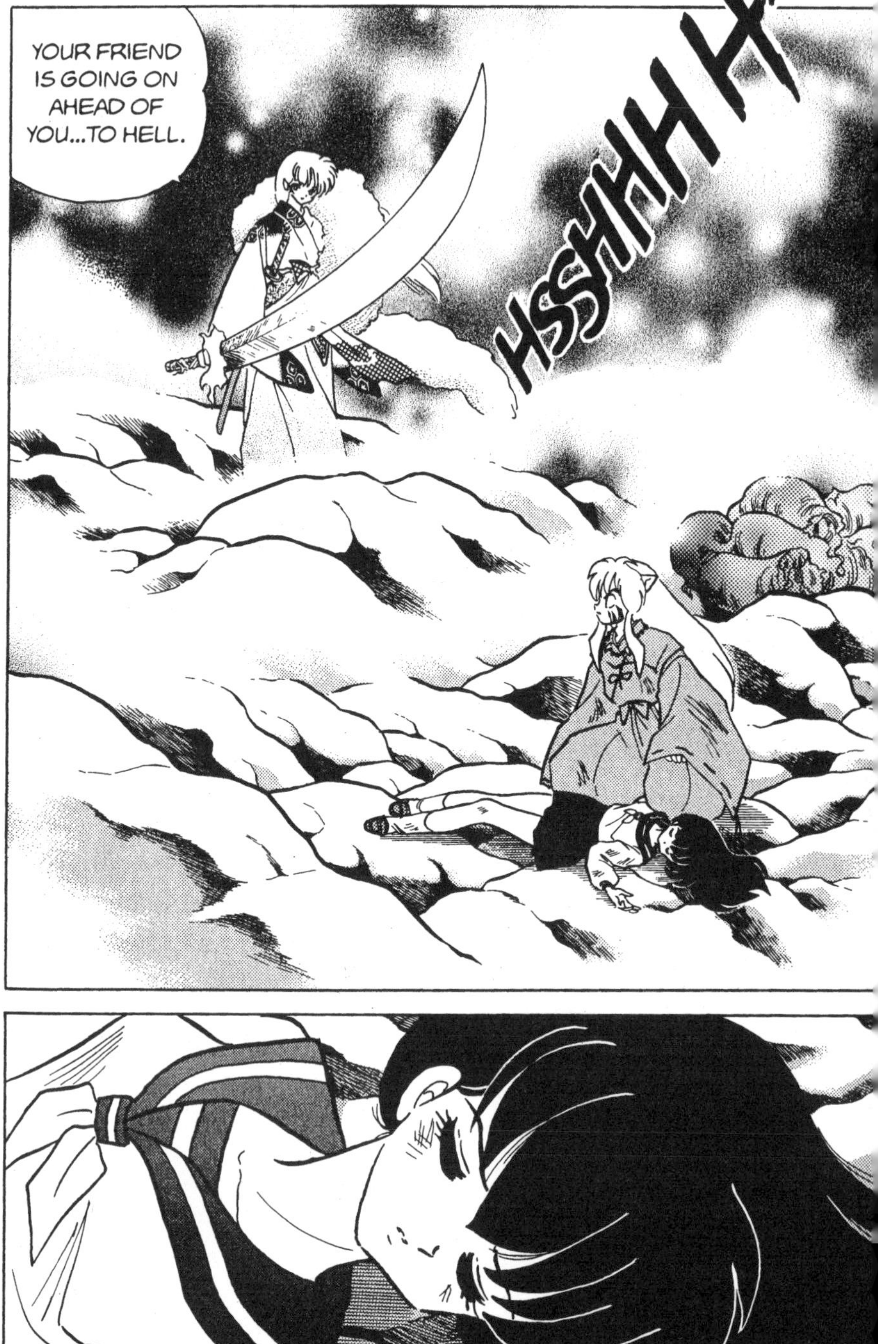
YOUR FRIEND IS GOING ON AHEAD OF YOU...TO HELL.
HSSHHH H...

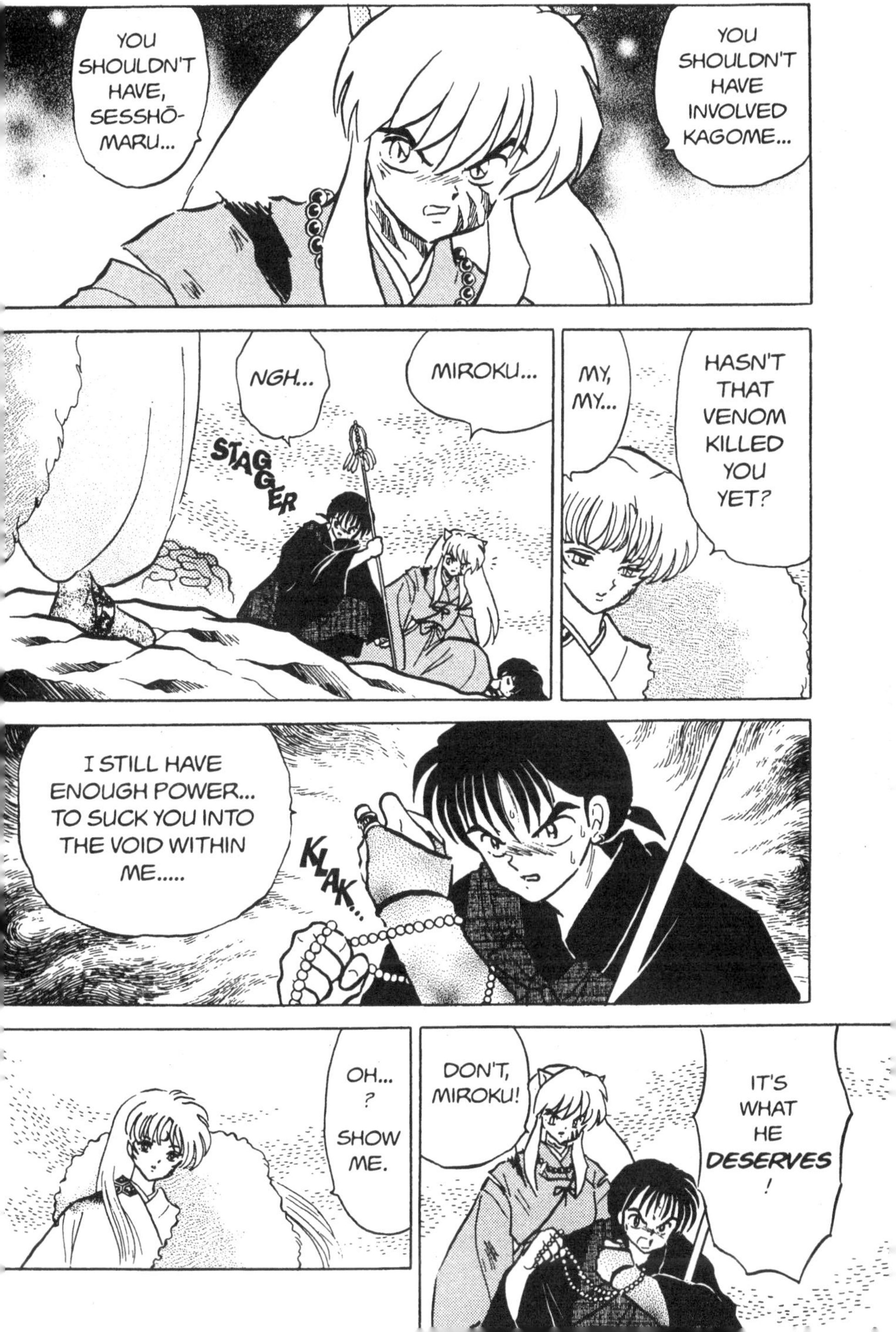
YOU SHOULDN'T HAVE, SESSHŌ-MARU...
YOU SHOULDN'T HAVE INVOLVED KAGOME...
NGH...
STAGGER
MIROKU...
MY, MY...
HASN'T THAT VENOM KILLED YOU YET?
I STILL HAVE ENOUGH POWER... TO SUCK YOU INTO THE VOID WITHIN ME.....
KLAK...
OH...? SHOW ME.
DON'T, MIROKU!
IT'S WHAT HE *DESERVES*!

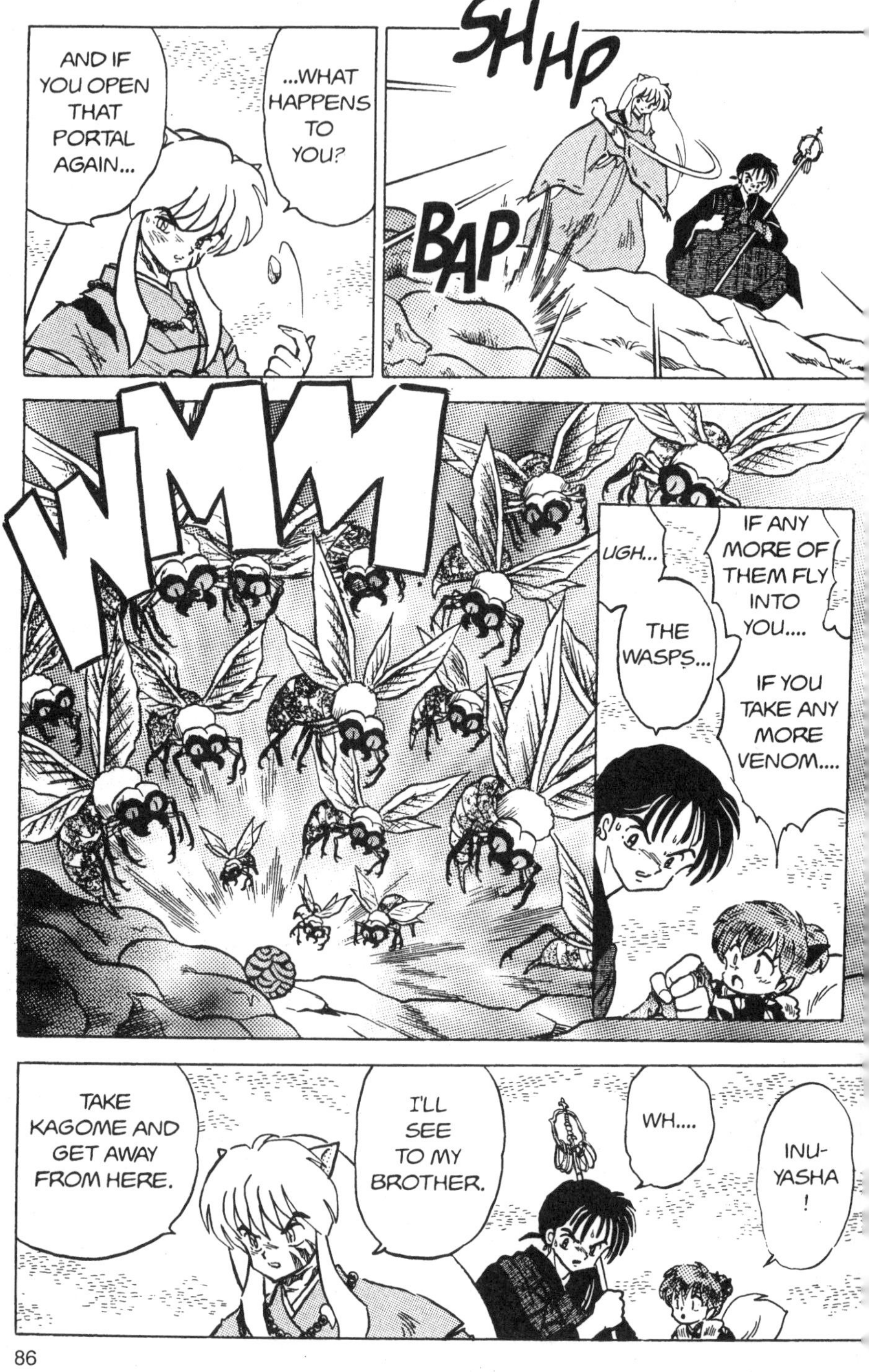
AND IF YOU OPEN THAT PORTAL AGAIN...
...WHAT HAPPENS TO YOU?
SHHP
BAP
WMM
UGH...
THE WASPS...
IF ANY MORE OF THEM FLY INTO YOU....
IF YOU TAKE ANY MORE VENOM....
TAKE KAGOME AND GET AWAY FROM HERE.
I'LL SEE TO MY BROTHER.
WH....
INU-YASHA!

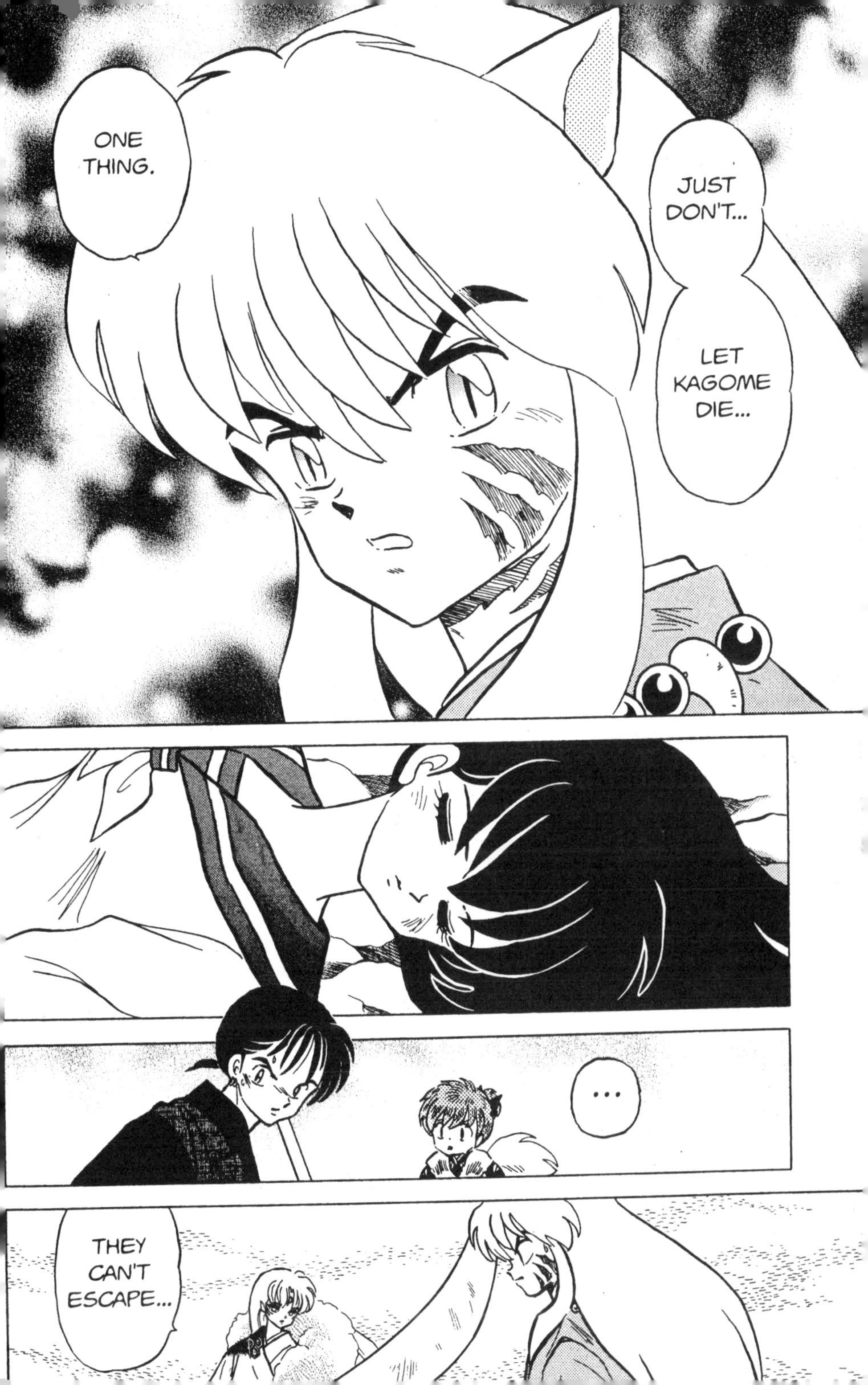
ONE THING.
JUST DON'T...
LET KAGOME DIE...
...
THEY CAN'T ESCAPE...

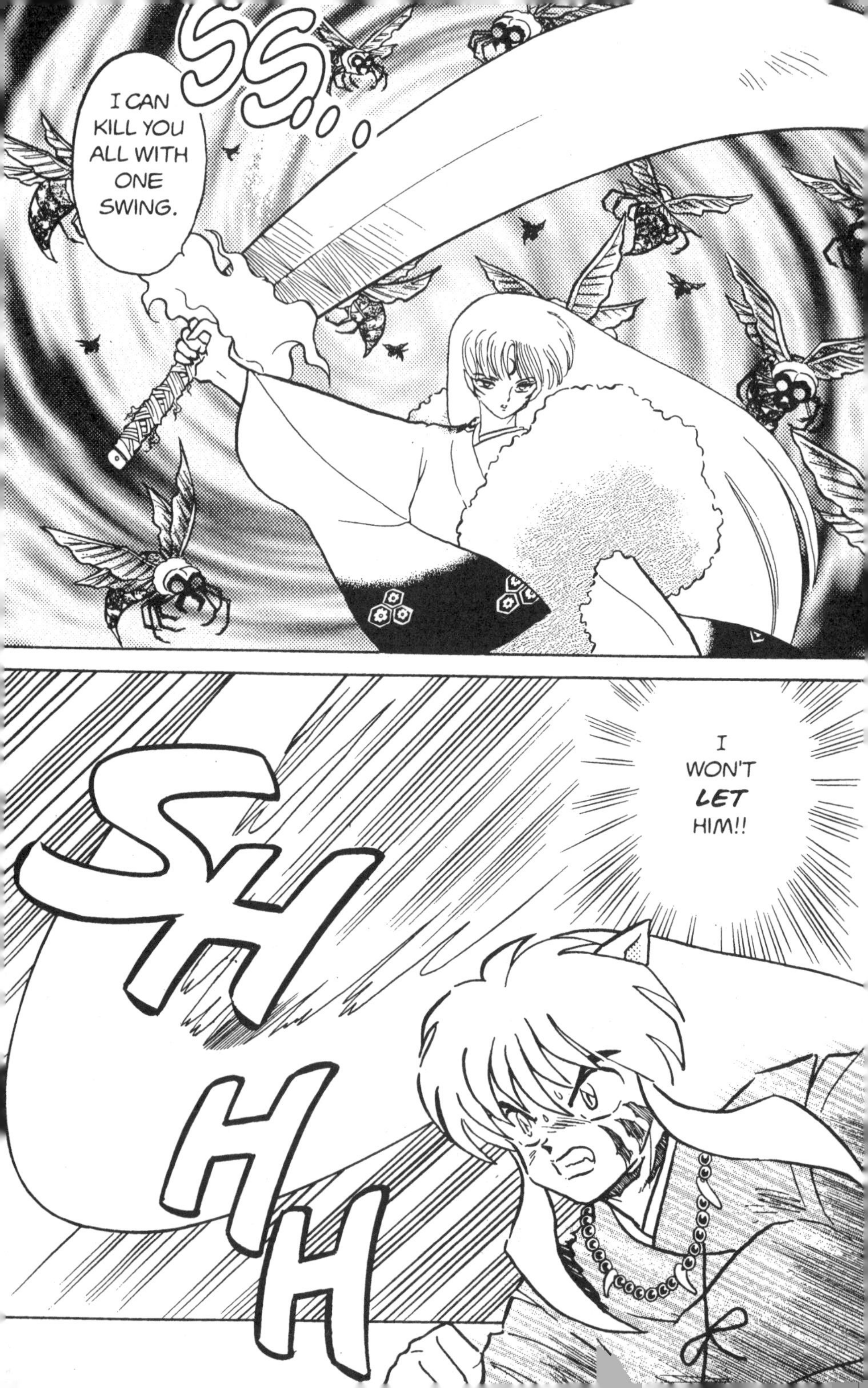
SS...
I CAN KILL YOU ALL WITH ONE SWING.
SHHH
I WON'T LET HIM!!

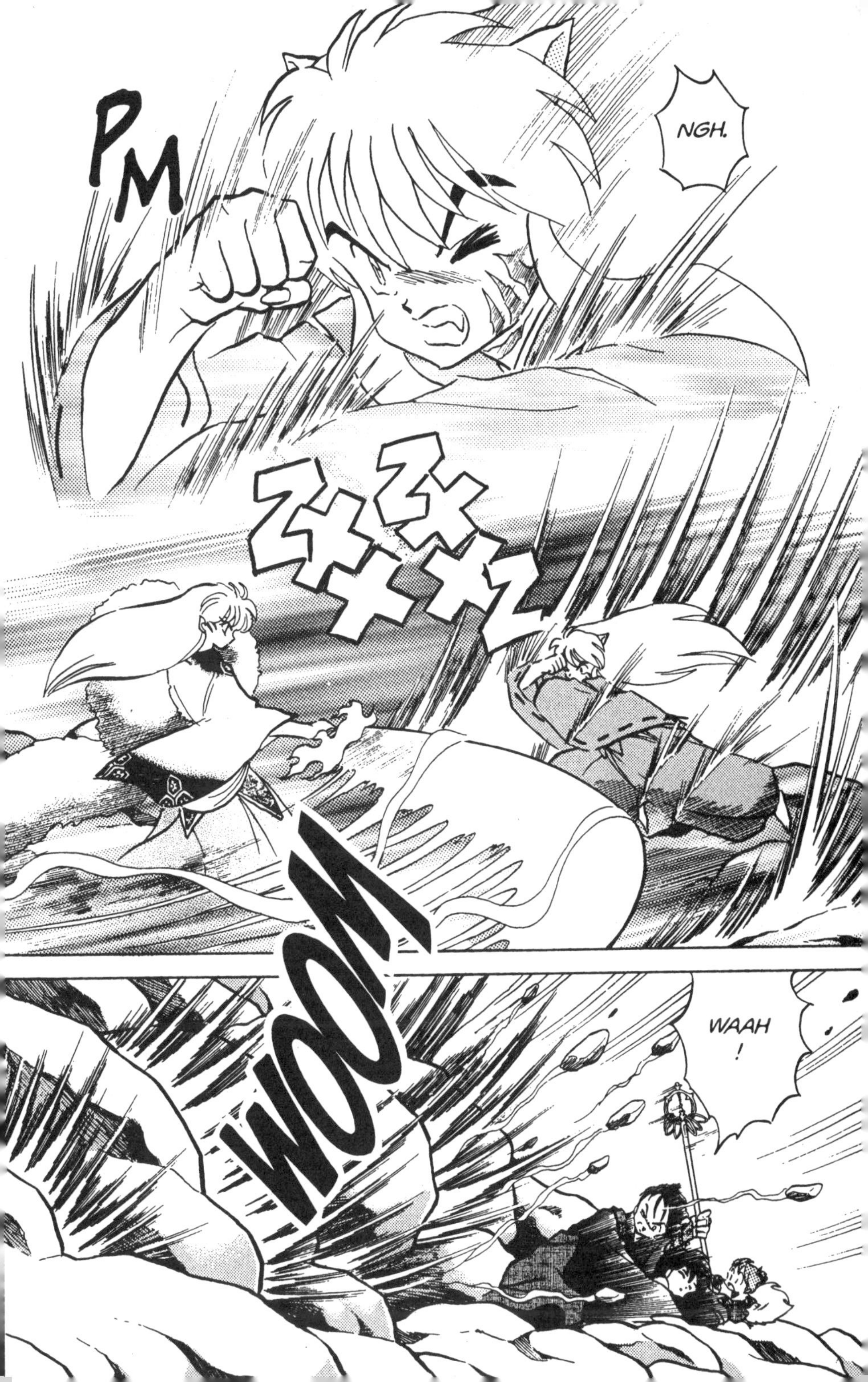
PM
NGH.
WOOM
WAAH!

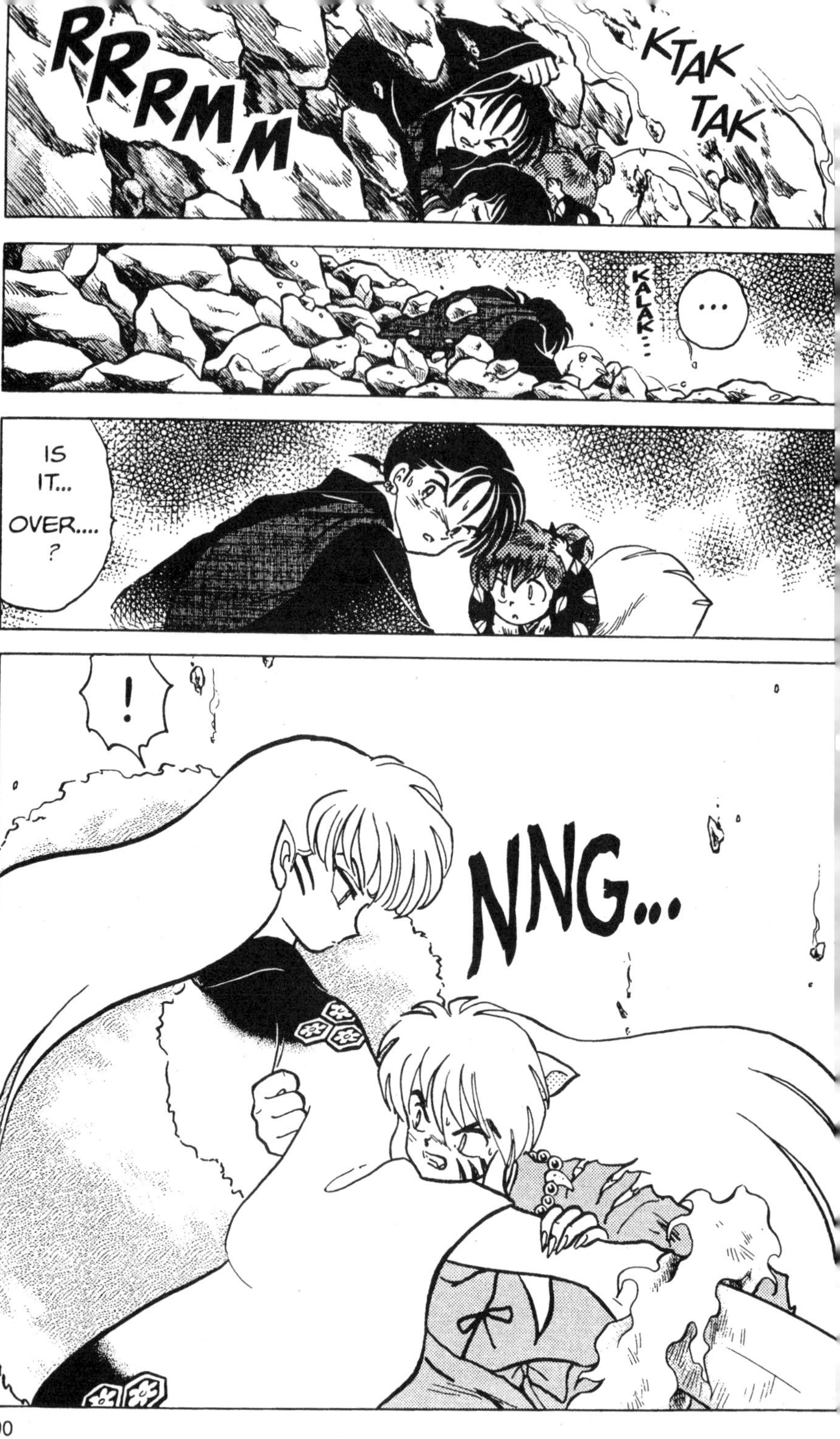
RRRMMM
KTAK TAK
KALAK...
...
IS IT... OVER.... ?
!
NNG...

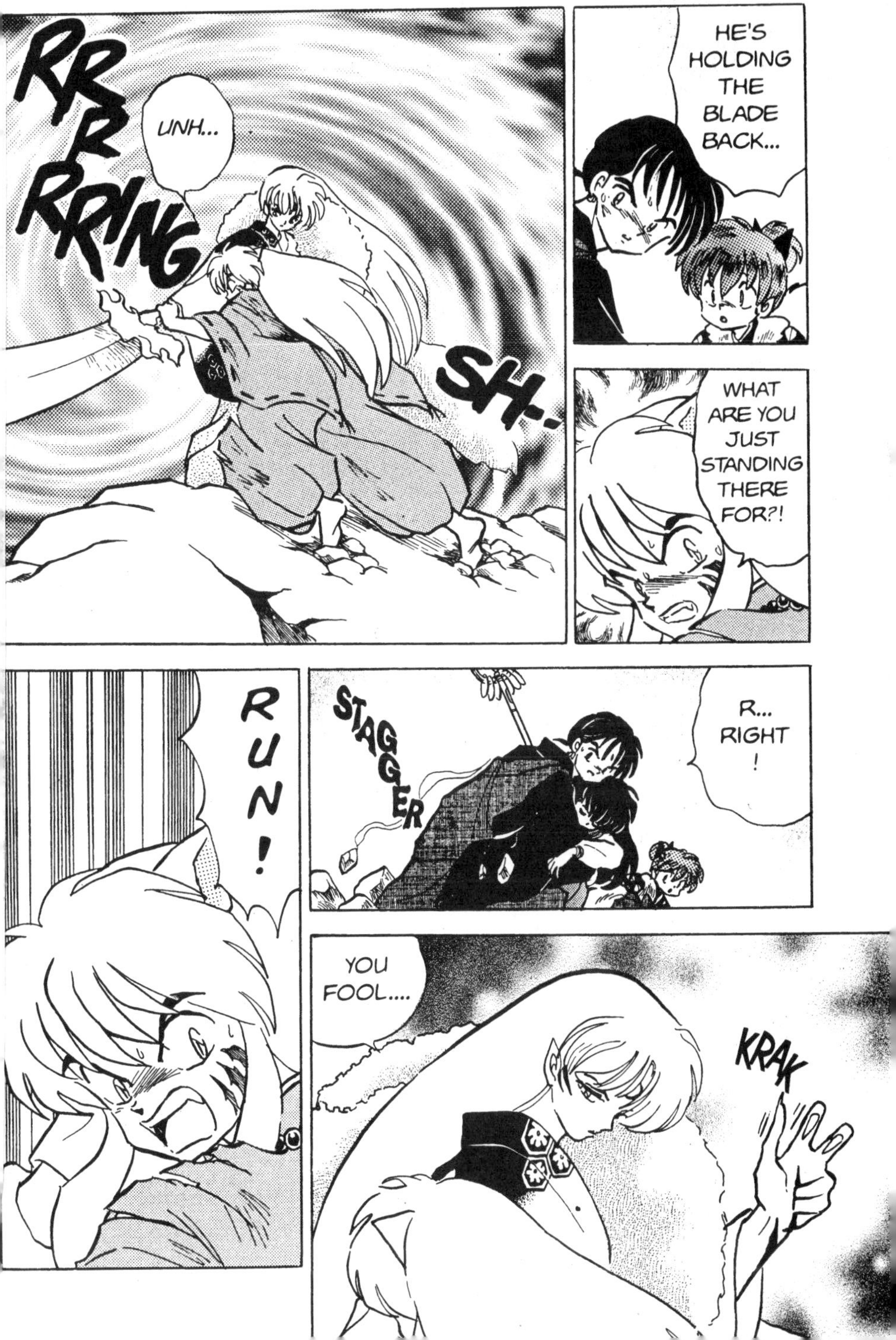
RRRRRING
UNH...
SH--
HE'S HOLDING THE BLADE BACK...
WHAT ARE YOU JUST STANDING THERE FOR?!
RUN!
STAGGER
R... RIGHT!
YOU FOOL....
KRAK

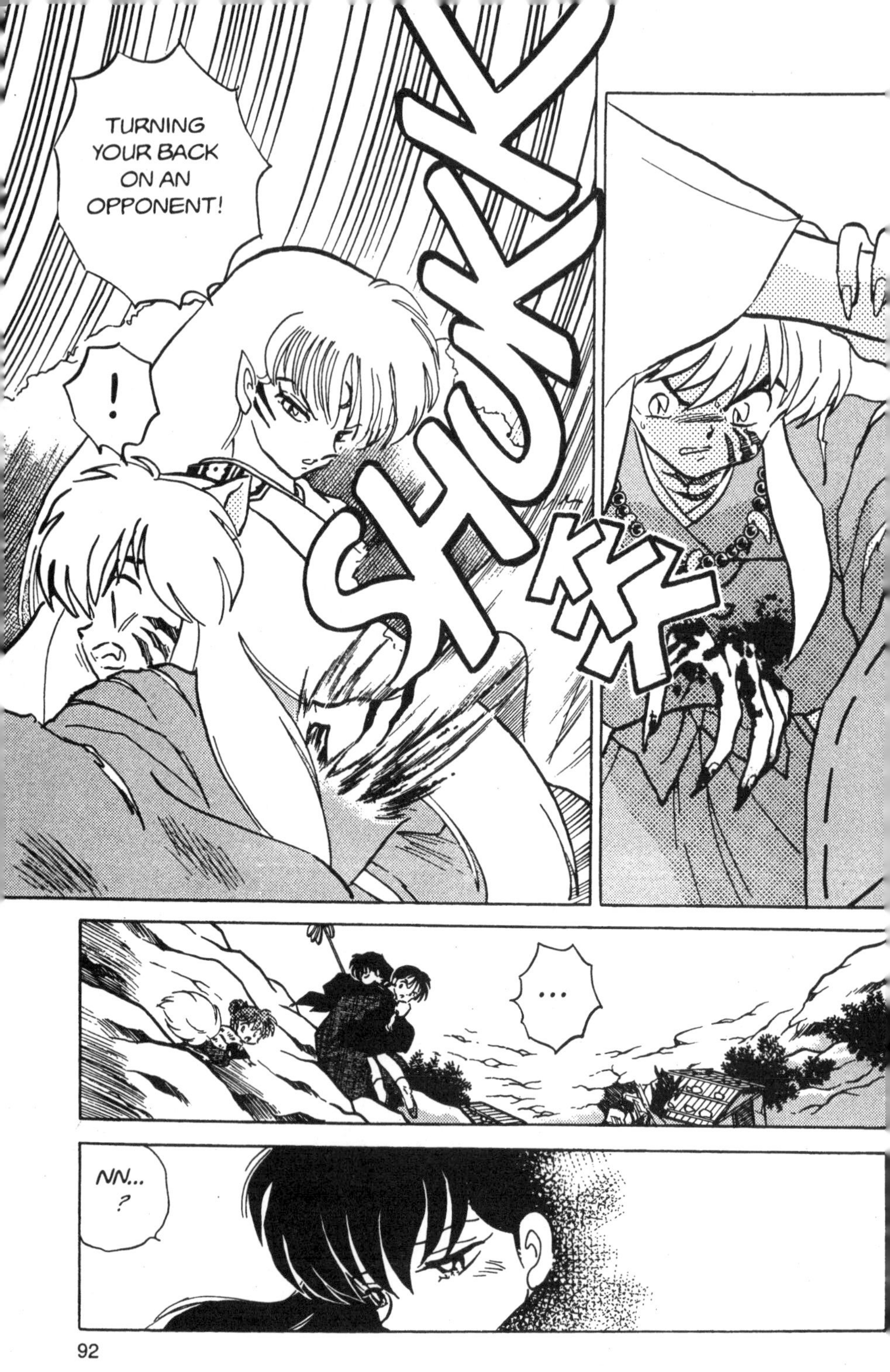
TURNING YOUR BACK ON AN OPPONENT!
!
SHUKK
...
NN... ?

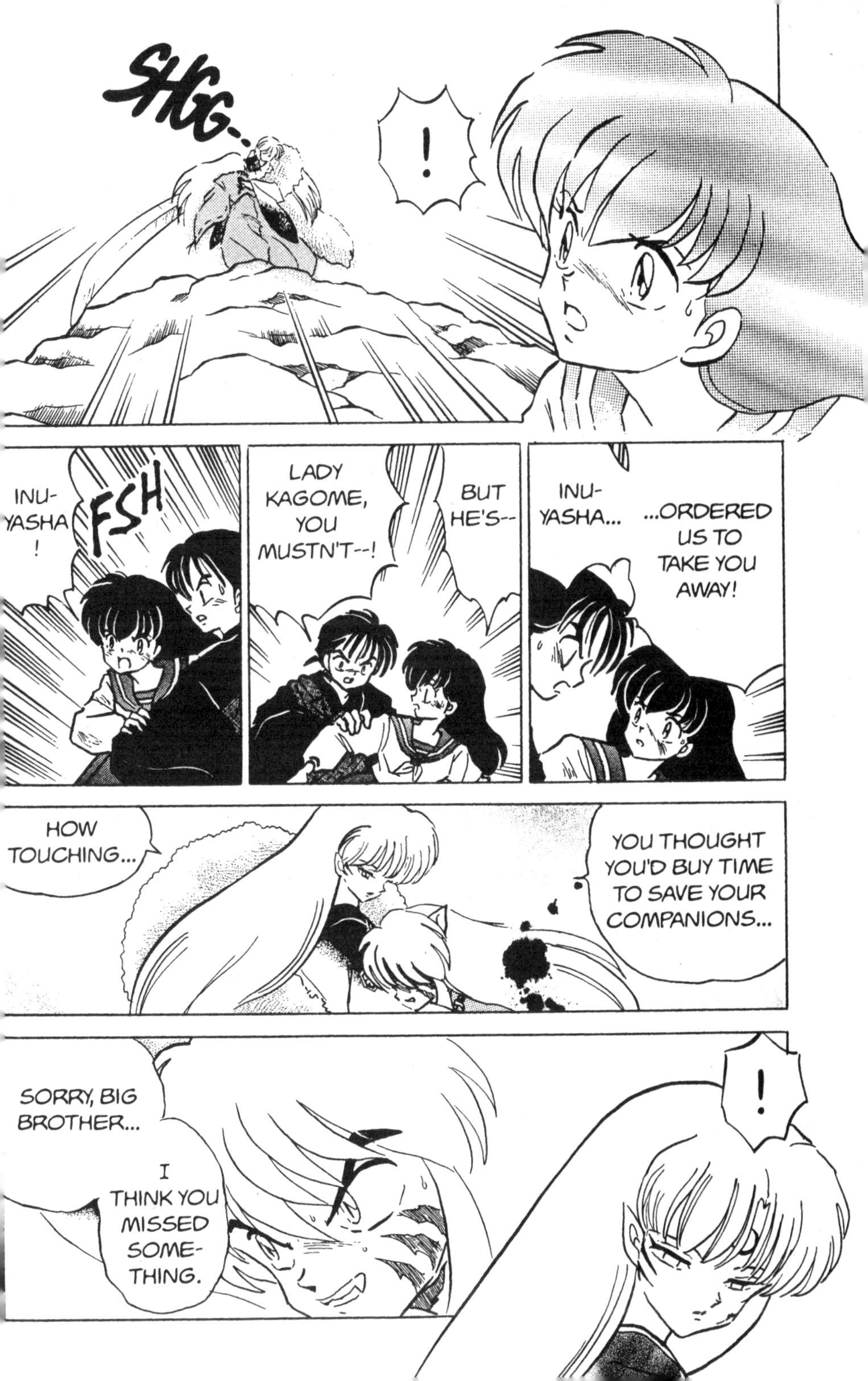
SHGG...
!
INU-YASHA!
FSH
LADY KAGOME, YOU MUSTN'T--!
BUT HE'S--
INU-YASHA...
...ORDERED US TO TAKE YOU AWAY!
HOW TOUCHING...
YOU THOUGHT YOU'D BUY TIME TO SAVE YOUR COMPANIONS...
SORRY, BIG BROTHER...
I THINK YOU MISSED SOME-THING.
!

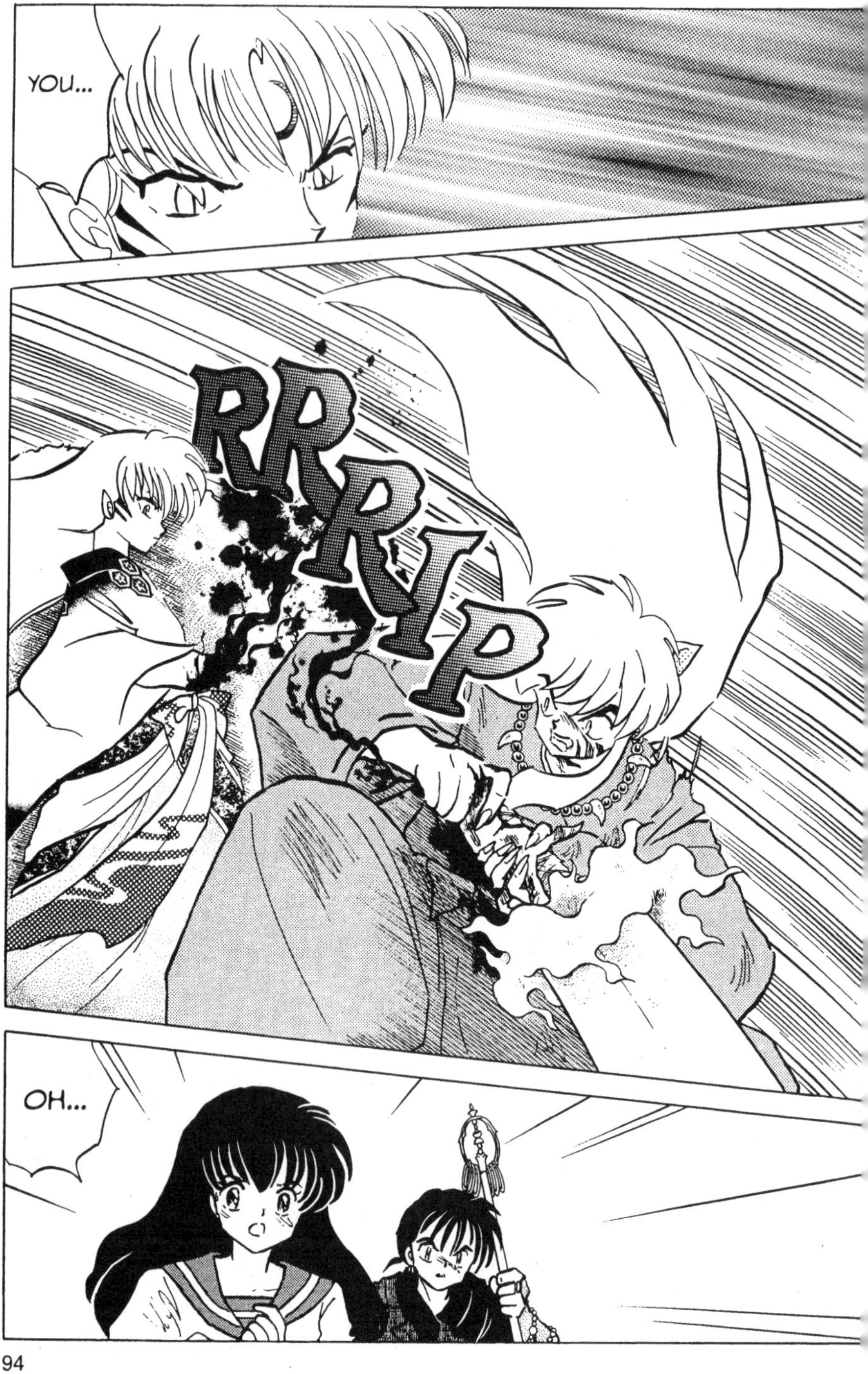
YOU...
RRRIP
OH...

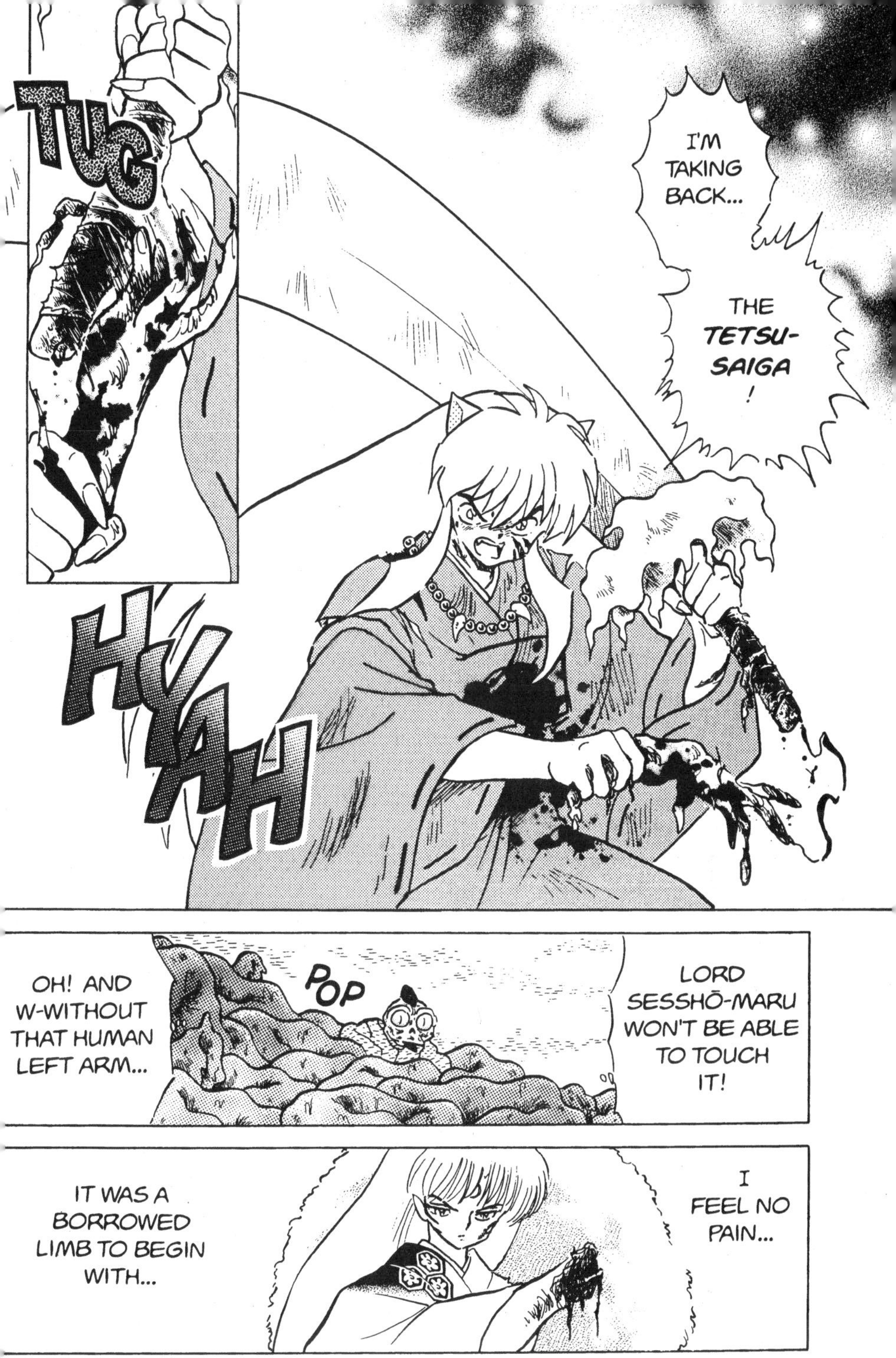
TUG
I'M TAKING BACK...
THE TETSU-SAIGA!
HYAH
OH! AND W-WITHOUT THAT HUMAN LEFT ARM...
POP
LORD SESSHŌ-MARU WON'T BE ABLE TO TOUCH IT!
IT WAS A BORROWED LIMB TO BEGIN WITH...
I FEEL NO PAIN...

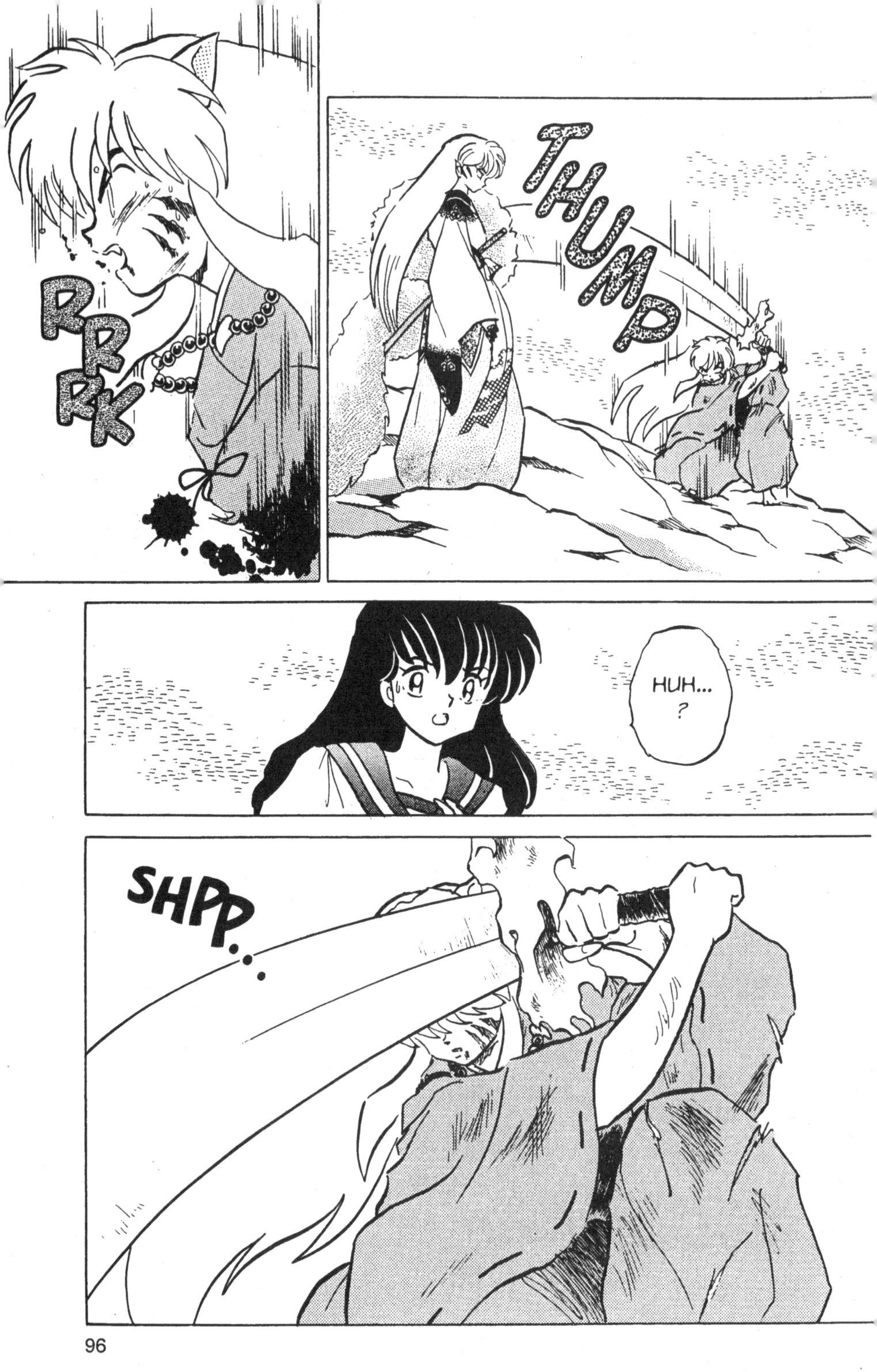
RRRK
THUMP
HUH... ?
SHPP...

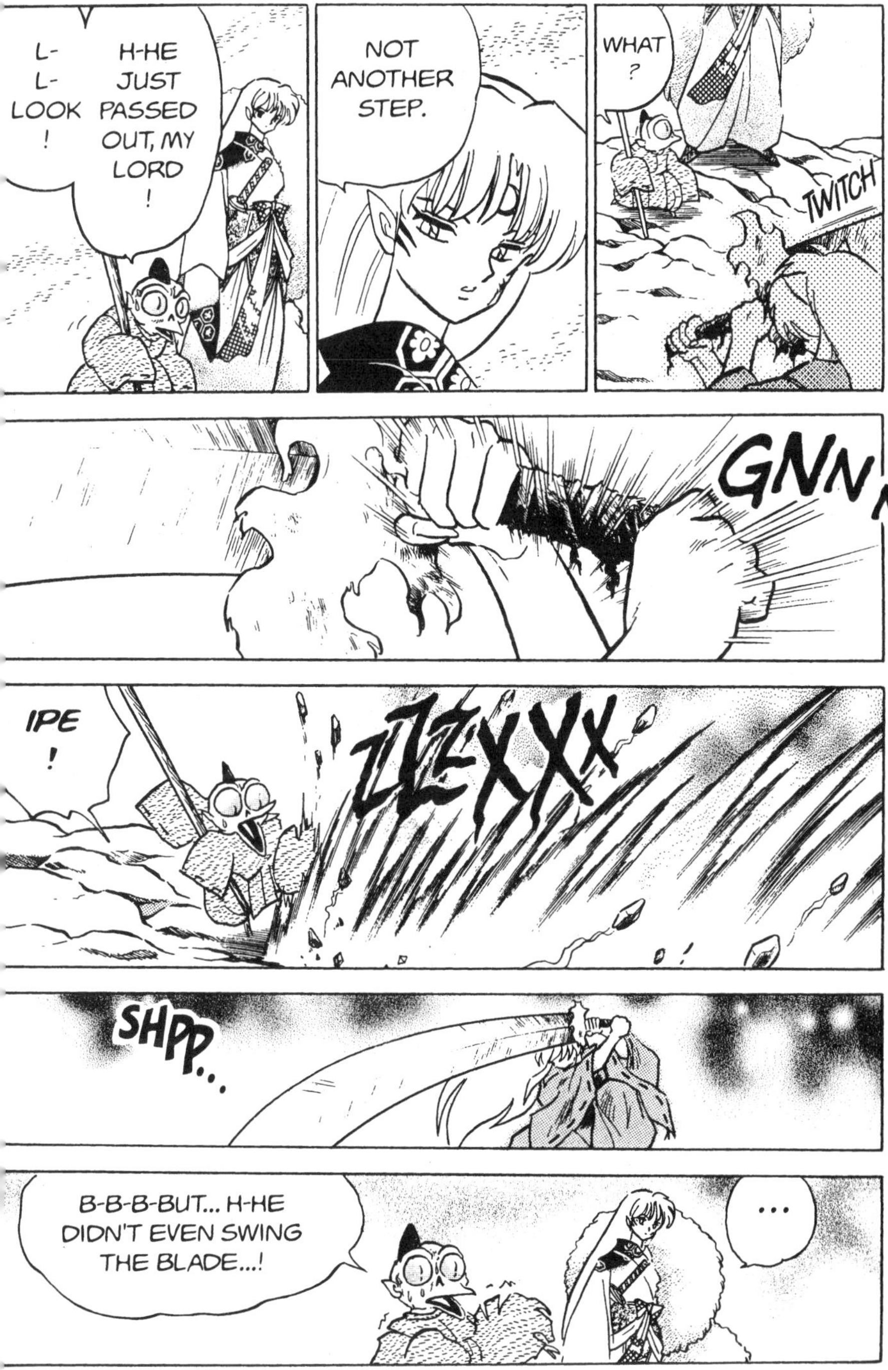
L- L- LOOK !
H-HE JUST PASSED OUT, MY LORD !
NOT ANOTHER STEP.
WHAT ?
TWITCH
GNNN
IPE !
ZZZXXX
SHPP...
B-B-B-BUT... H-HE DIDN'T EVEN SWING THE BLADE...!
...

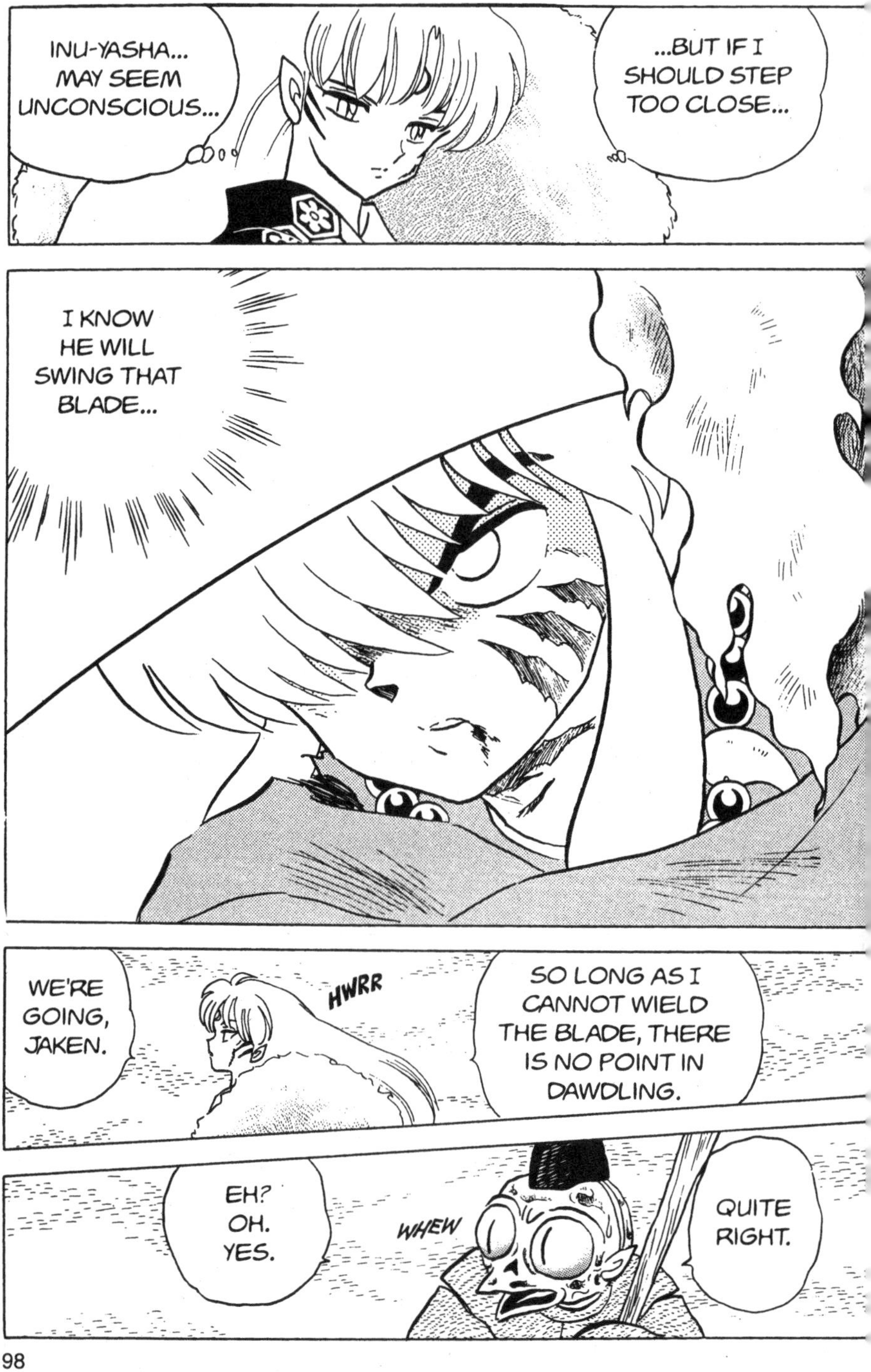
INU-YASHA... MAY SEEM UNCONSCIOUS...
...BUT IF I SHOULD STEP TOO CLOSE...
I KNOW HE WILL SWING THAT BLADE...
WE'RE GOING, JAKEN.
HWRR
SO LONG AS I CANNOT WIELD THE BLADE, THERE IS NO POINT IN DAWDLING.
EH? OH. YES.
WHEW
QUITE RIGHT.

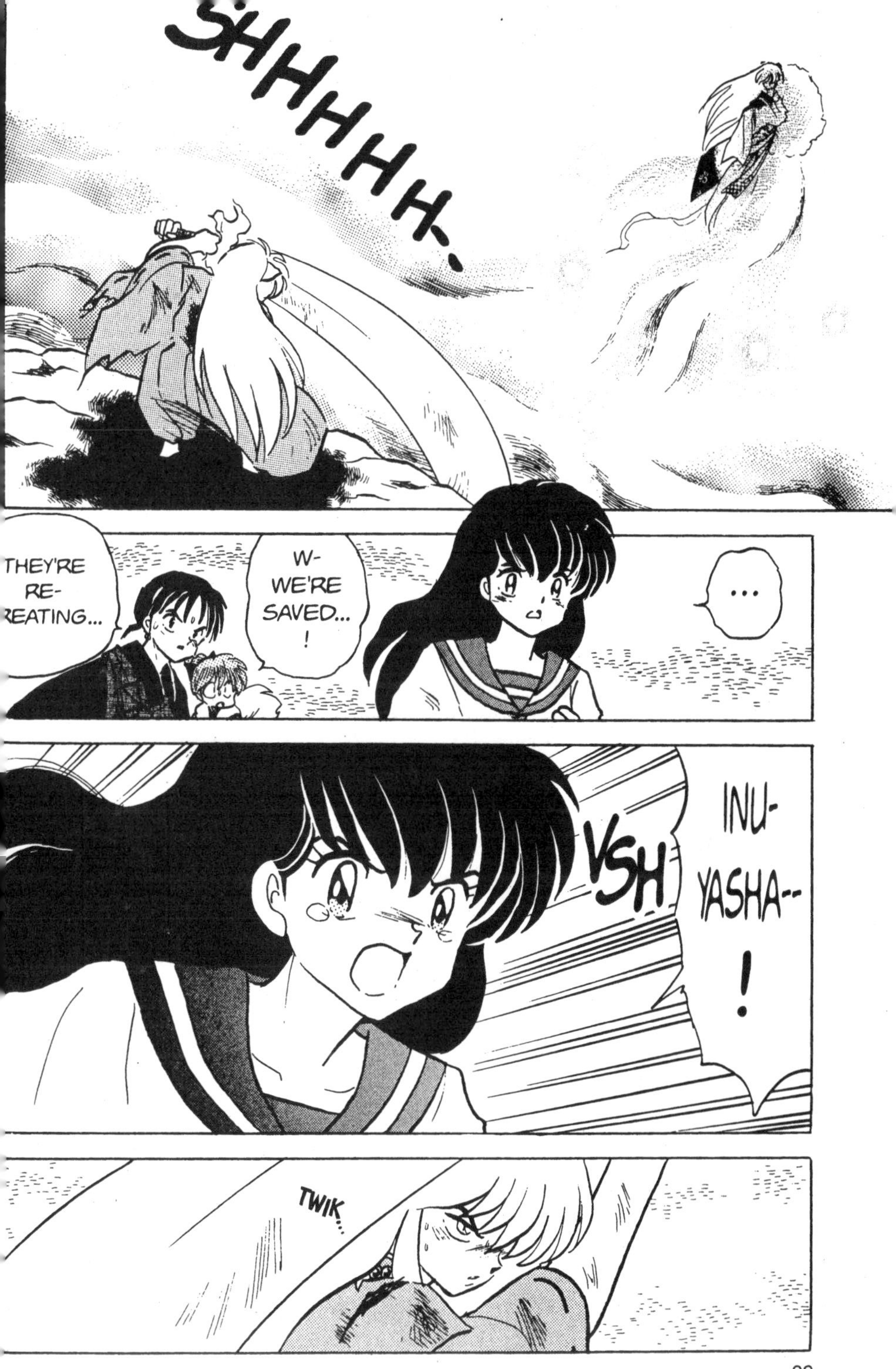
SHHHHHH...
THEY'RE RE- REATING...
W- WE'RE SAVED... !
...
VSH
INU- YASHA-- !
TWIK...

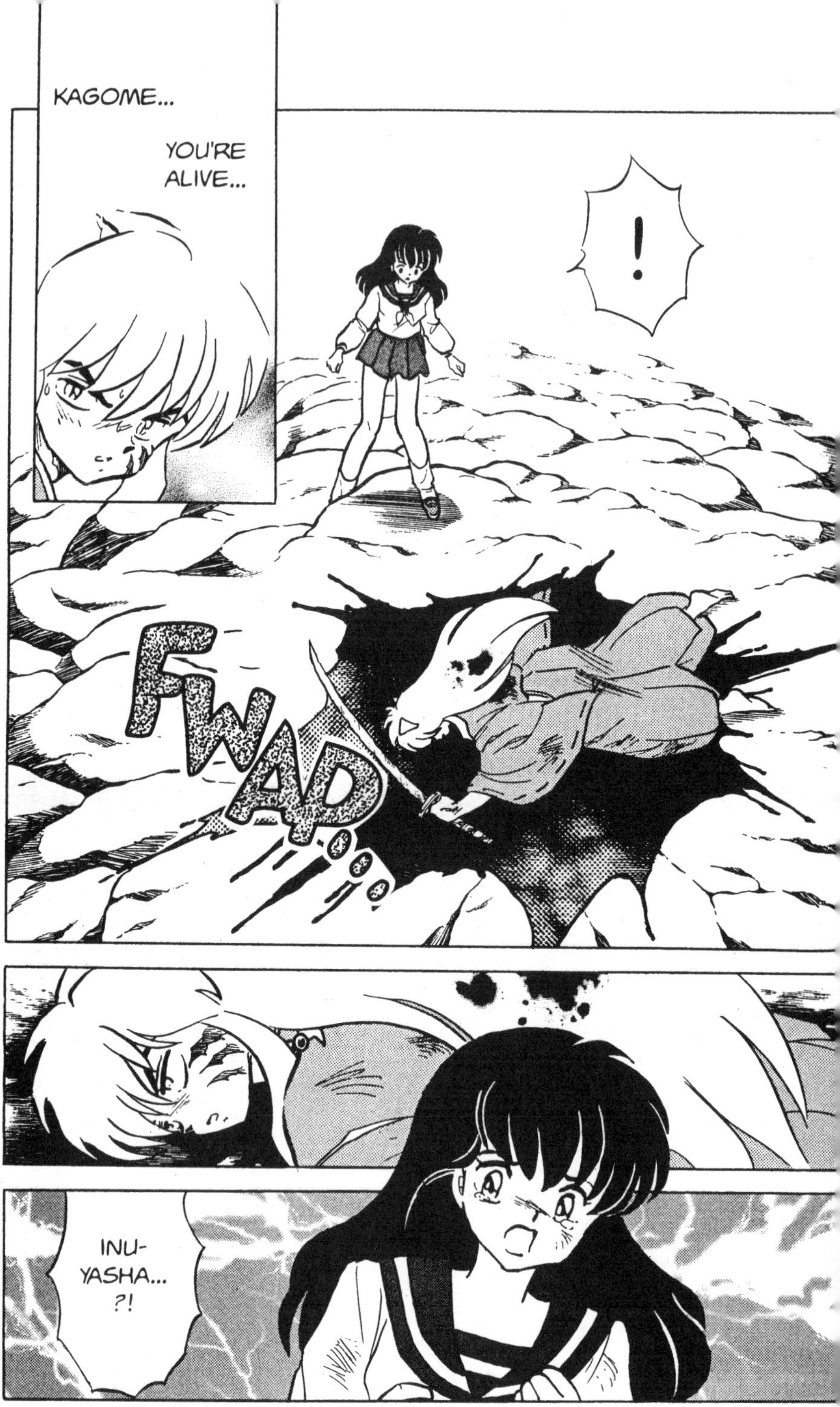
KAGOME...
YOU'RE ALIVE...
!
FWAP...
INU-YASHA...?!

SCROLL SIX

SEPARATE WAYS

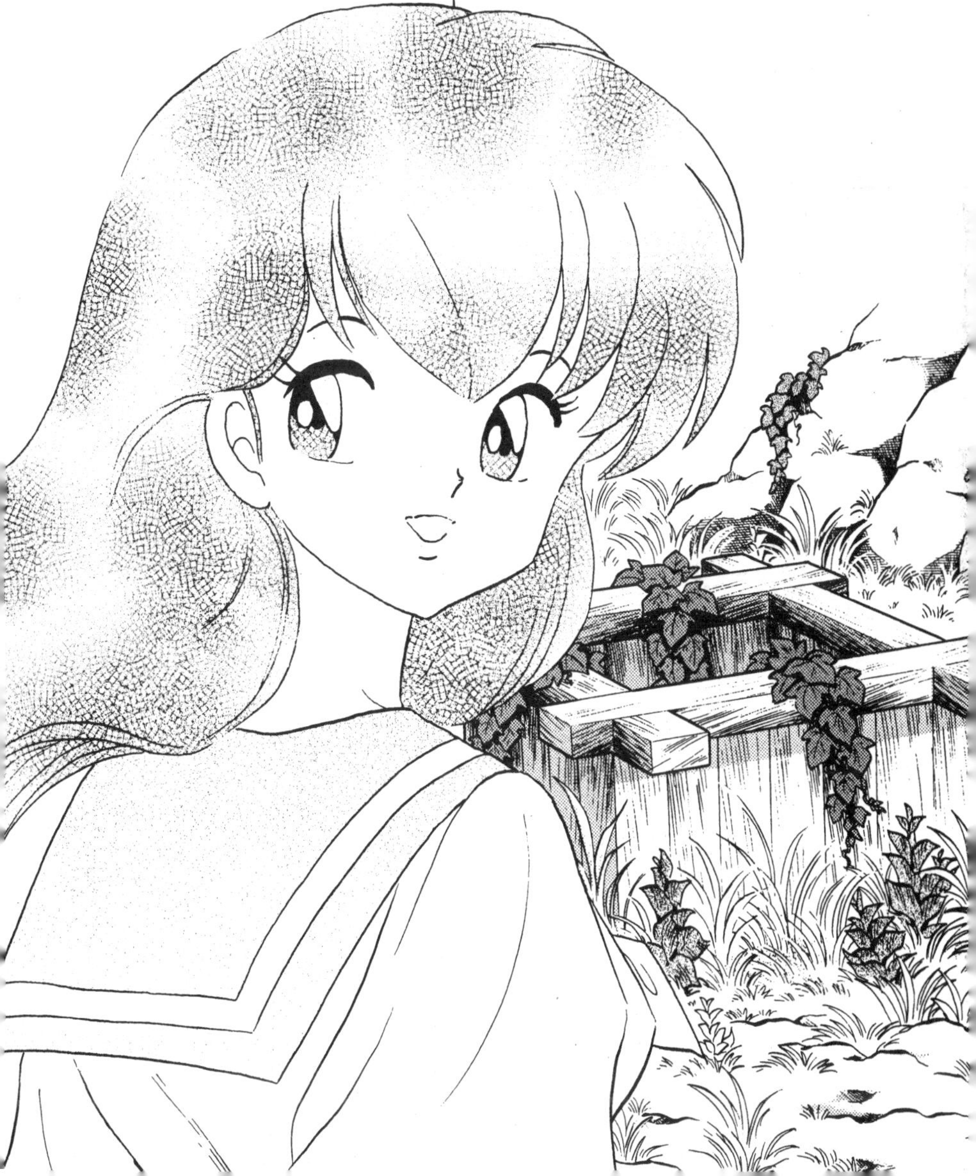

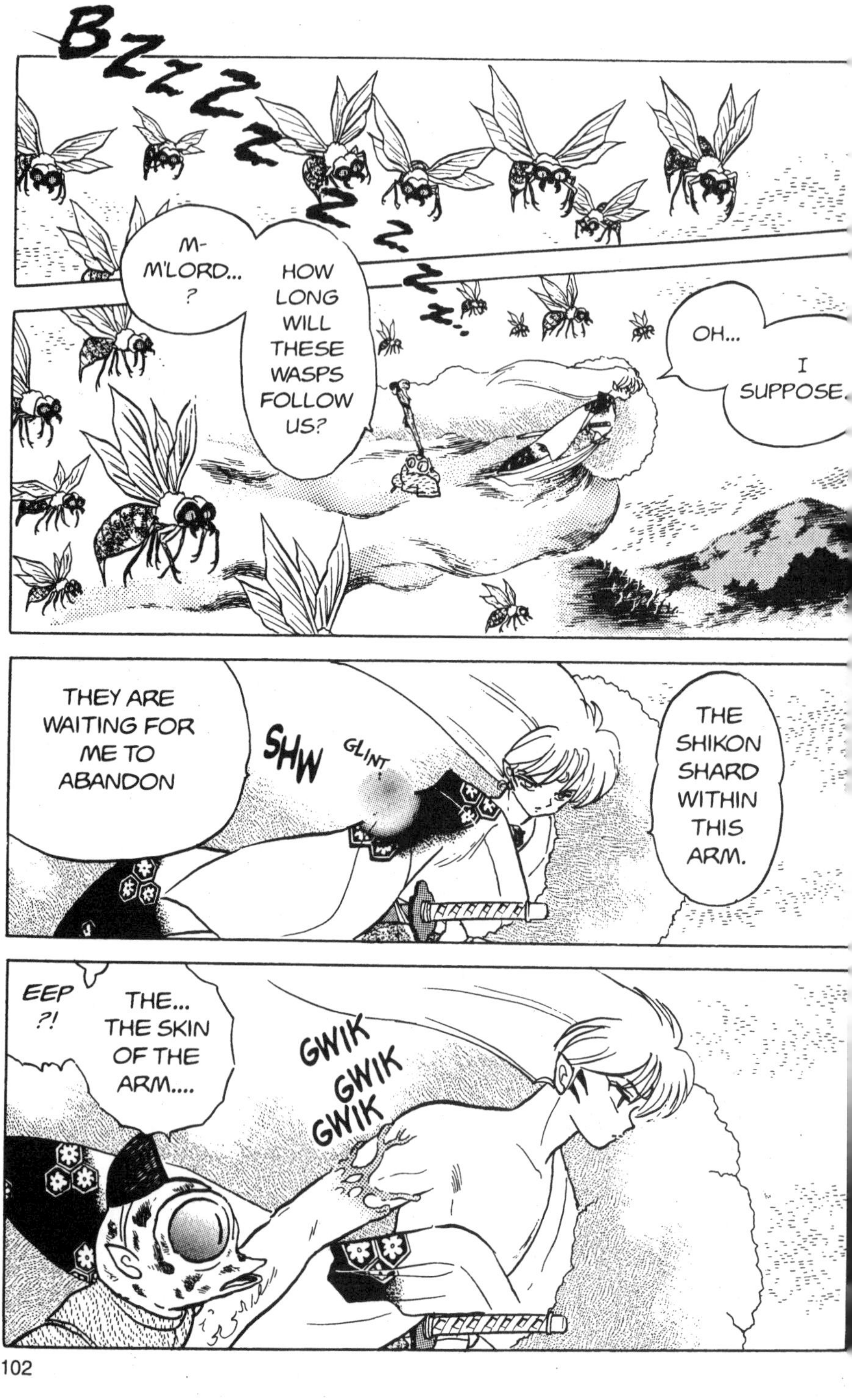
BZZZZZZZZ
M-M'LORD...?
HOW LONG WILL THESE WASPS FOLLOW US?
OH... I SUPPOSE.
THEY ARE WAITING FOR ME TO ABANDON
SHW
GLINT
THE SHIKON SHARD WITHIN THIS ARM.
EEP ?!
THE... THE SKIN OF THE ARM....
GWIK GWIK GWIK

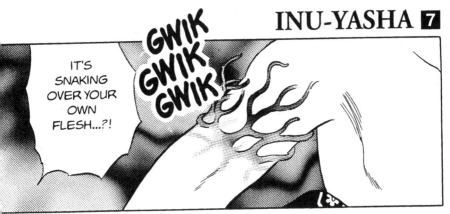

IT'S SNAKING OVER YOUR OWN FLESH...?!

GWIK GWIK GWIK

MM...

ATTEMPTING TO DEVOUR ME, I SEE...

SHLAP SNAP

WHSH

PIK

SHH...

BZZ...

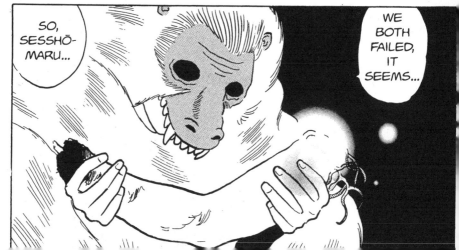

SO, SESSHŌ-MARU...

WE BOTH FAILED, IT SEEMS...

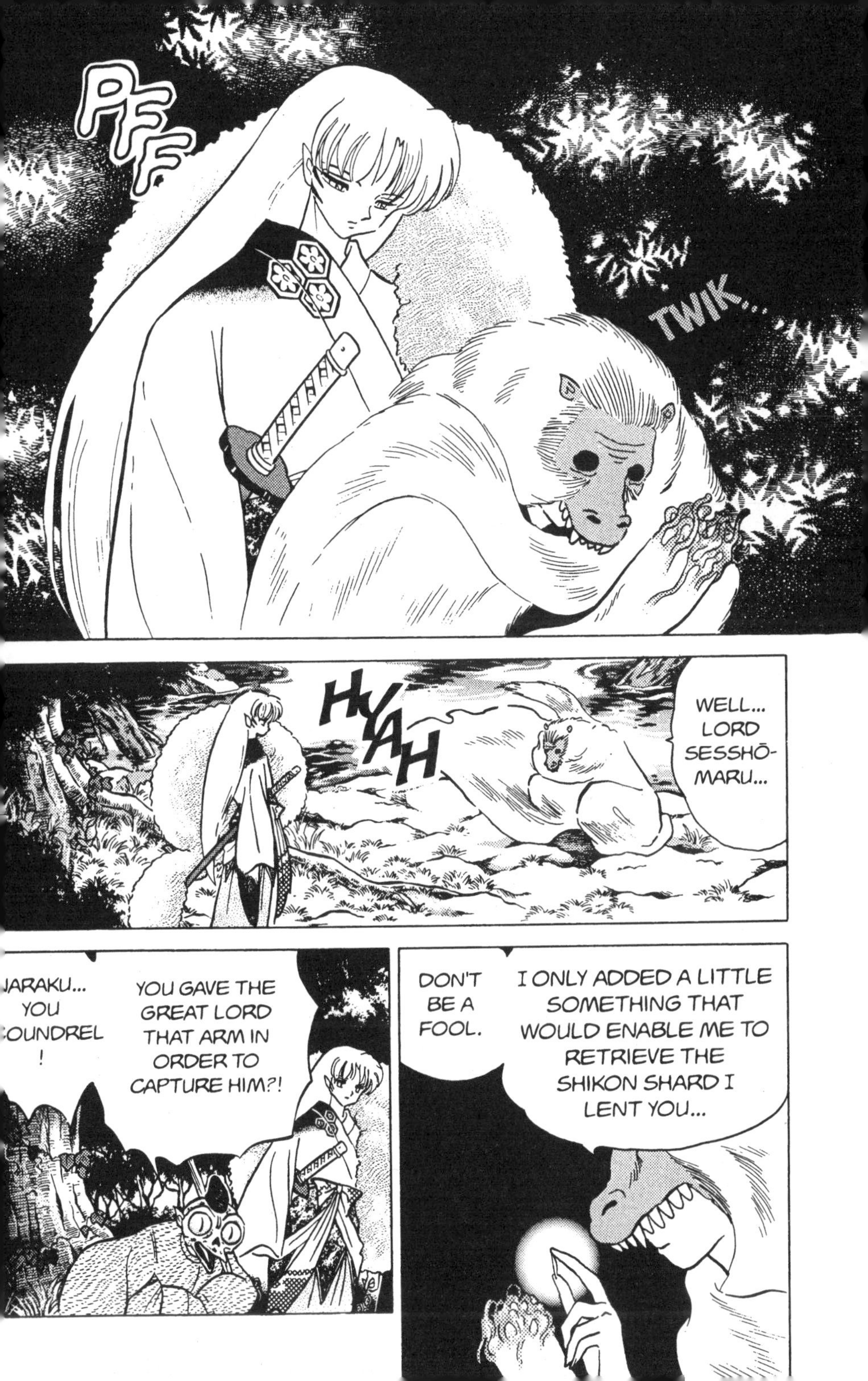
PFFF
TWIK...
HYAAH
WELL... LORD SESSHŌ-MARU...
NARAKU... YOU COUNDREL!
YOU GAVE THE GREAT LORD THAT ARM IN ORDER TO CAPTURE HIM?!
DON'T BE A FOOL.
I ONLY ADDED A LITTLE SOMETHING THAT WOULD ENABLE ME TO RETRIEVE THE SHIKON SHARD I LENT YOU...

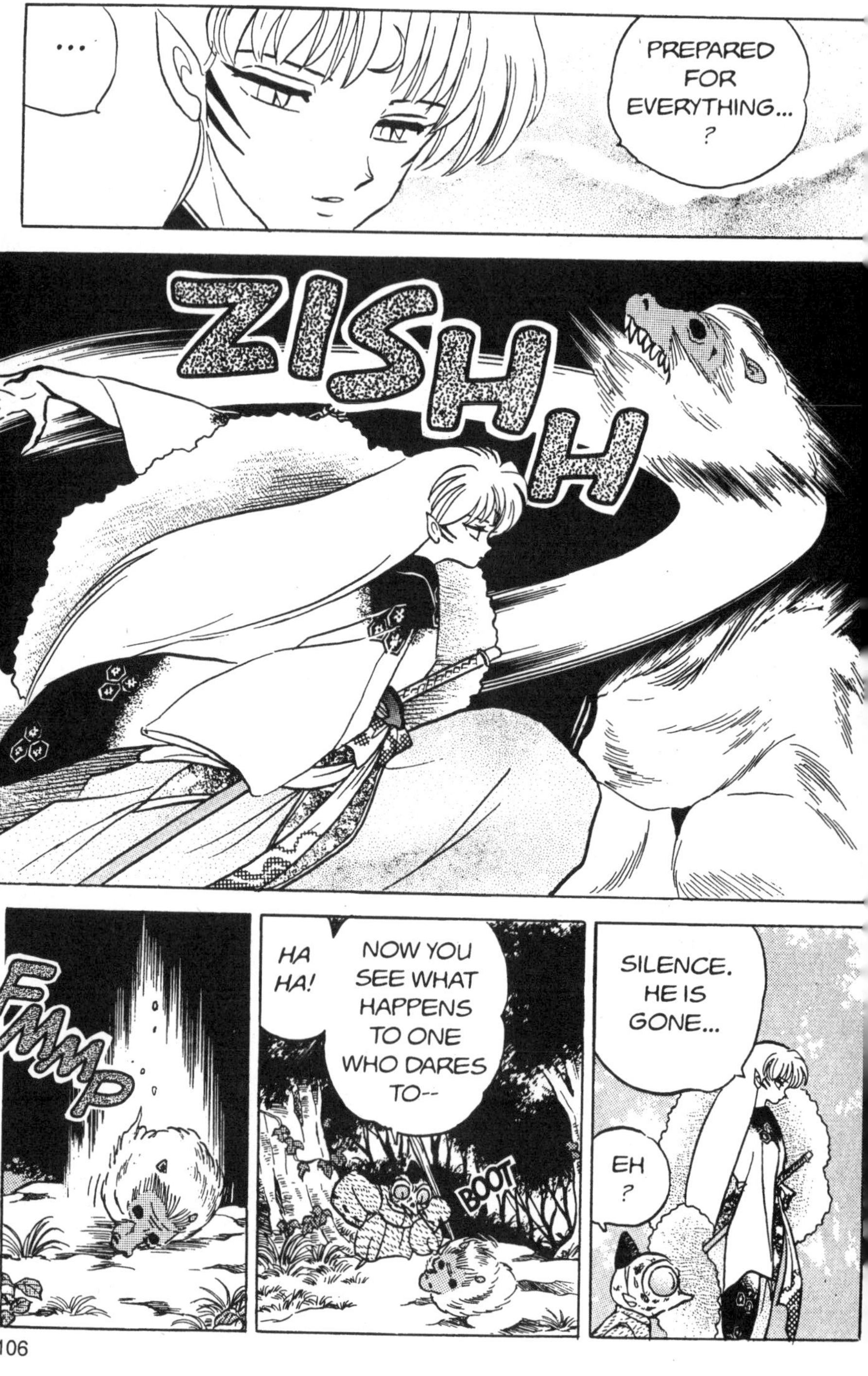
...
PREPARED FOR EVERYTHING... ?
ZISHH
FMMP
HA HA!
NOW YOU SEE WHAT HAPPENS TO ONE WHO DARES TO--
BOOT
SILENCE. HE IS GONE...
EH ?

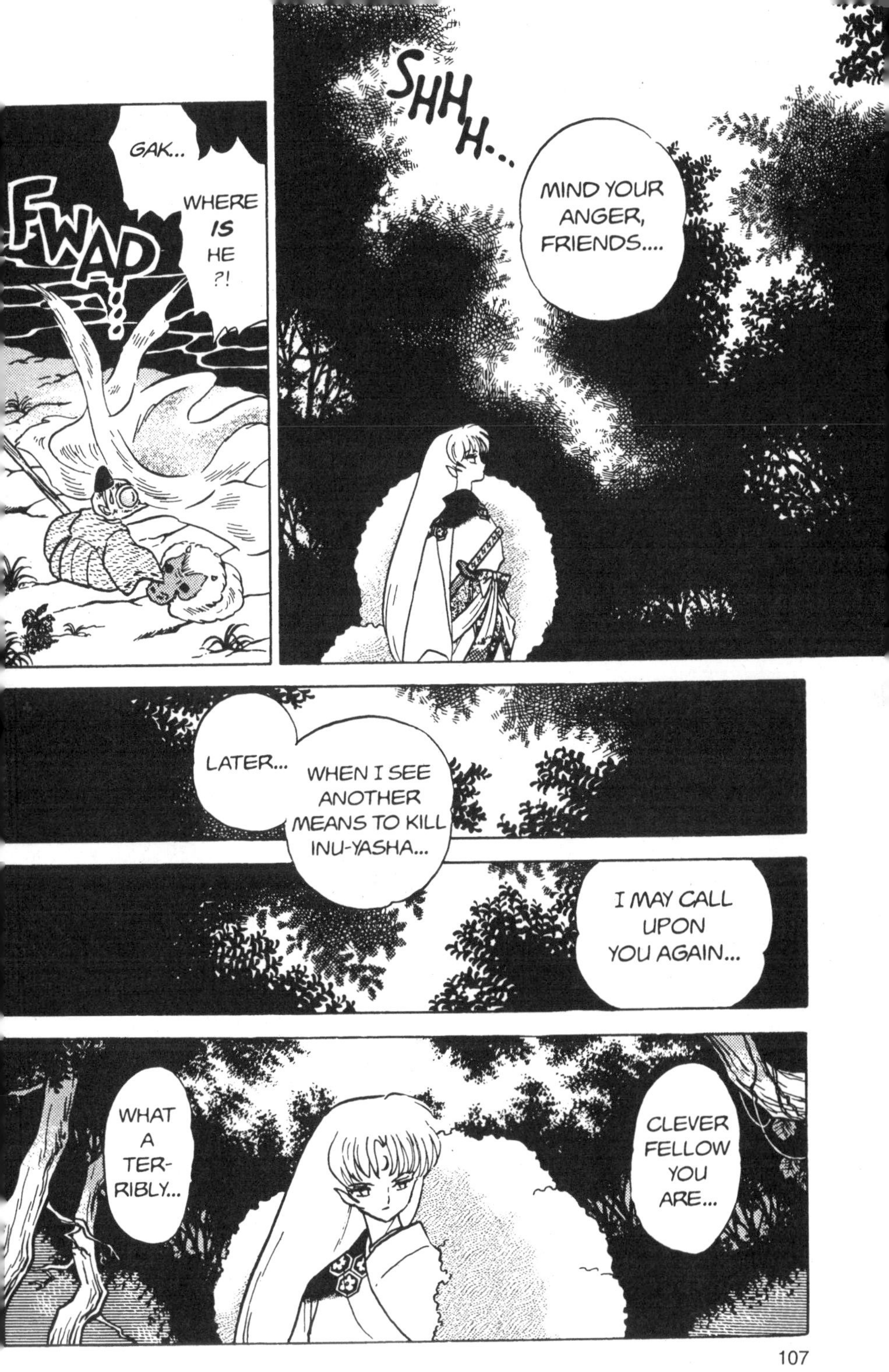
SHHH...
MIND YOUR ANGER, FRIENDS....
GAK...
WHERE IS HE ?!
FWAP
LATER...
WHEN I SEE ANOTHER MEANS TO KILL INU-YASHA...
I MAY CALL UPON YOU AGAIN...
WHAT A TER-RIBLY...
CLEVER FELLOW YOU ARE...

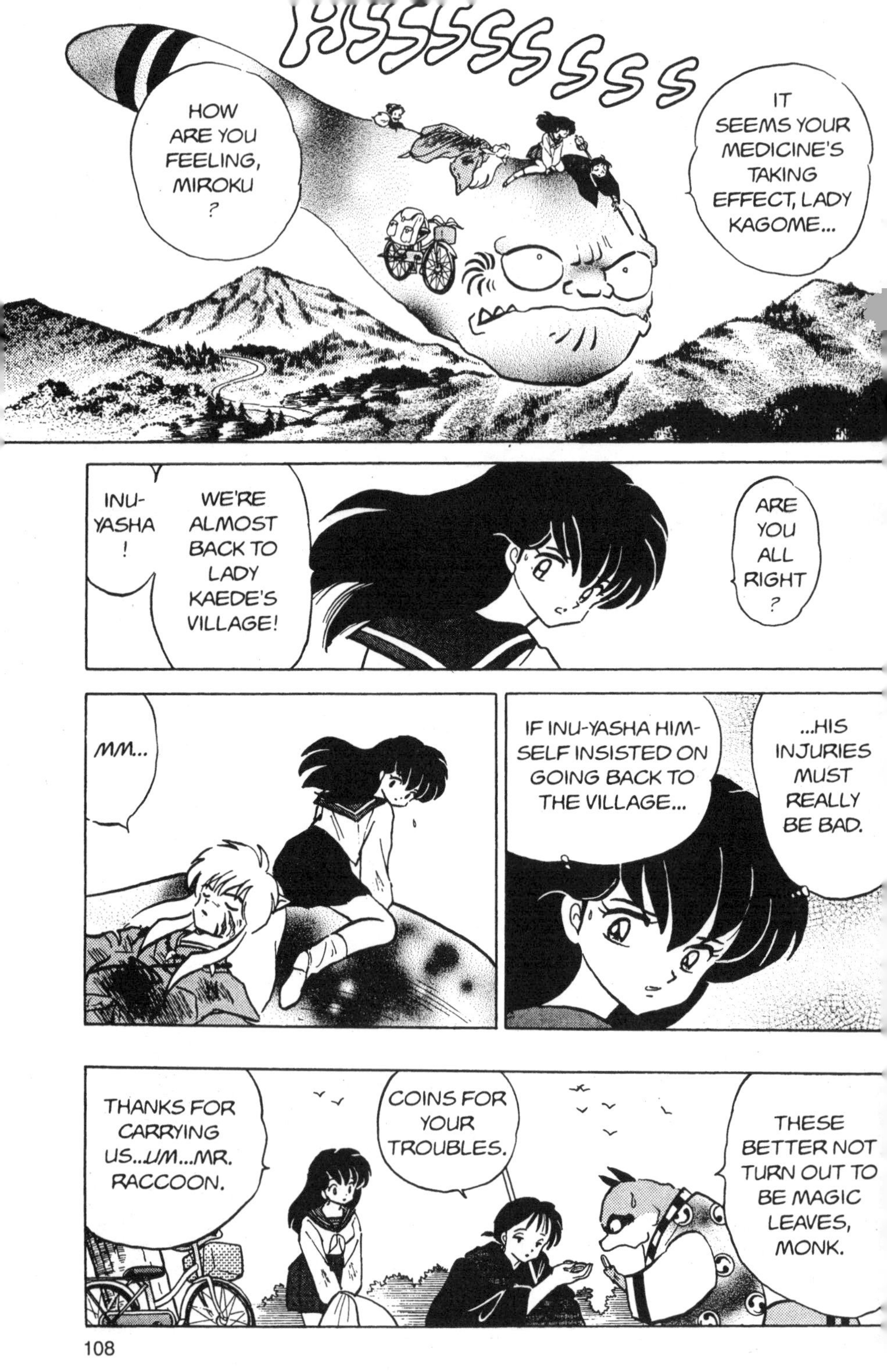
HSSSSSSSSS
HOW ARE YOU FEELING, MIROKU?
IT SEEMS YOUR MEDICINE'S TAKING EFFECT, LADY KAGOME...
INU-YASHA!
WE'RE ALMOST BACK TO LADY KAEDE'S VILLAGE!
ARE YOU ALL RIGHT?
MM...
IF INU-YASHA HIM-SELF INSISTED ON GOING BACK TO THE VILLAGE...
...HIS INJURIES MUST REALLY BE BAD.
THANKS FOR CARRYING US...UM...MR. RACCOON.
COINS FOR YOUR TROUBLES.
THESE BETTER NOT TURN OUT TO BE MAGIC LEAVES, MONK.

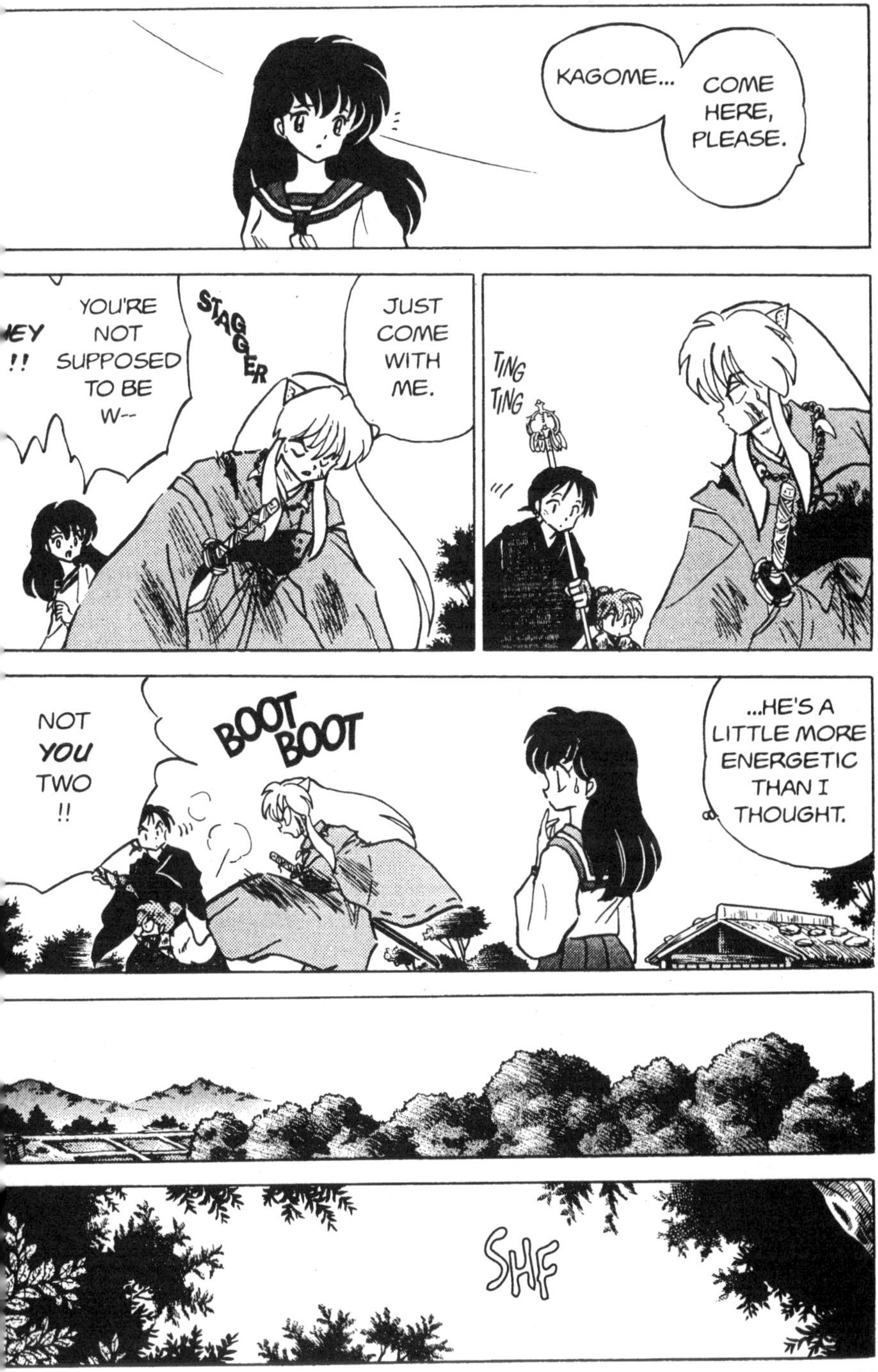
KAGOME...
COME HERE, PLEASE.
HEY !!
YOU'RE NOT SUPPOSED TO BE W--
STAGGER
JUST COME WITH ME.
TING TING
NOT YOU TWO !!
BOOT BOOT
...HE'S A LITTLE MORE ENERGETIC THAN I THOUGHT.
SHF

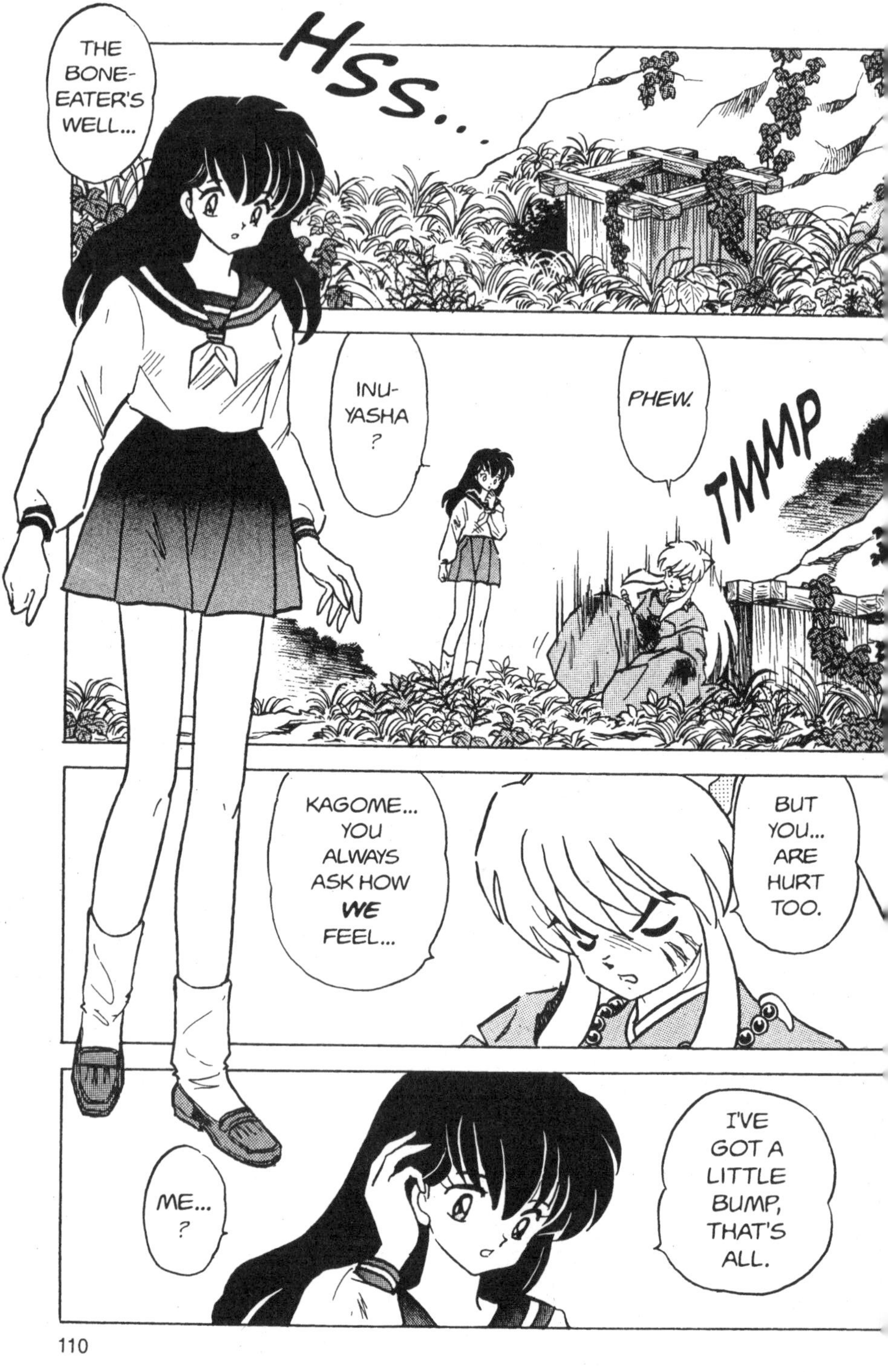
THE BONE-EATER'S WELL...
HSS...
INU-YASHA ?
PHEW.
TMMP
KAGOME... YOU ALWAYS ASK HOW WE FEEL...
BUT YOU... ARE HURT TOO.
ME... ?
I'VE GOT A LITTLE BUMP, THAT'S ALL.

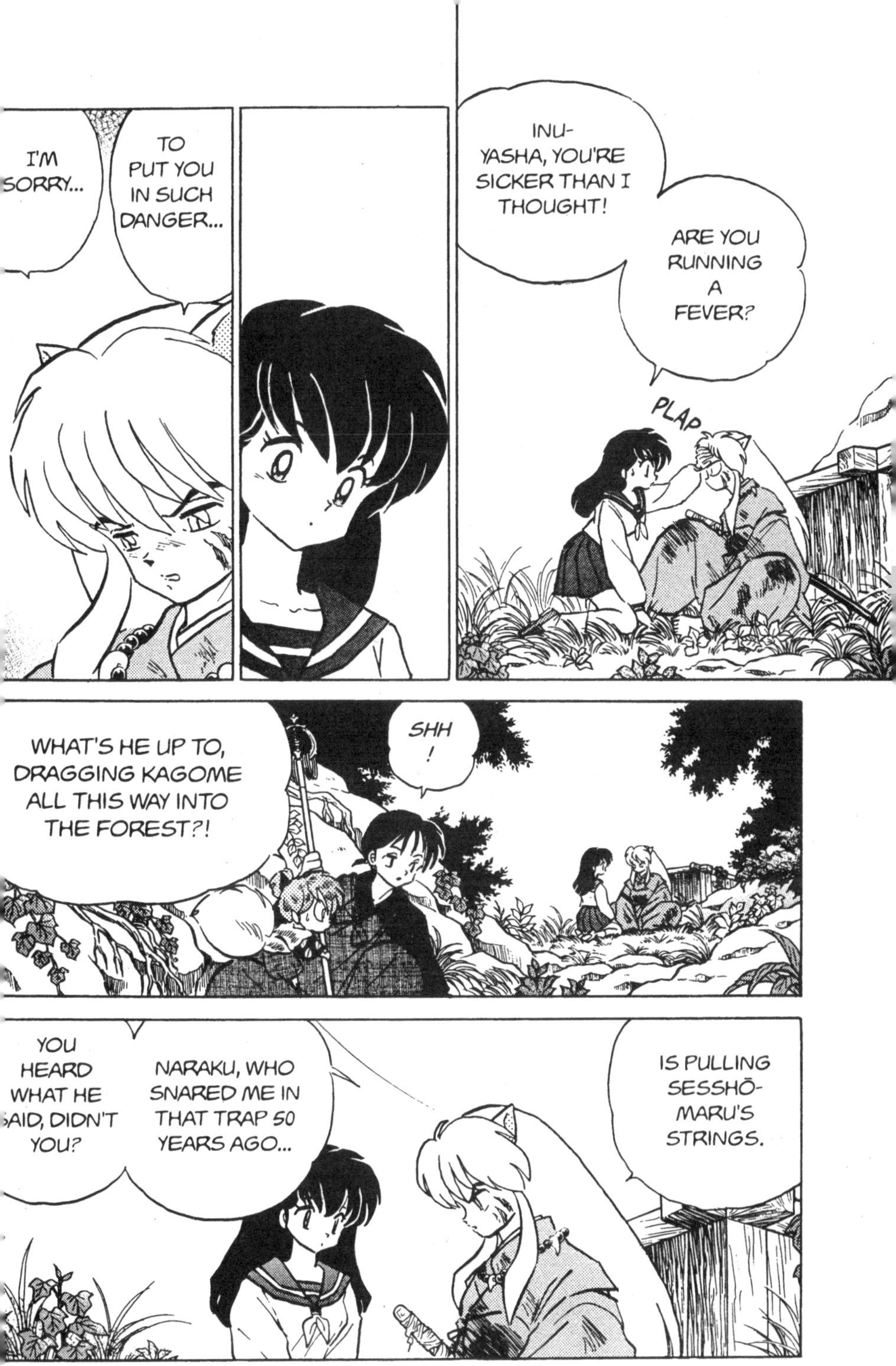
I'M SORRY...
TO PUT YOU IN SUCH DANGER...
INU-YASHA, YOU'RE SICKER THAN I THOUGHT!
ARE YOU RUNNING A FEVER?
PLAP
WHAT'S HE UP TO, DRAGGING KAGOME ALL THIS WAY INTO THE FOREST?!
SHH!
YOU HEARD WHAT HE SAID, DIDN'T YOU?
NARAKU, WHO SNARED ME IN THAT TRAP 50 YEARS AGO...
IS PULLING SESSHŌ-MARU'S STRINGS.

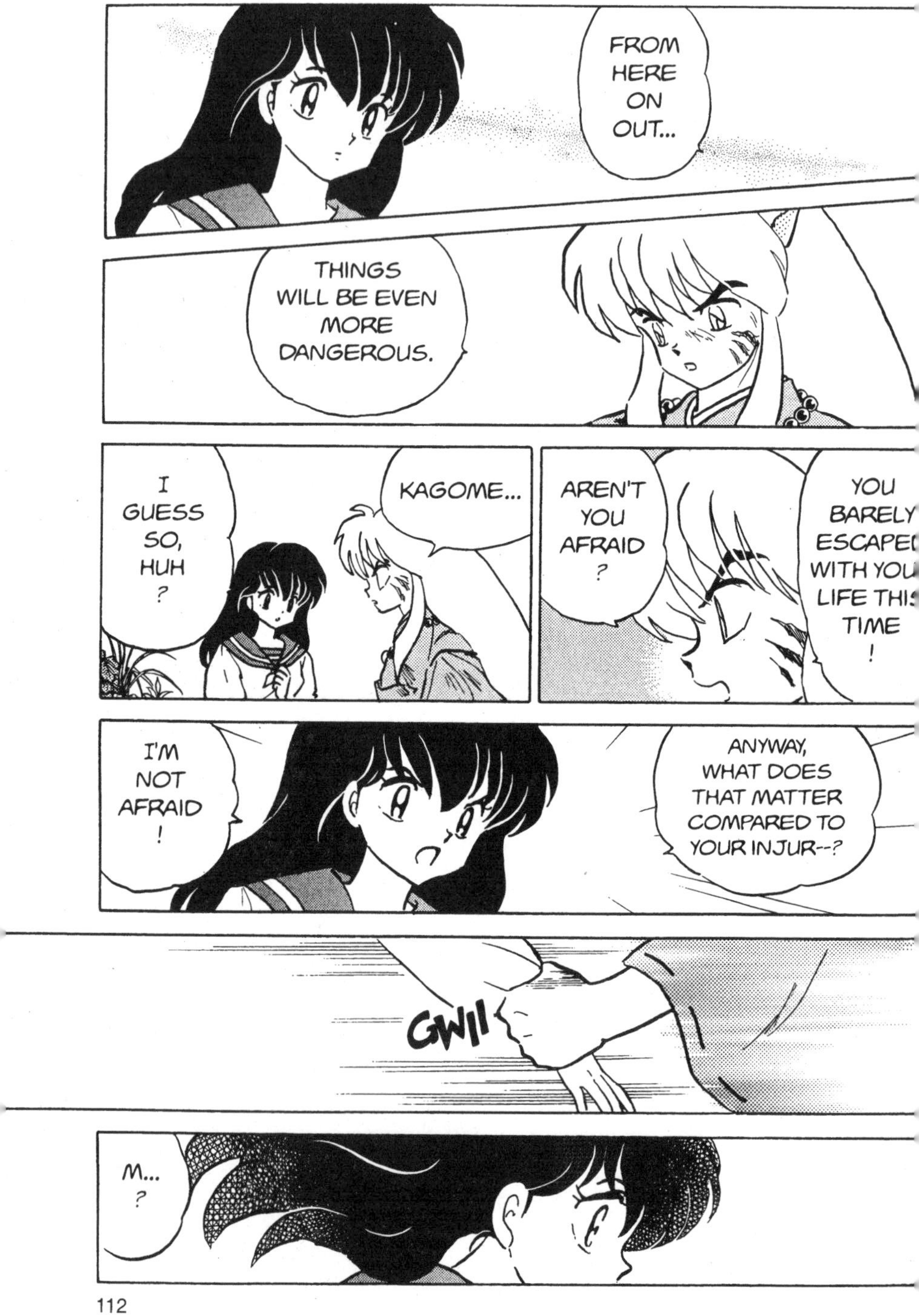
FROM HERE ON OUT...
THINGS WILL BE EVEN MORE DANGEROUS.
KAGOME...
I GUESS SO, HUH ?
YOU BARELY ESCAPED WITH YOUR LIFE THIS TIME !
AREN'T YOU AFRAID ?
I'M NOT AFRAID !
ANYWAY, WHAT DOES THAT MATTER COMPARED TO YOUR INJUR--?
GWIIl
M... ?

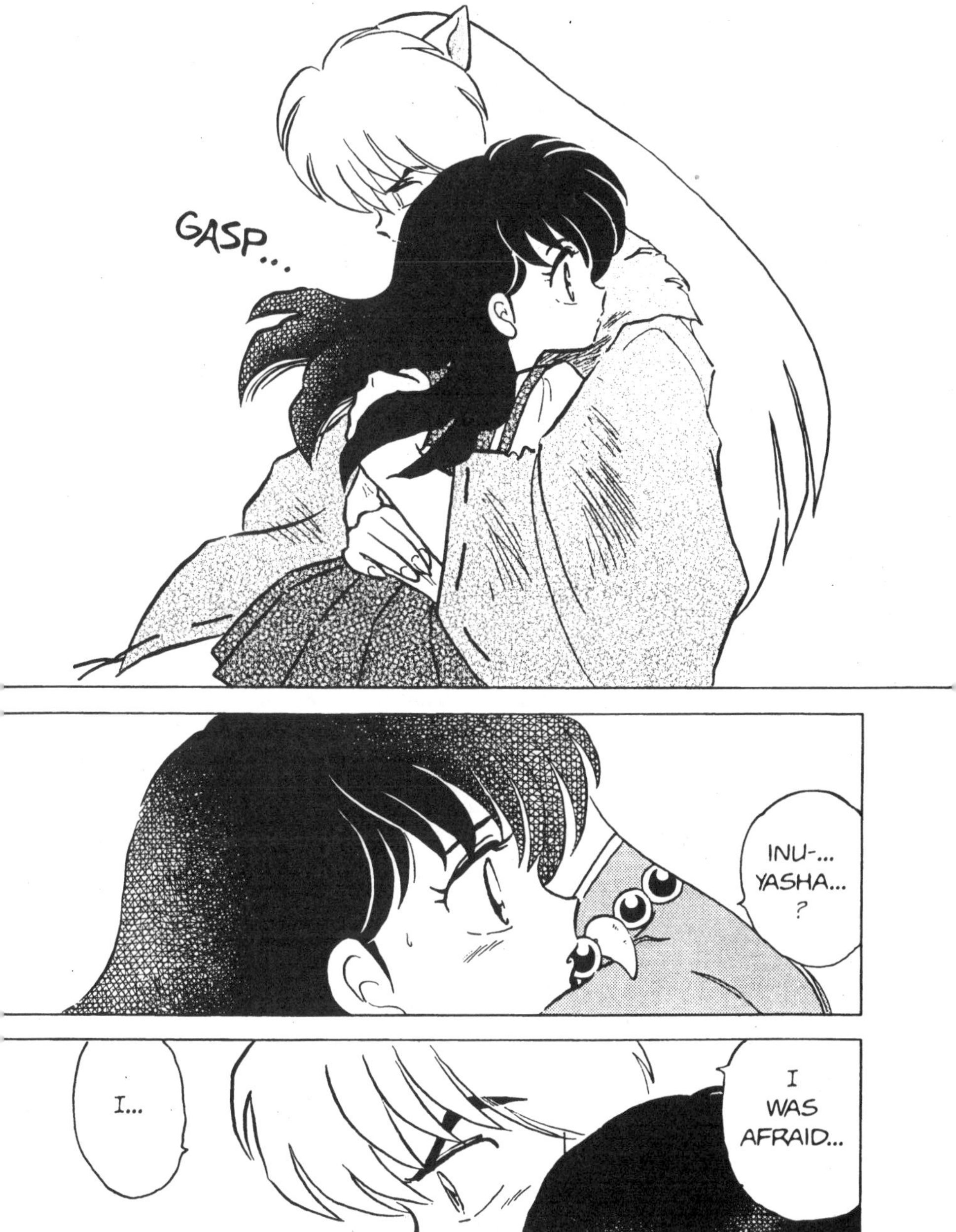
GASP...
INU-... YASHA... ?
I...
I WAS AFRAID...

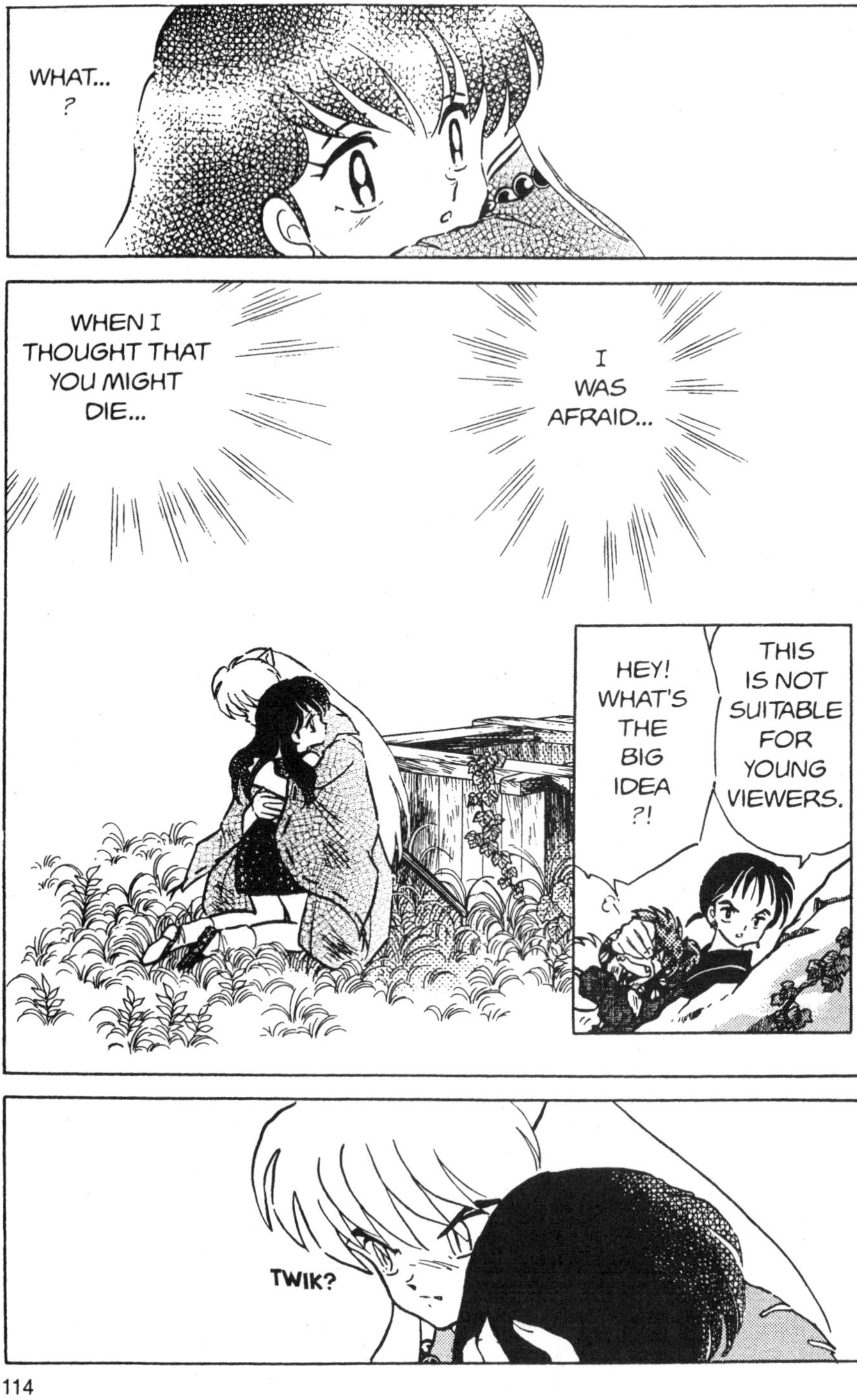
WHAT... ?
WHEN I THOUGHT THAT YOU MIGHT DIE...
I WAS AFRAID...
HEY! WHAT'S THE BIG IDEA ?!
THIS IS NOT SUITABLE FOR YOUNG VIEWERS.
TWIK?

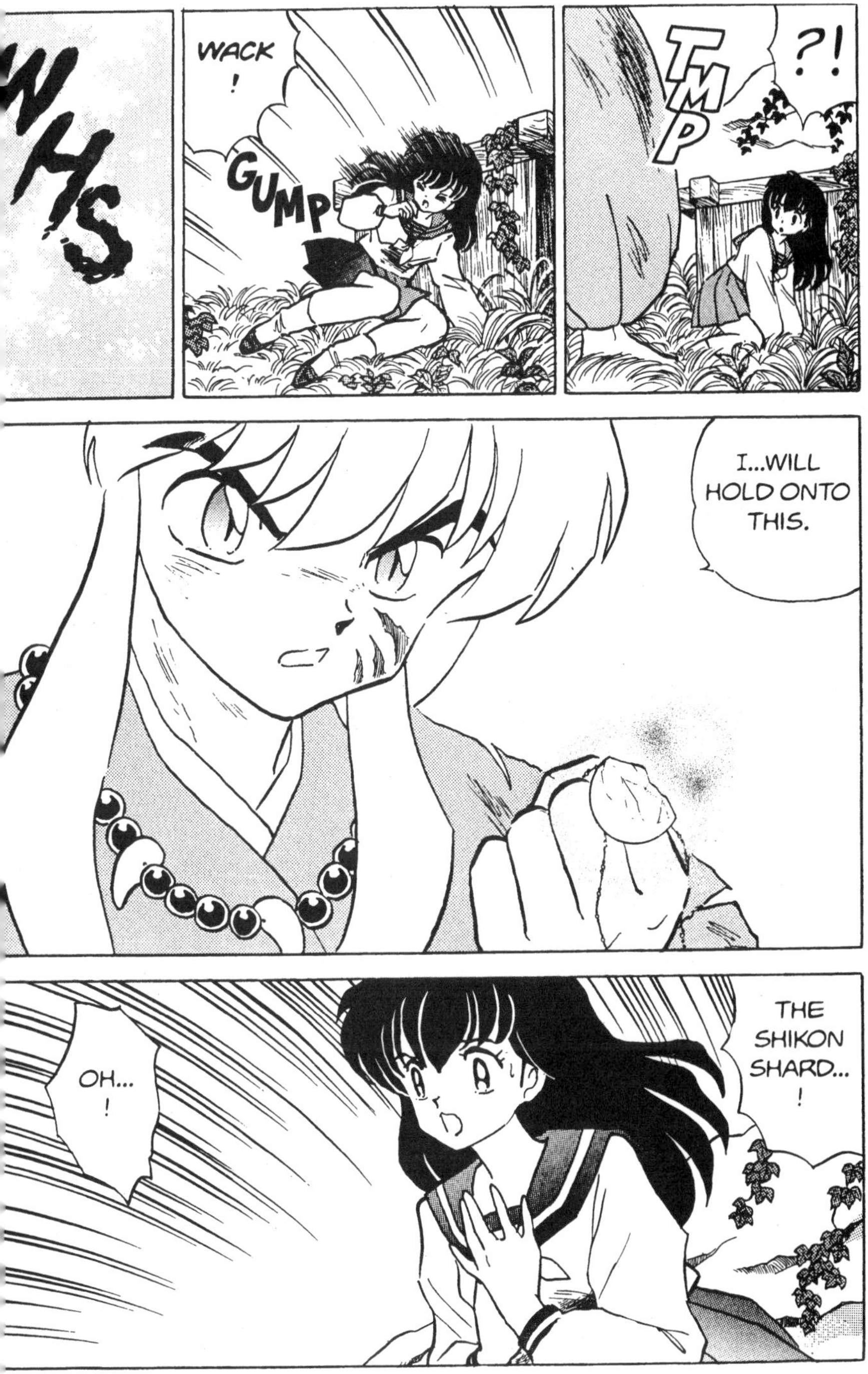
WHS
WACK
!
GUMP
TMP
?!
I...WILL HOLD ONTO THIS.
OH...
!
THE SHIKON SHARD...
!

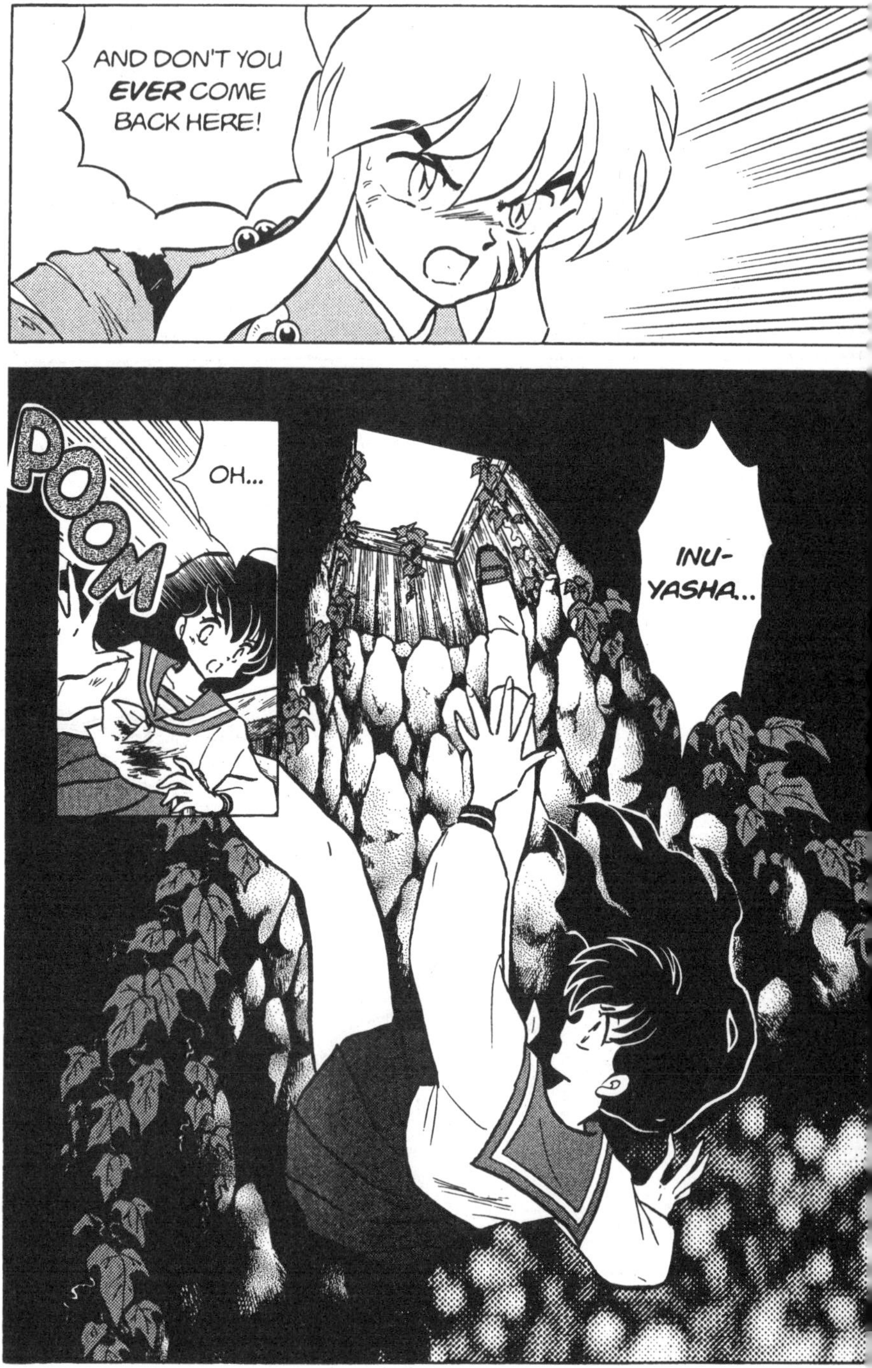
AND DON'T YOU EVER COME BACK HERE!
POOOM
OH...
INU-YASHA...

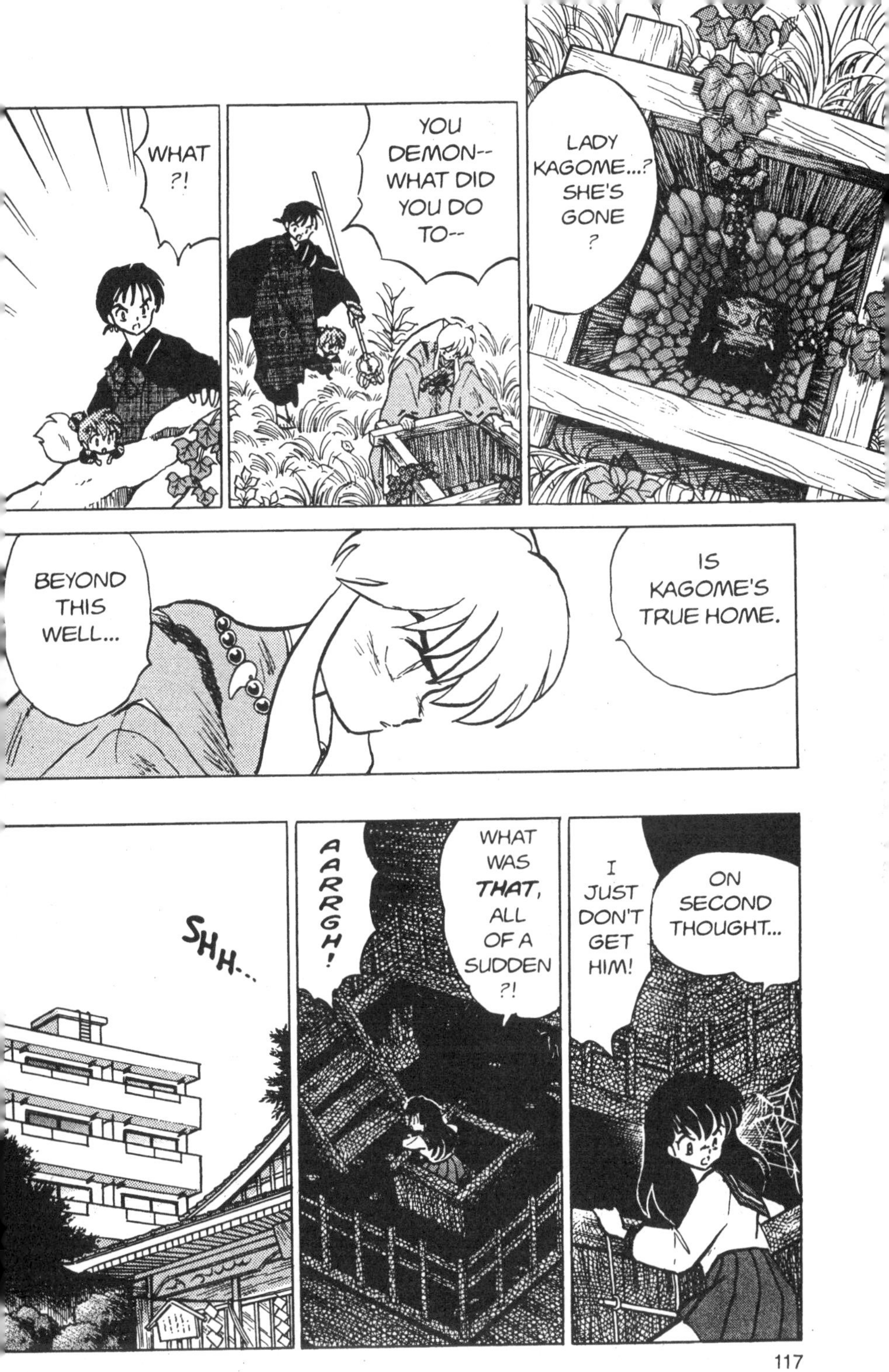
WHAT ?!
YOU DEMON-- WHAT DID YOU DO TO--
LADY KAGOME...? SHE'S GONE ?
BEYOND THIS WELL...
IS KAGOME'S TRUE HOME.
SHH...
AARRGH!
WHAT WAS *THAT*, ALL OF A SUDDEN ?!
I JUST DON'T GET HIM!
ON SECOND THOUGHT...

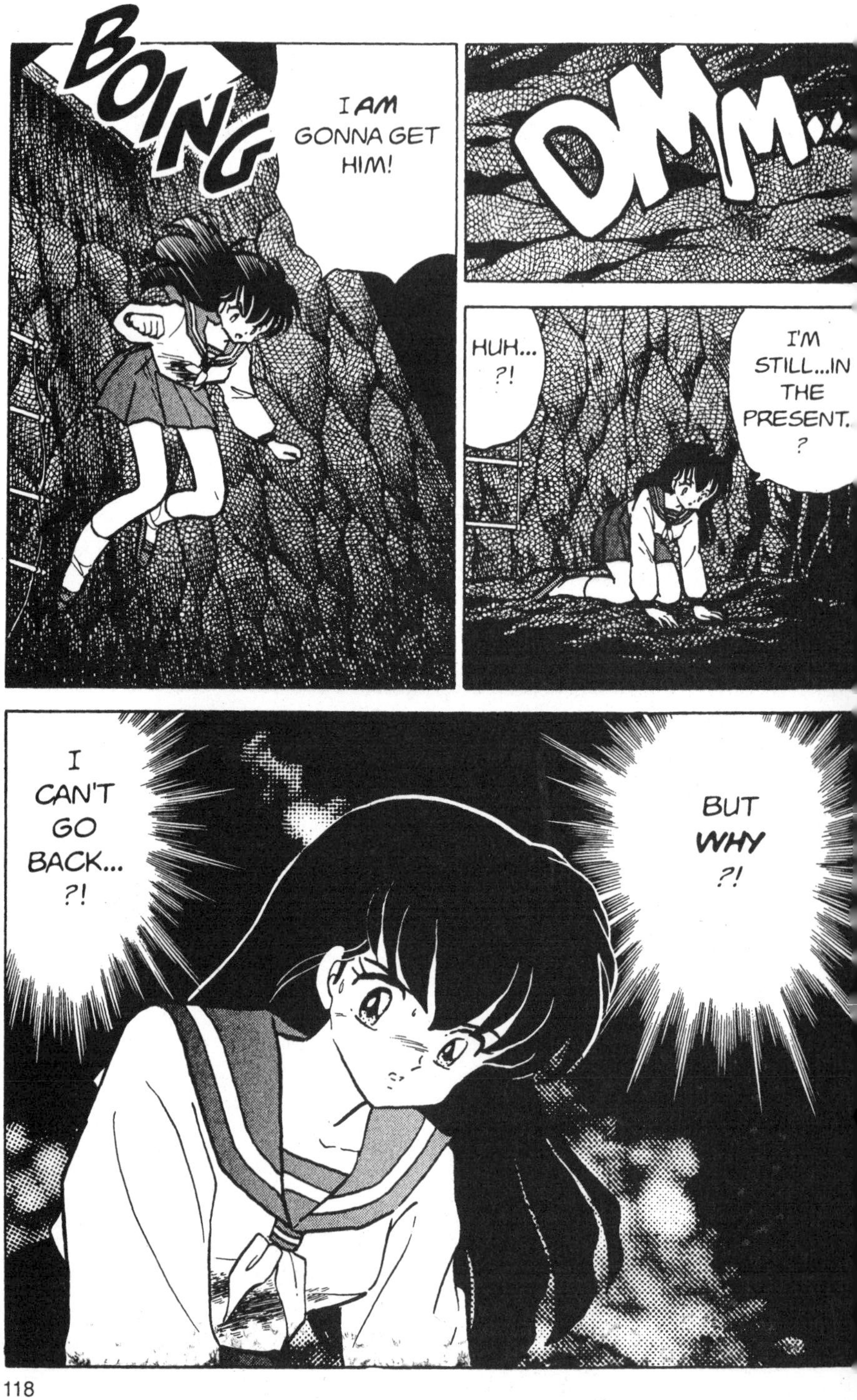
BOING
I AM GONNA GET HIM!
DMM...
HUH...?!
I'M STILL...IN THE PRESENT...?
I CAN'T GO BACK...?!
BUT WHY?!

SCROLL SEVEN

THE SPIDER'S LAIR

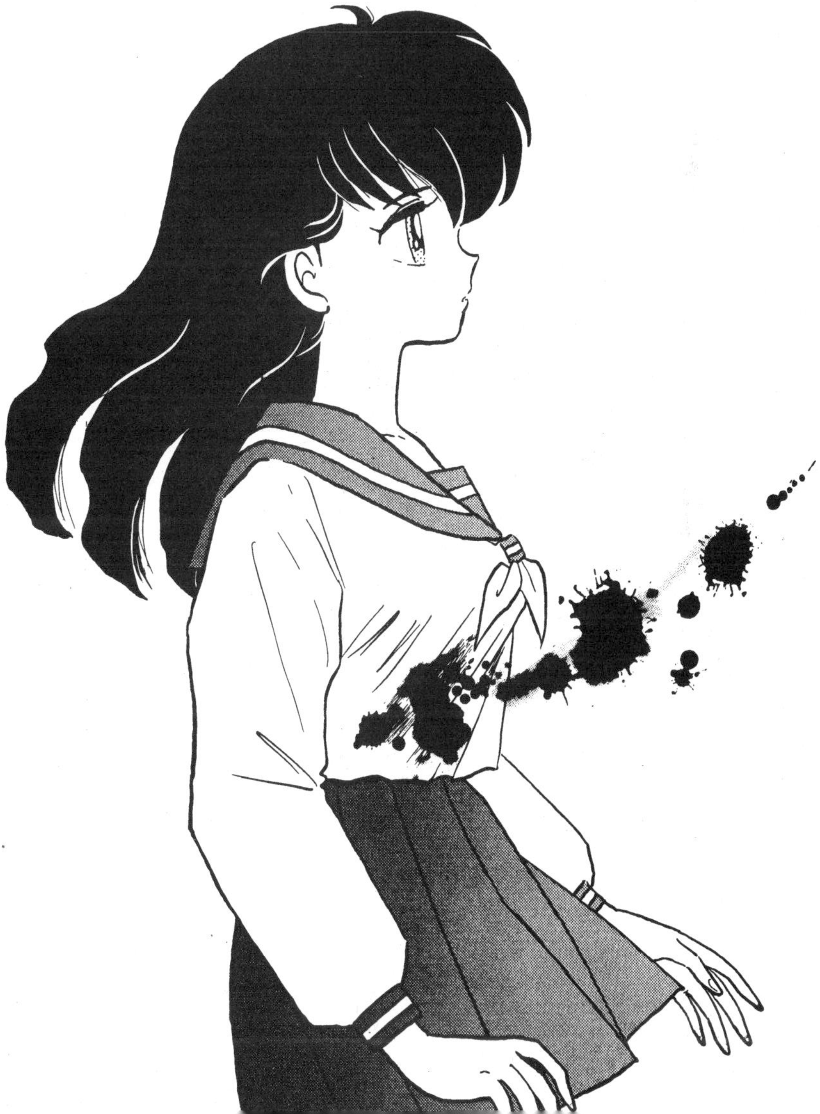

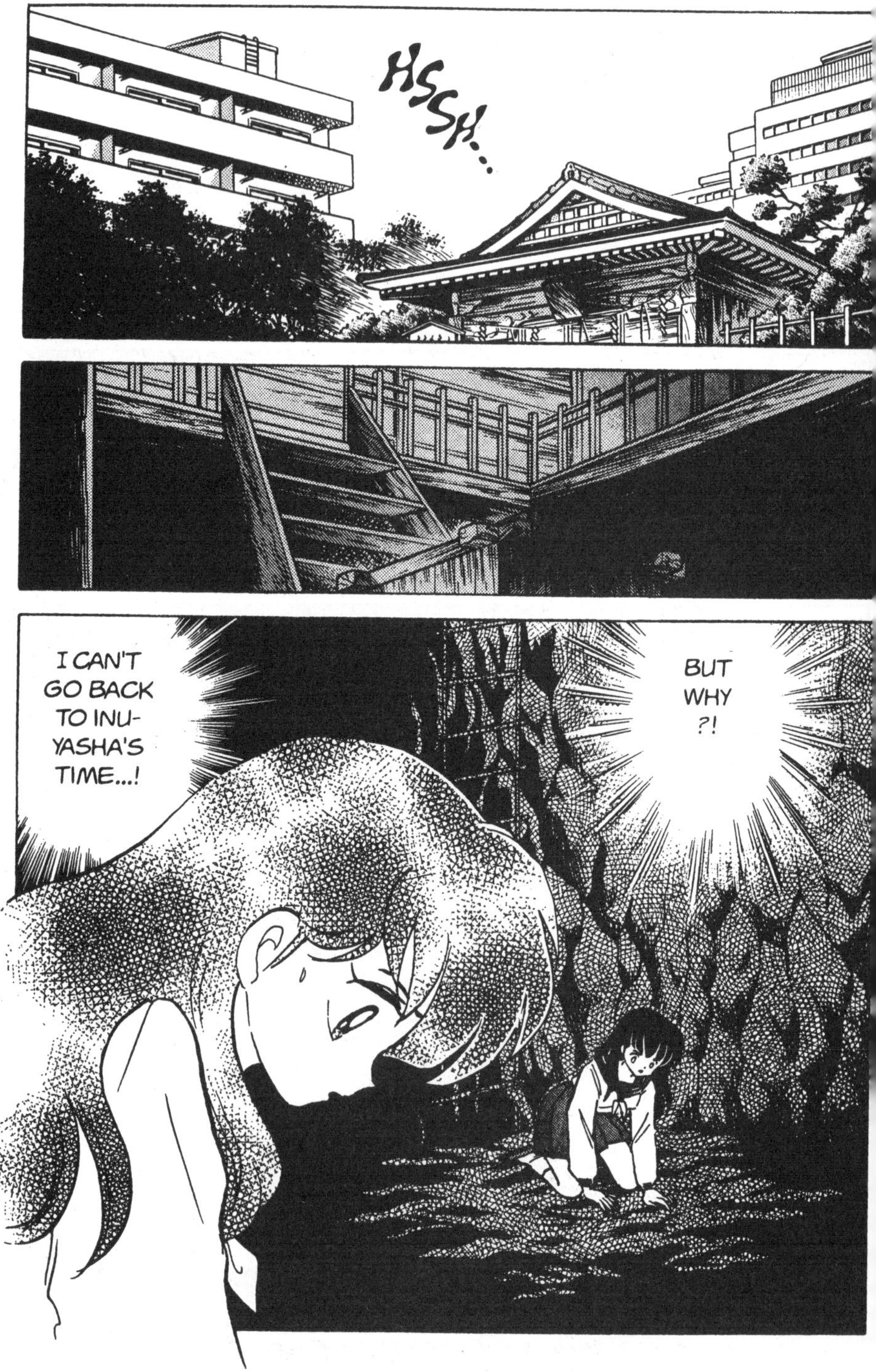
HSSH...
I CAN'T GO BACK TO INU-YASHA'S TIME...!
BUT WHY ?!

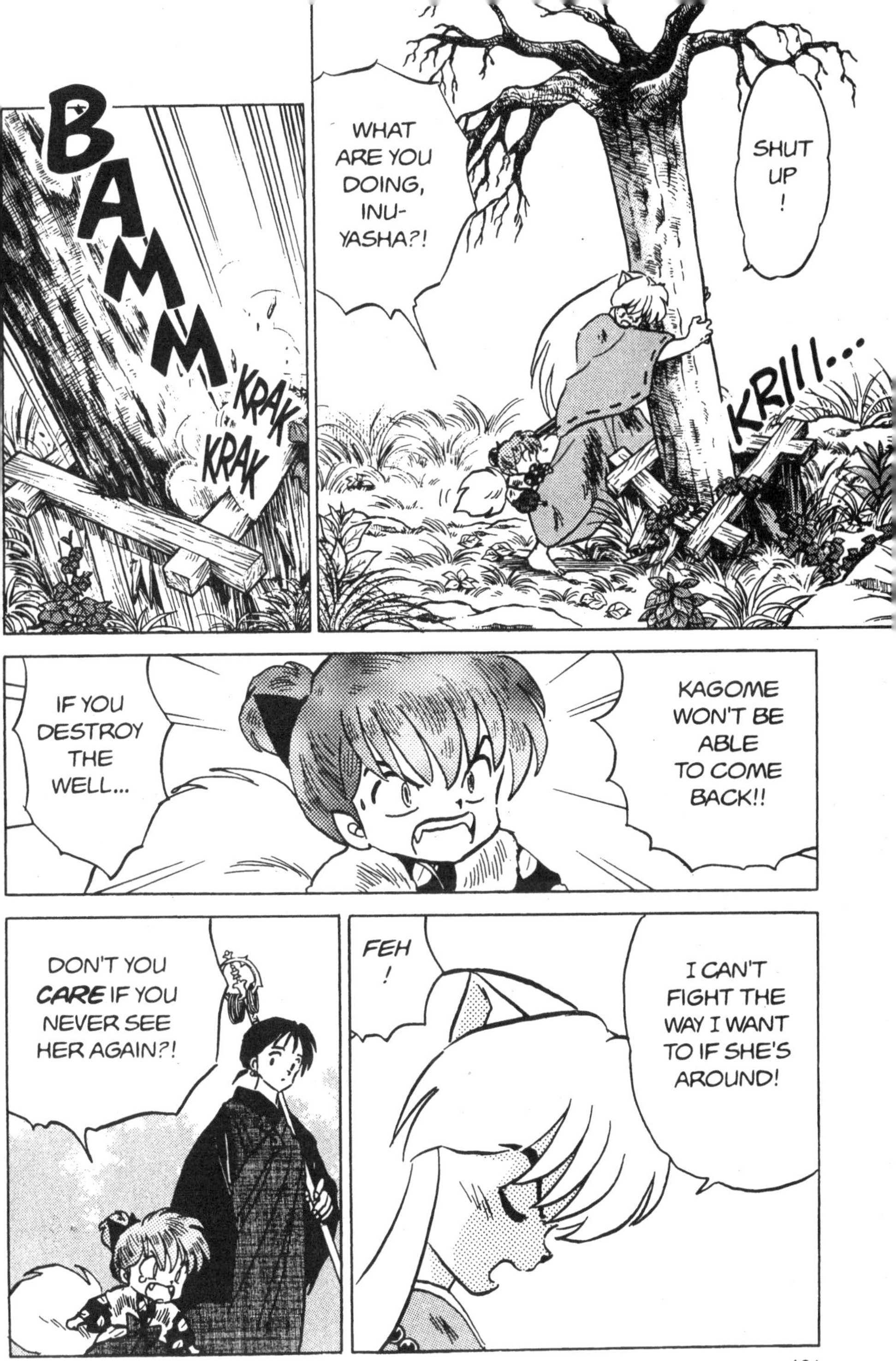
BAMMM
KRAK
KRAK
WHAT ARE YOU DOING, INU-YASHA?!
SHUT UP!
KRIII...
IF YOU DESTROY THE WELL...
KAGOME WON'T BE ABLE TO COME BACK!!
DON'T YOU CARE IF YOU NEVER SEE HER AGAIN?!
FEH!
I CAN'T FIGHT THE WAY I WANT TO IF SHE'S AROUND!

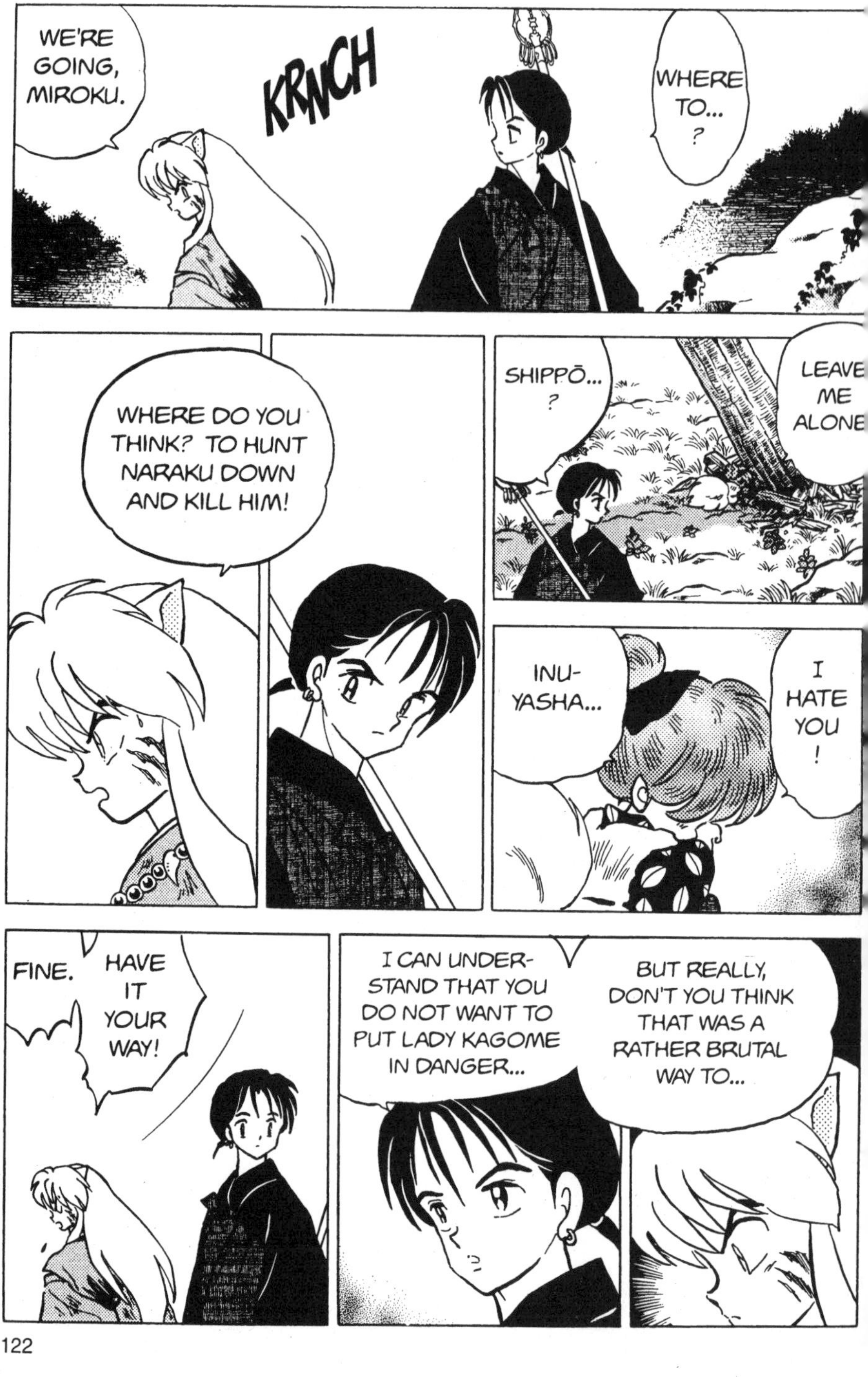
WE'RE GOING, MIROKU.
KRNCH
WHERE TO... ?
WHERE DO YOU THINK? TO HUNT NARAKU DOWN AND KILL HIM!
SHIPPŌ... ?
LEAVE ME ALONE
INU-YASHA...
I HATE YOU!
FINE.
HAVE IT YOUR WAY!
I CAN UNDER-STAND THAT YOU DO NOT WANT TO PUT LADY KAGOME IN DANGER...
BUT REALLY, DON'T YOU THINK THAT WAS A RATHER BRUTAL WAY TO...

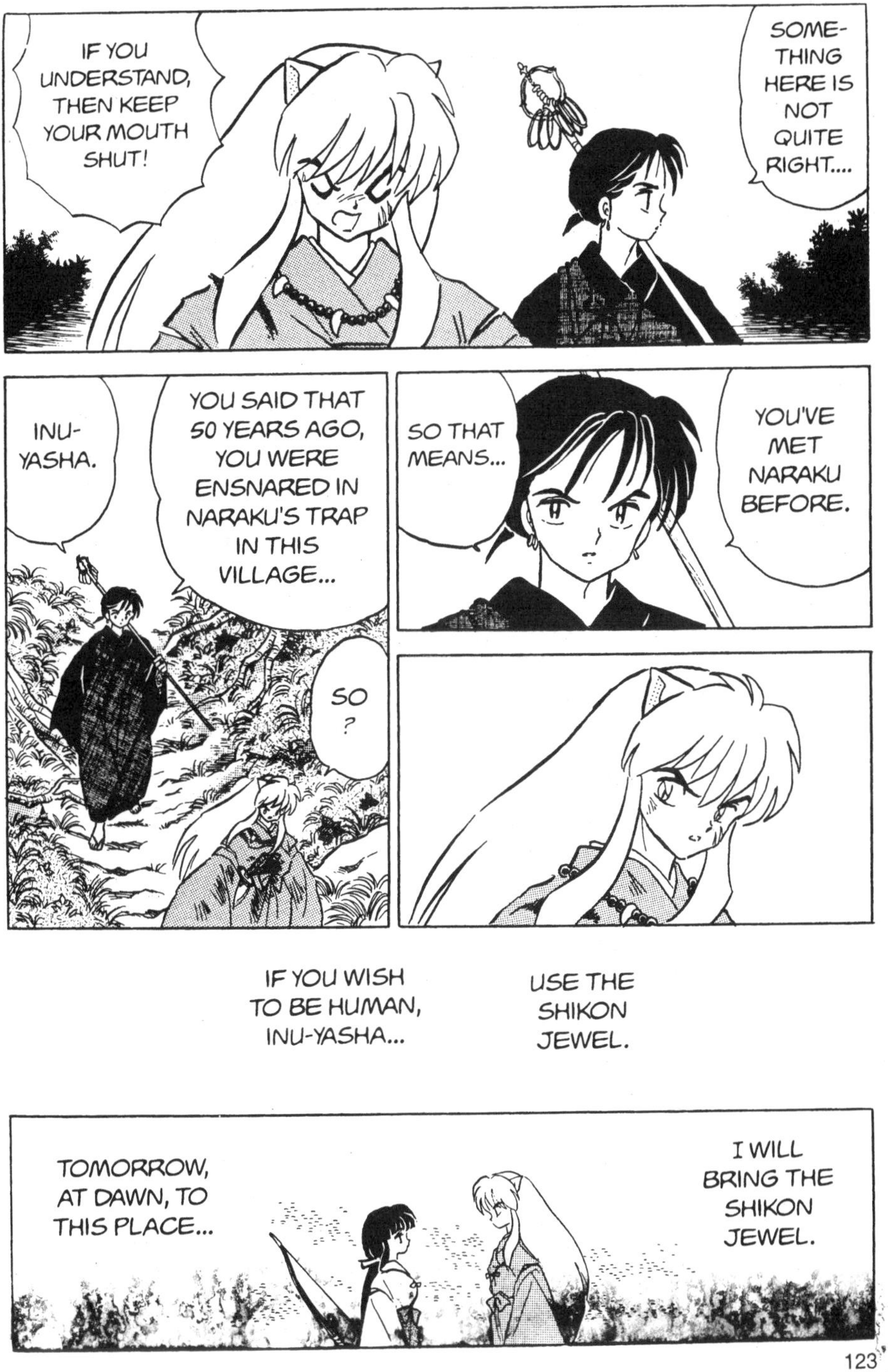
IF YOU UNDERSTAND, THEN KEEP YOUR MOUTH SHUT!
SOMETHING HERE IS NOT QUITE RIGHT....
INU-YASHA.
YOU SAID THAT 50 YEARS AGO, YOU WERE ENSNARED IN NARAKU'S TRAP IN THIS VILLAGE...
SO ?
SO THAT MEANS...
YOU'VE MET NARAKU BEFORE.
IF YOU WISH TO BE HUMAN, INU-YASHA...
USE THE SHIKON JEWEL.
TOMORROW, AT DAWN, TO THIS PLACE...
I WILL BRING THE SHIKON JEWEL.

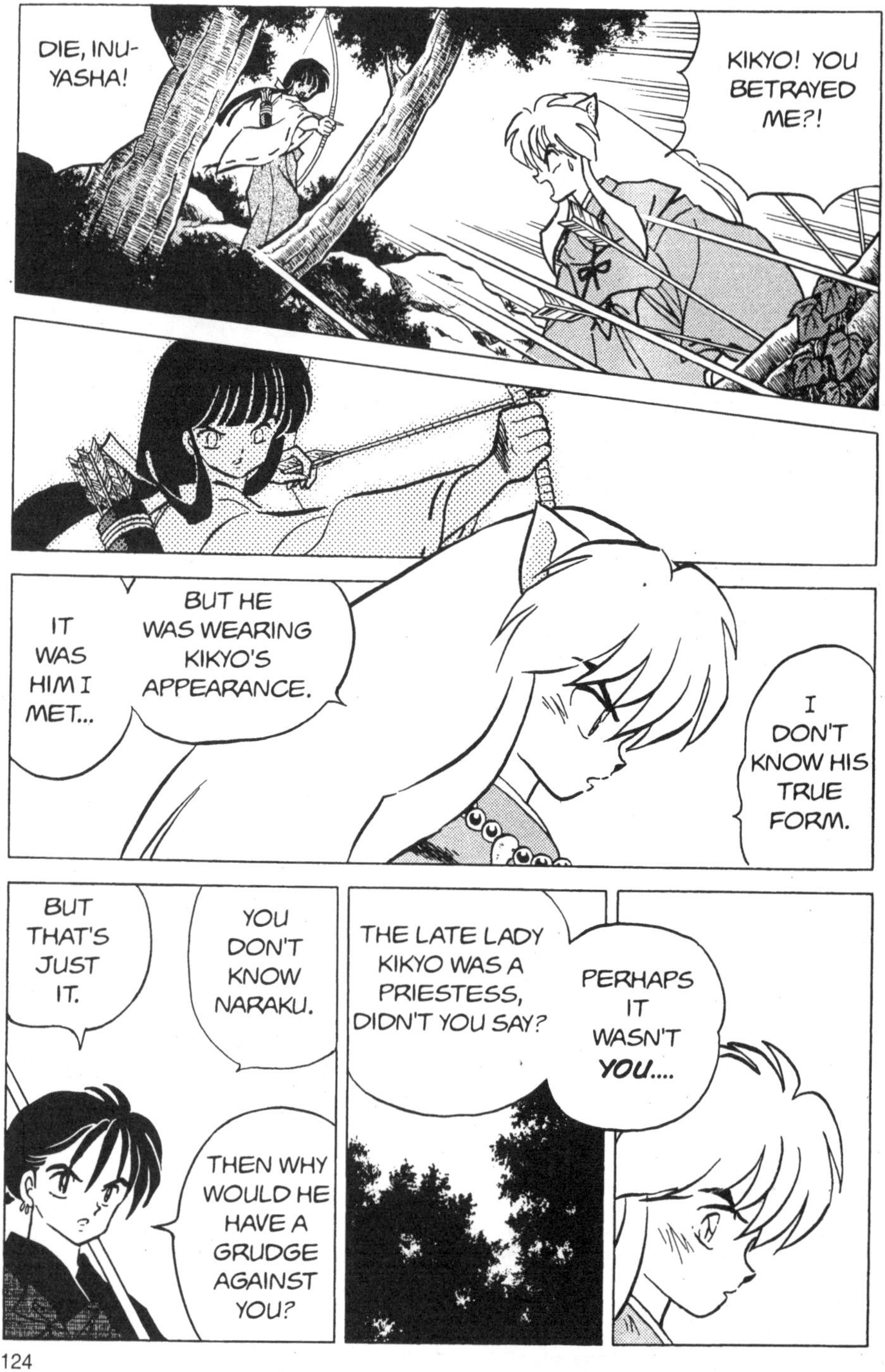
DIE, INU-YASHA!
KIKYO! YOU BETRAYED ME?!
IT WAS HIM I MET...
BUT HE WAS WEARING KIKYO'S APPEARANCE.
I DON'T KNOW HIS TRUE FORM.
BUT THAT'S JUST IT.
YOU DON'T KNOW NARAKU.
THEN WHY WOULD HE HAVE A GRUDGE AGAINST YOU?
THE LATE LADY KIKYO WAS A PRIESTESS, DIDN'T YOU SAY?
PERHAPS IT WASN'T **YOU**....

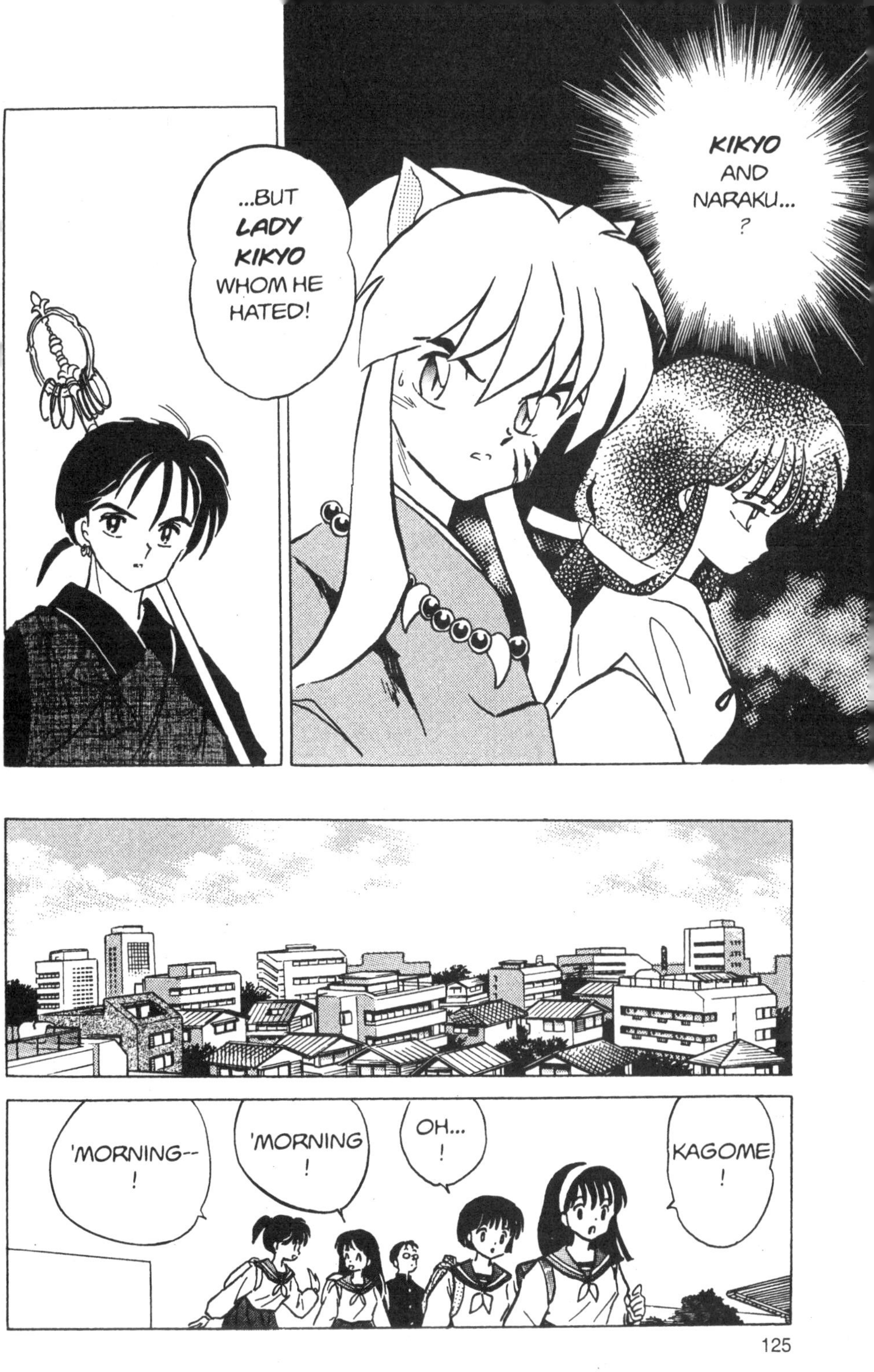
...BUT LADY KIKYO WHOM HE HATED!
KIKYO AND NARAKU...?
'MORNING--!
'MORNING!
OH...!
KAGOME!

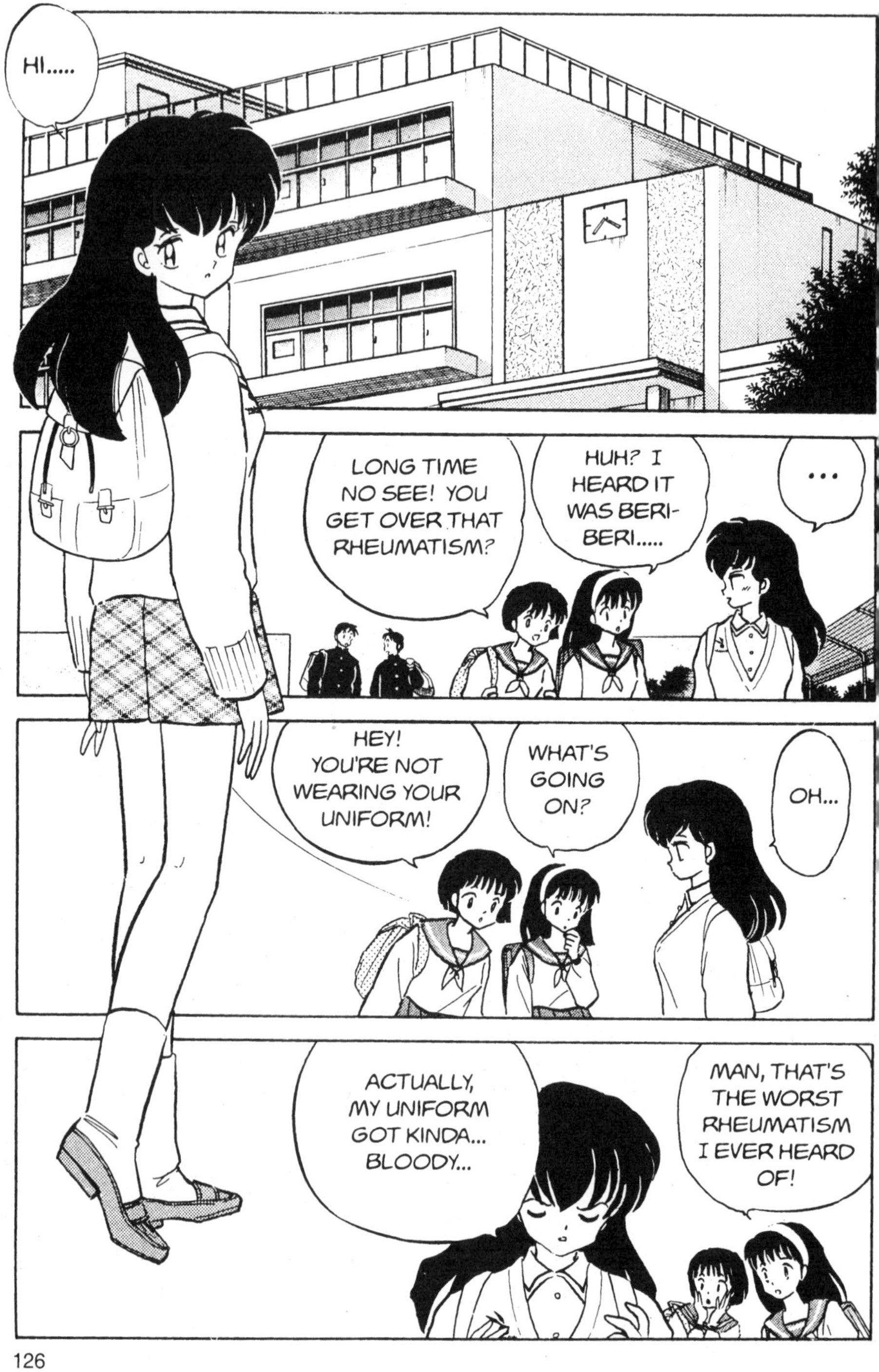
HI.....
LONG TIME NO SEE! YOU GET OVER THAT RHEUMATISM?
HUH? I HEARD IT WAS BERI-BERI.....
...
HEY! YOU'RE NOT WEARING YOUR UNIFORM!
WHAT'S GOING ON?
OH...
ACTUALLY, MY UNIFORM GOT KINDA... BLOODY...
MAN, THAT'S THE WORST RHEUMATISM I EVER HEARD OF!

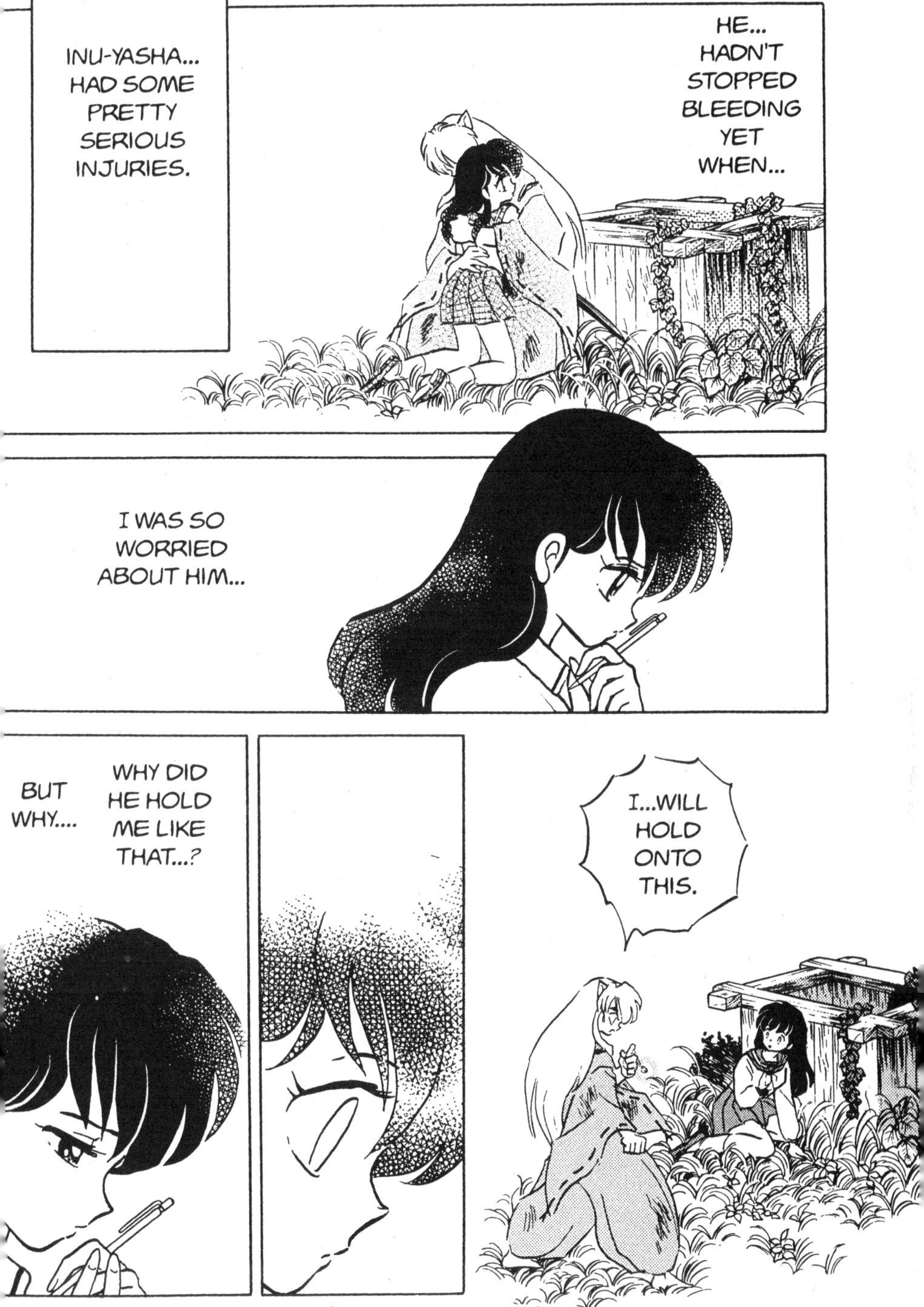
INU-YASHA... HAD SOME PRETTY SERIOUS INJURIES.
HE... HADN'T STOPPED BLEEDING YET WHEN...
I WAS SO WORRIED ABOUT HIM...
BUT WHY....
WHY DID HE HOLD ME LIKE THAT...?
I...WILL HOLD ONTO THIS.

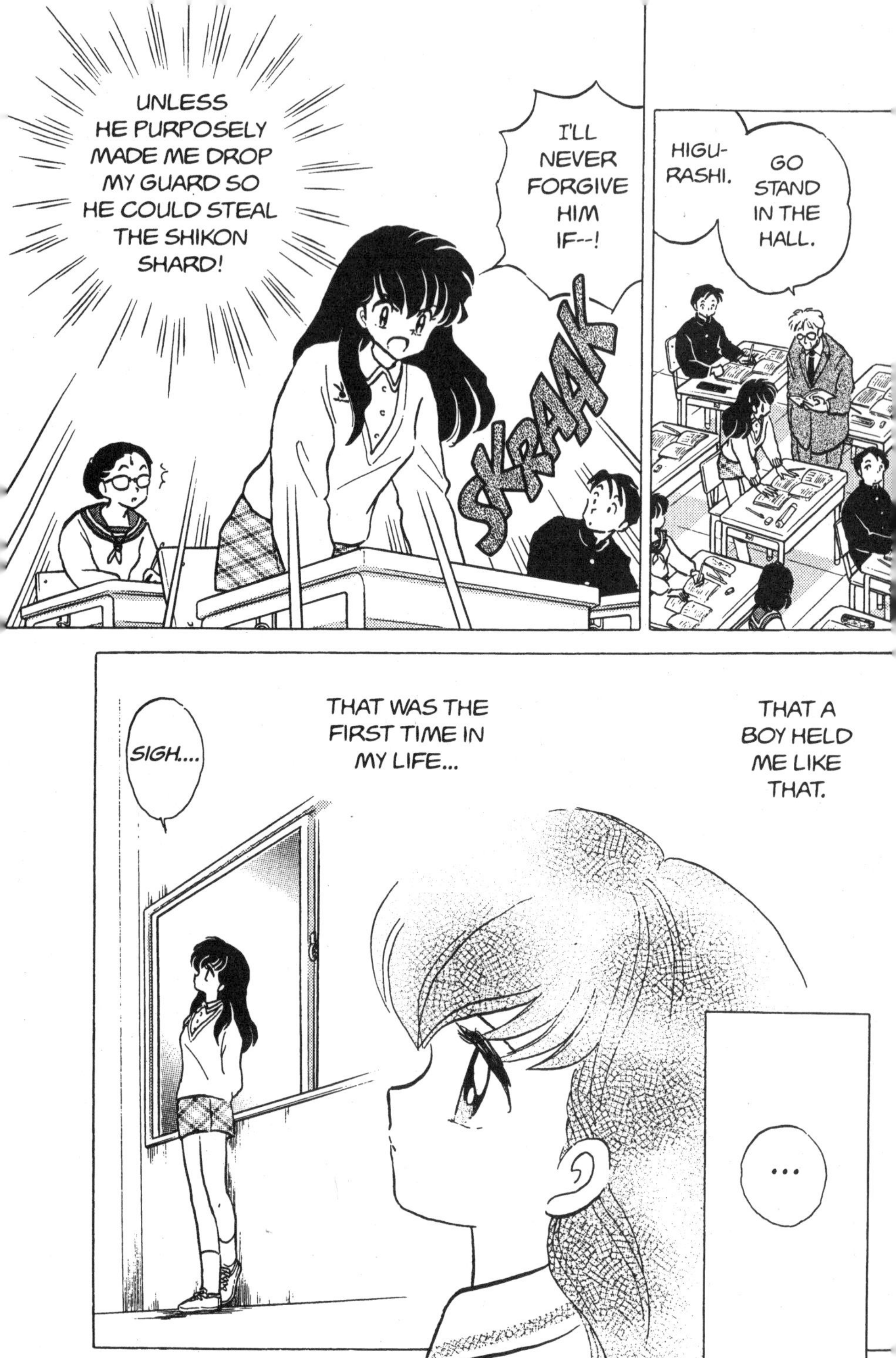
UNLESS HE PURPOSELY MADE ME DROP MY GUARD SO HE COULD STEAL THE SHIKON SHARD!
I'LL NEVER FORGIVE HIM IF--!
SKRAAK
HIGU-RASHI.
GO STAND IN THE HALL.
SIGH....
THAT WAS THE FIRST TIME IN MY LIFE...
THAT A BOY HELD ME LIKE THAT.
...

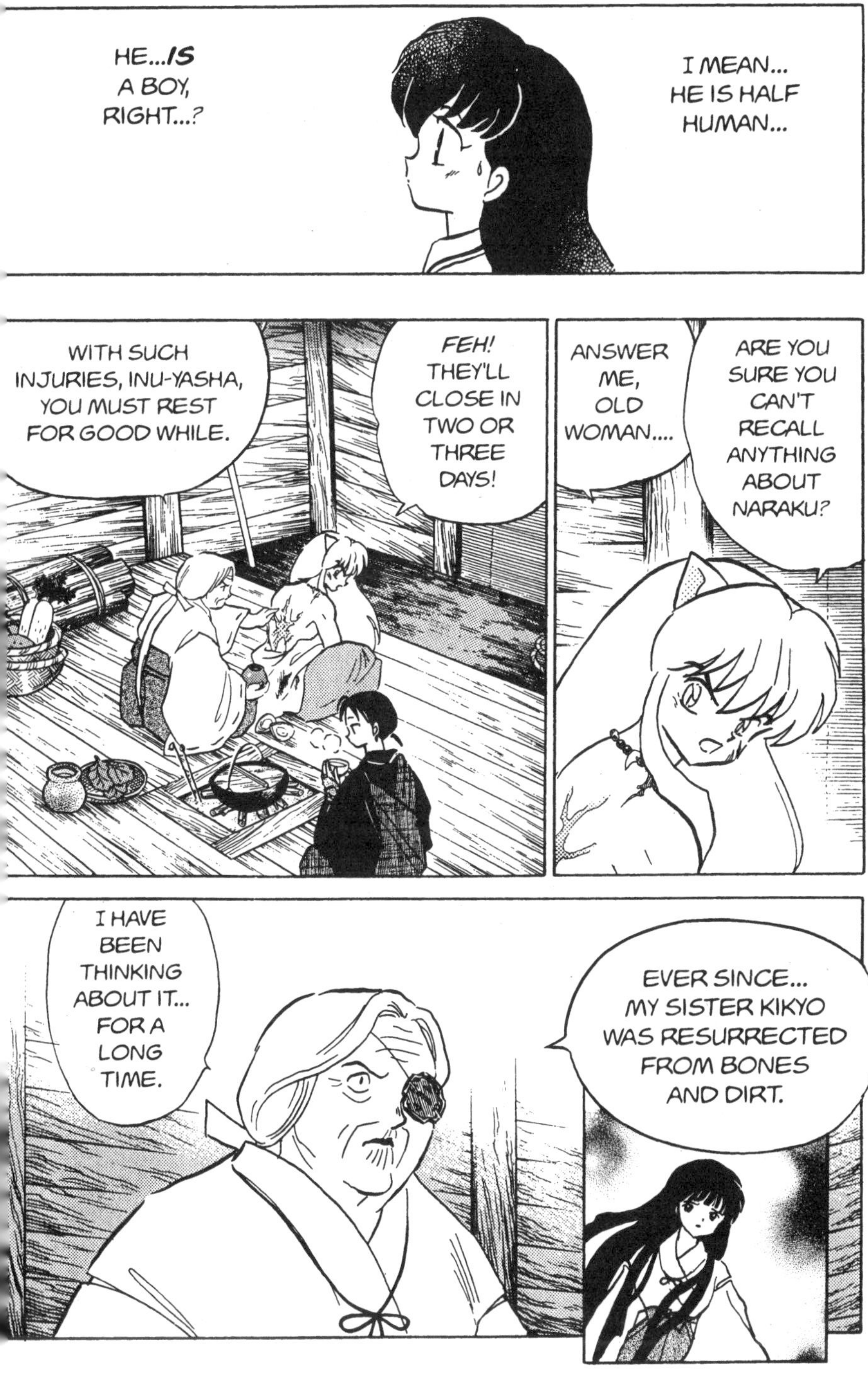
HE...*IS* A BOY, RIGHT...?
I MEAN... HE IS HALF HUMAN...
WITH SUCH INJURIES, INU-YASHA, YOU MUST REST FOR GOOD WHILE.
FEH! THEY'LL CLOSE IN TWO OR THREE DAYS!
ANSWER ME, OLD WOMAN....
ARE YOU SURE YOU CAN'T RECALL ANYTHING ABOUT NARAKU?
I HAVE BEEN THINKING ABOUT IT... FOR A LONG TIME.
EVER SINCE... MY SISTER KIKYO WAS RESURRECTED FROM BONES AND DIRT.

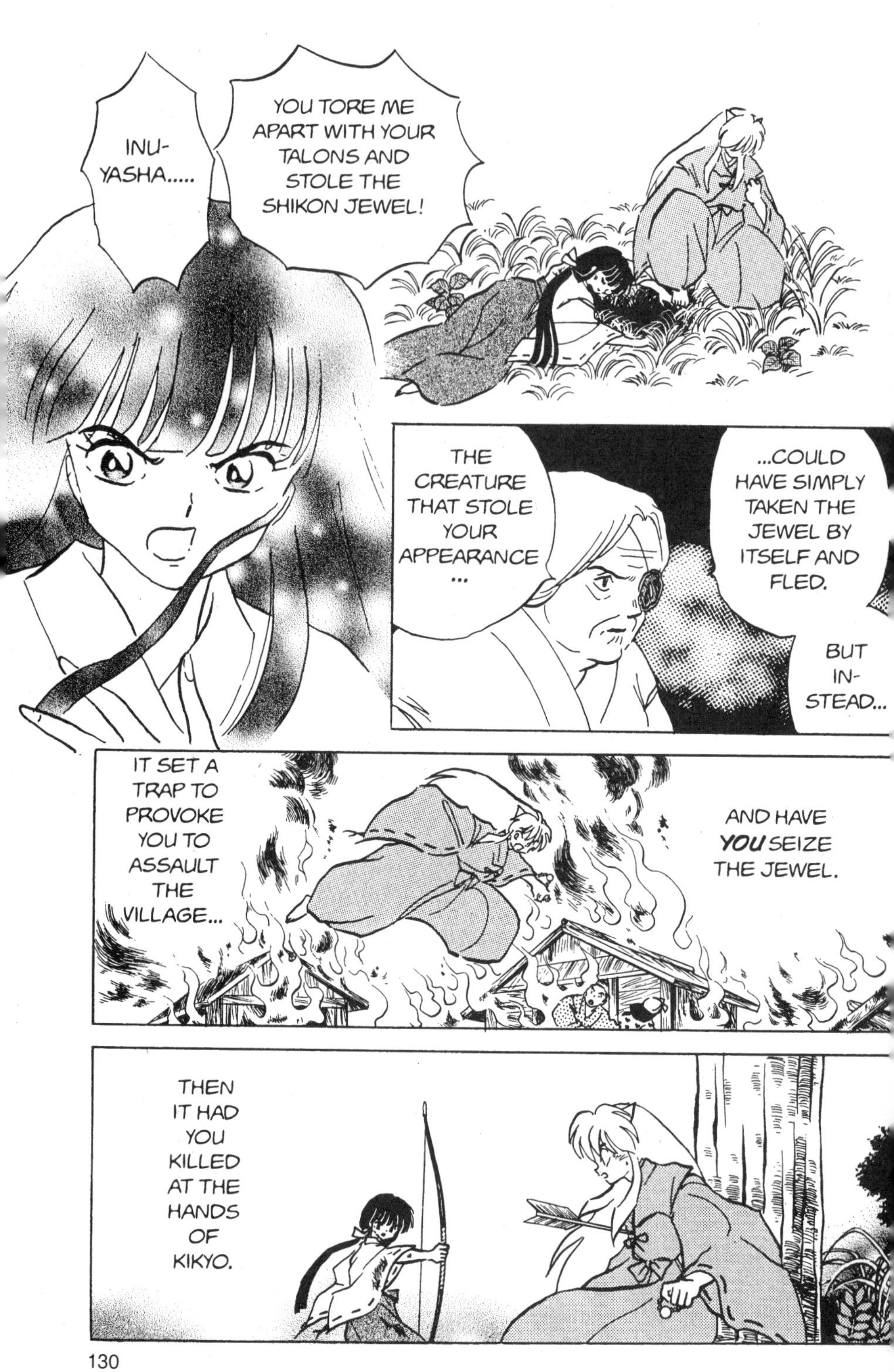
INU-YASHA.....
YOU TORE ME APART WITH YOUR TALONS AND STOLE THE SHIKON JEWEL!
THE CREATURE THAT STOLE YOUR APPEARANCE ...
...COULD HAVE SIMPLY TAKEN THE JEWEL BY ITSELF AND FLED.
BUT IN-STEAD...
IT SET A TRAP TO PROVOKE YOU TO ASSAULT THE VILLAGE...
AND HAVE ***YOU*** SEIZE THE JEWEL.
THEN IT HAD YOU KILLED AT THE HANDS OF KIKYO.

EITHER IT WANTED THE TWO OF YOU TO DESPISE ONE ANOTHER...

OR...

IT WANTED KIKYO'S HEART...

TO BECOME DEFILED WITH HATRED AND THE THIRST FOR VENGEANCE.

WHAT...?

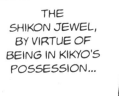

THE SHIKON JEWEL, BY VIRTUE OF BEING IN KIKYO'S POSSESSION...

WAS BEING PURIFIED.

WHEN MY SISTER'S HEART WAS DEFILED...

THE JEWEL WAS DEFILED AS WELL...AND ITS EVIL POWERS INCREASED.

AT THAT TIME, THERE WAS ONE FELLOW WHO DESIRED JUST THAT

!

WOULD YOU LIKE TO SEE...

WHERE THIS FELLOW USED TO BE...?

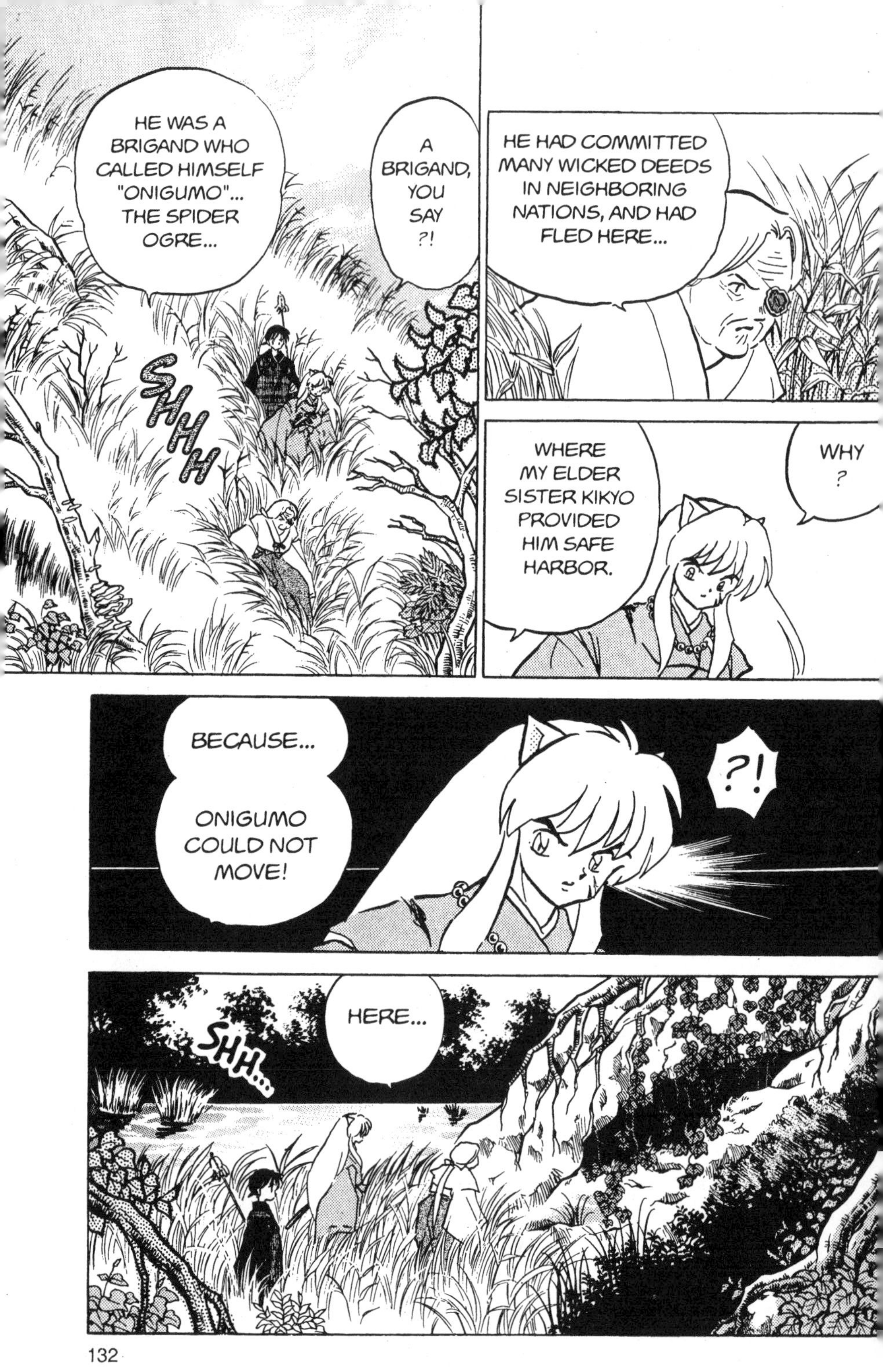
HE WAS A BRIGAND WHO CALLED HIMSELF "ONIGUMO"... THE SPIDER OGRE...
A BRIGAND, YOU SAY ?!
SHHHH
HE HAD COMMITTED MANY WICKED DEEDS IN NEIGHBORING NATIONS, AND HAD FLED HERE...
WHERE MY ELDER SISTER KIKYO PROVIDED HIM SAFE HARBOR.
WHY ?
BECAUSE...
ONIGUMO COULD NOT MOVE!
?!
HERE...
SHH...

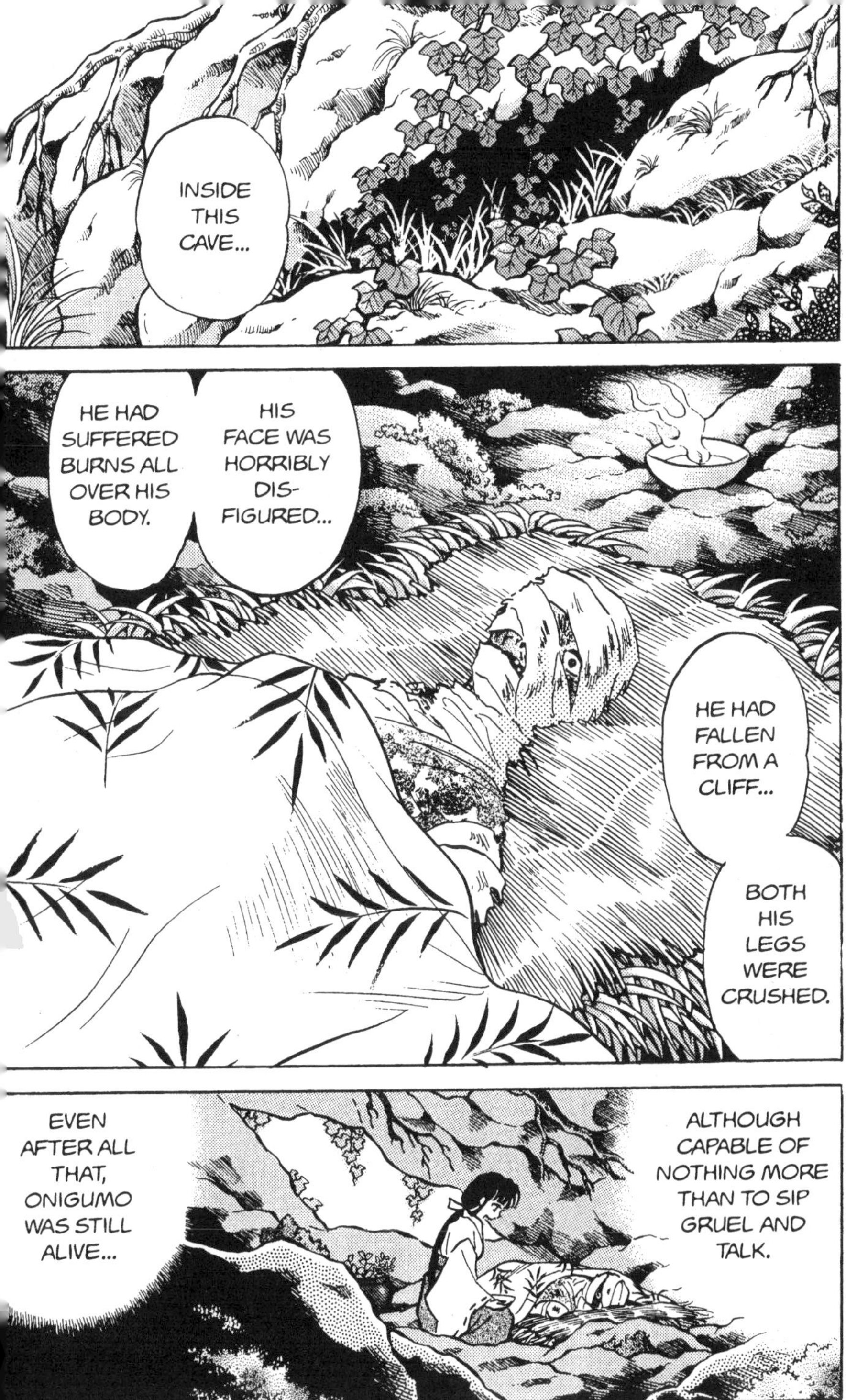
INSIDE THIS CAVE...
HE HAD SUFFERED BURNS ALL OVER HIS BODY.
HIS FACE WAS HORRIBLY DIS-FIGURED...
HE HAD FALLEN FROM A CLIFF...
BOTH HIS LEGS WERE CRUSHED.
EVEN AFTER ALL THAT, ONIGUMO WAS STILL ALIVE...
ALTHOUGH CAPABLE OF NOTHING MORE THAN TO SIP GRUEL AND TALK.

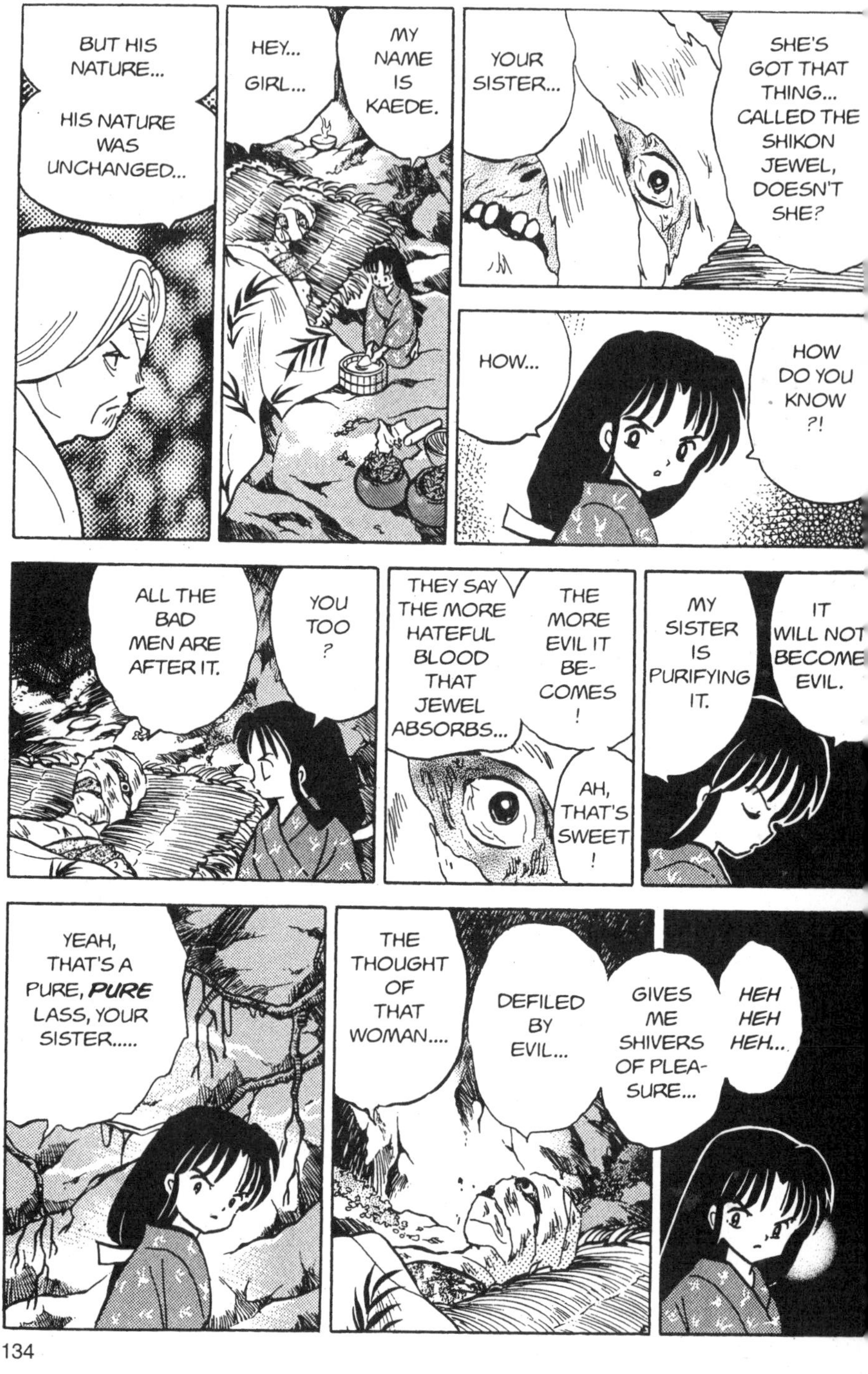
BUT HIS NATURE...
HIS NATURE WAS UNCHANGED...
HEY... GIRL...
MY NAME IS KAEDE.
YOUR SISTER...
SHE'S GOT THAT THING... CALLED THE SHIKON JEWEL, DOESN'T SHE?
HOW...
HOW DO YOU KNOW ?!
ALL THE BAD MEN ARE AFTER IT.
YOU TOO ?
THEY SAY THE MORE HATEFUL BLOOD THAT JEWEL ABSORBS...
THE MORE EVIL IT BE- COMES !
AH, THAT'S SWEET !
MY SISTER IS PURIFYING IT.
IT WILL NOT BECOME EVIL.
YEAH, THAT'S A PURE, PURE LASS, YOUR SISTER.....
THE THOUGHT OF THAT WOMAN....
DEFILED BY EVIL...
GIVES ME SHIVERS OF PLEA- SURE...
HEH HEH HEH...

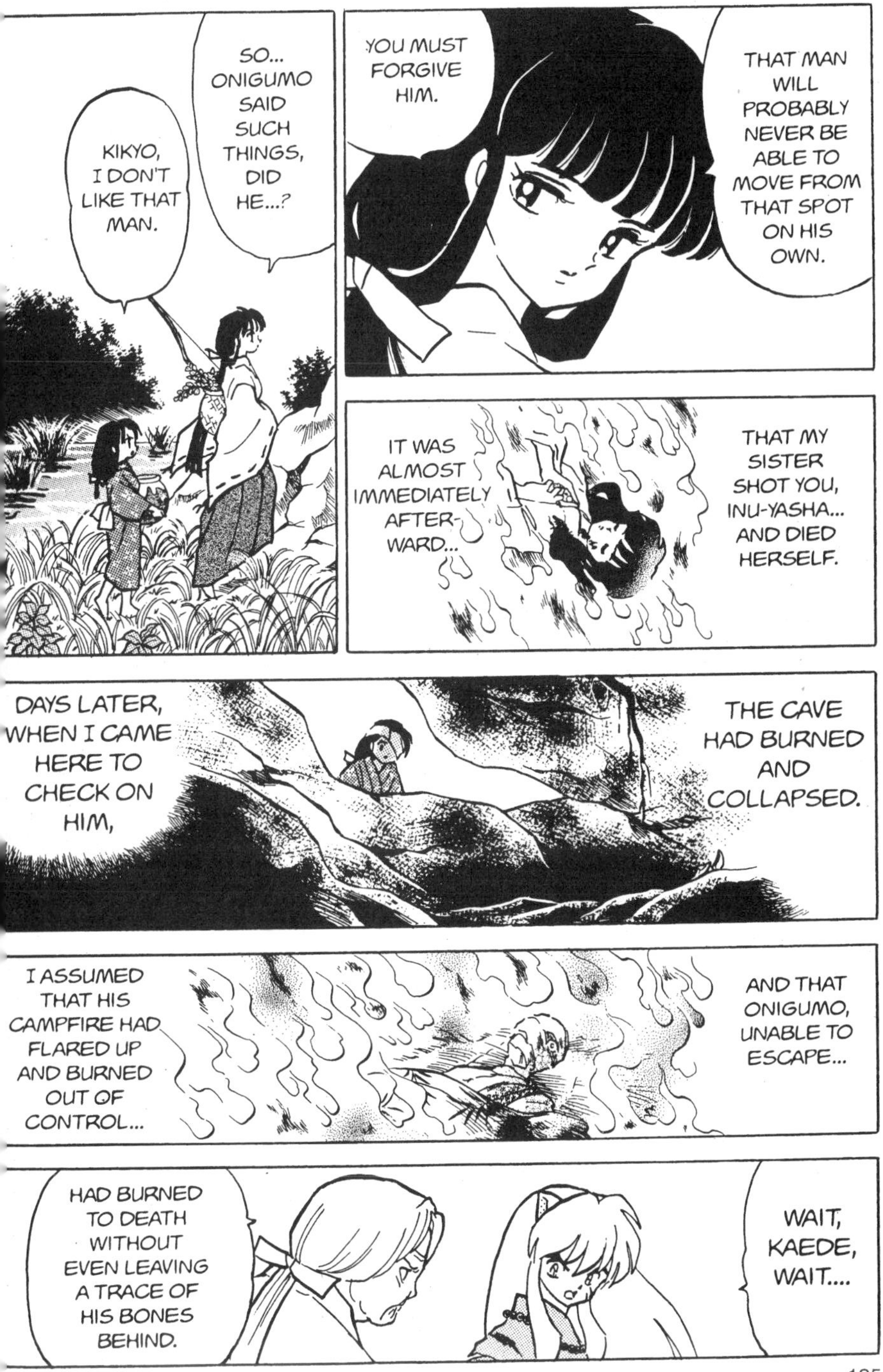
KIKYO, I DON'T LIKE THAT MAN.
SO... ONIGUMO SAID SUCH THINGS, DID HE...?
YOU MUST FORGIVE HIM.
THAT MAN WILL PROBABLY NEVER BE ABLE TO MOVE FROM THAT SPOT ON HIS OWN.
IT WAS ALMOST IMMEDIATELY AFTER-WARD...
THAT MY SISTER SHOT YOU, INU-YASHA... AND DIED HERSELF.
DAYS LATER, WHEN I CAME HERE TO CHECK ON HIM,
THE CAVE HAD BURNED AND COLLAPSED.
I ASSUMED THAT HIS CAMPFIRE HAD FLARED UP AND BURNED OUT OF CONTROL...
AND THAT ONIGUMO, UNABLE TO ESCAPE...
HAD BURNED TO DEATH WITHOUT EVEN LEAVING A TRACE OF HIS BONES BEHIND.
WAIT, KAEDE, WAIT....

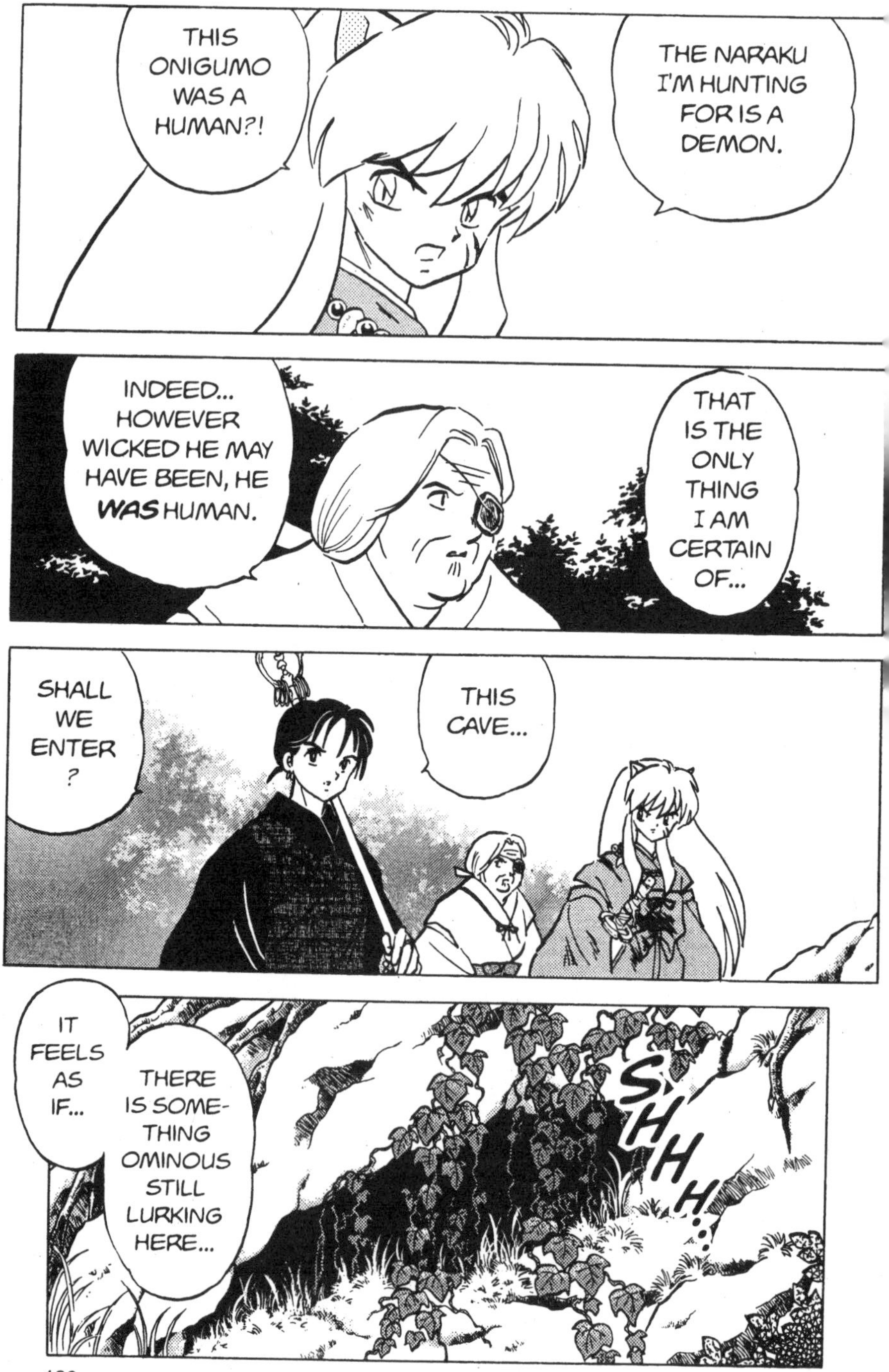
THIS ONIGUMO WAS A HUMAN?!
THE NARAKU I'M HUNTING FOR IS A DEMON.
INDEED... HOWEVER WICKED HE MAY HAVE BEEN, HE **WAS** HUMAN.
THAT IS THE ONLY THING I AM CERTAIN OF...
SHALL WE ENTER ?
THIS CAVE...
IT FEELS AS IF...
THERE IS SOME-THING OMINOUS STILL LURKING HERE...
SHHHH...

SCROLL EIGHT

THE SHADOW OF EVIL

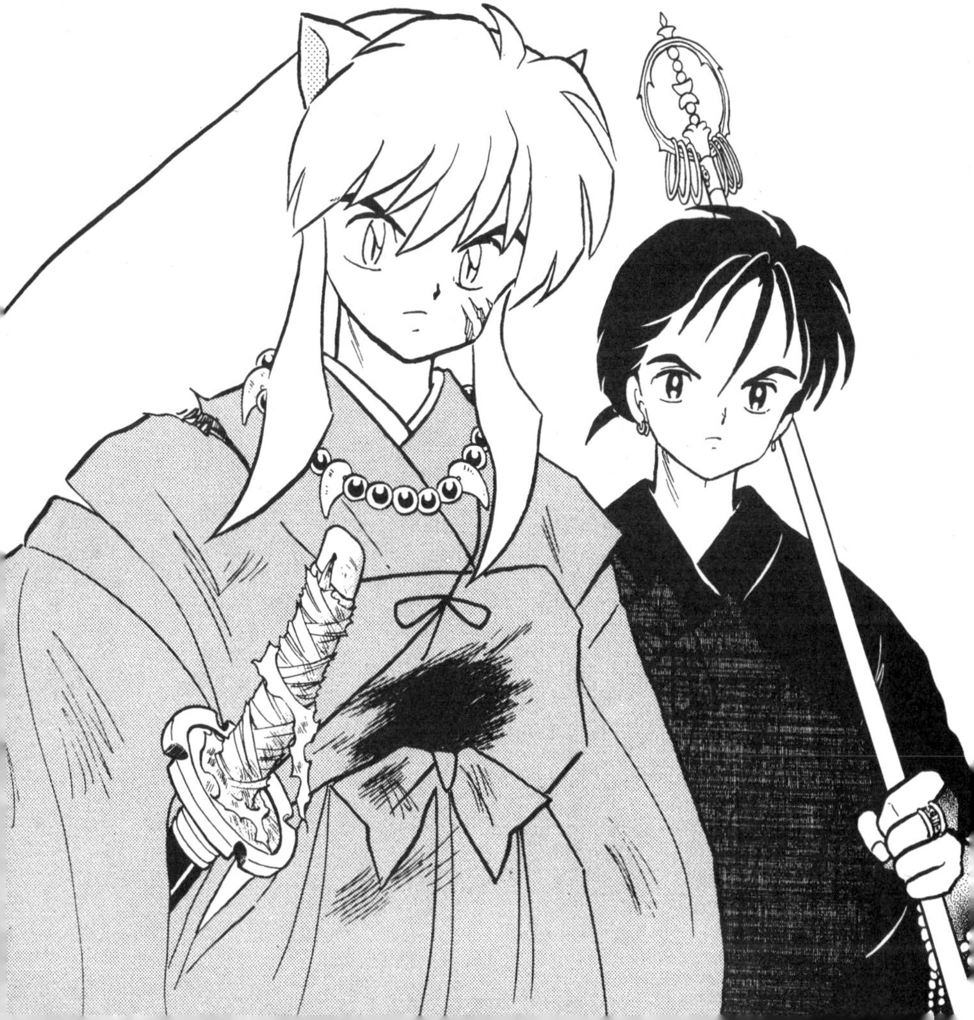

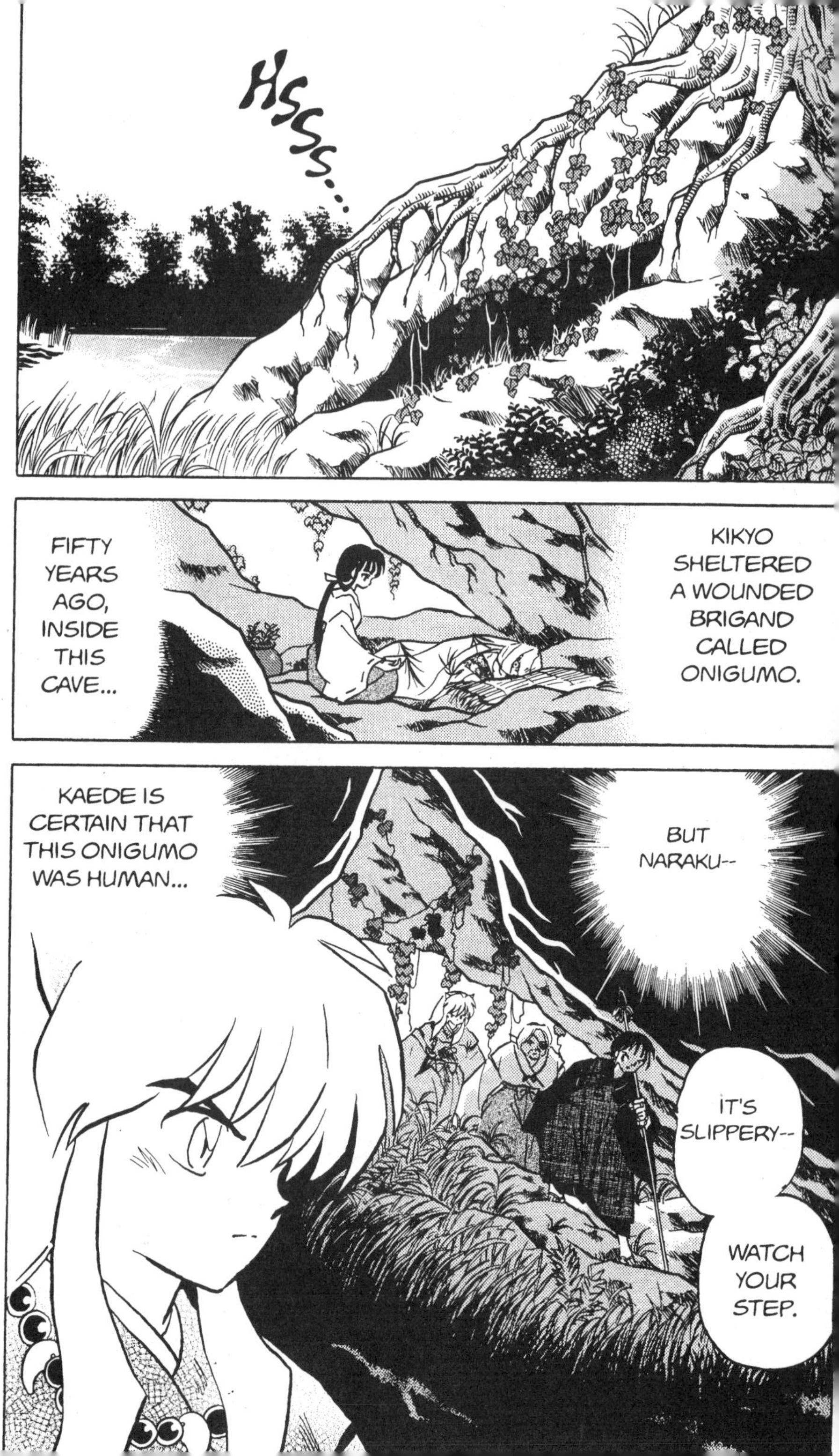
HSSS...
FIFTY YEARS AGO, INSIDE THIS CAVE...
KIKYO SHELTERED A WOUNDED BRIGAND CALLED ONIGUMO.
KAEDE IS CERTAIN THAT THIS ONIGUMO WAS HUMAN...
BUT NARAKU--
IT'S SLIPPERY--
WATCH YOUR STEP.

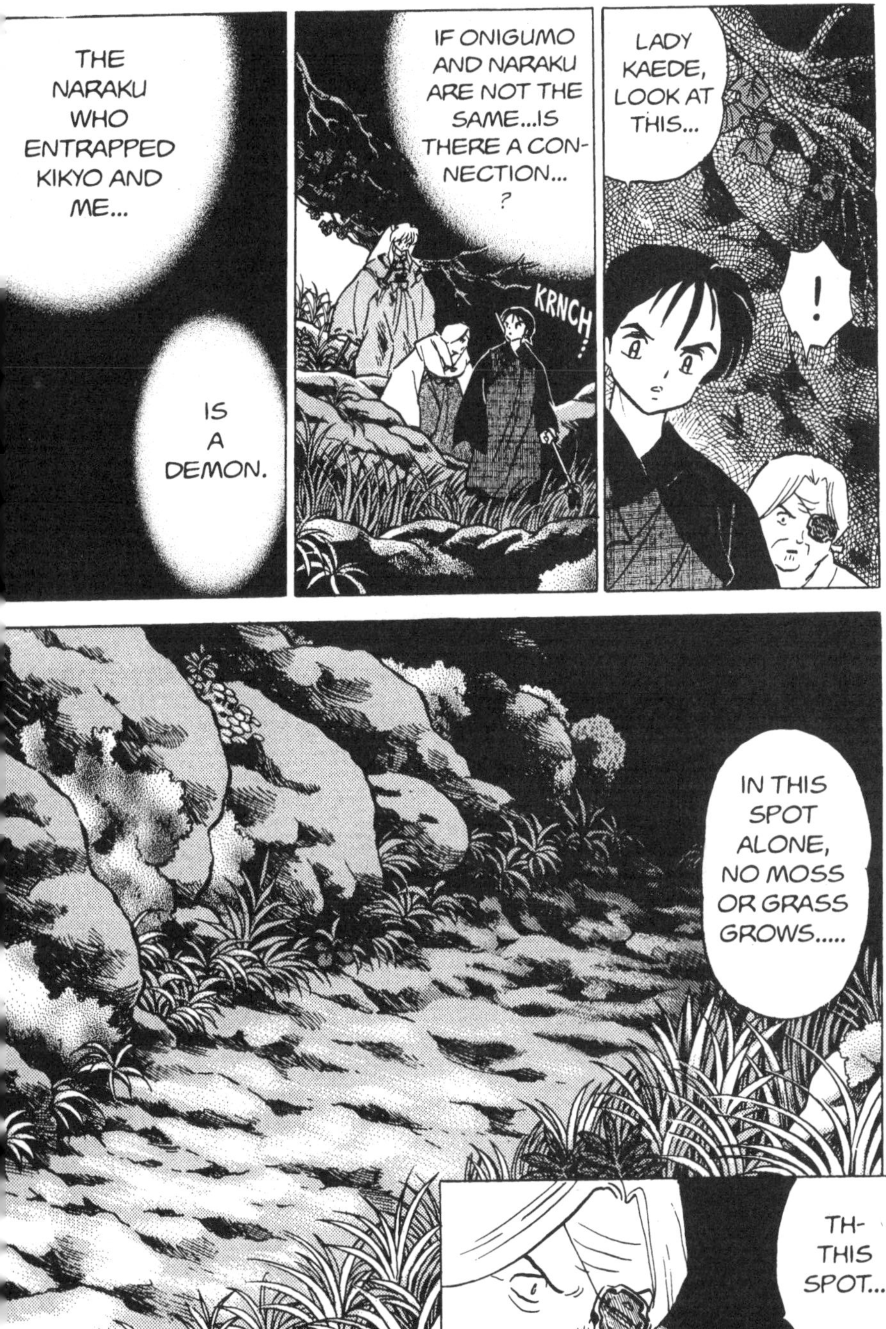
THE NARAKU WHO ENTRAPPED KIKYO AND ME...
IS A DEMON.
IF ONIGUMO AND NARAKU ARE NOT THE SAME...IS THERE A CONNECTION... ?
KRNCH!
LADY KAEDE, LOOK AT THIS...
!
IN THIS SPOT ALONE, NO MOSS OR GRASS GROWS.....
TH-THIS SPOT...

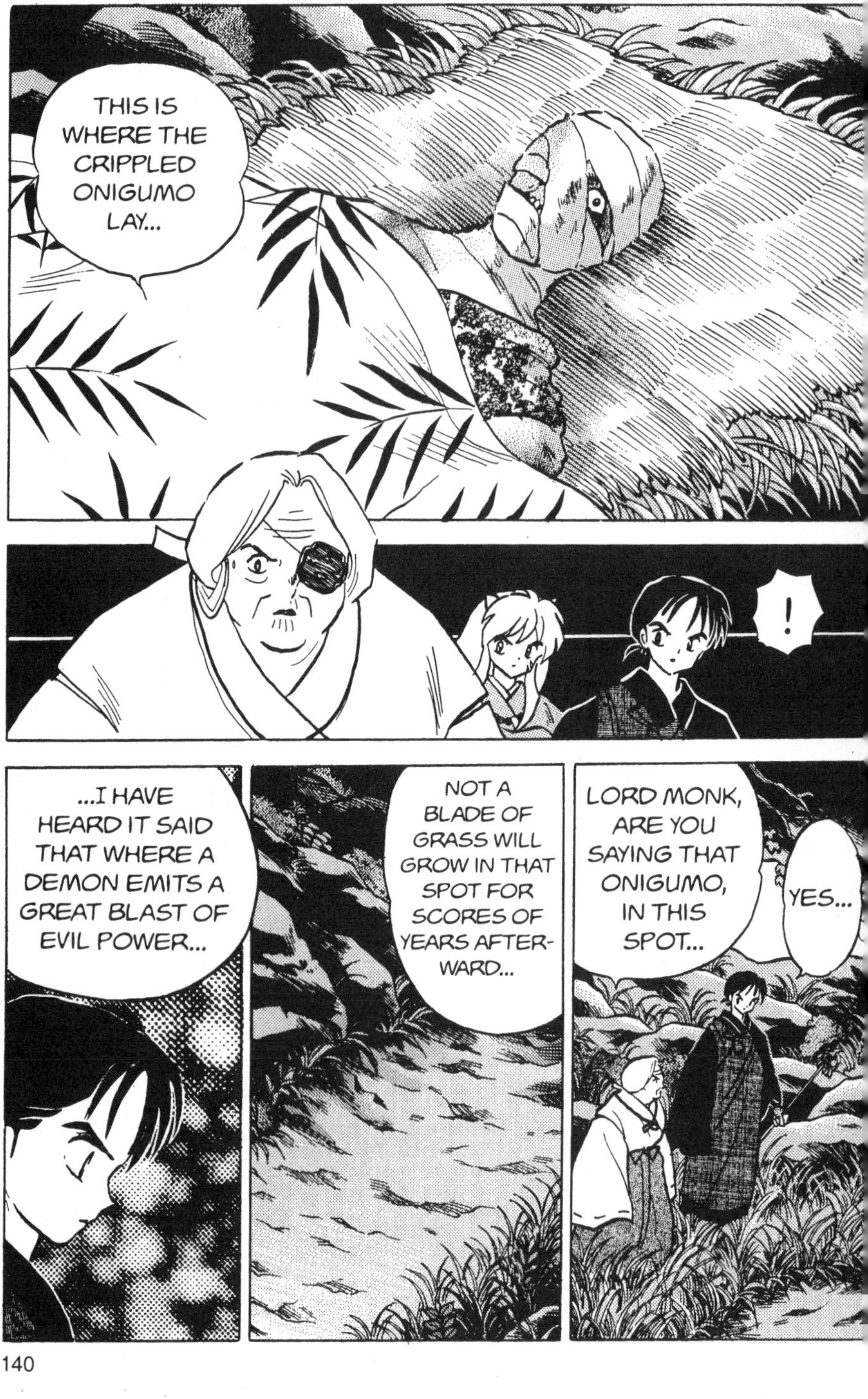
THIS IS WHERE THE CRIPPLED ONIGUMO LAY...
!
...I HAVE HEARD IT SAID THAT WHERE A DEMON EMITS A GREAT BLAST OF EVIL POWER...
NOT A BLADE OF GRASS WILL GROW IN THAT SPOT FOR SCORES OF YEARS AFTER-WARD...
LORD MONK, ARE YOU SAYING THAT ONIGUMO, IN THIS SPOT...
YES...

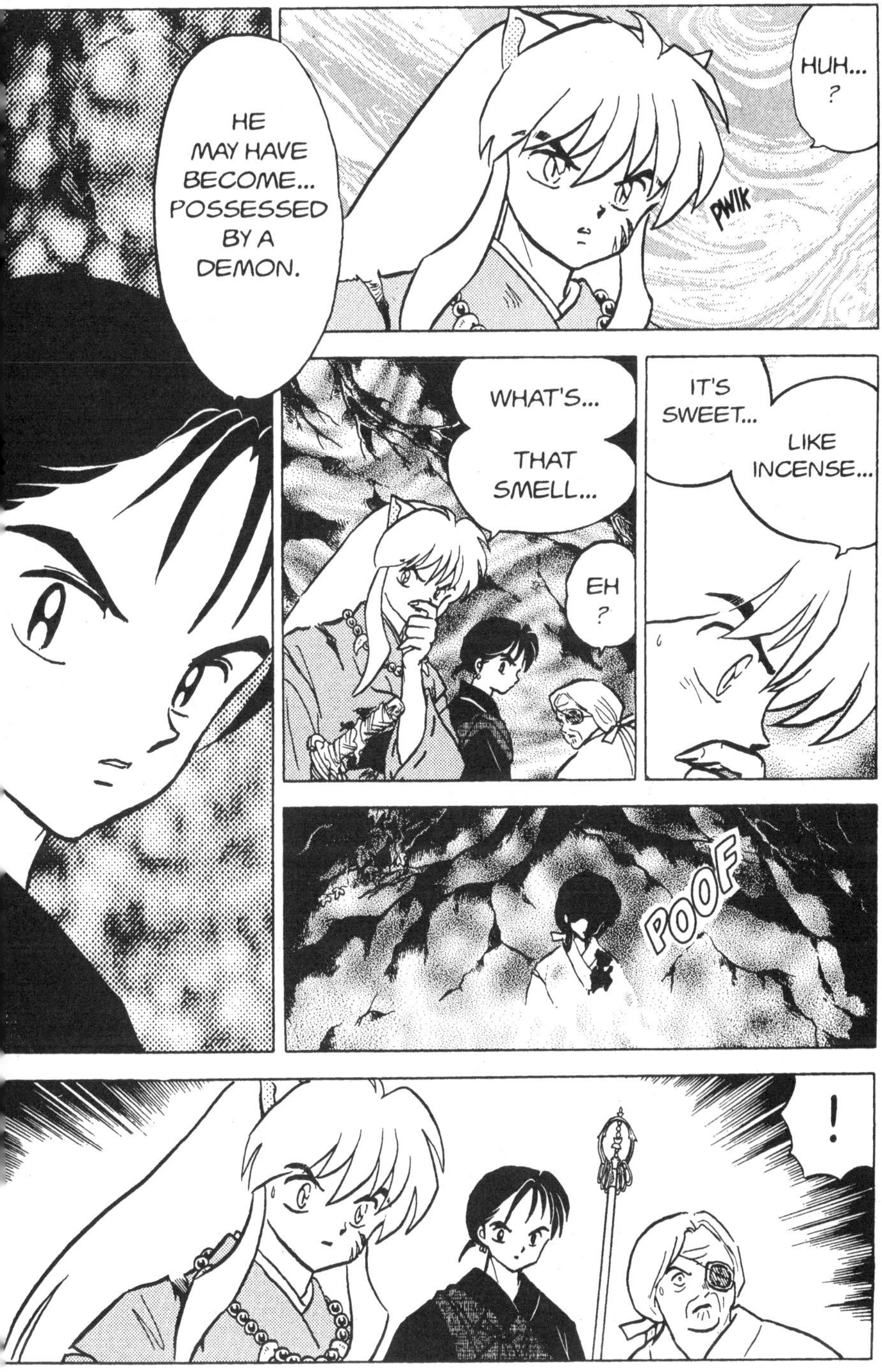
HE MAY HAVE BECOME... POSSESSED BY A DEMON.
HUH... ?
PWIK
WHAT'S...
THAT SMELL...
EH ?
IT'S SWEET...
LIKE INCENSE...
POOF
!

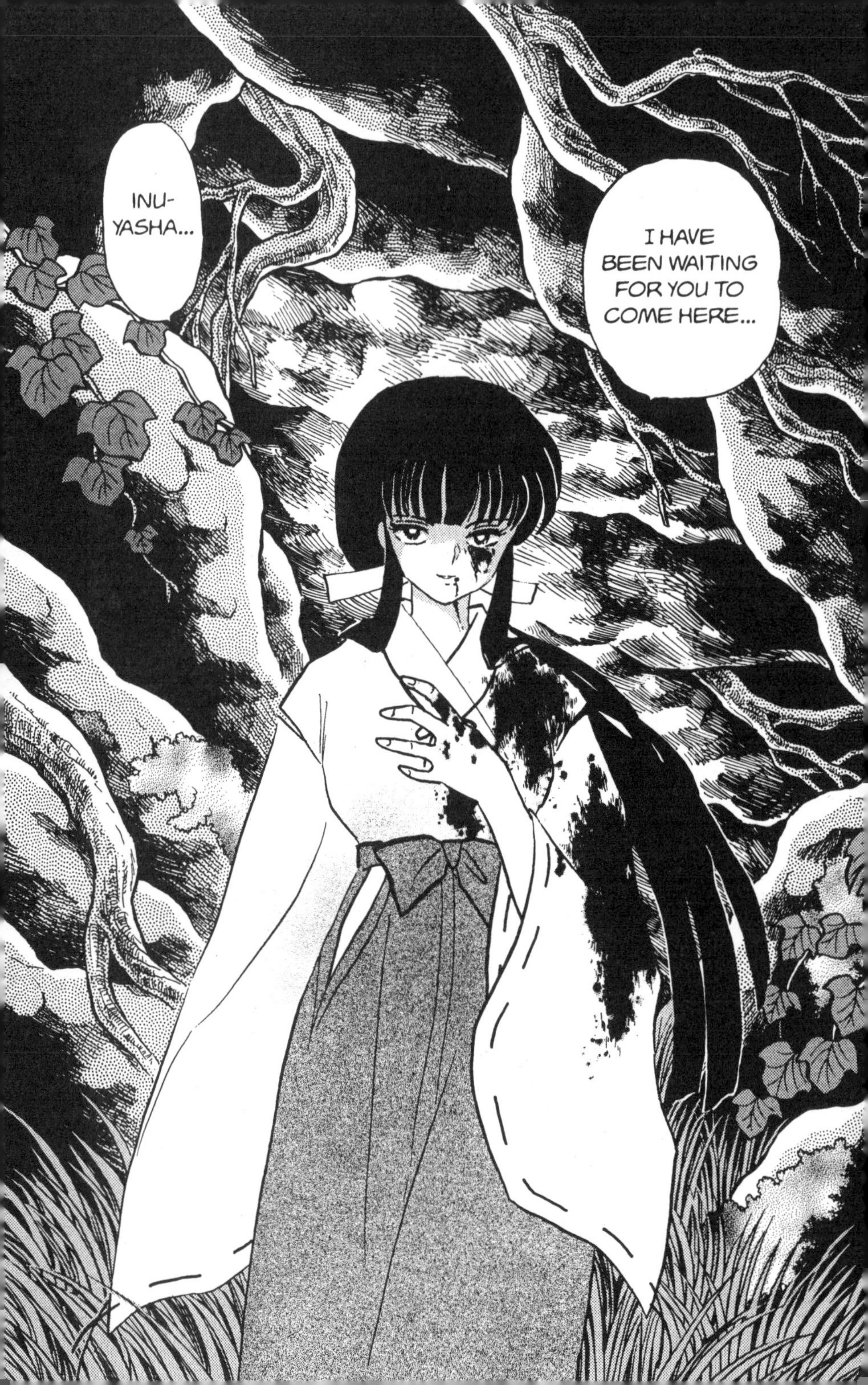
INU-
YASHA...
I HAVE
BEEN WAITING
FOR YOU TO
COME HERE...

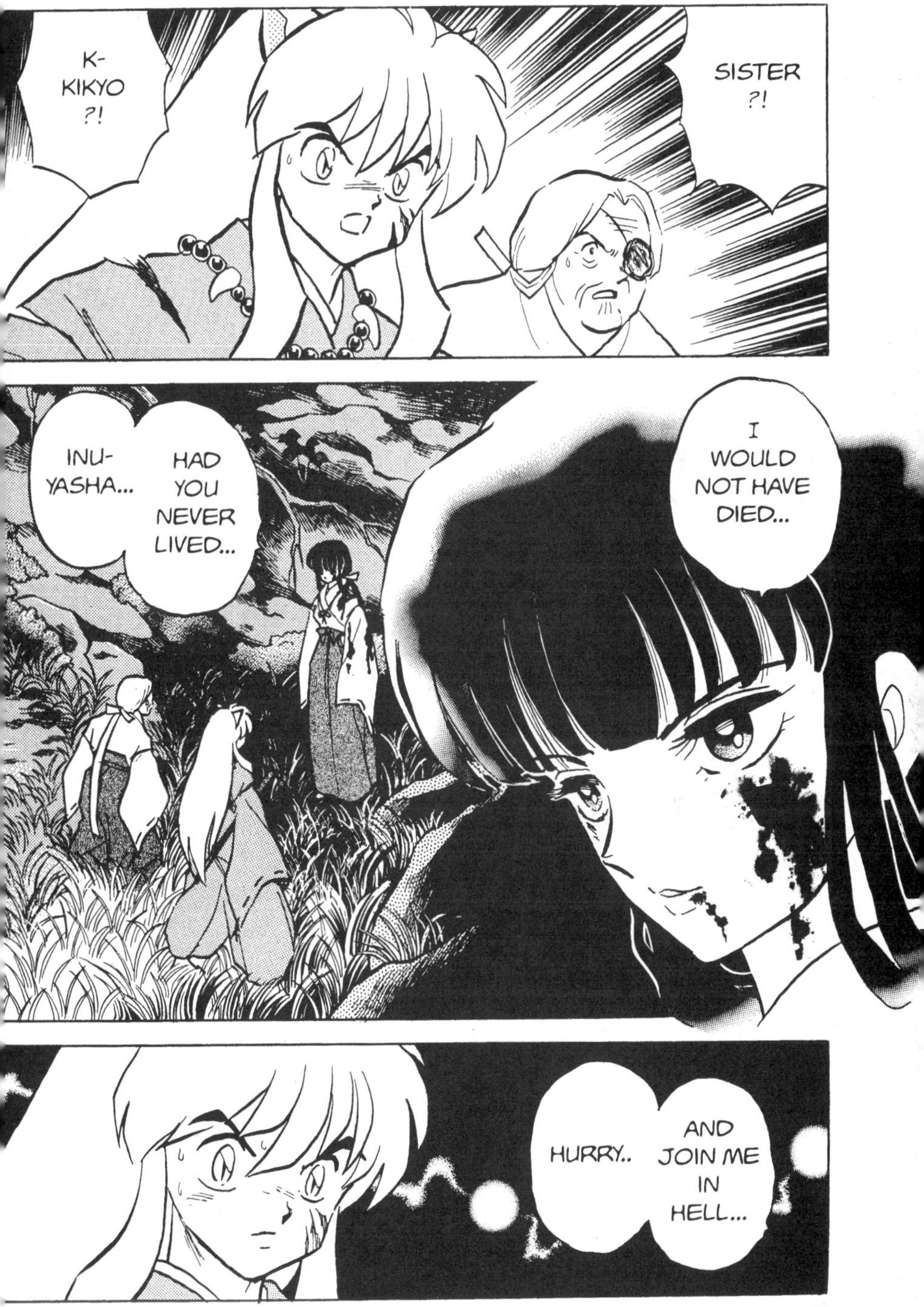
K-
KIKYO
?!
SISTER
?!
INU-
YASHA...
HAD
YOU
NEVER
LIVED...
I
WOULD
NOT HAVE
DIED...
HURRY..
AND
JOIN ME
IN
HELL...

fff

DNK

!

HMPH.
A
CHILD'S
TRICK.

INCENSE OF
ILLUSION WAS
PLACED INSIDE
THIS LIZARD'S
ABDOMEN.

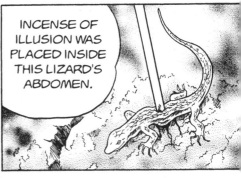

ANTICIPATING
THAT WE
WOULD COME
HERE...?

SO
IT
SEEMS.

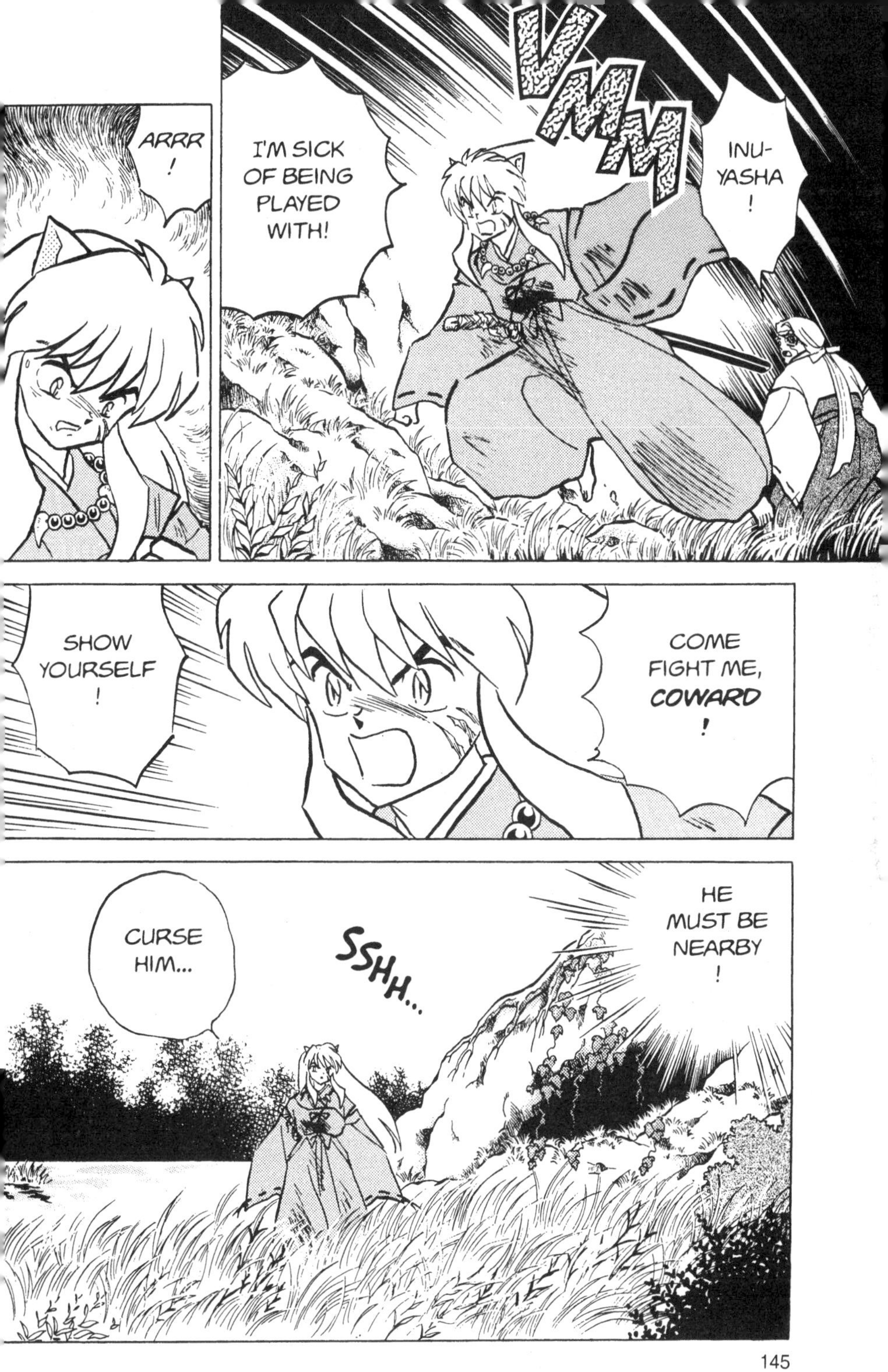
ARRR!
I'M SICK OF BEING PLAYED WITH!
VMM
INU-YASHA!
SHOW YOURSELF!
COME FIGHT ME, **COWARD**!
CURSE HIM...
SSHH...
HE MUST BE NEARBY!

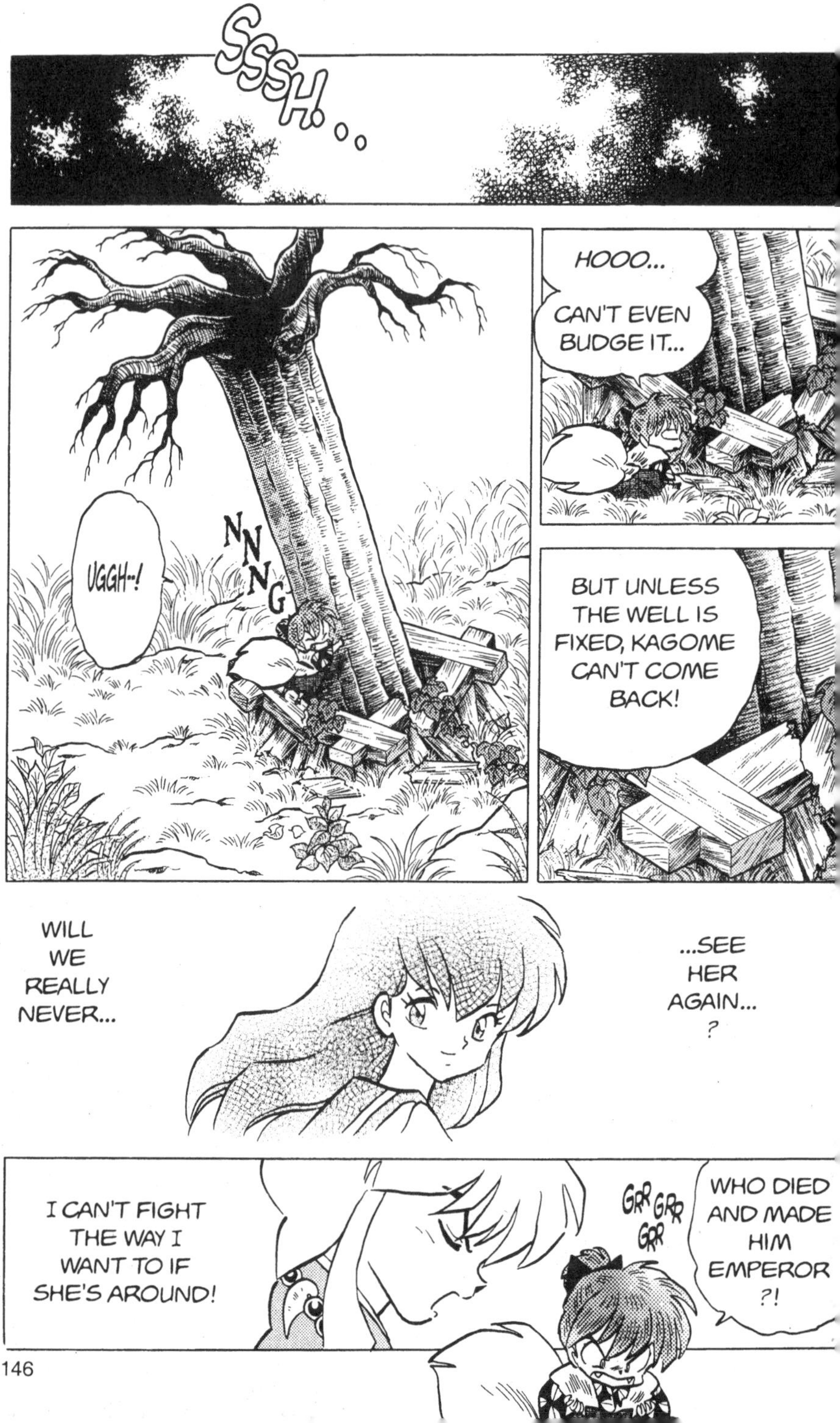
SSSH...
UGGH--!
NNNG
HOOO...
CAN'T EVEN BUDGE IT...
BUT UNLESS THE WELL IS FIXED, KAGOME CAN'T COME BACK!
WILL WE REALLY NEVER...
...SEE HER AGAIN...?
I CAN'T FIGHT THE WAY I WANT TO IF SHE'S AROUND!
GRR GRR GRR
WHO DIED AND MADE HIM EMPEROR?!

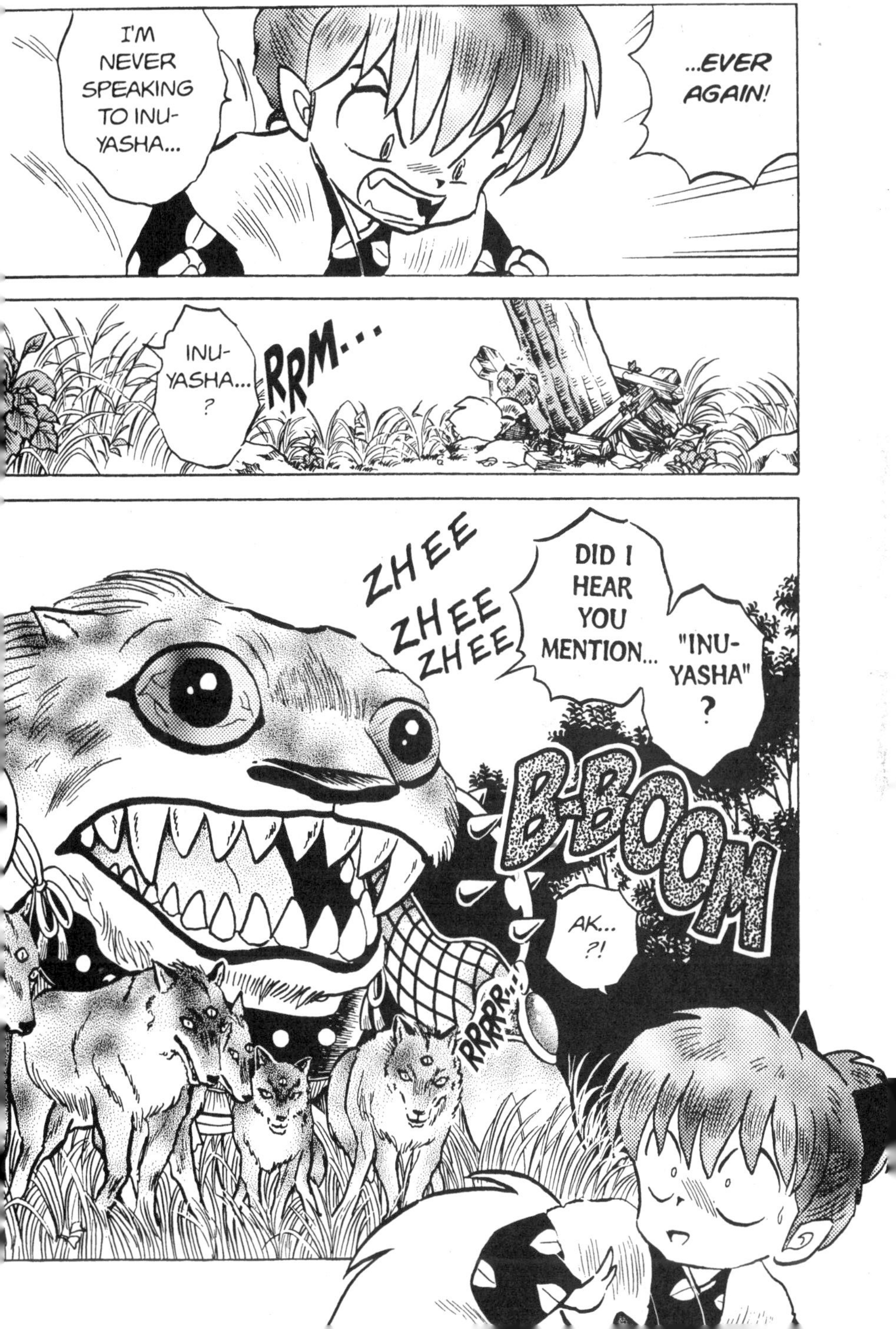
I'M NEVER SPEAKING TO INU-YASHA...
...EVER AGAIN!
INU-YASHA... ?
RRM...
ZHEE ZHEE ZHEE
DID I HEAR YOU MENTION...
"INU-YASHA" ?
B-BOOM
AK... ?!
RRRRR...

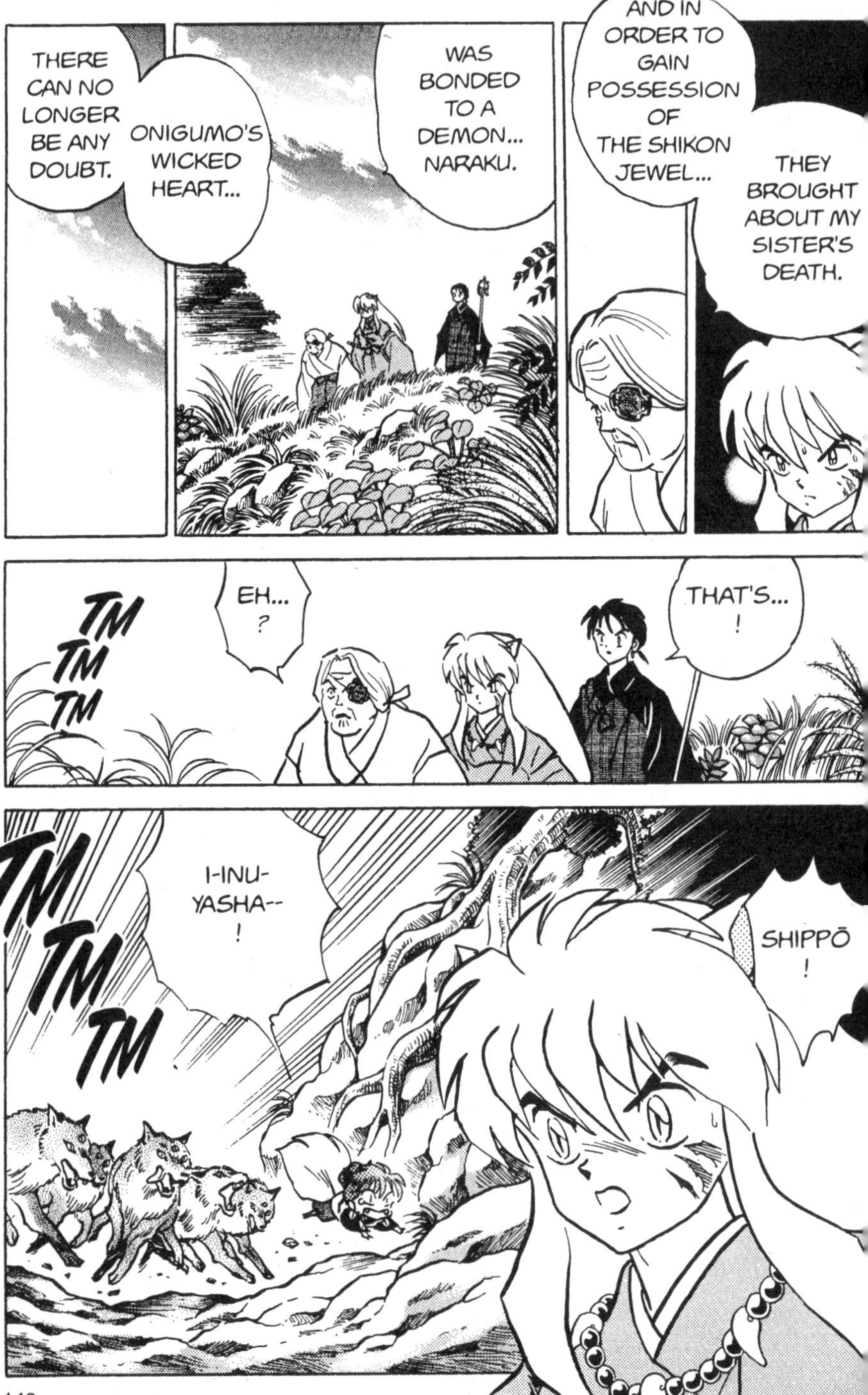
THERE CAN NO LONGER BE ANY DOUBT.
ONIGUMO'S WICKED HEART...
WAS BONDED TO A DEMON... NARAKU.
AND IN ORDER TO GAIN POSSESSION OF THE SHIKON JEWEL...
THEY BROUGHT ABOUT MY SISTER'S DEATH.
TM TM TM
EH... ?
THAT'S... !
TM TM TM
I-INU-YASHA-- !
SHIPPŌ !

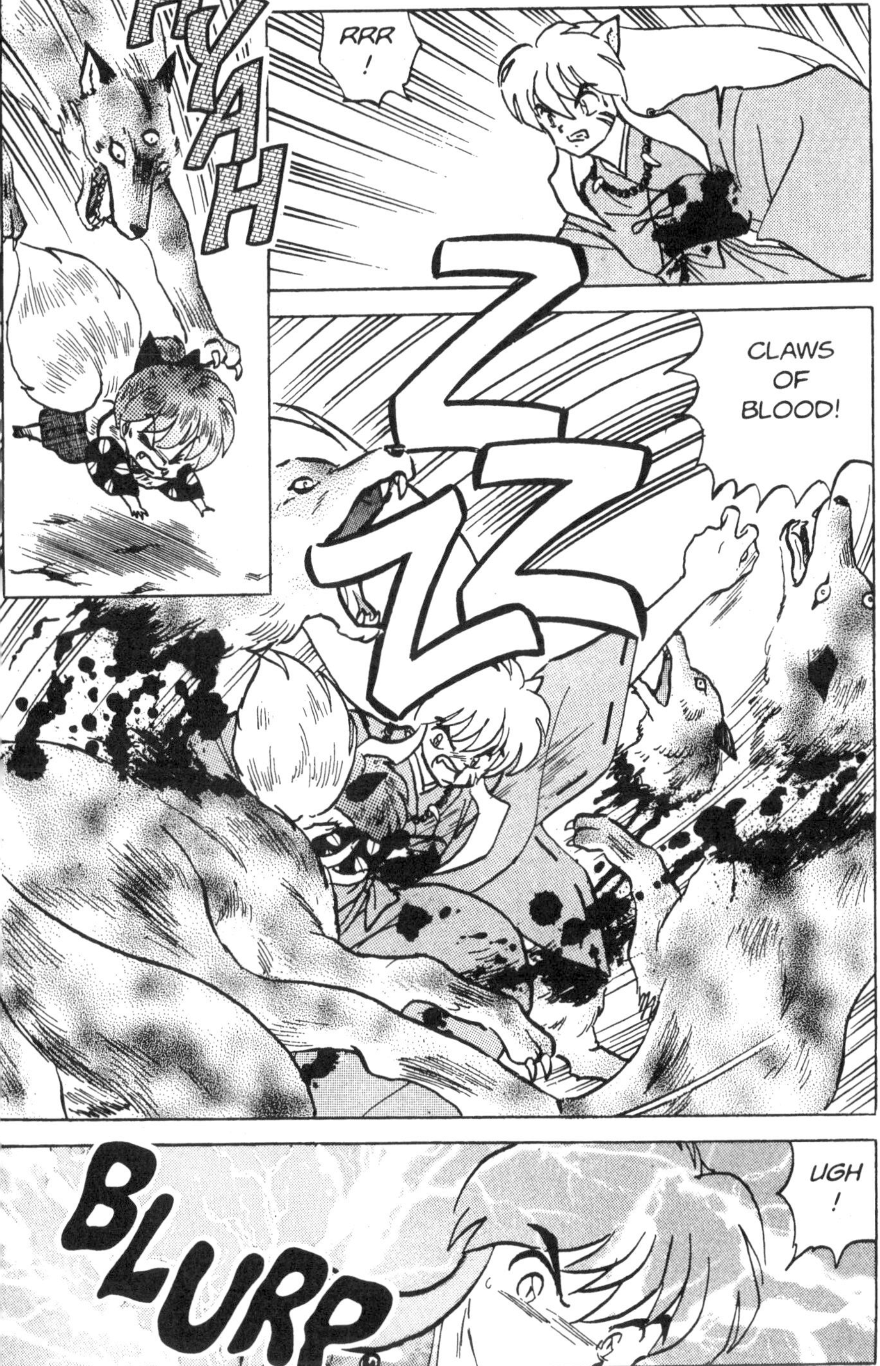
HYAH
RRR !
ZZZ
CLAWS OF BLOOD!
BLURP
UGH !

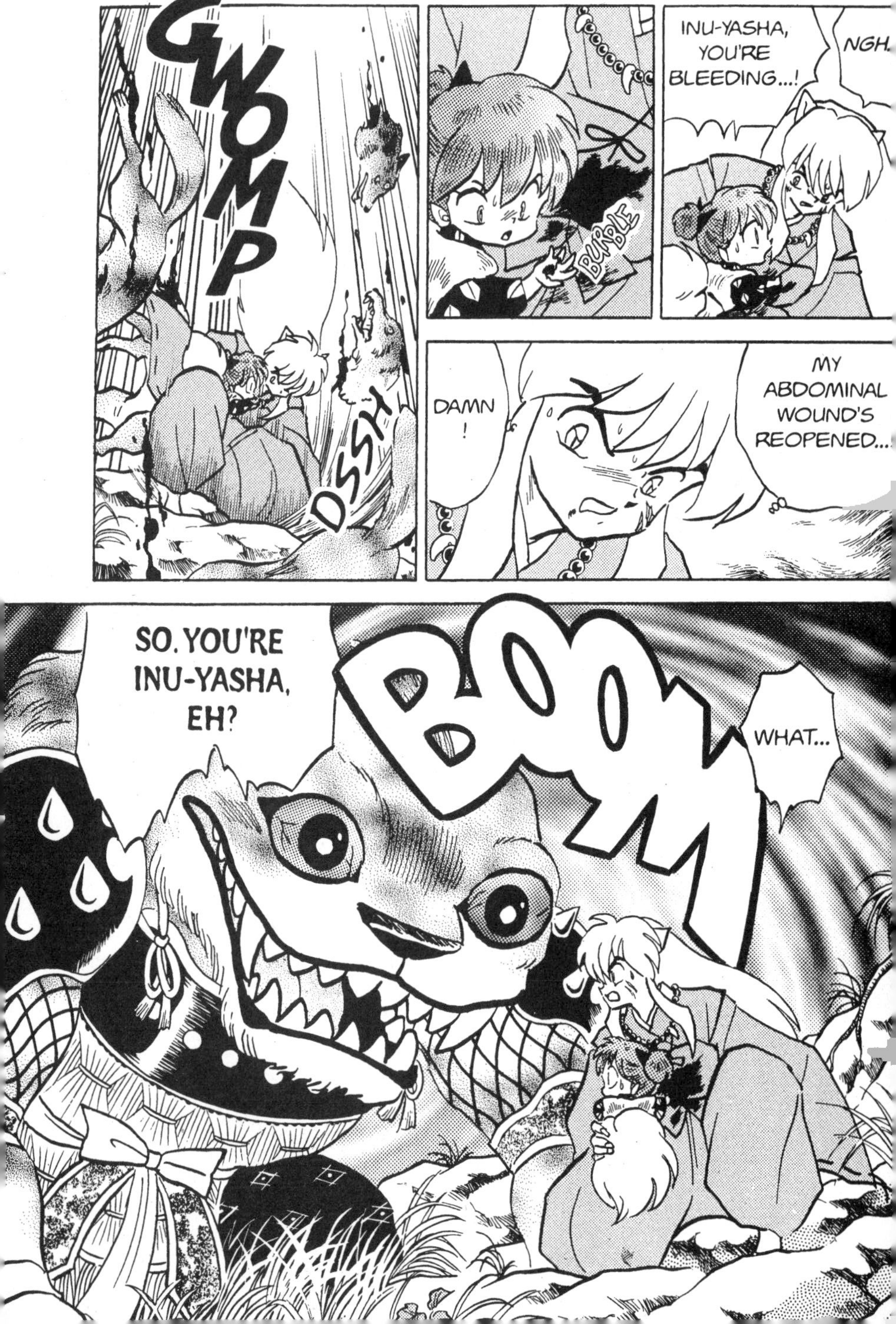
GWOMP
DSSH
BURBLE
INU-YASHA, YOU'RE BLEEDING...!
NGH.
DAMN !
MY ABDOMINAL WOUND'S REOPENED...
SO. YOU'RE INU-YASHA, EH?
BOOM
WHAT...

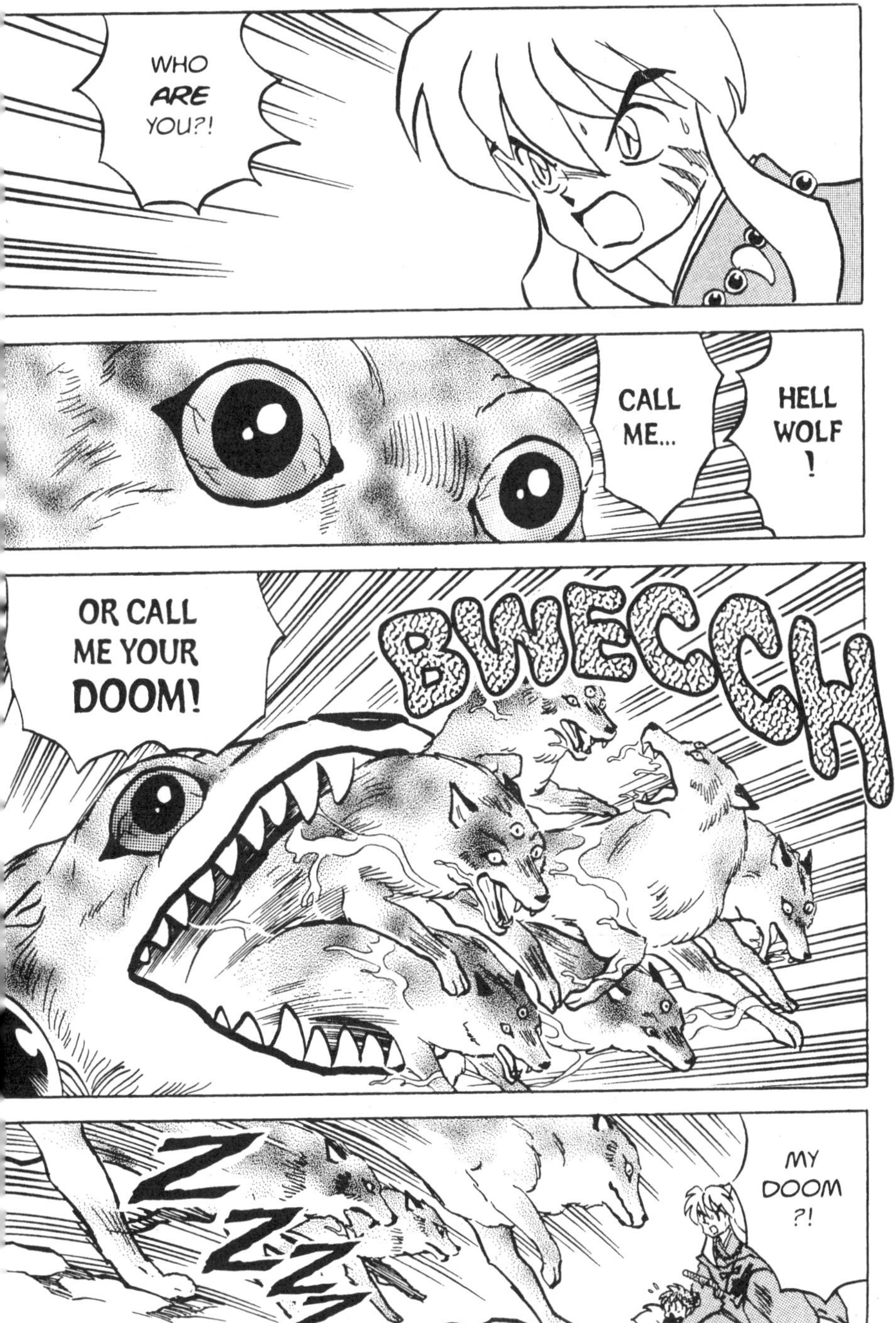
WHO ARE YOU?!
CALL ME...
HELL WOLF!
OR CALL ME YOUR DOOM!
BWECCH
ZZZZZ
MY DOOM?!

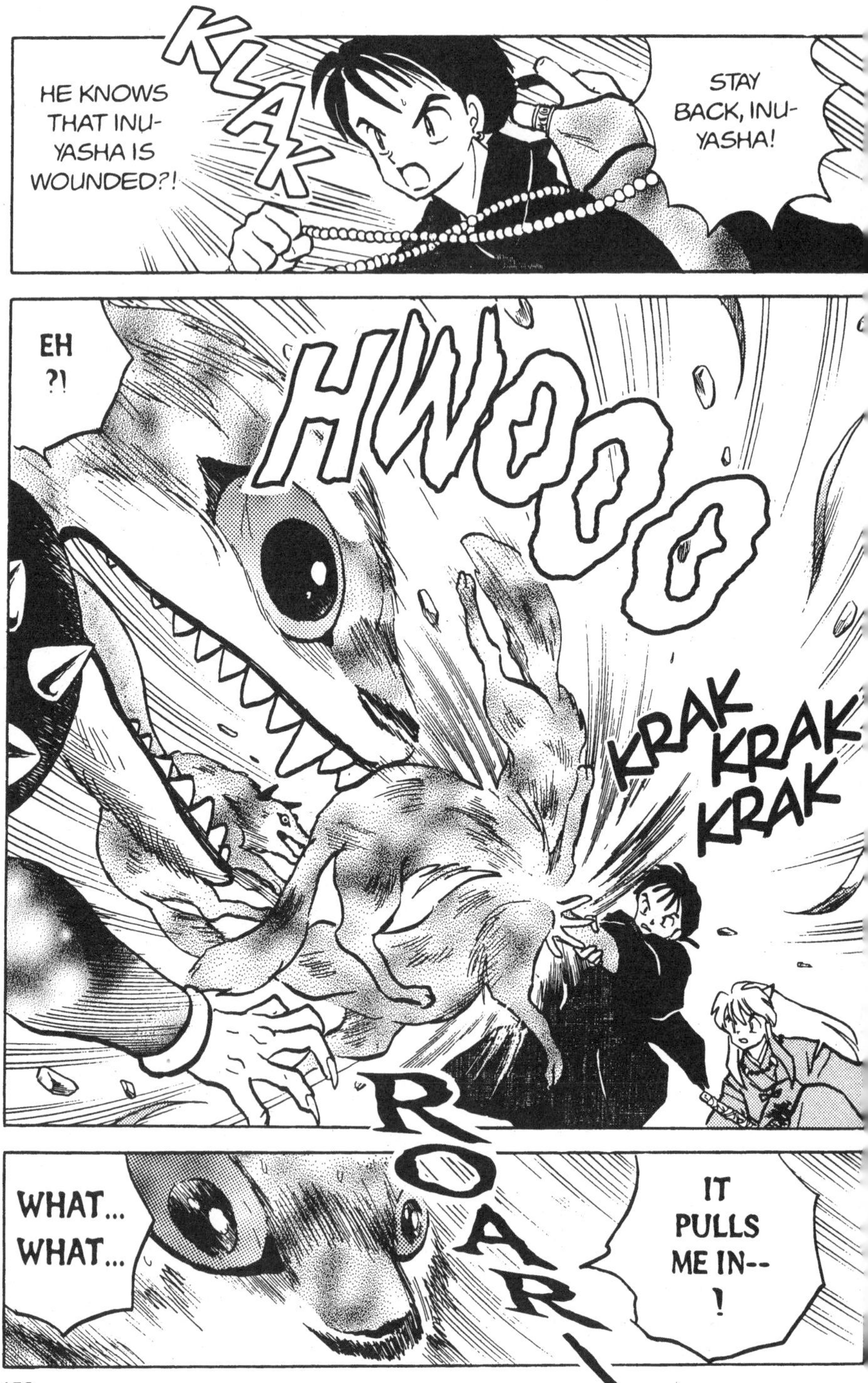
KLAK
HE KNOWS THAT INU-YASHA IS WOUNDED?!
STAY BACK, INU-YASHA!
EH ?!
HWOOOO
KRAK KRAK KRAK
ROAR!...
WHAT... WHAT...
IT PULLS ME IN-- !

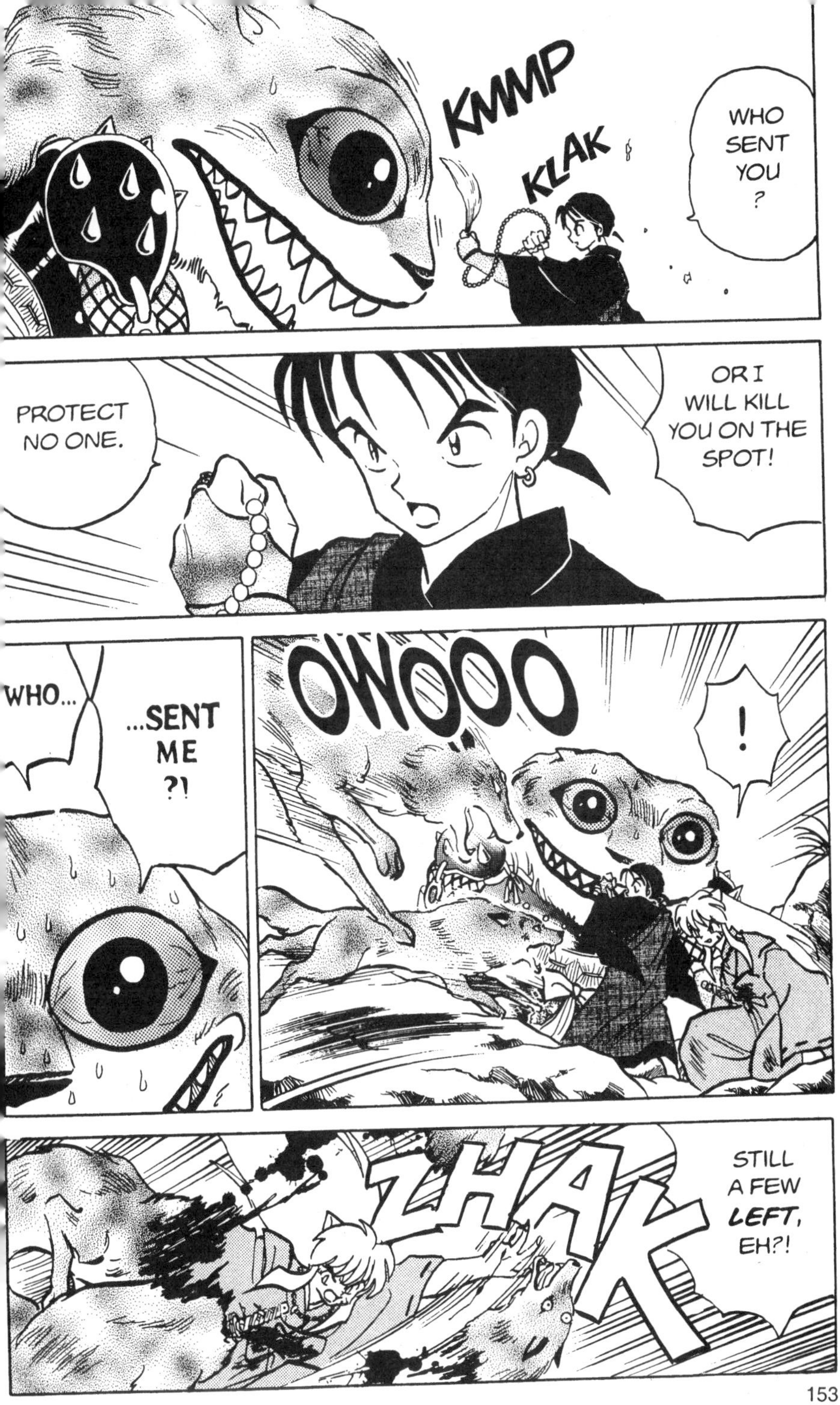
KMMP
KLAK
WHO SENT YOU ?
PROTECT NO ONE.
OR I WILL KILL YOU ON THE SPOT!
WHO...
...SENT ME ?!
OWOOO
!
ZHAK
STILL A FEW LEFT, EH?!

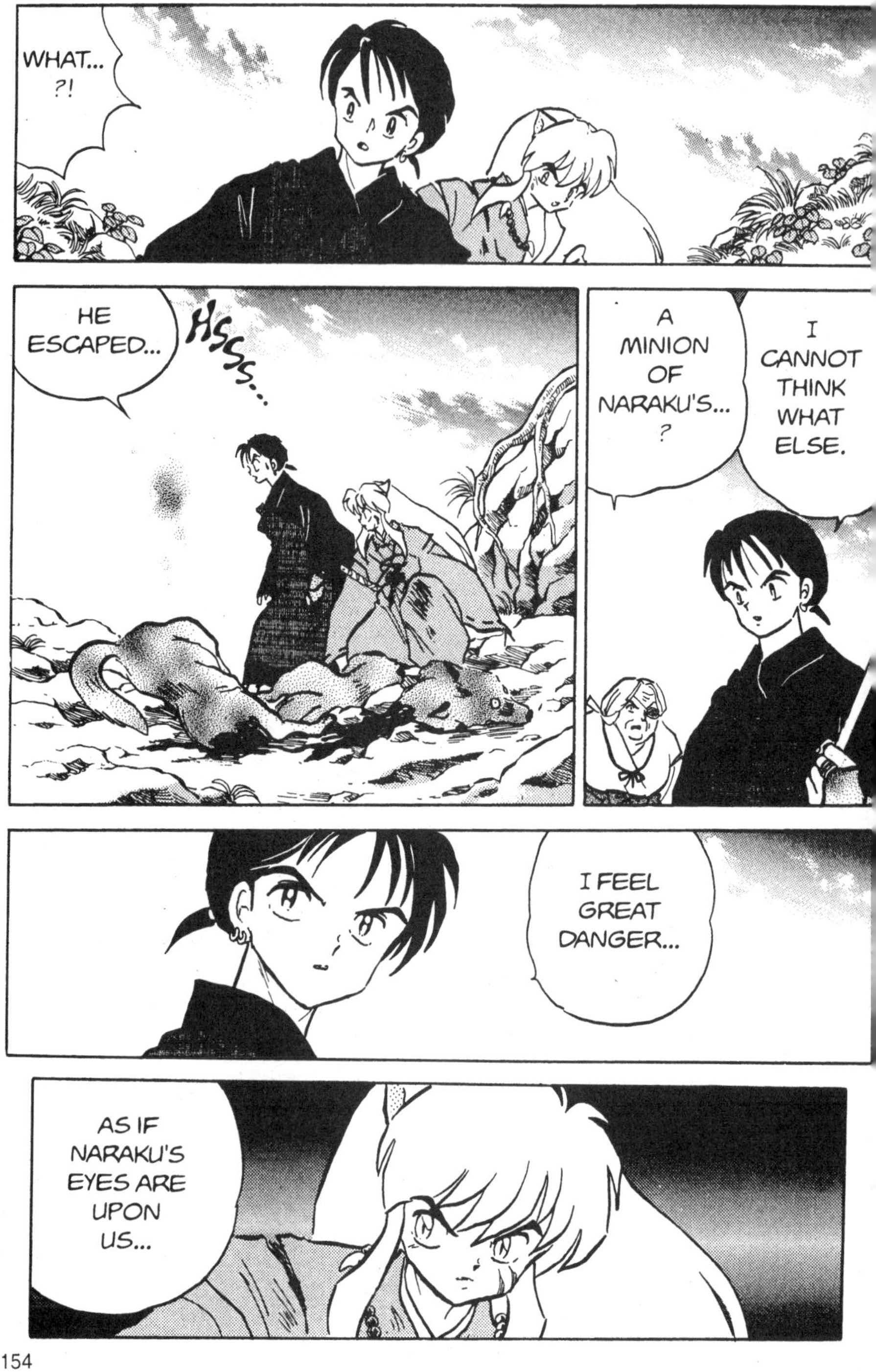

WHAT... ?!
HE ESCAPED...
HSSSS...
A MINION OF NARAKU'S...?
I CANNOT THINK WHAT ELSE.
I FEEL GREAT DANGER...
AS IF NARAKU'S EYES ARE UPON US...

SCROLL NINE

WHEN WE ARE TWO

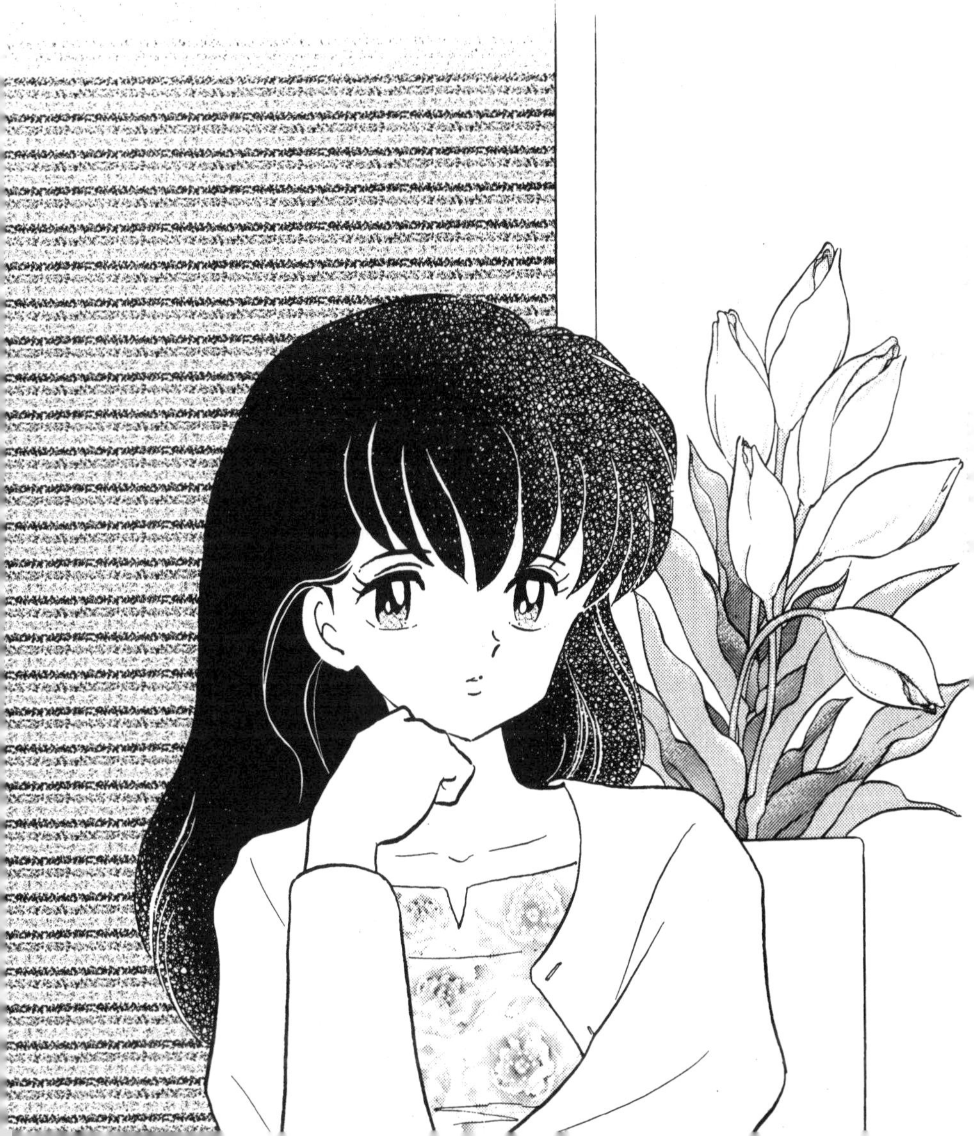

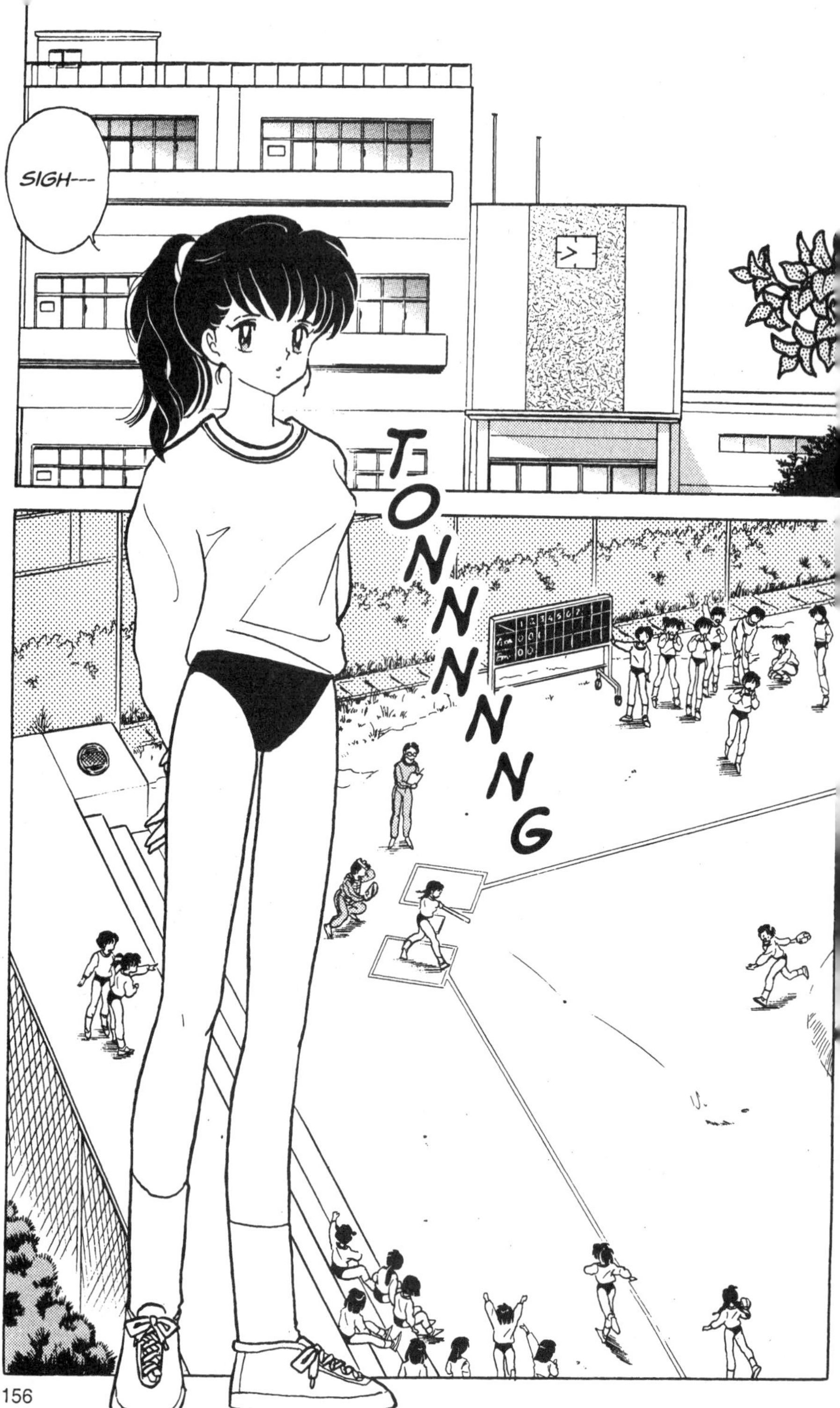
SIGH---
TONNNNG

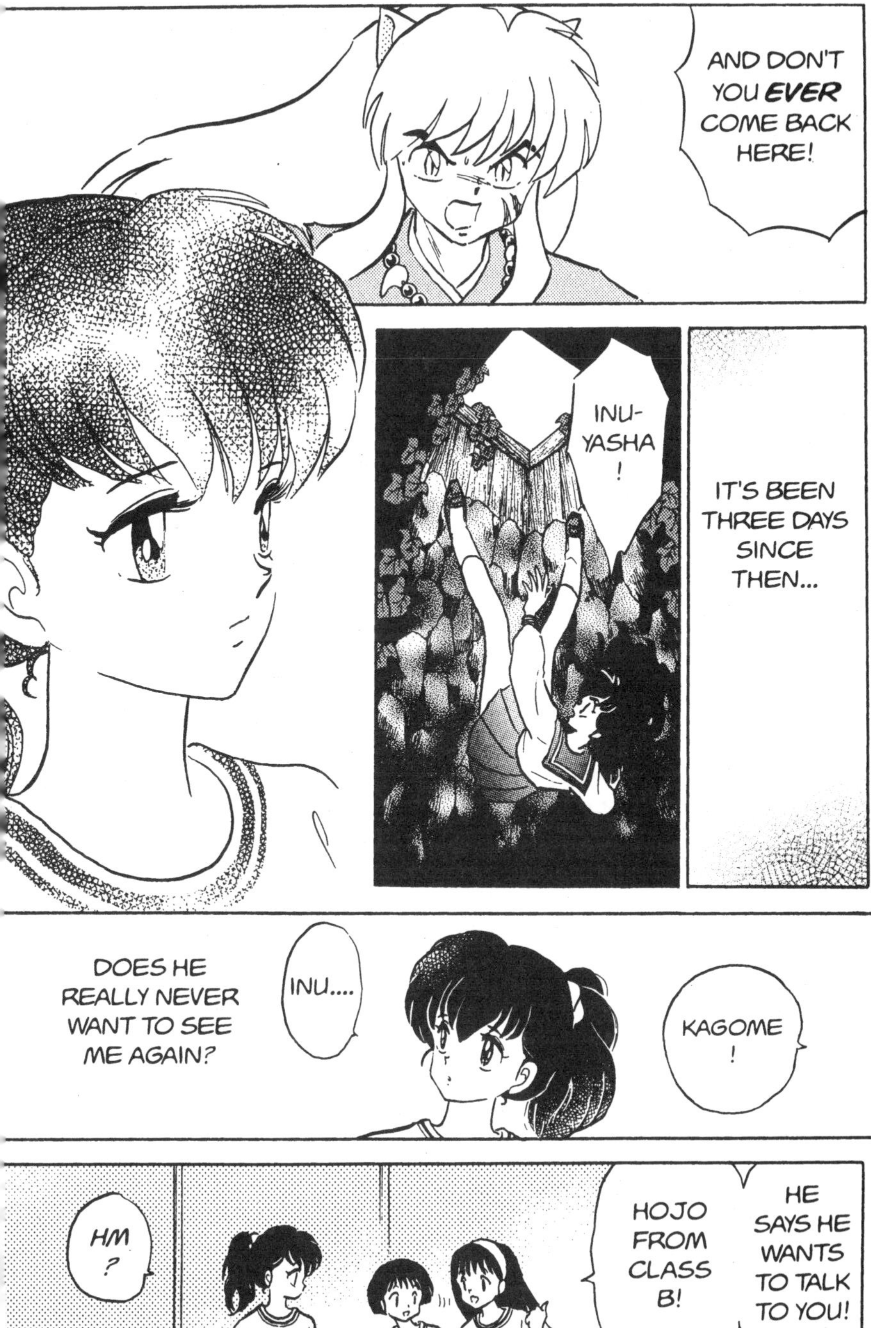
AND DON'T YOU **EVER** COME BACK HERE!
INU-YASHA!
IT'S BEEN THREE DAYS SINCE THEN...
DOES HE REALLY NEVER WANT TO SEE ME AGAIN?
INU....
KAGOME!
HM?
HOJO FROM CLASS B!
HE SAYS HE WANTS TO TALK TO YOU!

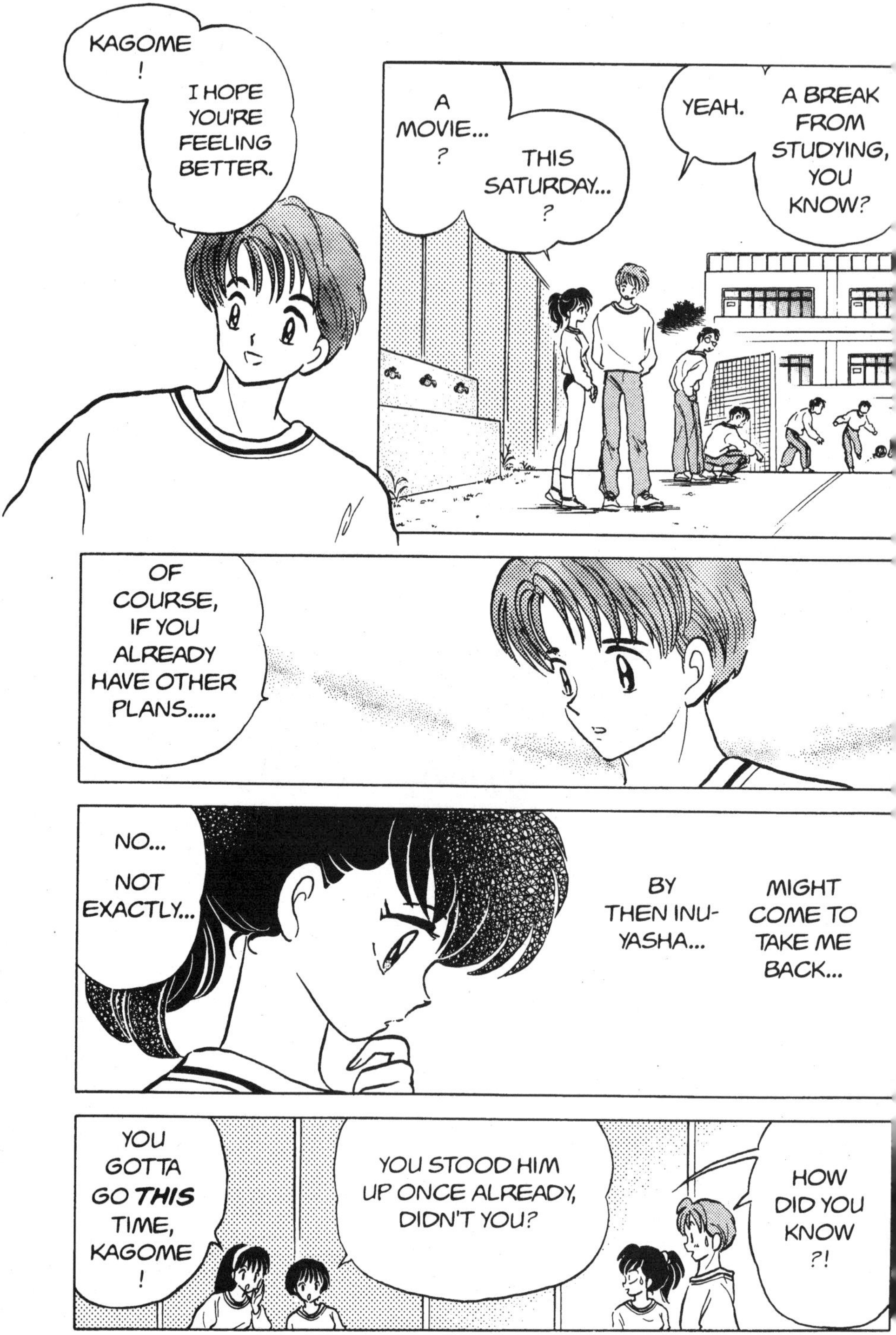
KAGOME! I HOPE YOU'RE FEELING BETTER.
A MOVIE...? THIS SATURDAY...?
YEAH. A BREAK FROM STUDYING, YOU KNOW?
OF COURSE, IF YOU ALREADY HAVE OTHER PLANS.....
NO... NOT EXACTLY...
BY THEN INU-YASHA...
MIGHT COME TO TAKE ME BACK...
YOU GOTTA GO **THIS** TIME, KAGOME!
YOU STOOD HIM UP ONCE ALREADY, DIDN'T YOU?
HOW DID YOU KNOW?!

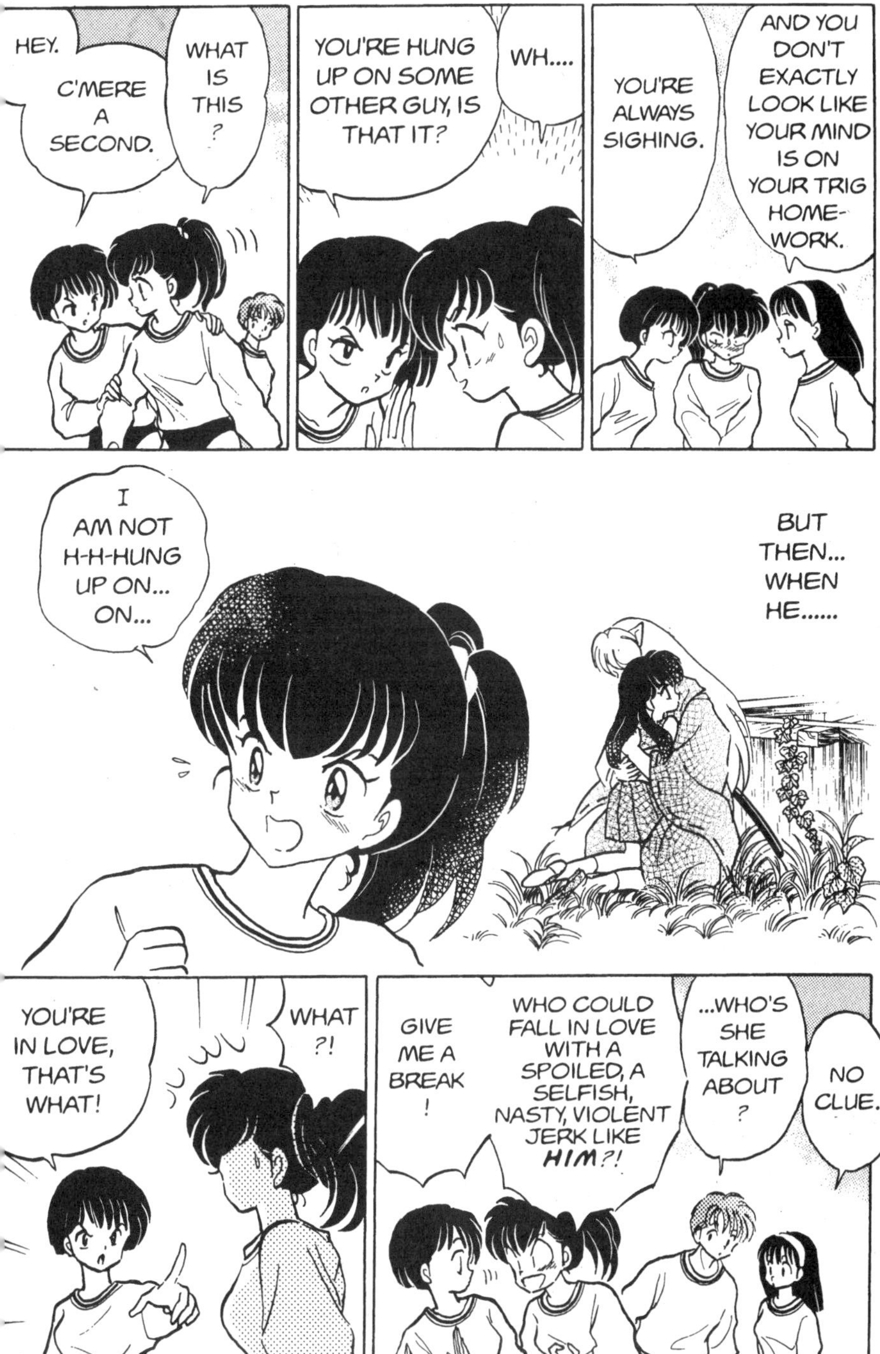
HEY. C'MERE A SECOND.
WHAT IS THIS ?
YOU'RE HUNG UP ON SOME OTHER GUY, IS THAT IT?
WH....
YOU'RE ALWAYS SIGHING.
AND YOU DON'T EXACTLY LOOK LIKE YOUR MIND IS ON YOUR TRIG HOME-WORK.
I AM NOT H-H-HUNG UP ON... ON...
BUT THEN... WHEN HE......
YOU'RE IN LOVE, THAT'S WHAT!
WHAT ?!
GIVE ME A BREAK !
WHO COULD FALL IN LOVE WITH A SPOILED, A SELFISH, NASTY, VIOLENT JERK LIKE HIM?!
...WHO'S SHE TALKING ABOUT ?
NO CLUE.

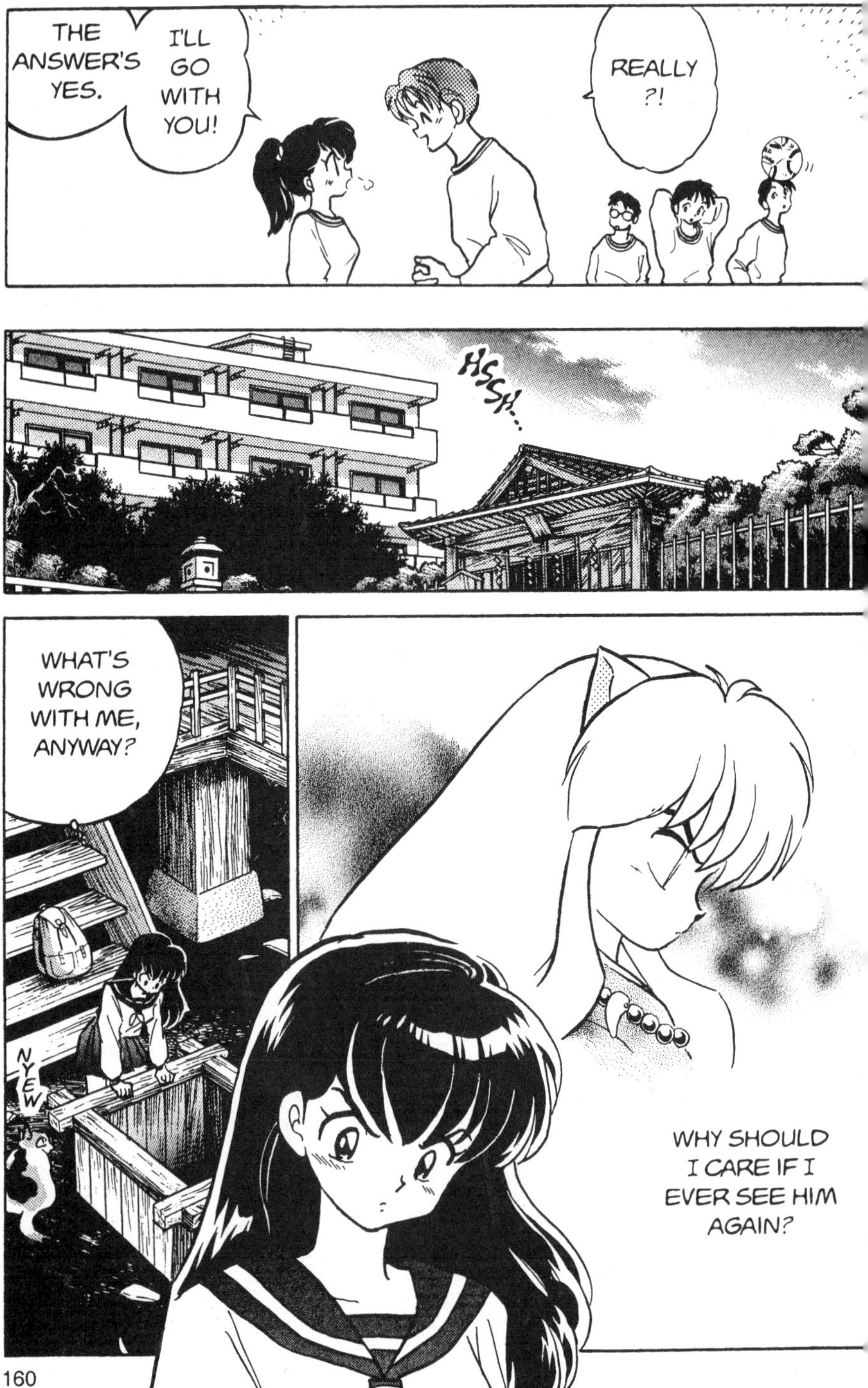
THE ANSWER'S YES.
I'LL GO WITH YOU!
REALLY ?!
HSSH...
WHAT'S WRONG WITH ME, ANYWAY?
NYEW
WHY SHOULD I CARE IF I EVER SEE HIM AGAIN?

...

WMM

HYAH!

NNNKH

MROWR

STILL NO USE...

INU-YASHA...

I WONDER WHAT YOU'RE DOING RIGHT NOW...

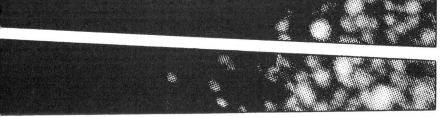

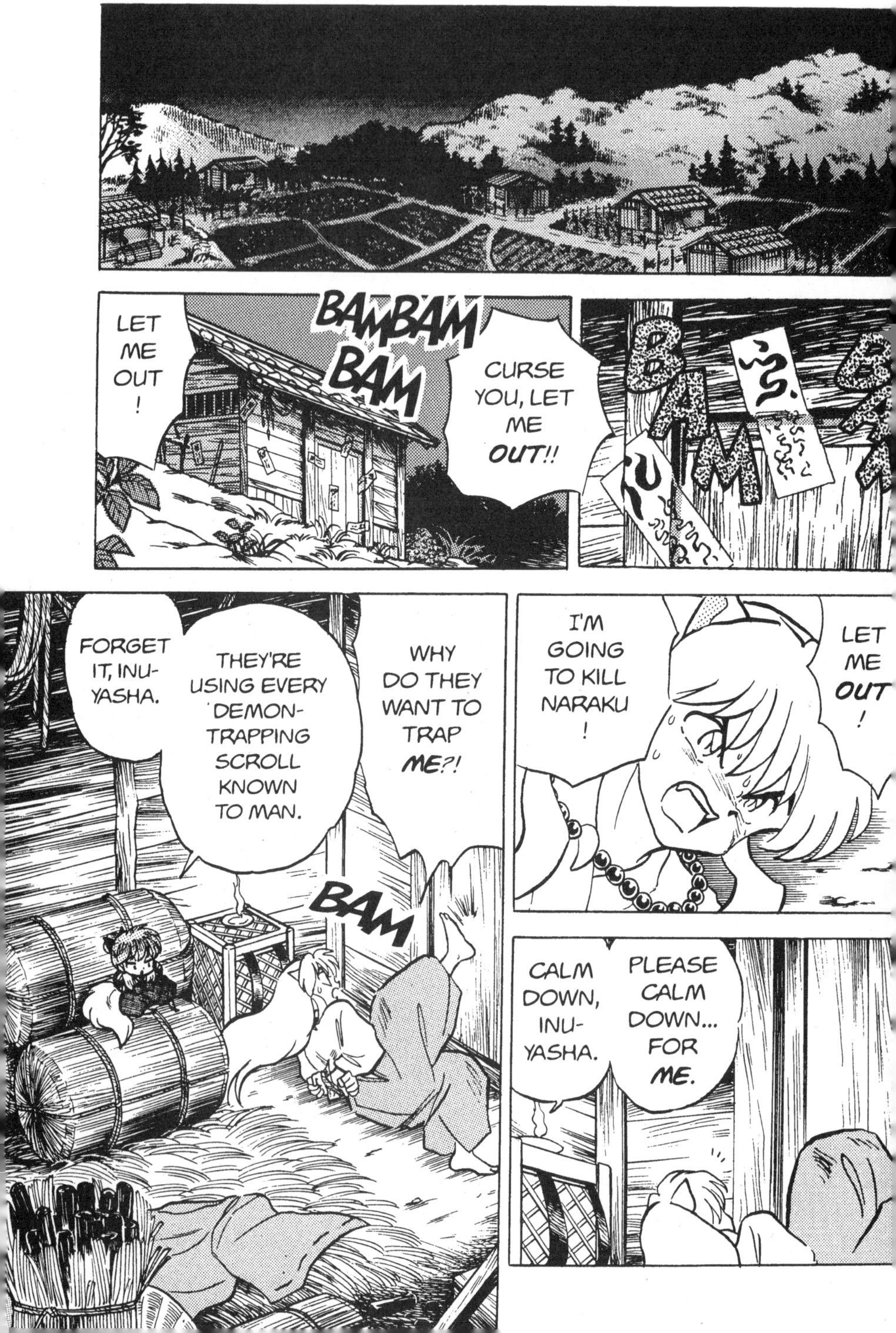
LET ME OUT!
BAMBAM BAM
CURSE YOU, LET ME OUT!!
BAM
BAM
FORGET IT, INU-YASHA.
THEY'RE USING EVERY DEMON-TRAPPING SCROLL KNOWN TO MAN.
WHY DO THEY WANT TO TRAP ME?!
BAM
I'M GOING TO KILL NARAKU!
LET ME OUT!
CALM DOWN, INU-YASHA.
PLEASE CALM DOWN... FOR ME.

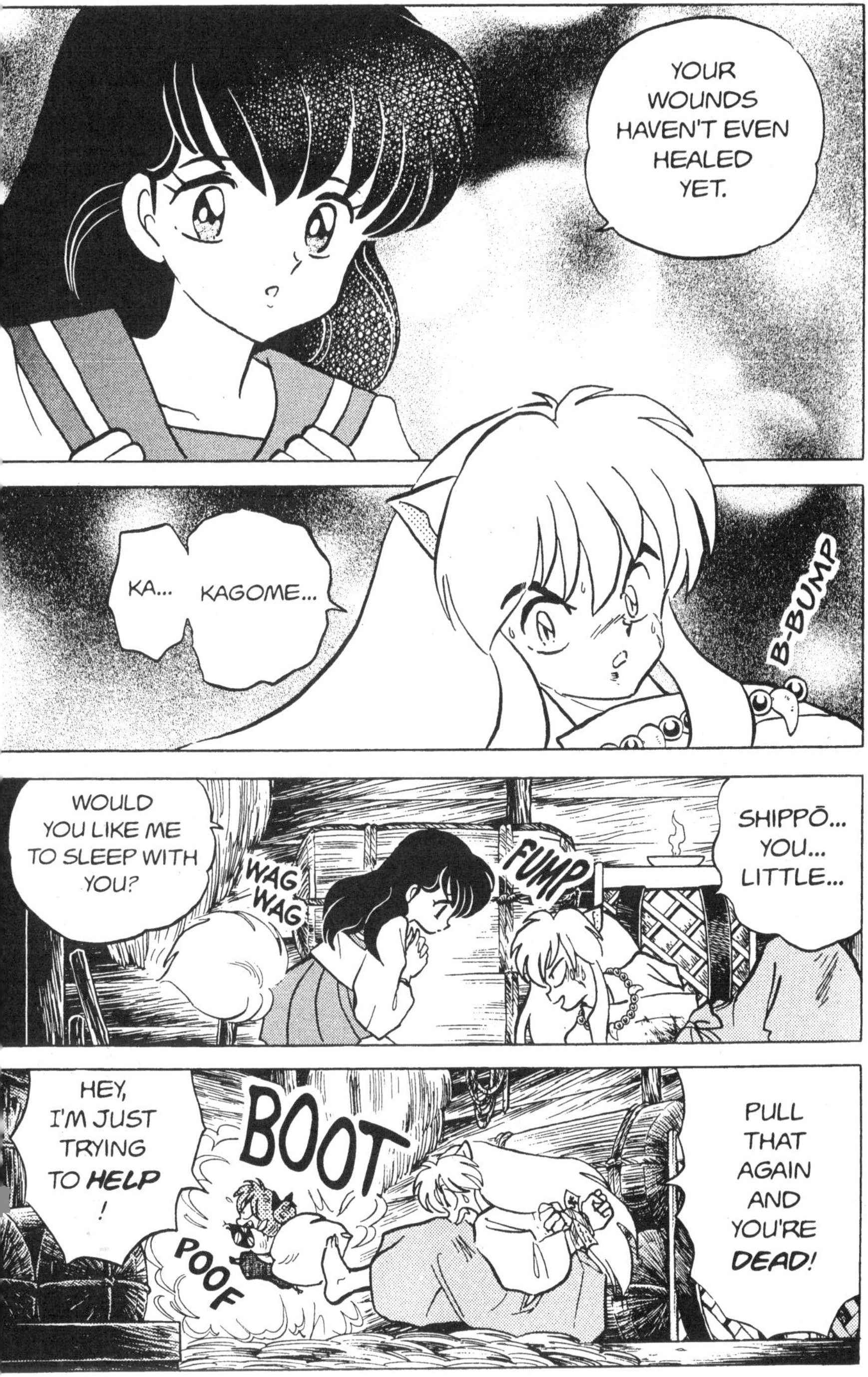
YOUR WOUNDS HAVEN'T EVEN HEALED YET.
KA... KAGOME...
B-BUMP
WOULD YOU LIKE ME TO SLEEP WITH YOU?
WAG WAG
FUMP
SHIPPŌ... YOU... LITTLE...
HEY, I'M JUST TRYING TO **HELP**!
BOOT
POOF
PULL THAT AGAIN AND YOU'RE **DEAD**!

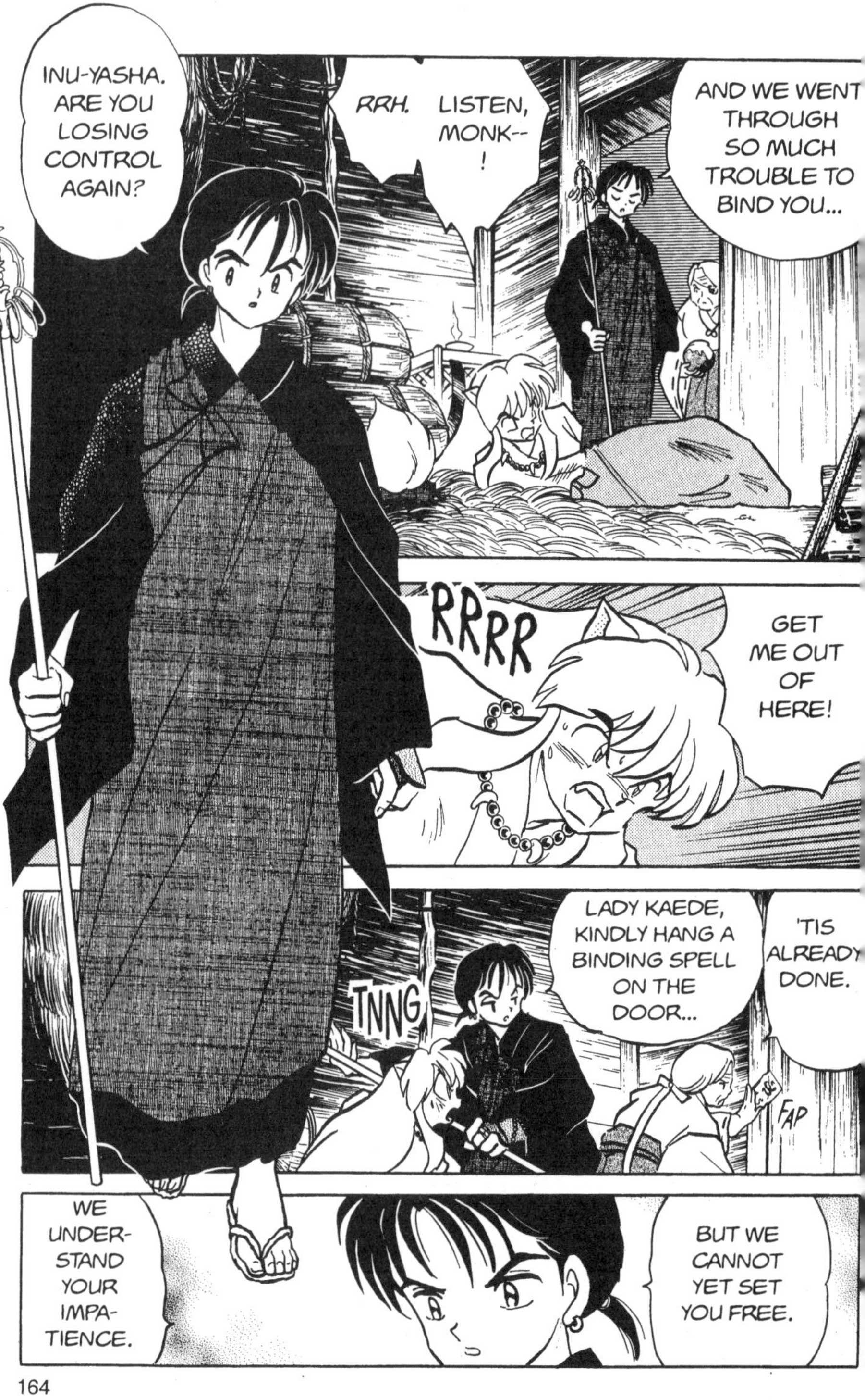
INU-YASHA. ARE YOU LOSING CONTROL AGAIN?
RRH.
LISTEN, MONK-- !
AND WE WENT THROUGH SO MUCH TROUBLE TO BIND YOU...
RRRR
GET ME OUT OF HERE!
TNNG
LADY KAEDE, KINDLY HANG A BINDING SPELL ON THE DOOR...
'TIS ALREADY DONE.
FAP
WE UNDER-STAND YOUR IMPA-TIENCE.
BUT WE CANNOT YET SET YOU FREE.

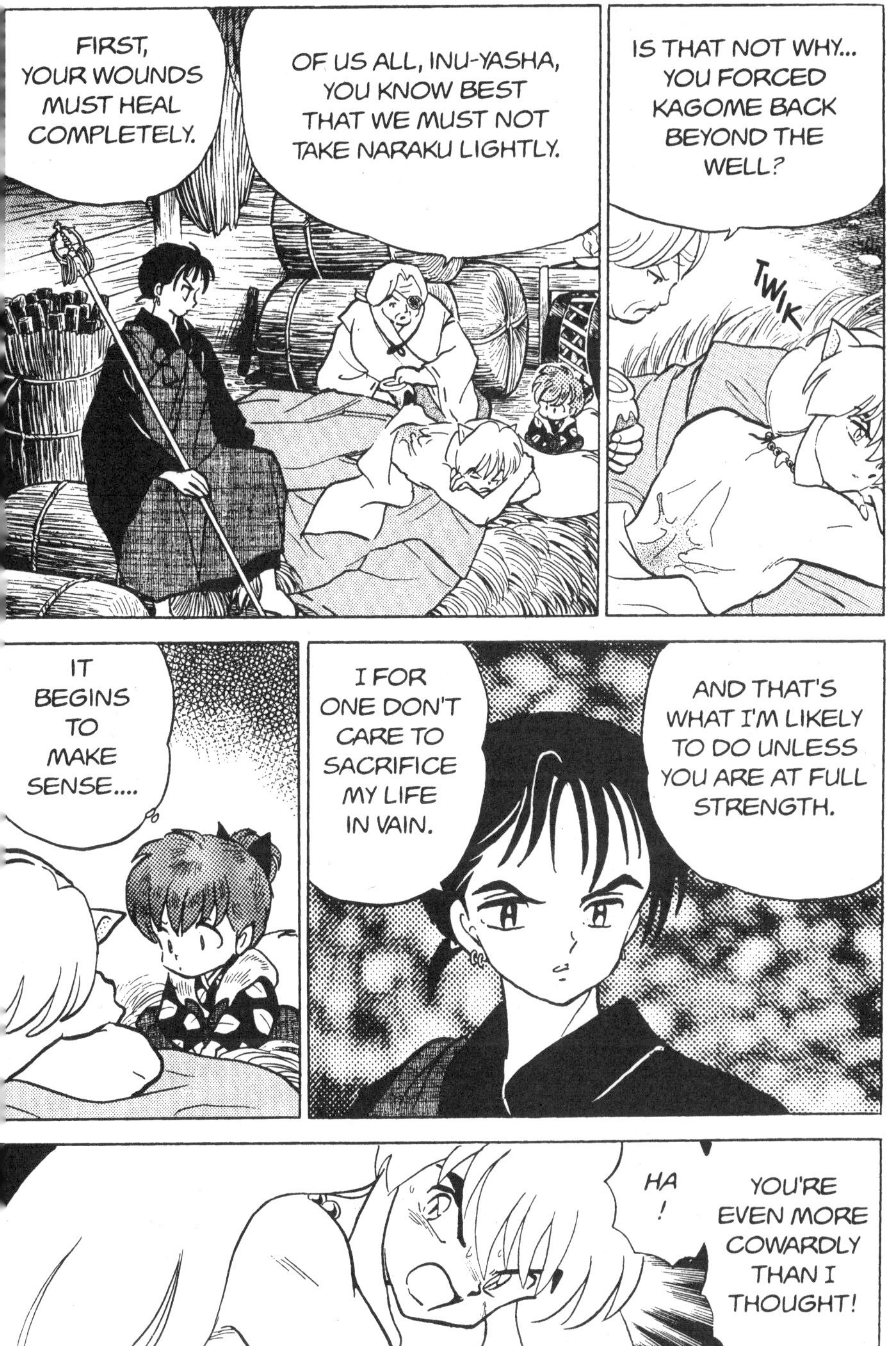
FIRST, YOUR WOUNDS MUST HEAL COMPLETELY.
OF US ALL, INU-YASHA, YOU KNOW BEST THAT WE MUST NOT TAKE NARAKU LIGHTLY.
IS THAT NOT WHY... YOU FORCED KAGOME BACK BEYOND THE WELL?
TWIK
IT BEGINS TO MAKE SENSE....
I FOR ONE DON'T CARE TO SACRIFICE MY LIFE IN VAIN.
AND THAT'S WHAT I'M LIKELY TO DO UNLESS YOU ARE AT FULL STRENGTH.
HA!
YOU'RE EVEN MORE COWARDLY THAN I THOUGHT!

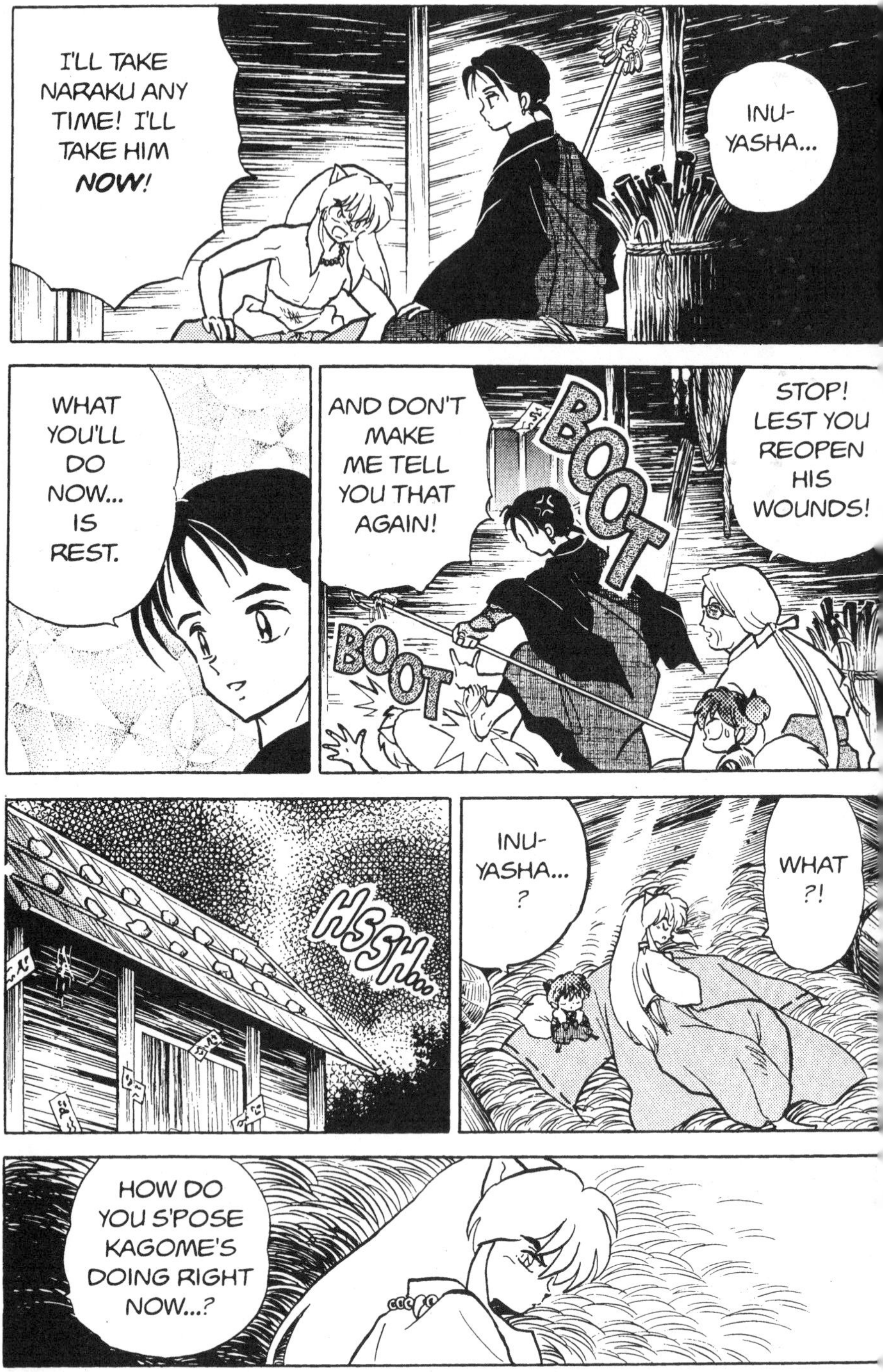
I'LL TAKE NARAKU ANY TIME! I'LL TAKE HIM NOW!
INU-YASHA...
WHAT YOU'LL DO NOW... IS REST.
AND DON'T MAKE ME TELL YOU THAT AGAIN!
BOOT
BOOT
STOP! LEST YOU REOPEN HIS WOUNDS!
HSSH...
INU-YASHA...?
WHAT?!
HOW DO YOU S'POSE KAGOME'S DOING RIGHT NOW...?

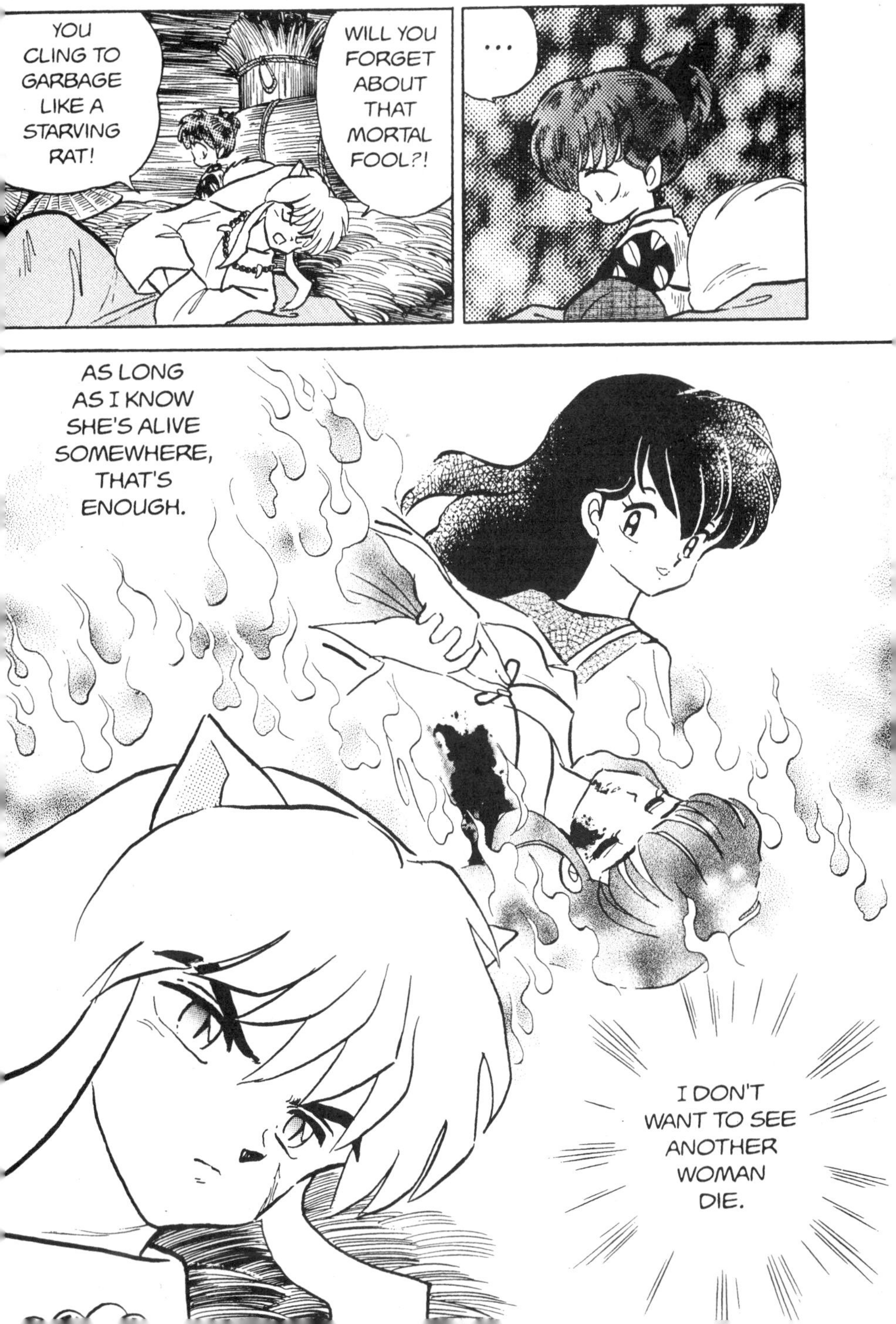
YOU CLING TO GARBAGE LIKE A STARVING RAT!
WILL YOU FORGET ABOUT THAT MORTAL FOOL?!
...
AS LONG AS I KNOW SHE'S ALIVE SOMEWHERE, THAT'S ENOUGH.
I DON'T WANT TO SEE ANOTHER WOMAN DIE.

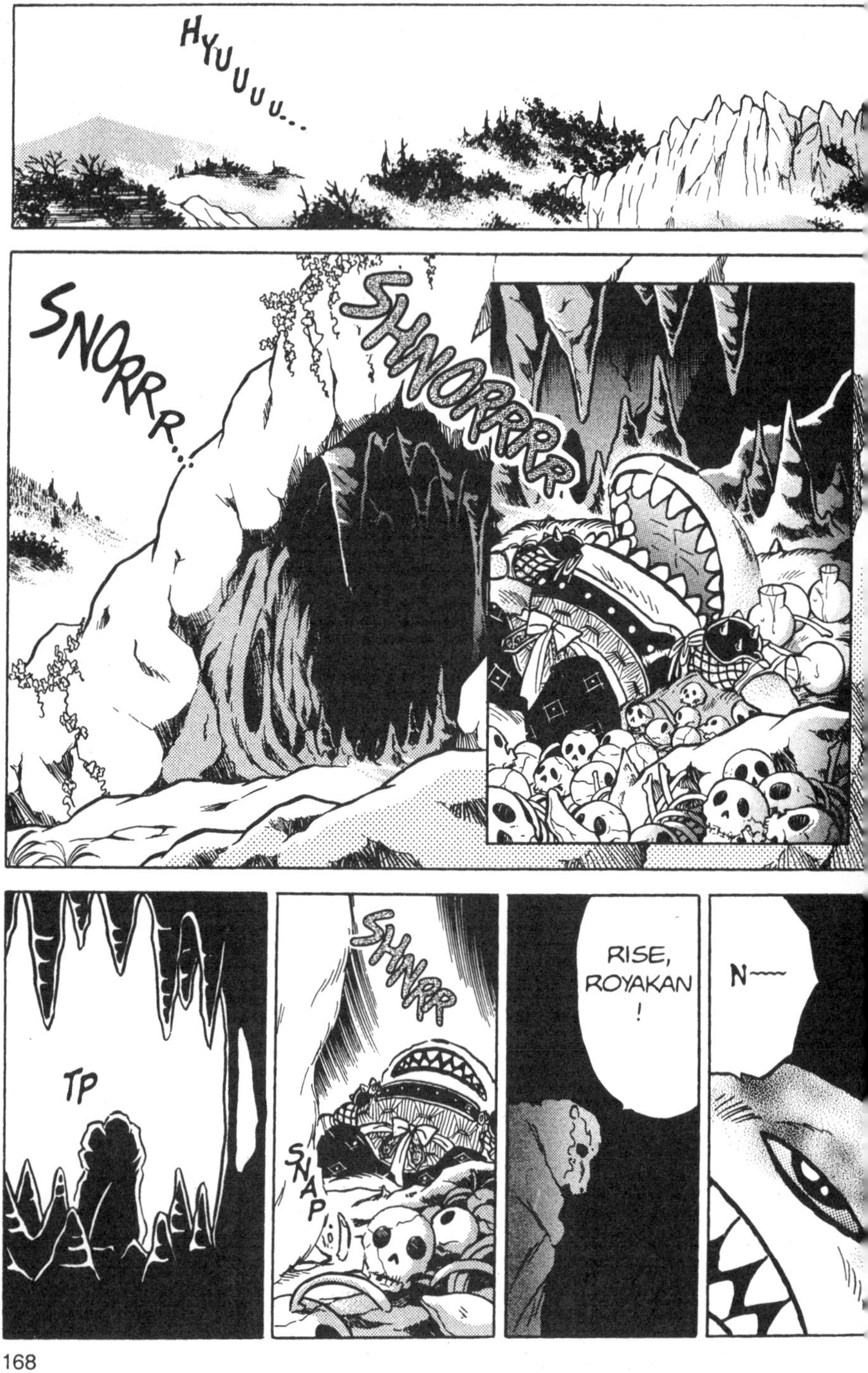

HYUUUU...
SNORRRR...
SHNORRRR
TP
SHNRR
SNAP
RISE, ROYAKAN!
N~~~

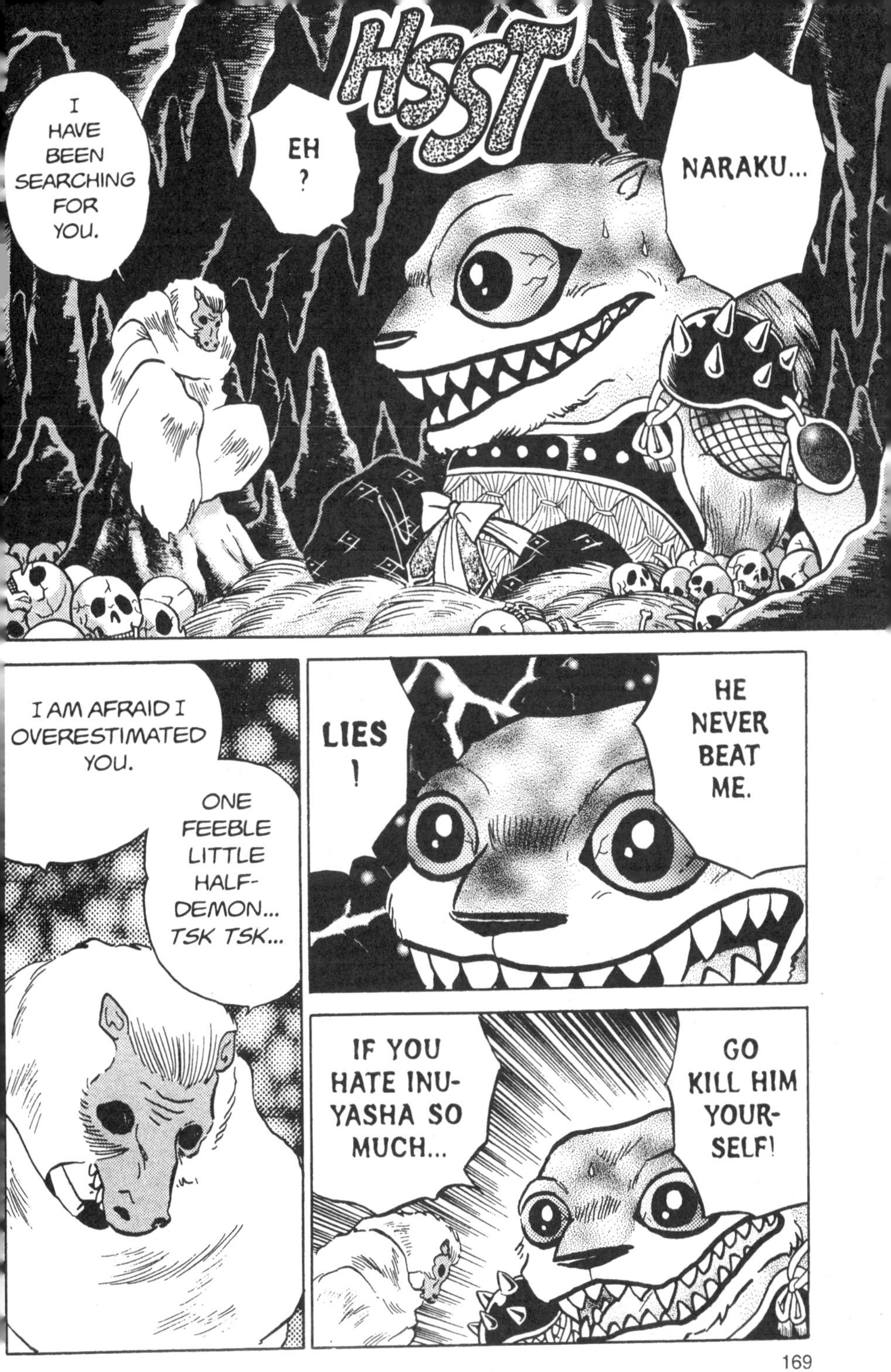
I HAVE BEEN SEARCHING FOR YOU.
EH?
HSST
NARAKU...
I AM AFRAID I OVERESTIMATED YOU.
ONE FEEBLE LITTLE HALF-DEMON... TSK TSK...
LIES!
HE NEVER BEAT ME.
IF YOU HATE INU-YASHA SO MUCH...
GO KILL HIM YOUR-SELF!

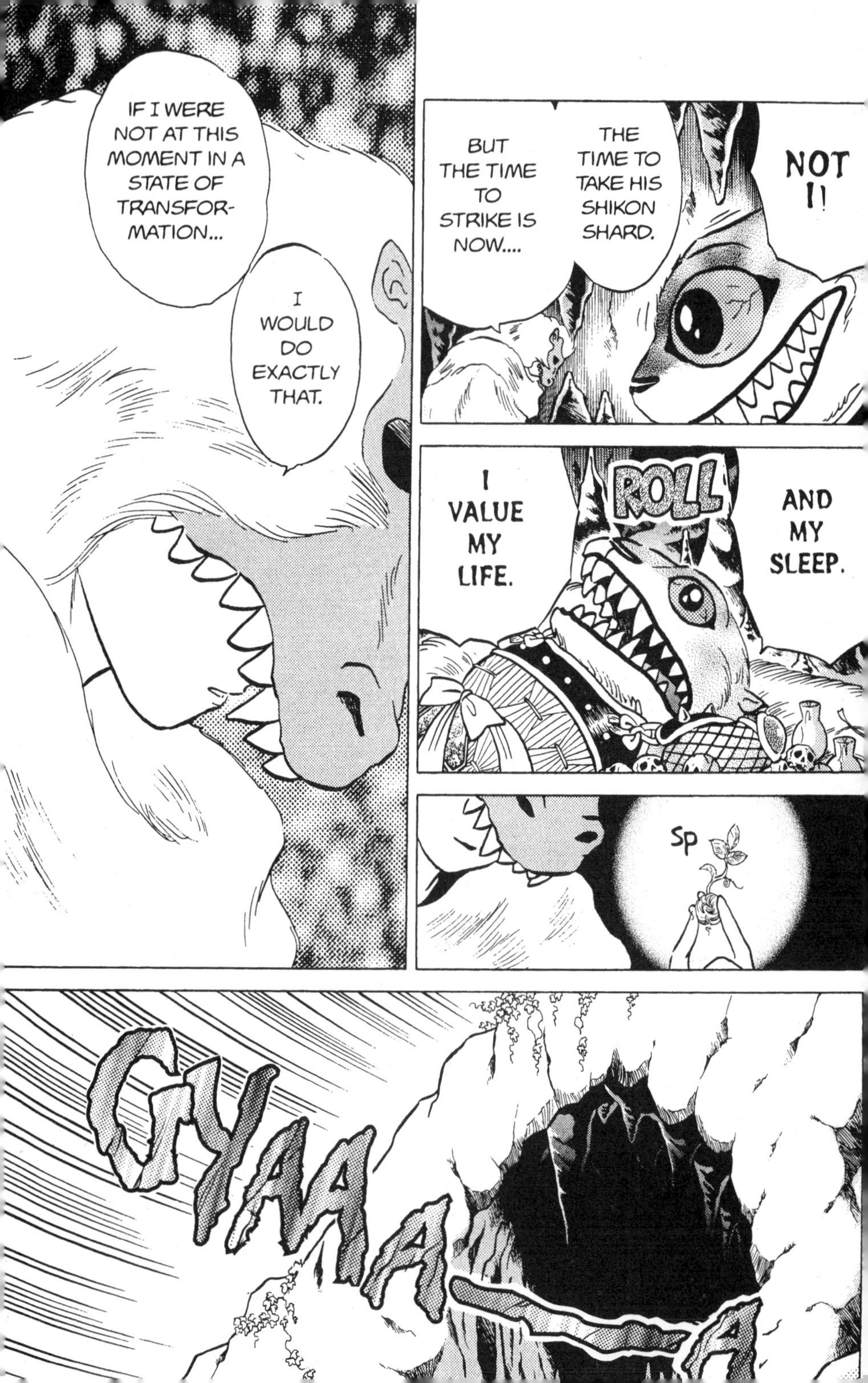
IF I WERE NOT AT THIS MOMENT IN A STATE OF TRANSFORMATION...
I WOULD DO EXACTLY THAT.
BUT THE TIME TO STRIKE IS NOW....
THE TIME TO TAKE HIS SHIKON SHARD.
NOT I!
I VALUE MY LIFE.
ROLL
AND MY SLEEP.
Sp
GYAAA-A

IT'S HOT!

MY~ HEAD!

EH ?!

SUU...

IN THAT SPROUT IS BURIED A SHIKON SHARD.

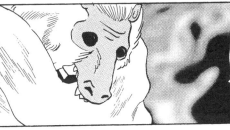

LEFT ALONE, ITS ROOTS WILL SPREAD AND TEAR YOUR SKULL APART.

NO!

I'LL PULL IT OUT!

DO SO, AND YOU WILL DIE.

YOU!

TAKE IT OUT!

I WILL BE HAPPY TO... AFTER YOU'VE DEFEATED INU-YASHA.

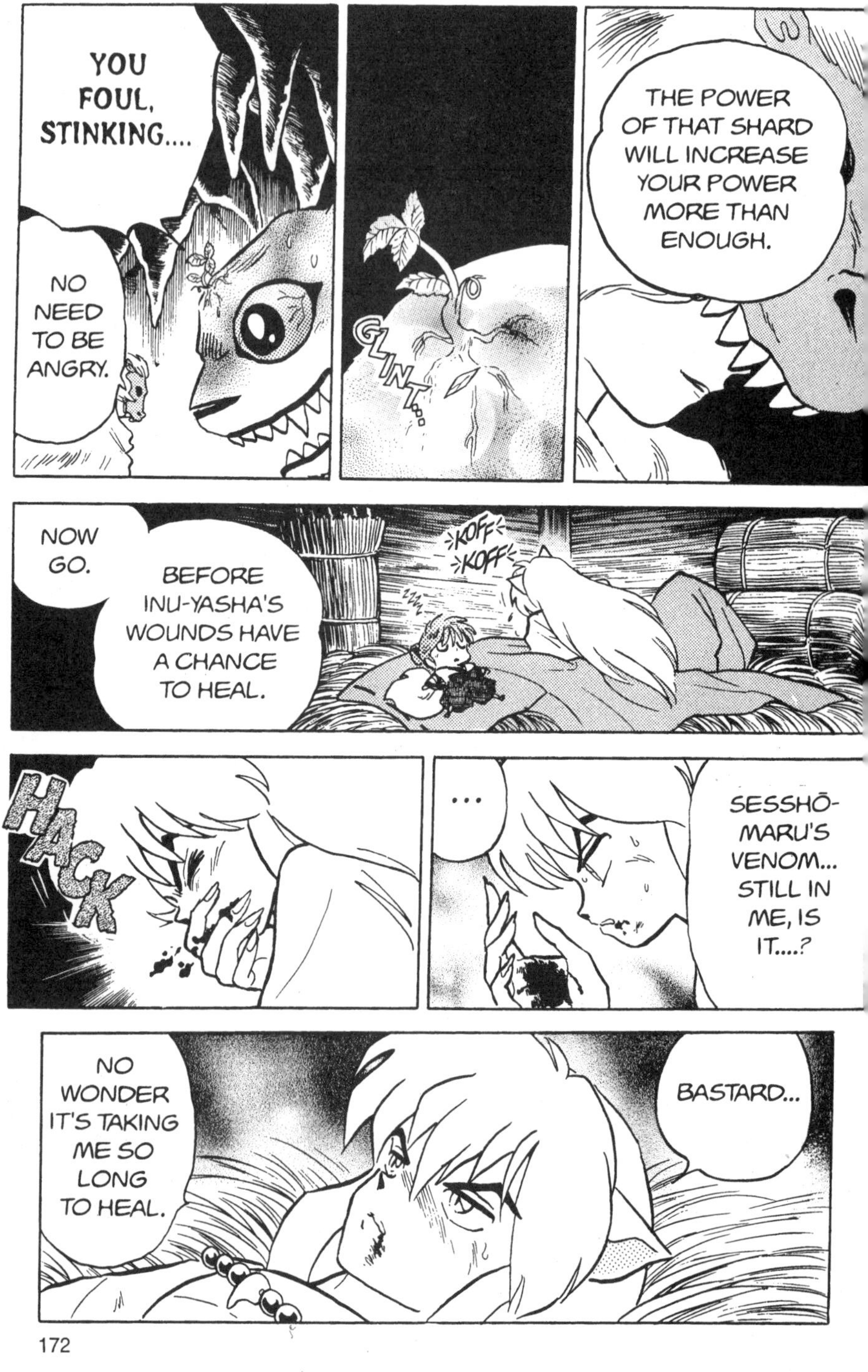
YOU FOUL, STINKING....
NO NEED TO BE ANGRY.
GLINT...
THE POWER OF THAT SHARD WILL INCREASE YOUR POWER MORE THAN ENOUGH.
NOW GO.
BEFORE INU-YASHA'S WOUNDS HAVE A CHANCE TO HEAL.
KOFF KOFF
HACK
...
SESSHŌ-MARU'S VENOM... STILL IN ME, IS IT....?
NO WONDER IT'S TAKING ME SO LONG TO HEAL.
BASTARD...

SCROLL TEN

THE PIERCED WALL

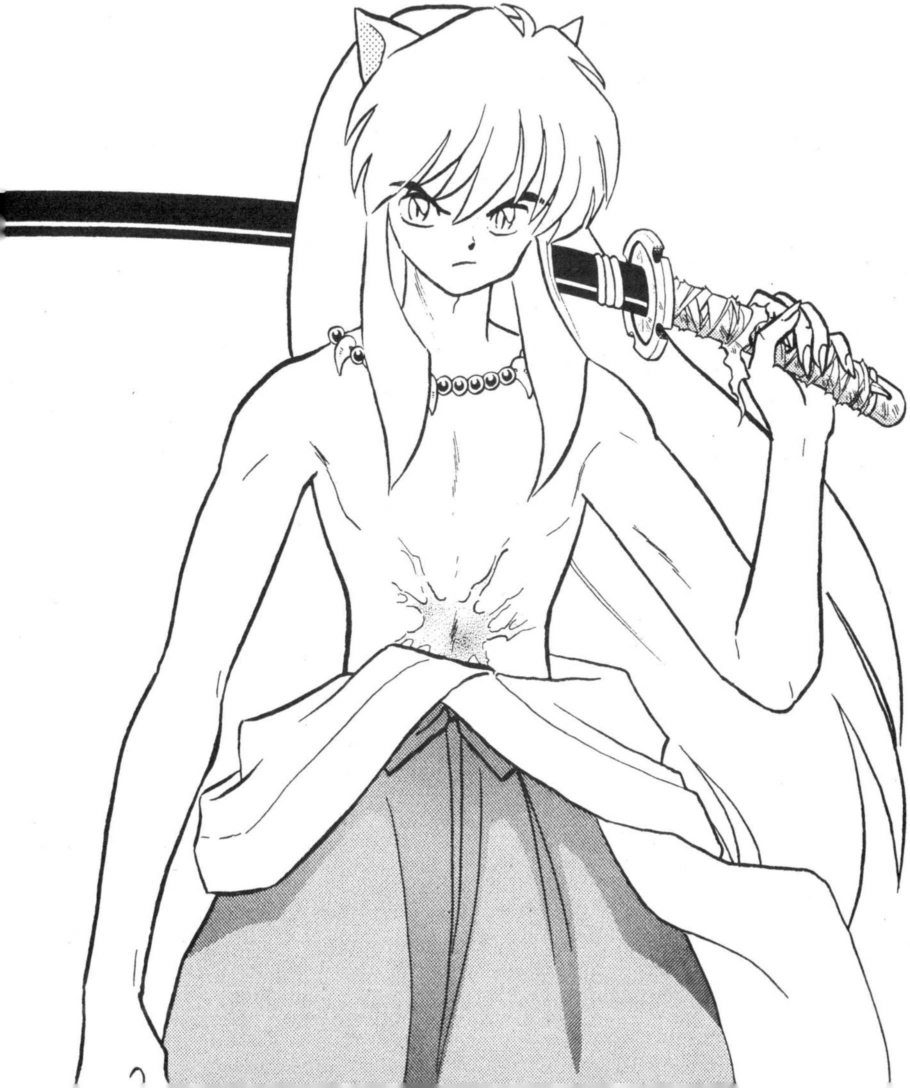

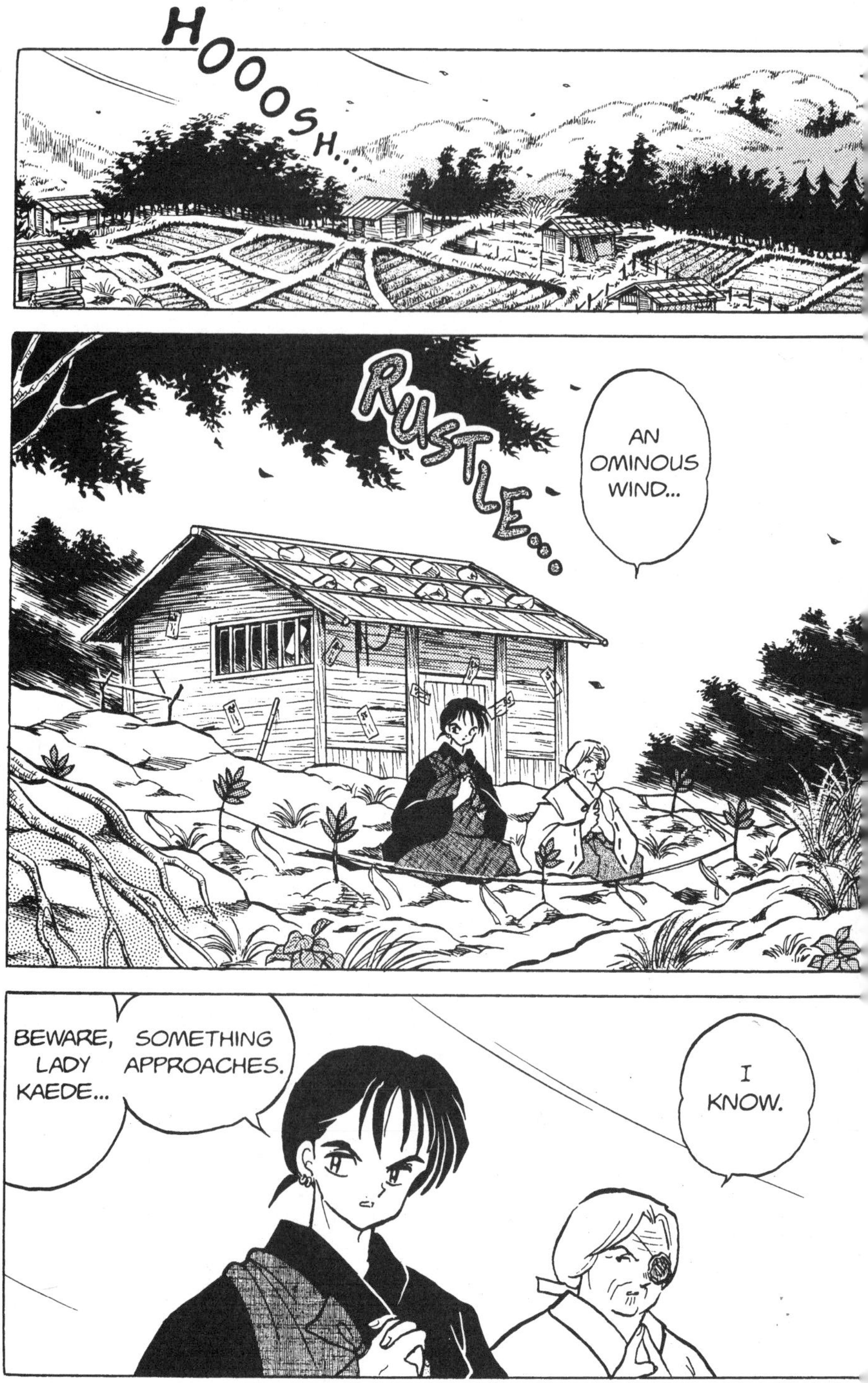
HOOOSH...
RUSTLE...
AN OMINOUS WIND...
BEWARE, LADY KAEDE...
SOMETHING APPROACHES.
I KNOW.

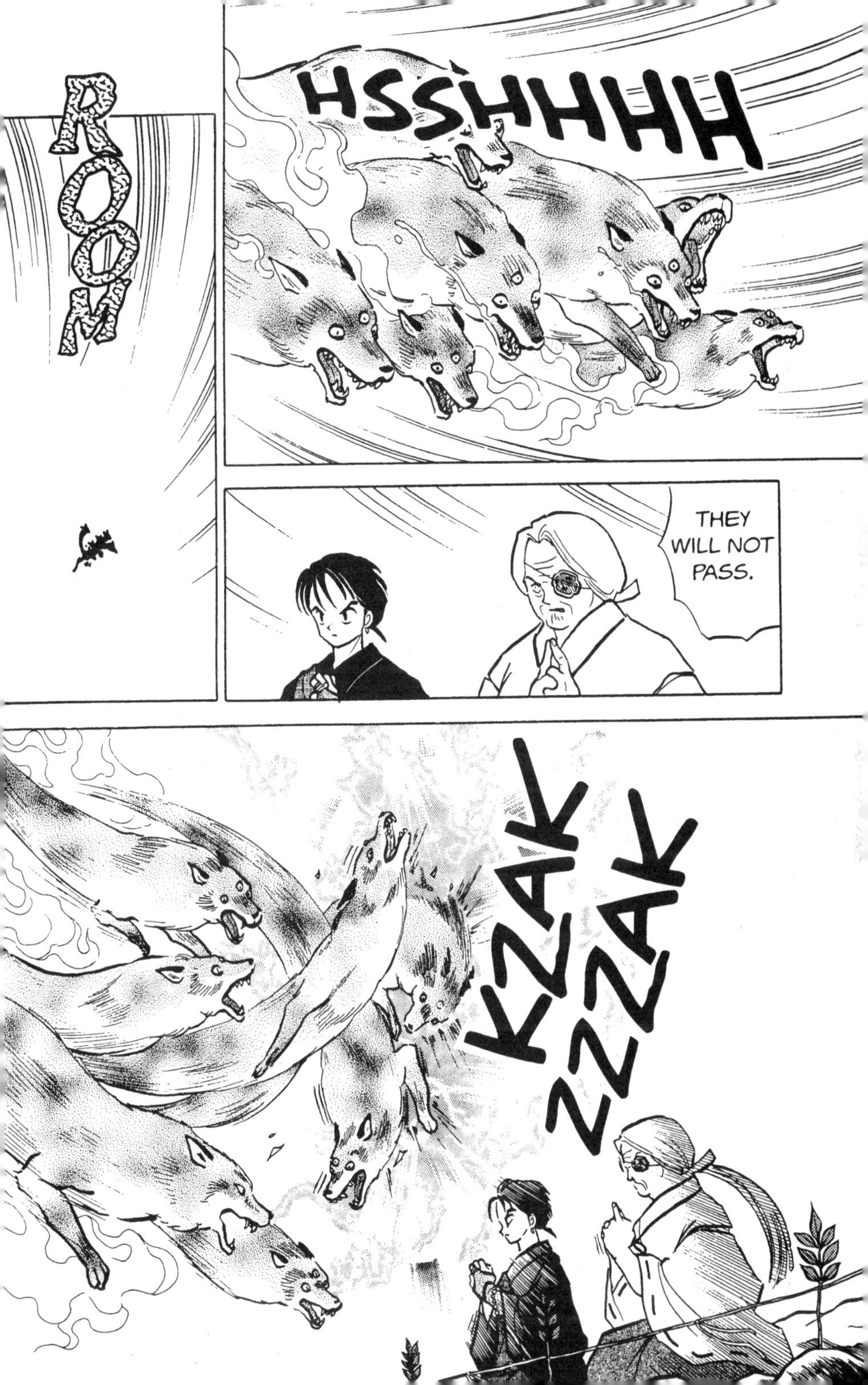
ROOM
HSSHHHH
THEY WILL NOT PASS.
KZAK
ZZZAK

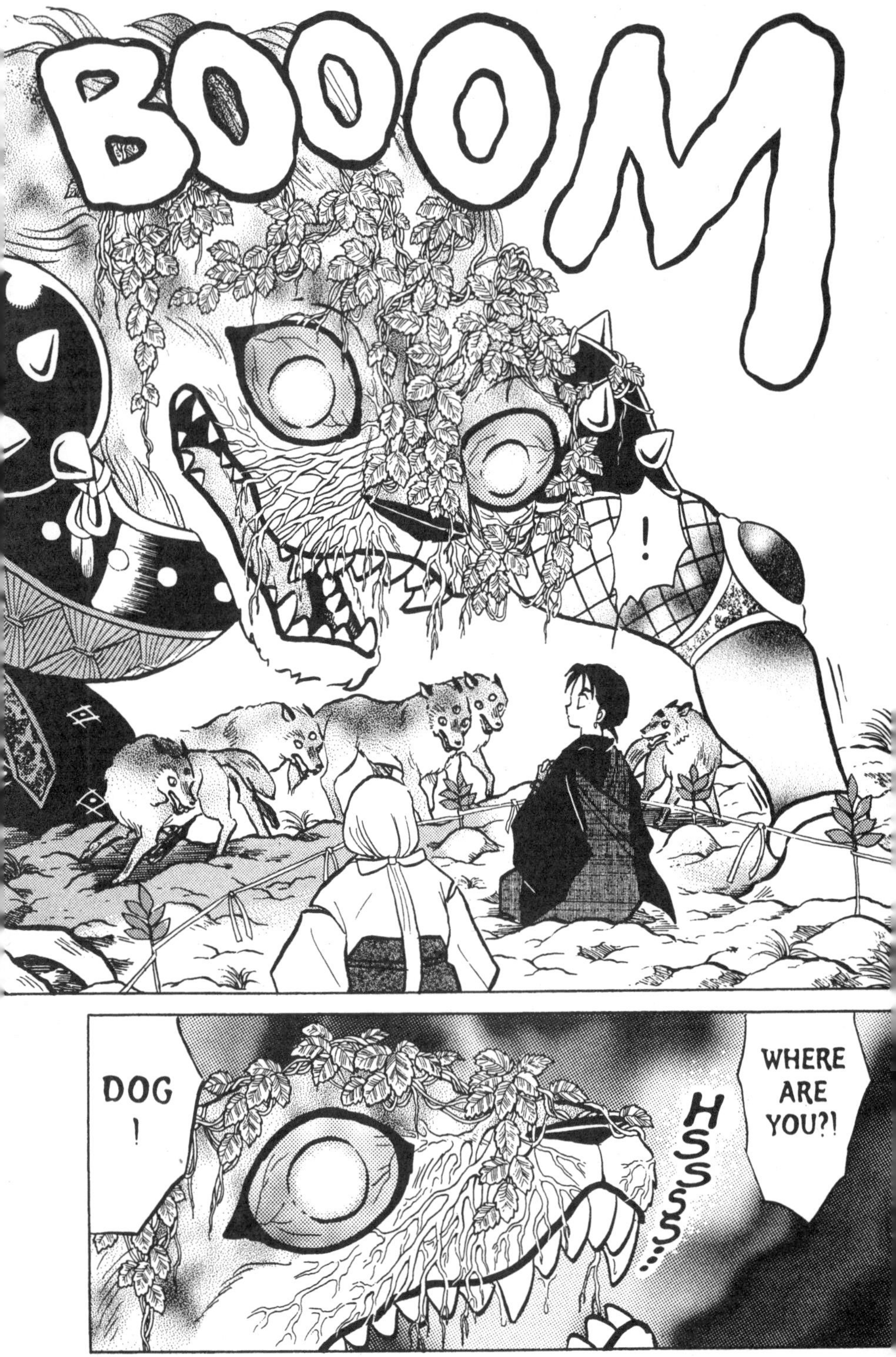
BOOOM
!
DOG !
HSSSS...
WHERE ARE YOU?!

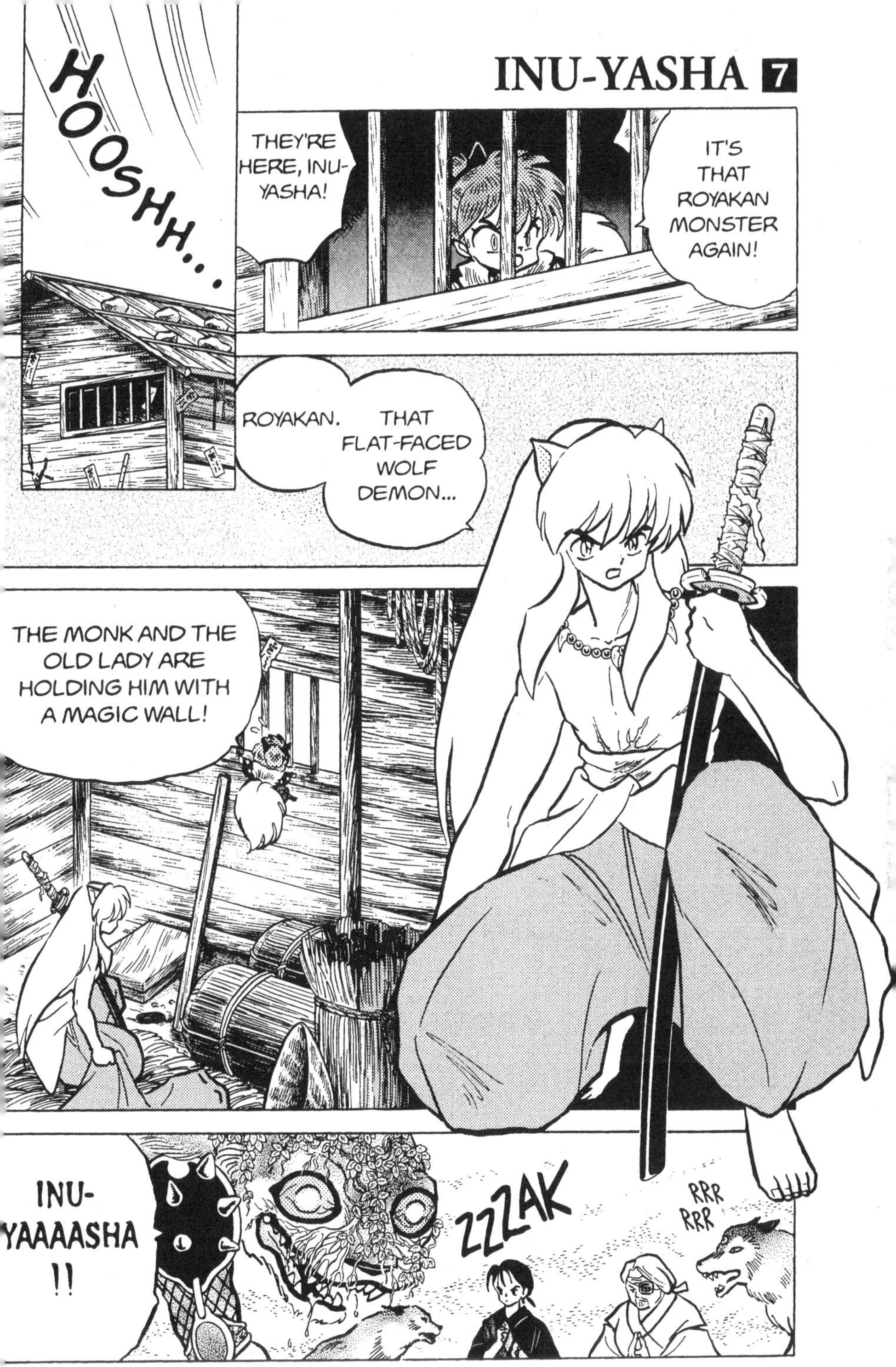
HOOSHH...
THEY'RE HERE, INU-YASHA!
IT'S THAT ROYAKAN MONSTER AGAIN!
ROYAKAN.
THAT FLAT-FACED WOLF DEMON...
THE MONK AND THE OLD LADY ARE HOLDING HIM WITH A MAGIC WALL!
INU-YAAAASHA !!
ZZZAK
RRR RRR

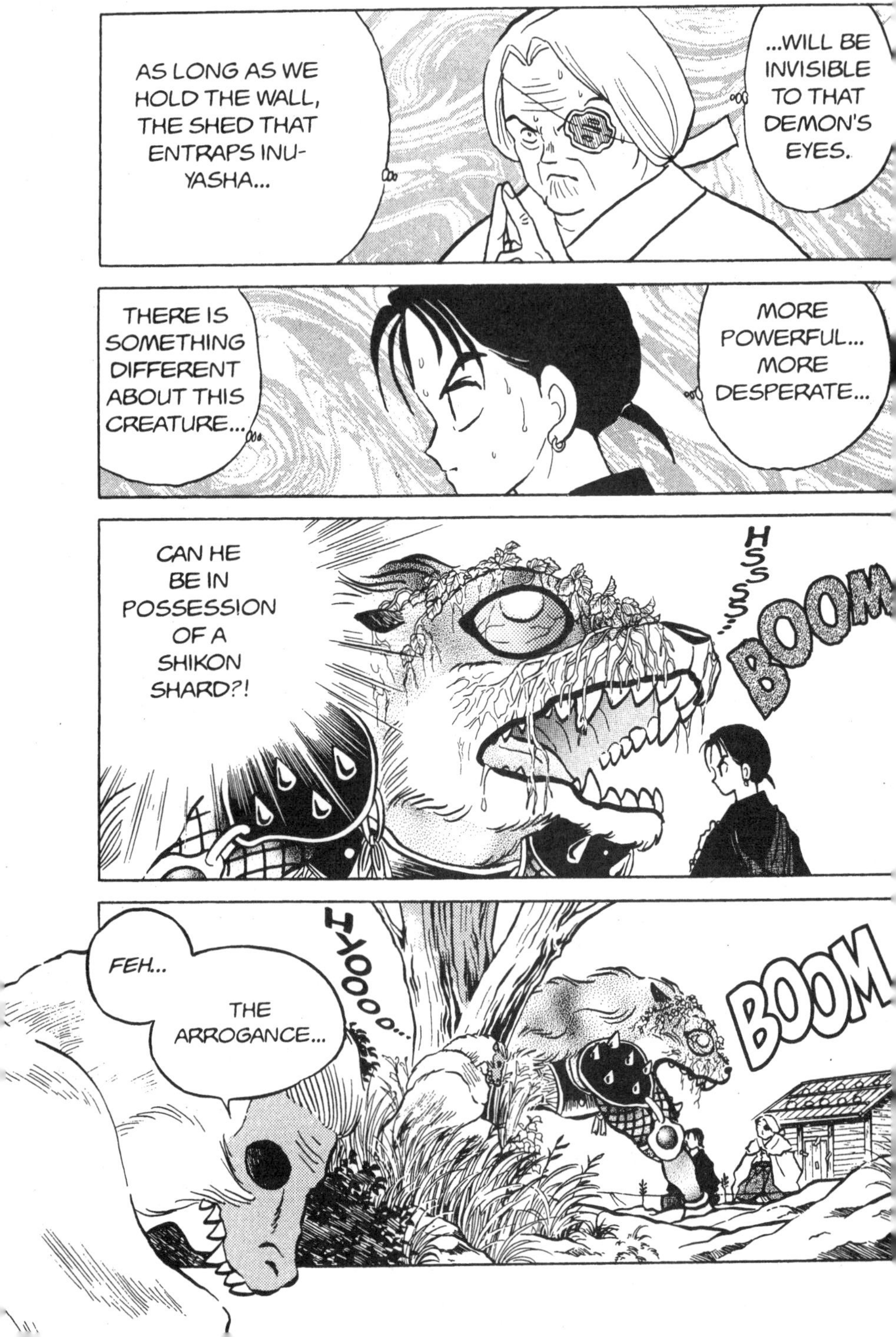
AS LONG AS WE HOLD THE WALL, THE SHED THAT ENTRAPS INU-YASHA...
...WILL BE INVISIBLE TO THAT DEMON'S EYES.
THERE IS SOMETHING DIFFERENT ABOUT THIS CREATURE...
MORE POWERFUL... MORE DESPERATE...
CAN HE BE IN POSSESSION OF A SHIKON SHARD?!
HSSSS...
BOOM
FEH...
THE ARROGANCE...
HYOOOOO...
BOOM

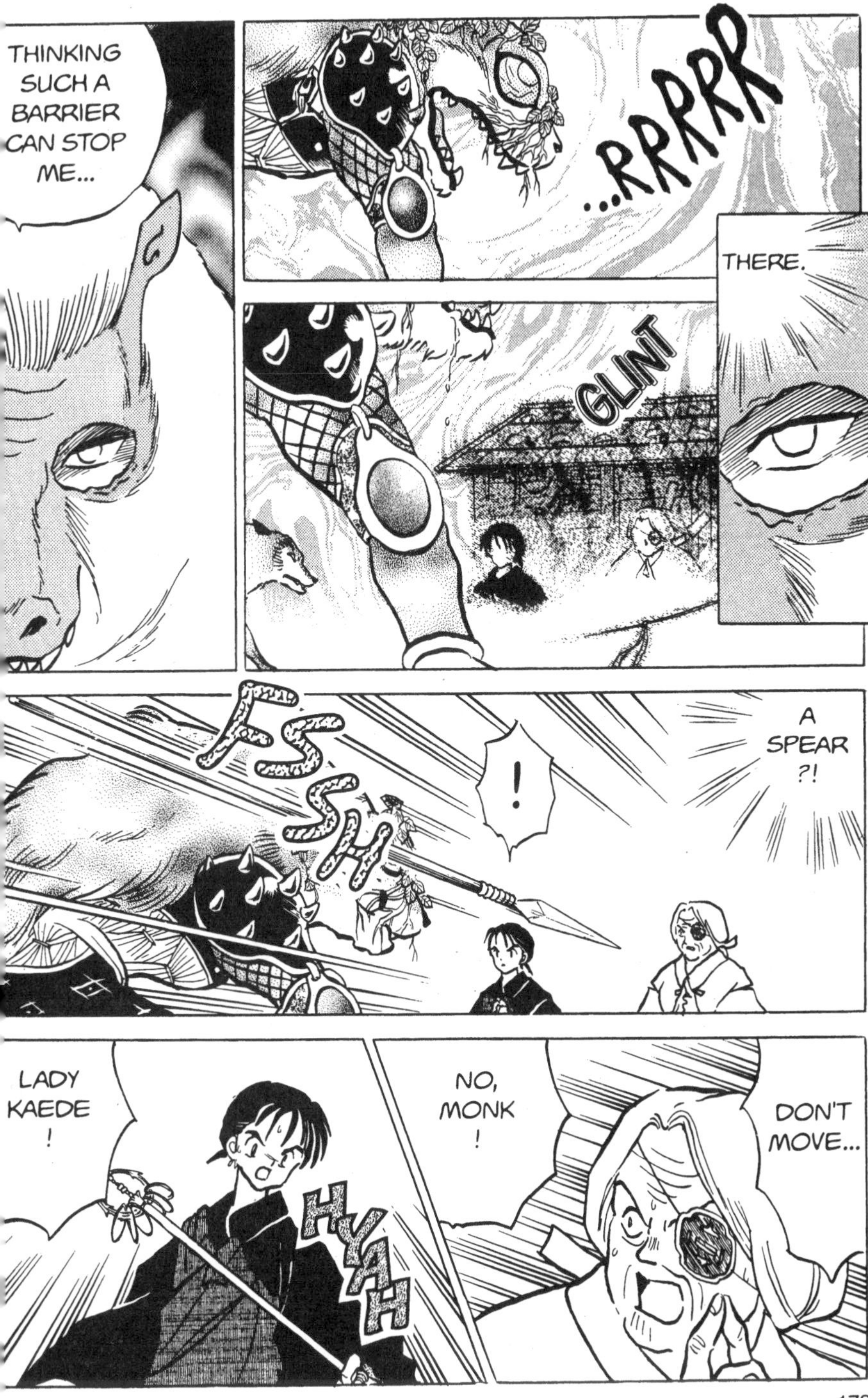
THINKING SUCH A BARRIER CAN STOP ME...
...RRRRR
GLINT
THERE.
FSSH
!
A SPEAR ?!
LADY KAEDE !
HYAH
NO, MONK !
DON'T MOVE...

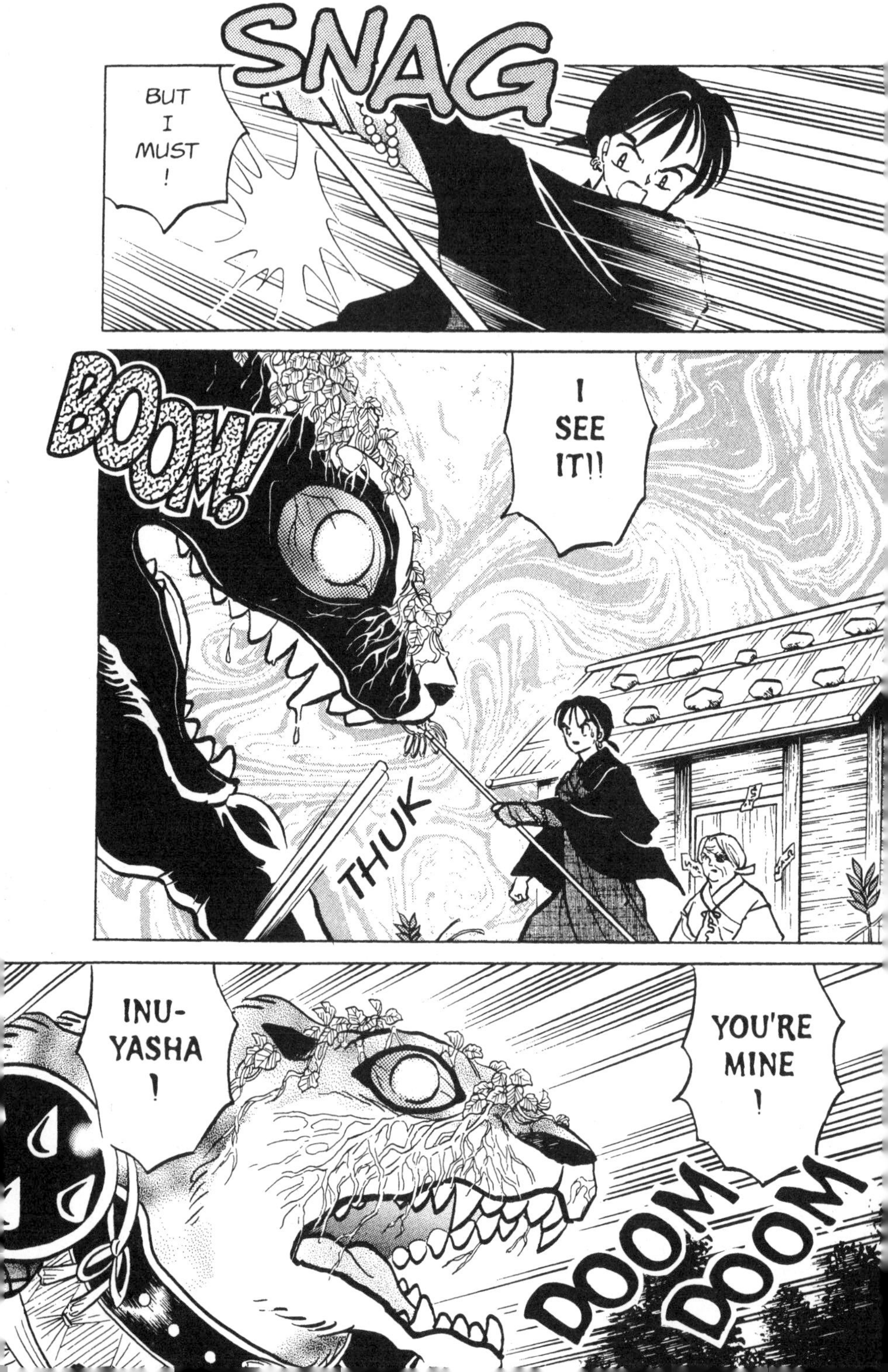
SNAG
BUT I MUST!
BOOM!
I SEE IT!!
THUK
INU-YASHA!
YOU'RE MINE!
DOOM DOOM

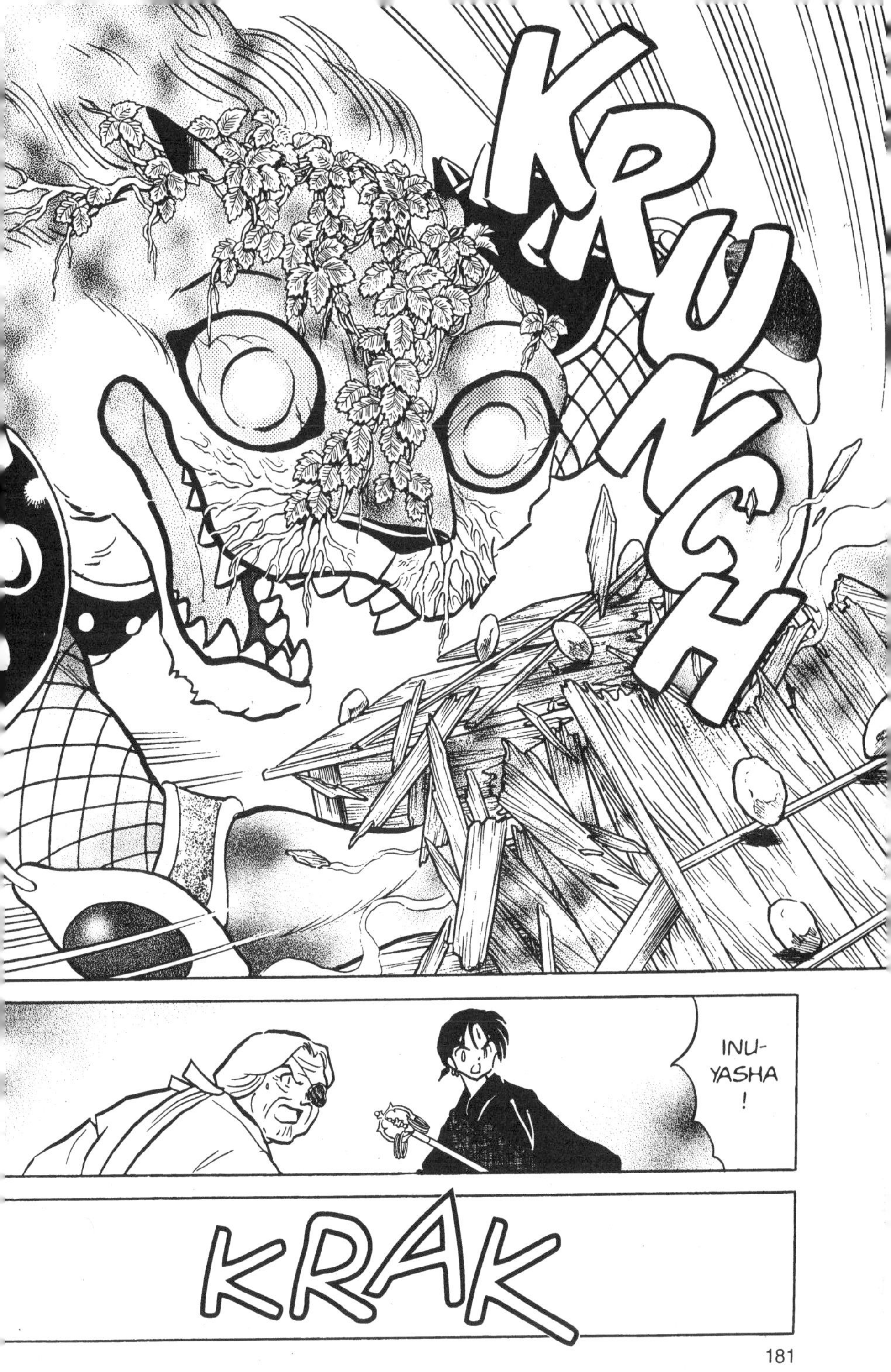
KRUNCH
INU-YASHA!
KRAK

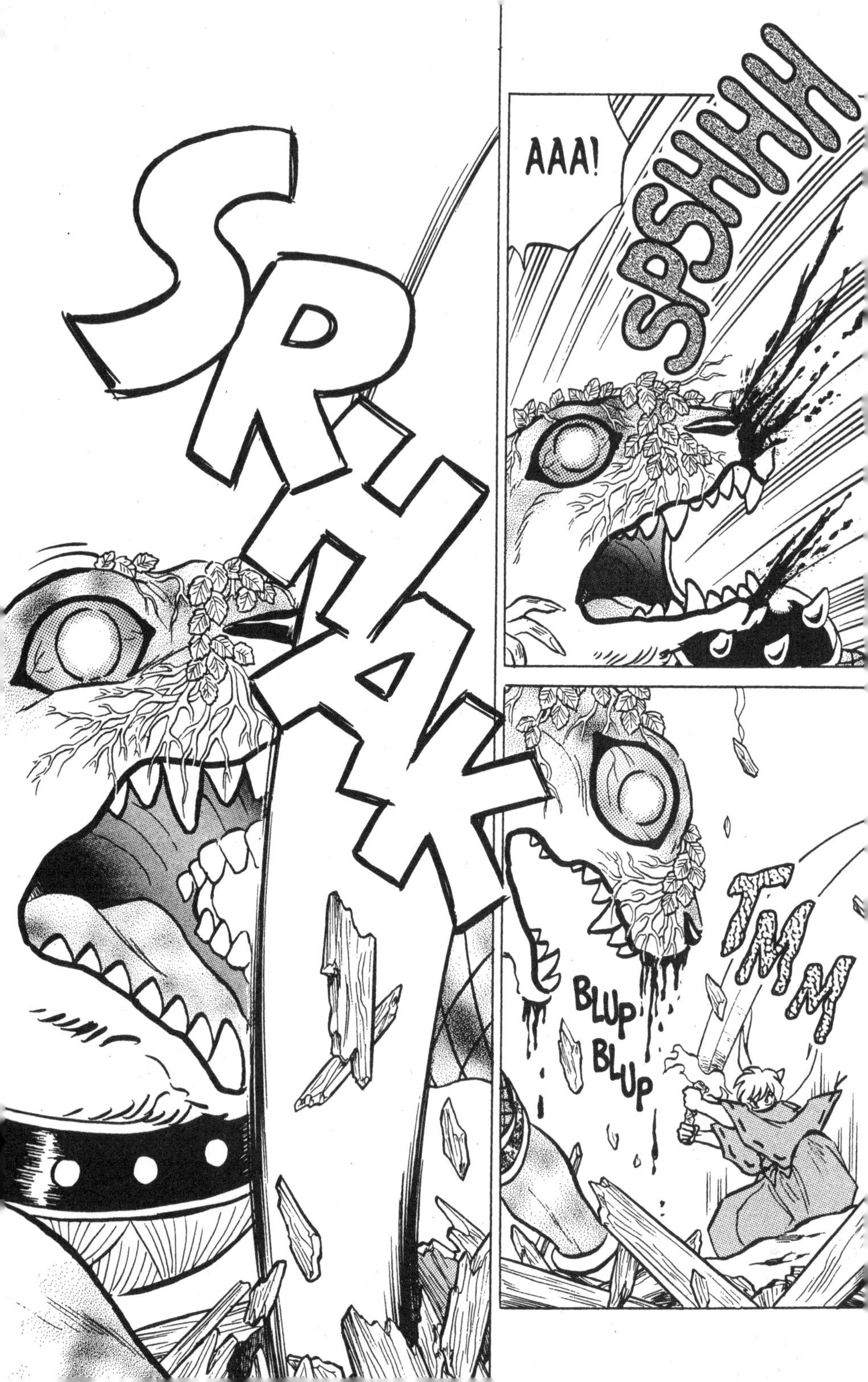
AAA!
SPSHHH
BLUP
BLUP
TMM

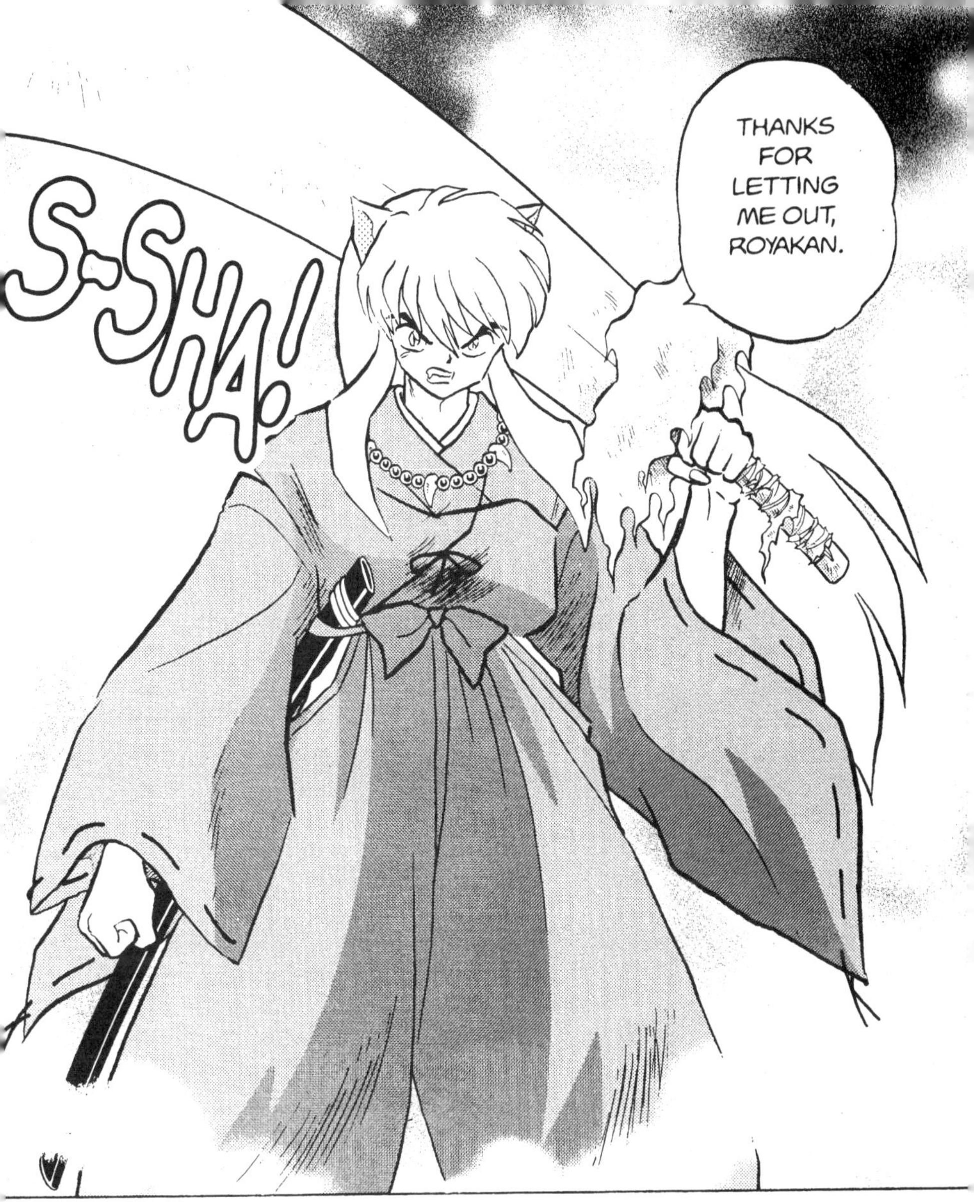
S-SHA!
THANKS FOR LETTING ME OUT, ROYAKAN.

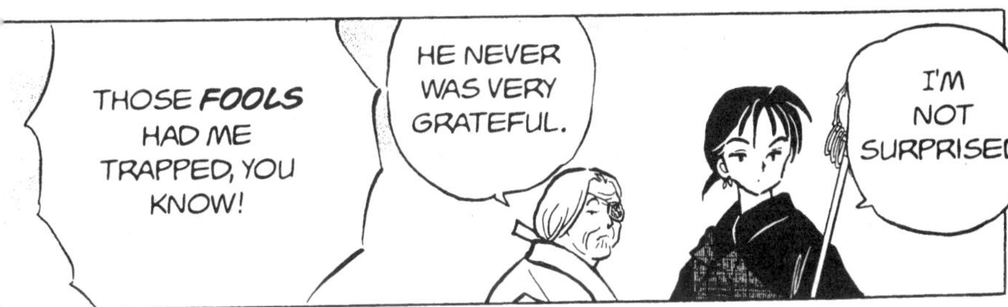
THOSE **FOOLS** HAD ME TRAPPED, YOU KNOW!
HE NEVER WAS VERY GRATEFUL.
I'M NOT SURPRISED.

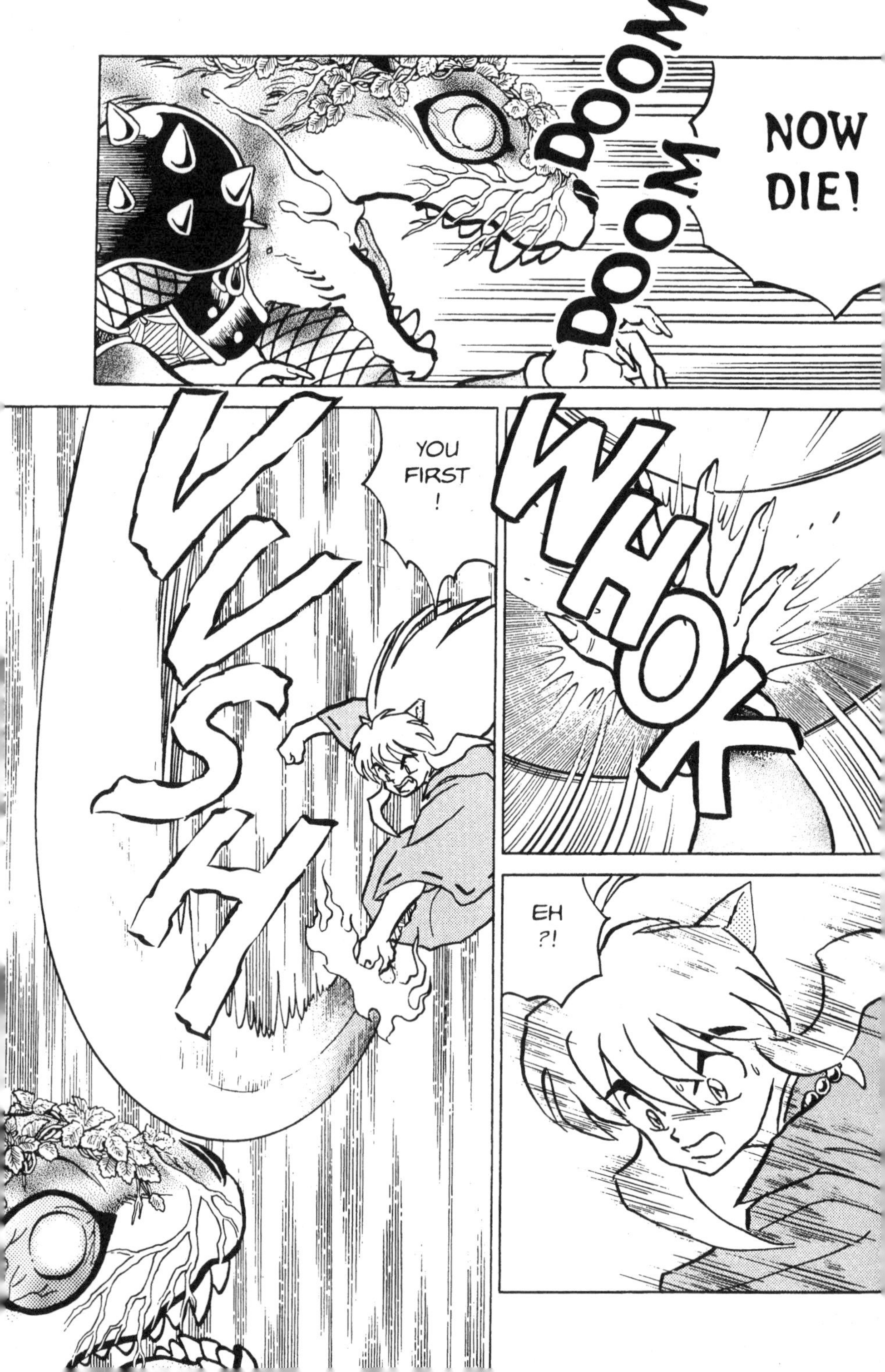
DOOM DOOM
NOW DIE!
YOU FIRST !
WHOK
EH ?!

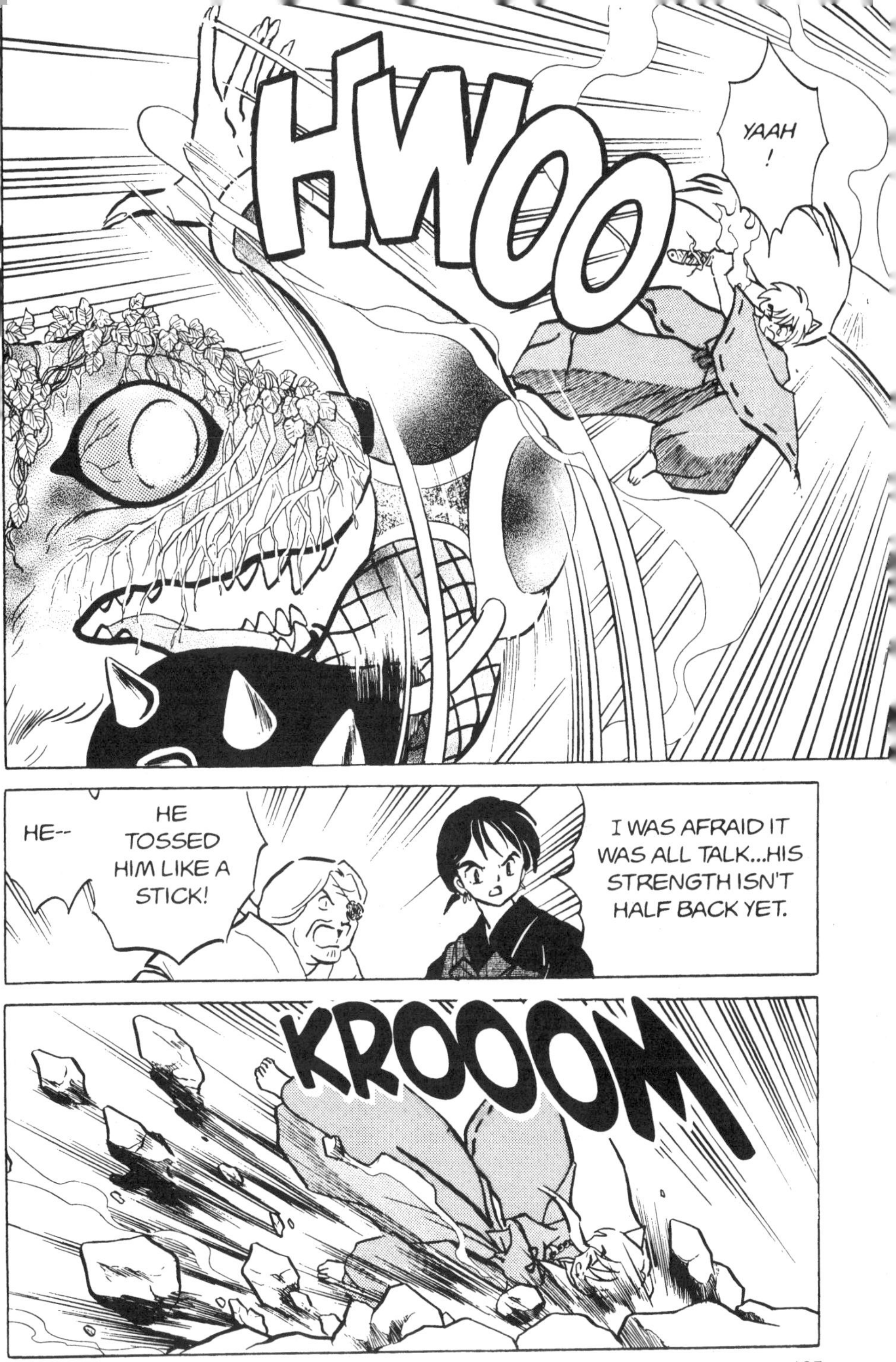
HWOO
YAAH!
HE--
HE TOSSED HIM LIKE A STICK!
I WAS AFRAID IT WAS ALL TALK...HIS STRENGTH ISN'T HALF BACK YET.
KROOOM

SHHHHHH

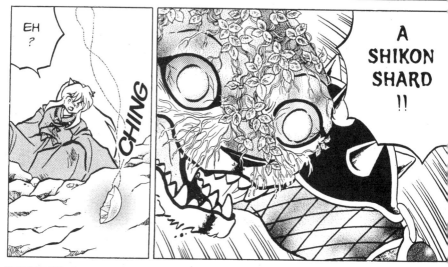

EH
?

CHING

A SHIKON SHARD !!

BAM

ZZZIP

IT'S NOT FOR YOU!

ZZZ

SHIPPŌ...!

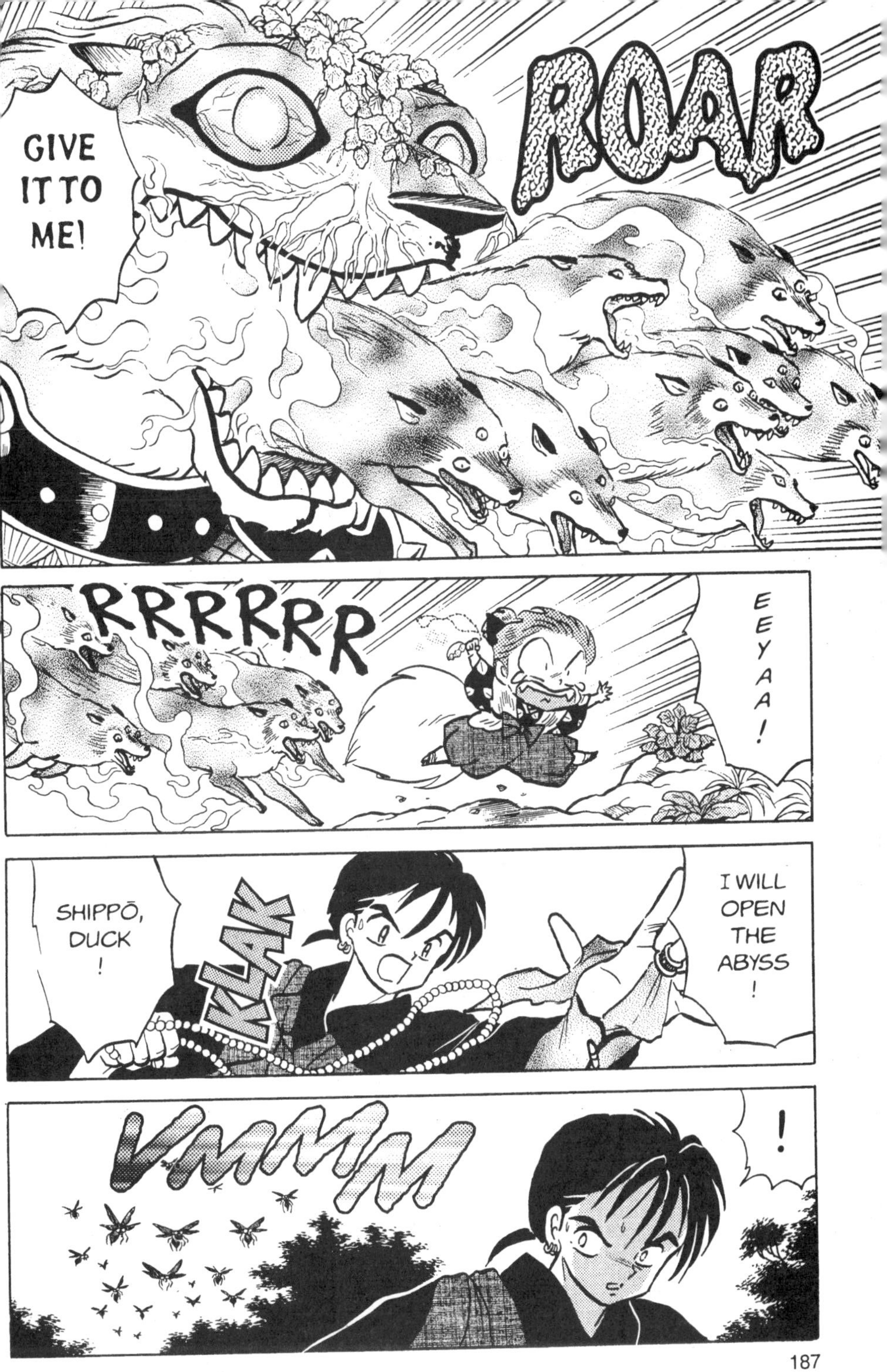
GIVE IT TO ME!
ROAR
RRRRRR
EEYAAA!
SHIPPŌ, DUCK!
KLAK
I WILL OPEN THE ABYSS!
VMMM
!

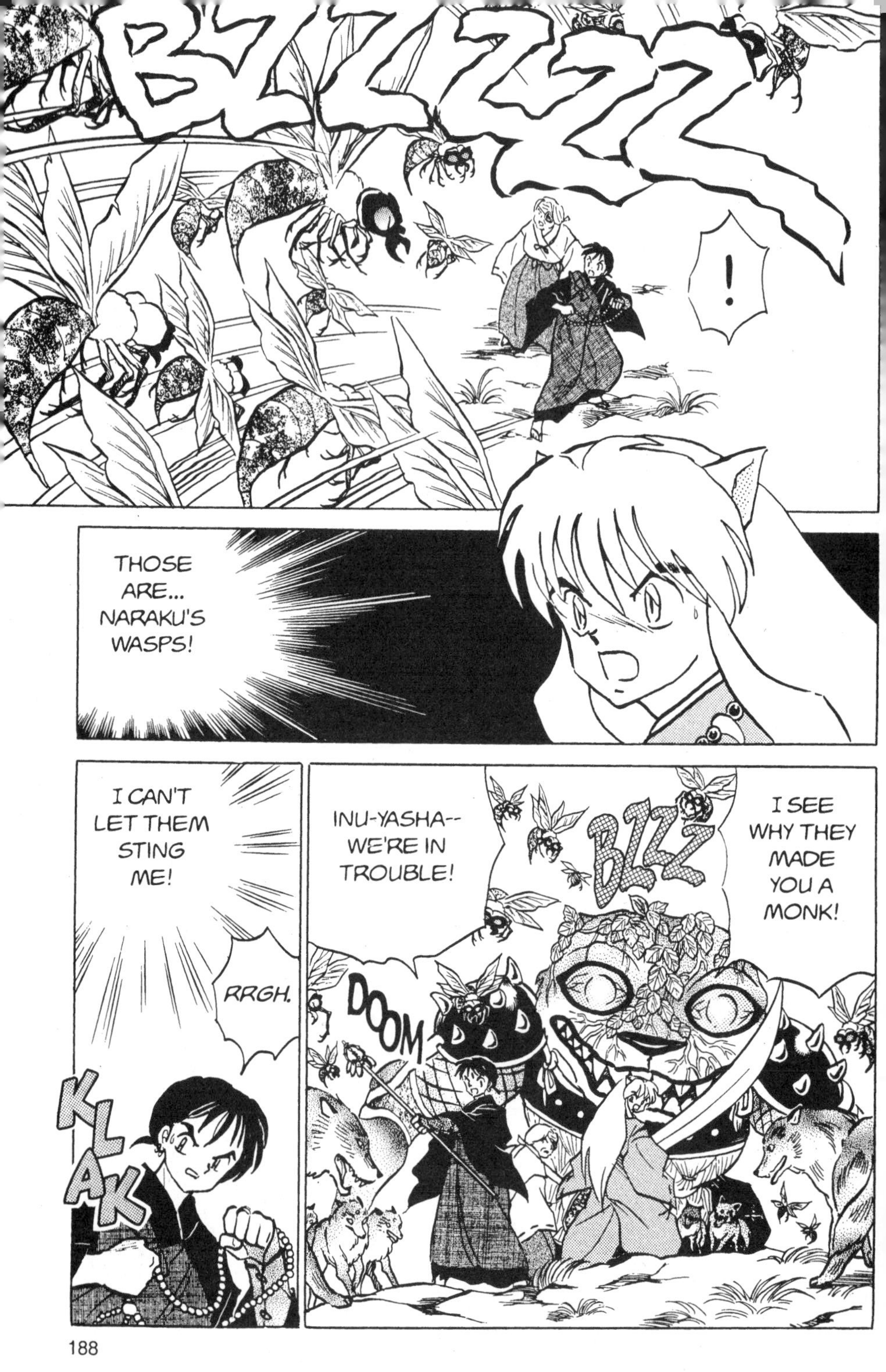
BZZZZZ
!
THOSE ARE... NARAKU'S WASPS!
I CAN'T LET THEM STING ME!
RRGH.
KLAK
INU-YASHA-- WE'RE IN TROUBLE!
BZZ
I SEE WHY THEY MADE YOU A MONK!
DOOM

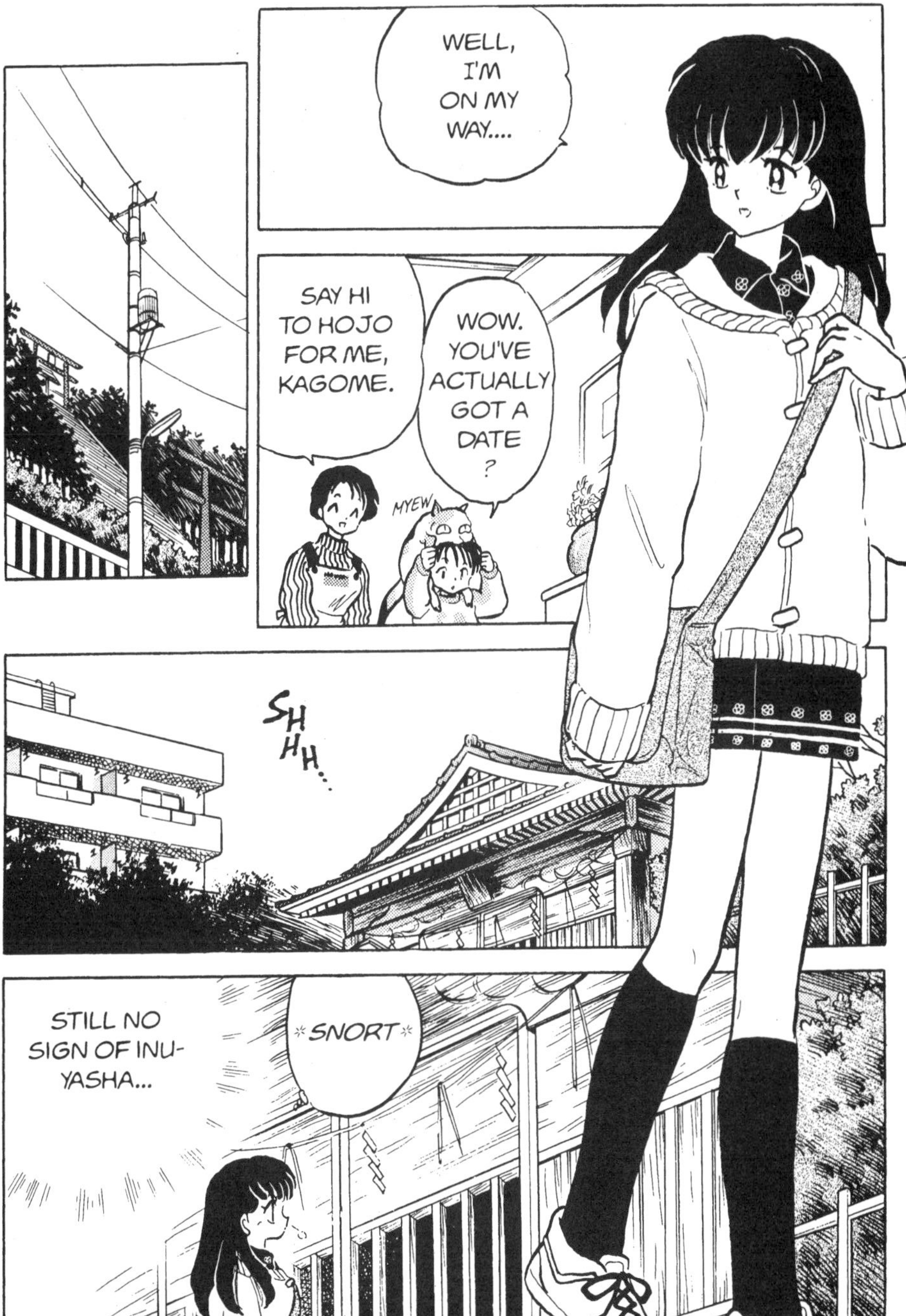
WELL, I'M ON MY WAY....
SAY HI TO HOJO FOR ME, KAGOME.
WOW. YOU'VE ACTUALLY GOT A DATE?
MYEW
SHHH...
STILL NO SIGN OF INU-YASHA...
SNORT

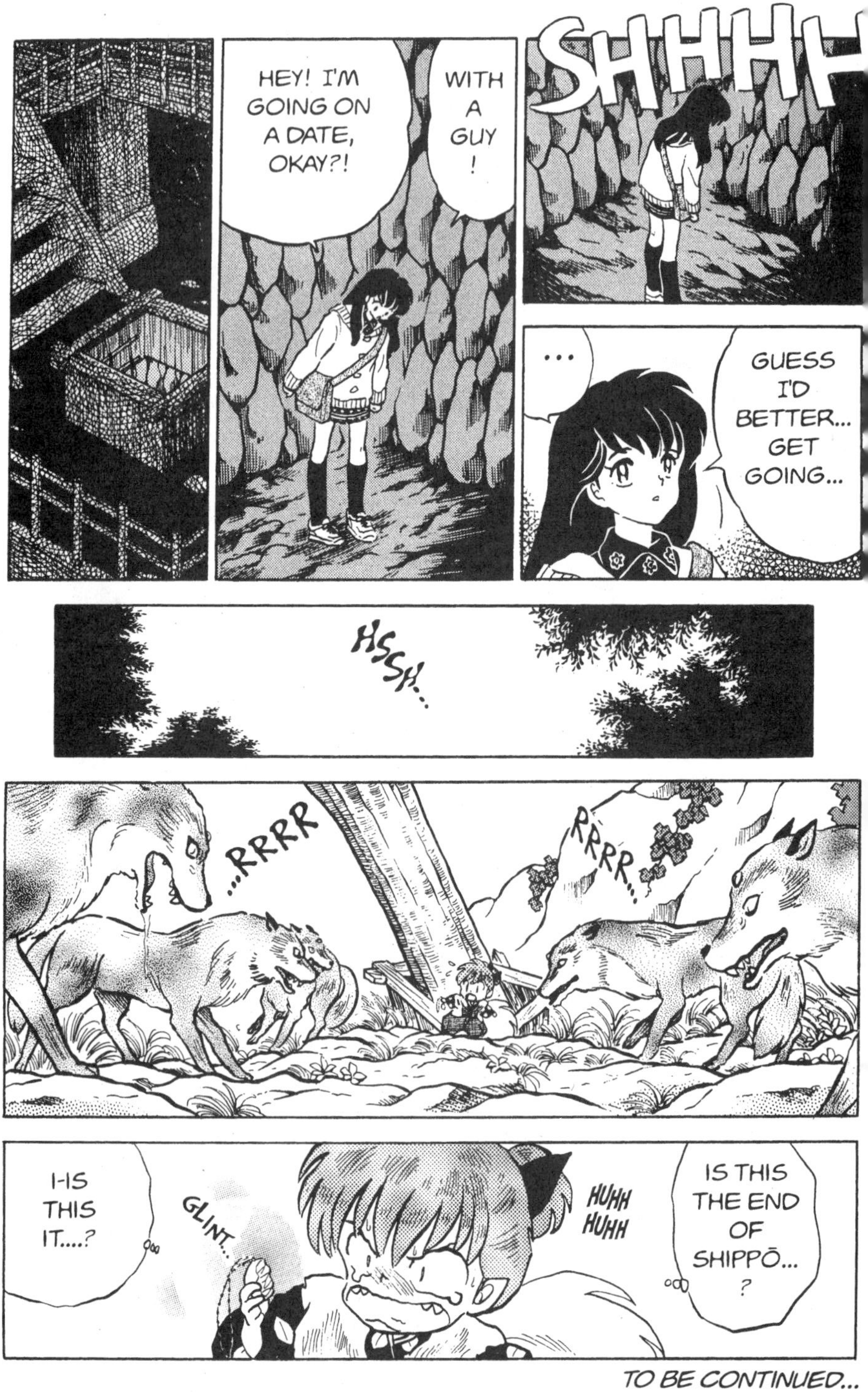
HEY! I'M GOING ON A DATE, OKAY?!
WITH A GUY!
SHHHH
...
GUESS I'D BETTER... GET GOING...
HSSH...
...RRRR
RRRR...
I-IS THIS IT....?
GLINT...
HUHH HUHH
IS THIS THE END OF SHIPPŌ...?

TO BE CONTINUED...